The Road to Rose Bend

NAIMA SIMONE

The Road to
Rose Bend

ISBN-13: 978-1-335-43047-2

The Road to Rose Bend

This edition published by arrangement with Harlequin Books S.A.

For questions and comments about the quality of this book, please contact us
at CustomerService@Harlequin.com.

HQN
22 Adelaide St. West, 40th Floor
Toronto, Ontario M5H 4E3, Canada
www.Harlequin.com

Printed in U.S.A.

To Gary. 143.

To the real "Moe" and "Eva," Lucille "Moe" Alston and Eva Lee Butts. You taught me kindness, selflessness, sacrifice, generosity, how to cheat at cards and how to creatively use, uh, agitated adjectives. You both showed me what it was to live life loud and full of laughter. You encouraged me to dream big and supported me every step of the way, whether it was going to college, traveling to another country for the first time or writing a book. You were—still are—the matriarchs who exemplified pride, courage and beauty in grace. I couldn't have asked for better examples of womanhood and dignity. Most important, you loved me. God, how you loved me. I will miss you both for the rest of my life.

The Road to Rose Bend

CHAPTER ONE

There's no place like home.

Huh.

Obviously, Dorothy hadn't gotten out much.

Sydney Collins stared at the majestic Monument Mountain and Mount Everett, the breathtaking sentinels that soared above the picturesque town of Rose Bend, Massachusetts. Dorothy's bewildering need to return to boring, sepia-toned Kansas couldn't be found among the trees that covered their peaks, though.

Sydney could still remember sitting in the living room and watching *The Wizard of Oz* for the first time when she'd been seven years old. While her parents and her sister, Carlin, had been rooting for Dorothy to click those ruby heels and make it back home, Sydney had jumped to her feet and yelled, "Are you crazy, Dorothy? Keep your ass in Oz!"

Well, her parents hadn't been too happy with the language—they'd later had words with Uncle Travis about watching his mouth around her—but Carlin, resting in her special recliner, had quietly snickered.

Carlin…

A dusty, too-familiar feeling weaved through Sydney, burrowing deep in her heart. From experience, she knew no amount of meditation, Come-to-Jesus talks or Sunday sermons explaining how "God moves in mysterious ways," could dig it out.

Sydney's fingers curved around her slightly rounded belly, the mound and life within keeping her grounded here, in the present.

God. She hadn't been back home for fifteen minutes, and already the memories were smothering her, seeking to drag her back.

Well, the past wasn't exactly *dragging* her back. As of yesterday morning, when she'd left Charlotte, North Carolina, to start the twelve-hour drive to the Berkshires, she'd willingly returned to her hometown located in the Southern Berkshires.

The hometown she'd vowed—eight years earlier—to never step foot in again.

Had it been only about her, she still might be settled in her Ballentyne condo.

But it was no longer only about her.

Sydney splayed her fingers wider over her stomach. Seventeen weeks, her doctor had confirmed the day before yesterday.

Love, so deep, so fierce it was terrifying, welled up inside her as it did every time she thought of the tiny, vulnerable person growing inside her. Love and…fear. Oh God, Sydney was scared. Not only for herself, but for the life she would soon be responsible for. On her own. Yes, it was her choice to raise her child as a single mother, just as it'd been her choice to divorce her ex-husband, Daniel. But those decisions didn't make the future any less daunting. They didn't mean she wasn't questioning if she was doing the right thing.

Shaking her head, as if the abrupt motion could dislodge her doubts, she inhaled a deep breath. Released it.

"I'm doing this," she said to the mountains. To no one. "I'm really doing this."

Was she reminding herself…or questioning her sanity? Yeah,

she had no clue. But with her apartment lease canceled, all her belongings either packed away in storage or piled inside this vehicle, with her ties cut, she had no choice but to go forward. Literally and figuratively.

She closed her eyes and tipped her head back. Up here, the air didn't contain the mugginess of the South. Though she'd lived almost a decade in Charlotte, North Carolina, she'd never quite become accustomed to the humidity that clung to her skin like a layer of clothing. Here, though, summer had truly arrived. A high seventies temperature with a fresh breeze that brushed over her skin like a loving caress.

The Southern Berkshires in mid-June were simply…breathtaking. As much as she resented the place where she'd grown up, she couldn't deny the beauty of it. Centuries-old trees seemed to preen with their vividly green, lush leaves. Wide fields rolled into hills that were only eclipsed by the majesty of mountains and endless blue sky. As a child, she'd stared up at those great sentinels, imagined they'd been stacked there by lightning-bolt-wielding gods and fierce Titans. And as a teen, she'd studied them, dreaming about what lay on the other side. They'd been her friends, her guardians. And they'd been the only thing she'd waved goodbye to as she'd left Rose Bend eight years ago.

But now she was back.

Tears stung her eyes, and Sydney blinked against them. Stupid hormones. She'd never been much of a crier—she'd learned at an early age that tears solved nothing—but since she'd been pregnant, they popped up like stray hairs on a chin.

Family. Acceptance. A sense of belonging. Those had never been hers to have in her hometown. Hell, there was a very good chance they still might not be hers now. But for her baby, it could be different. The burdens of Sydney's childhood didn't have to be her child's. She wouldn't *let* it be.

But she wasn't in the habit of fooling herself. While she hoped—prayed—for a nurturing haven for her child, and truly believed she would find it here, she also wanted that for *herself*, for Sydney "That Girl" Collins. On that latter point, she knew better. Nothing changed in Rose Bend. Not the houses. Not the townspeople. Not the opinions. Not the hearts.

That's why she stood on this hill behind St. John's Catholic Church, the oldest church in Rose Bend, instead of driving to her parents' home. It was an ancient institution.

Carlin was buried at the newer cemetery on the other side of town. Undoubtedly Sydney's parents still visited her older sister's resting place, while Sydney hadn't been there since they lowered Carlin into the ground. Eighteen years. What kind of sister did it make her that she hadn't visited Carlin in almost two decades?

A shitty one.

The answer popped into her mind, clear and adamant. And curiously, the voice sounded very similar to her mother's. She huffed out a rough, jagged laugh. That criticism and more awaited her once she arrived at her parents' house.

Focus on the bigger picture. You're here to raise your child in a warmer and safer environment. To give your baby a place where she's not a passing strange face, but a part of a loving family and community. True and true. While Sydney and her parents had a strained relationship that might be impossible to heal after years of too-cold politeness and stinging disapproval, she believed—had to believe—that they would accept their grandchild. Love their grandchild.

But now that the idea was cold reality and no longer theory? Well, she would be a liar if she claimed her stomach wasn't bolting for her throat. And the feeling had absolutely nothing to do with morning sickness.

Oh God, she'd made a mistake. What the hell had she been thinking returning here? She should leave right now. It wasn't too late—

"Stop it, dammit," she hissed at herself. "Get a hold of yourself and woman-the-fuck-up."

Sydney shook her head, and a whisper of movement out of

her peripheral vision snagged her attention. Surprise crackled through her as she spotted a lone, tall figure standing in the newer section of the graveyard. The leaves of a soaring, ancient red oak cast shadows over him, concealing his identity at this distance. Not that she would've called out if she recognized him. He was obviously here for solitude, just like her.

With one last glance in the mourner's direction, she concentrated on the view before her once more.

Peace settled over her, like an old friend eagerly welcoming her back. As she'd known it would. The people in Rose Bend might not be the most receptive to her being back. They might not ever accept her. But this place? It knew her heart. Closing her eyes, Sydney tipped her head back, allowing the fat sun sitting low in the sky to warm her skin with its last rays. This had been her special place after Carlin died. Here, she could be alone. Away from the censure and overwhelming grief she'd glimpsed in her parents' eyes. Here, she could shed the I-don't-give-a-fuck persona she'd adorned, because *God*…she gave so many fucks.

Here, she could be Sydney and not sink in the shame of being *alive*.

"Sydney?"

Well, damn.

Irritation flashed through her, but years of living in the South already had her lips curling into a polite smile. Until she turned her head and met a pair of stunning amber eyes. A very familiar pair of stunning amber eyes that she hadn't forgotten in the eight years she'd been gone.

Astonishment ricocheted through her, robbing her of coherent speech.

"Cole?" The shallow rasp was all she could squeeze past her constricted lungs.

A full, sensual mouth curved at the corners, that bottom lip heavy, and for a moment, his smile briefly banished the shadows lurking in his gaze. And it was that smile that confirmed the tall, wide-shouldered, powerfully built man standing before her was indeed Coltrane "Cole" Dennison. The man she'd hopelessly crushed on so many years ago stared down at her now, that jeweled gaze filled with confusion, surprise and delight.

Delight.

Coltrane Dennison was delighted to see her. Then again, her childhood friend's older brother had always been nice to the foolish and reckless teenager she'd been. Even though she and his sister Leontyne had gotten into some scrapes that could squarely be placed at Sydney's feet. Now...some might still call her reckless. But at twenty-six, she'd learned discipline and restraint. The hard way.

"It *is* you," he said in a voice that landed somewhere between the smooth glide of water over pebbles and thunder rolling across an inky sky.

Damn. Not only had pregnancy turned her into an emotional Tilt-a-Whirl and caused hair to sprout in places it really had no business growing, but it'd apparently transformed her from grant writer to poet. Cole shifted closer, effectively cutting off her scolding of herself. Clearing her throat, she forced herself to adopt a carefree smile that was a flat-out lie.

"It's me," she said, slipping her hands into the pockets of her billowy red-and-gold maxi dress. "Guilty," she added with a chuckle that sounded way too self-deprecating for her comfort.

Seemed she was always on the verge of apologizing for something.

For not saving her older sister's life.

For not being the perfect daughter.

For not giving her baby a two-parent home.

Yep. That was her. The Queen of I'm Sorry.

He moved forward again, and before she could brace herself, his arms encircled her, his wide, hard chest pressed against her cheek and his scent wrapped around her. Her lashes fluttered then lowered, her hands raising to flatten against the strong muscles of his back. She slowly released her pent-up breath, and for the shortest of moments, she caved. Yielded to the pleasure of his—of anyone's—genuine joy in seeing her again. Capitulated to the thrill of being welcomed instead of scorned.

Surrendered to the need for human contact, for being close to someone, held by them. Touched by them.

She stiffened. Jesus, what was she doing?

Being a damn glutton for punishment, that's what. Hadn't it been giving in to that last need that had led to her current state of impending single motherhood? Yes, a bottle of Moscato and a boatload of being-up-in-her-feelings had guided the way to unwise sex with her ex-husband, but still… It'd been that desire for intimacy, for emotional and physical connection, that had greased it. And that desire, the fear of being alone, had kept her in her marriage long past its expiration date.

Hours and hours on a therapist's couch had granted her insight into the whys. Distant parents. Lack of affirmation. Viewing her looks as her primary value. Validation. Yada, yada, yada.

It all boiled down to one thing: she needed to keep dicks out of her pants because it led to nothing but trouble.

Not that Cole, her best friend's brother, wanted her… Good God. She was devolving.

Easing out of his arms, she dropped hers to her sides.

"It's good to see you again. God, how many years has it been? Seven? Eight?" If her abrupt retreat confused him, his voice didn't betray it. His smile didn't slip, and he dipped his head in a nod. "I just saw your mom this morning at her store. She didn't mention you were coming in for a visit."

Because she doesn't know.

A shiver of anxiety quivered through her at the thought of showing up on her parents' doorstep, her life packed in her car. "Unhappy" would be a serious understatement for the confusion, disappointment and anger that would greet Sydney's news.

Shrugging a shoulder, she glanced away from him and refocused on the view so she didn't have to lie to his face. "I'm sure she just had other things on her mind. And it's been eight years since the Black Sheep of Rose Bend left." What in the hell had possessed her to add *that*? Because she was a master of deflection, she switched the subject. "What are you doing out here anyway? The back of a church isn't exactly a hot spot on a Friday night," she teased.

She waited for a husky chuckle or his playful response, but only silence replied to her. No, it screamed at her so loudly she jerked her head to the side and peered at Cole.

The utter *desolation* in his gaze punched the air from her lungs. She lifted a hand to her chest and pressed her knuckles to the ache there. How could those eyes contain so much pain and yet he still stood? Still breathed? She was having a difficult time doing both just witnessing it.

His lashes lowered, and he slid his hands into the pockets of his black, tailored pants. He turned toward the sun and the sky that bled lavender and gray. His white dress shirt clung to his taut shoulders and back. And for the first time, the shock of seeing him again ebbed enough for her to catalog the smaller details about Cole.

As long as she'd known him—and in a town the size of Rose Bend, that was all her life—his dark hair had tumbled around his face in loose curls and waves. But no strands flirted with his cheekbones or jaw. They were gone, shorn into a closely cropped cut that framed his head and exposed his sharply hewn profile. Golden wheat skin that proudly proclaimed his Puerto Rican heritage stretched across cheekbones that could slice air, but his strong, patrician facial features were more pronounced, more severe than she remembered. As if he'd lost some weight recently and the whittling down had emphasized the bold bones of his cheeks, the slant of his nose, the sensuous curves of his mouth, the slash of his clean-shaven jaw.

The same with his big body. Still tall, still a swimmer's build with the expanse of shoulders and chest and a tapered waist, lean hips and powerful thighs. But whereas before he'd carried a sense of peace she'd always envied, now a fine tension seemed to hum from his motionless frame. As if even when not moving, he was on the verge of it. Or needed to be moving. She understood that. Because putting her hands to something, losing herself in action, prevented thinking.

Was that it? Was Cole running from his own thoughts, desperate to get out of his head?

"I was visiting my wife and son," he said, his voice ground glass and gravel.

Pain blasted her in a fiery backdraft.

She swayed, the world expanding then contracting like a snapped rubber band. He'd been the person in the cemetery. The man standing under the tree, alone. Grieving.

Lovely, kind Tonia. His love since high school.

She was dead.

And son. Another wave of stunned pain swelled and broke over her. Her hand rose toward her own belly. Cole had not only lost the love of his life, but a son, too.

Only a hard hand clasped above her elbow prevented her from stumbling backward.

"Sydney." The sharp whip of her name penetrated the roar clouding her head, steadied her trembling knees. Cole gripped her other arm, and she lifted her head, scanning his frown and the worry darkening his eyes. "Sydney, are you okay? Do you need to sit down? Can I get you—"

"No, no," she interrupted him, shaking her head, embarrassment and pain mingling like the best of friends. "I'm fine. I just…" She trailed off.

What could she say? What was there to say in this situation? She flashed back to when Carlin died. The platitudes of "I'm so sorry for your loss" and "She's in a better place" and "God works in mysterious ways" had bombarded her, and Sydney had wanted to howl her fury and agony at every person who'd uttered those inadequate condolences. They'd been acid poured into an open wound.

Because Carlin had belonged there with Sydney, with their parents who loved her more than anything—more than the daughter they'd been left with. And what merciful God would allow a thirteen-year-old to suffer for years from cancer only to take her away? Sydney hadn't—didn't—call His ways mysterious; she called them cruel.

"I didn't know," she finally murmured. "I'm sorry. How long?"

"Two years." Those shadows in his gaze thickened, swallowing the gold for a moment.

She nodded. Licked her suddenly dry lips. "I don't know exactly the depth of the grief you've suffered, but with…" Again, she trailed off. She might have thought of Carlin over and over again since she'd crossed the town limits, but she hadn't spoken her sister's name in eighteen long years. "I won't lie and promise you that it goes away completely. But it does become tolerable after a while. And then there will be the day when you only think about them five times instead of fifty." The corner of her mouth lifted in a faint half smile. "And then, there will come the time when their memory brings more happiness than pain and guilt. When you get there, you'll let me know how it feels, okay?"

Because she hadn't yet reached that plateau. But Cole had always been strong, seemingly indomitable. With the huge, loving Dennison clan behind him, she had zero doubts he would get there. She should know. His sister Leontyne had been a wonderful friend to Sydney before she left Rose Bend.

His lashes briefly lowered, and he squeezed her arms before releasing her. "How long are you in town?" he asked, not answering her question. "Leo is going to lose her mind when she finds out you're here. Maybe you can do something about dragging her away from the inn. God knows, she's twenty-seven going on seventy-seven with all the responsibility she piles on herself."

"Leo? I-faked-the-swine-flu-to-get-out-of-work Leo?" Sydney gaped. "Did Rose Bend drop into an alternate universe while I was away? And did you check the seams along her hairline to make sure it's really her and not some body-snatching clone?"

He snorted, and though it wasn't a laugh, for a second, the shadows thinned. "You know what? I didn't check. I'll have to get Wolf to help me yank her away from the laundry and hold her down so we can make sure." An evil glint gleamed in his gaze, and Sydney laughed at the image of Cole and his older brother wrestling Leo to the ground. That would be a battle she'd pay ticket fare to see.

"Whatever you do, don't tell her I suggested it. I know some things might've changed here, but somehow I'm doubting her bloodthirsty need for payback is one of them."

"Not even a little bit," he agreed. "But back to you. How long are you here? A week? Two?"

The sigh escaped her before she could trap it. "I don't know," she hedged, glancing down and sweeping her hand down her baby bump. Just touching her rounded stomach comforted her, grounded her. "But since I have a good part of my life stashed away in my car, I'm guessing more than one or two weeks," she drawled with a soft chuckle.

But like before, her teasing slammed against a wall of silence.

Wary, she tipped her head back.

Stark agony widened his haunted gaze, tautened his light brown skin and flattened his full lips into a grim line.

His gaze fastened on her belly.

Understanding crashed into her. He'd lost a child; she couldn't imagine how that affected him. How he could bear being around children when all he probably thought about was his son who should be there with him.

"Cole," she whispered.

"You're pregnant," he stated the obvious, tone flat.

Just moments ago, delight had colored his voice, his smile, his eyes. Now, there was nothing.

An ache bloomed in her chest. As inappropriate as it might be, she missed that happiness. How many people in this town would greet her return with joy instead of curiosity, side-eye and gossip? She could count them on one hand and still have about two fingers left over.

Before she left this place to go to her parents and face their disappointment, she *needed* that pleasure lighting his amber eyes again.

Hell, even his pain was preferable to this, this…emptiness.

"Yes." She lifted her chin. Curling her hand around her stomach, she cradled the swell. As if protecting her baby from his coldness. His rejection. "I'm a little over four months along."

His expression remained shuttered, a smooth, blank mask. But the muscle along his jaw bounced like a jackhammer.

"Congratulations."

"Thank you," she murmured. Then, on a sigh, she swept her hand over her head, fingers bumping into the large, bound puff at the top. "Listen, Cole…"

"Welcome home, Sydney," he interrupted. "I need to go, but it was good seeing you again."

He didn't grant her the opportunity to reply. With a last nod, he pivoted on his heel and strode away, back down the rise, past the cemetery, disappearing from sight.

She continued to stare at the empty path for several seconds. What the hell had just happened? Spinning back around, she focused her gaze upon the now rapidly setting sun. But the peace and solitude of the view and the churchyard had vanished like early morning mist.

"It's going to be okay," she quietly reassured her baby as if he or she could hear her fervent words. Some books said babies could hear in the womb, though probably not this early in her pregnancy. But Sydney could still pretend the words were for her child instead of for herself. Pretend that Cole's abrupt switch toward her hadn't caused hurt to echo through her.

Lifting her shoulders high, she rolled them back. Envisioning his aloofness and cold dismissal tumbling away from shoulders that already carried too much. She didn't have room for anything else.

So, Coltrane Dennison would have to take a back seat to her pending single motherhood, enduring her parents' anger and frustration, establishing a new home, a new future. Finding her place.

Forcing her shoulders to remain straight, she followed the path Cole had taken. Past the church. Back through town. To her car.

To her reckoning.

Another thing pregnancy had apparently transformed her into: dramatic.

Shaking her head, she slid into the driver's seat and cranked the engine.

Still… If this first encounter was any indication of how her return to Rose Bend would go, she would need to buckle up.

Because this ride was going to be bumpy as hell.

CHAPTER TWO

Coltrane slammed his wrapped fists into the punching bag. The jarring impact of each blow vibrated up his wrists and arms, settling into his shoulders. Bouncing on the balls of his feet, he circled the suspended bag. His brain comprehended that he jabbed the equipment over and over. But in his soul—where he disappeared when the pain, grief and anger swelled so high he imagined drowning under its destructive lure—he swung at the Fates, at Life, at the merciless universe that had flipped his world on its ass. Then laughed.

He drew short of cursing God.

His biological mom and his adoptive mom were both stalwart Catholics, and going off on God was a blasphemous line he couldn't bring himself to cross. Besides, he wasn't some biblical Jacob, wrestling with the Lord until He blessed him. Cole had already been cursed, condemned. Instead of giving him a disjointed hip, God had left him dislocated from the fairy-tale life he'd lived with his wife, Tonia, and their soon-to-be-born and already adored son. Cole's existence had been broken into two halves. Heaven and hell.

And hell was this gray place, devoid of joy, of peace. He'd become a full-time resident of that place.

His hard breaths reverberated off the cement walls of his rental cottage as he shifted away from the swinging bag. He dragged an arm over his forehead, swiping away the sweat dripping into his eyes. Usually, exercise grounded him, allowed him to release the overwhelming emotion that built up inside him like a seething, rumbling volcano. Right after Tonia and their son—Mateo Seamus Dennison, named after both of Cole's fathers—died in childbirth, and Cole had sat, curled up in the corner of the nursery they'd decorated together, with a gun clasped in his hands, he'd admitted he needed to find a way to relieve the pressure, to release his grief and rage. The next day, he'd turned the gun in to the local police station, moved out of the house he'd shared with Tonia into one of his parents' rental cottages and hung the punching bag in the garage. And he'd thrown himself back into his family law practice.

That's where he should be now. Or down at the town hall where he had his own office as Rose Bend's newly elected mayor. The town's first nonwhite mayor. Damn, he'd been in the position for almost a year now, and at times, he still asked himself, *How in the hell did I get here?* But he knew the how and the why.

He was no longer a husband whose purpose was to protect his wife and their world. So now, he'd channeled that instinct into protecting the community that had been so important to both of them. He intended to do everything he could to make Rose Bend grow and continue to be a safe, beautiful and thriving haven for its residents.

Everything he did came back to Tonia and Mateo.

Besides, his law practice and mayoral responsibilities kept him busy and, more importantly, distracted. At least during his waking hours. It was those lonely, seemingly endless hours of the night when the silence deafened him, and the right side of the bed taunted him with its cruel emptiness. Then, his mind

raced and refused to slow down. That's when the memories—
no longer kept at bay by duties, phone calls and people—crept
in. He recoiled from the pain of them, even as he stretched ravenous fingers toward them.

Grief was like a drug.

It trapped him in its claws, dragging him down so deep, he
couldn't see his way out of it. Didn't want to. Didn't want to
leave the dark bosom even as it slowly asphyxiated him. Slowly
stole who he once was, until he was an insubstantial shadow of
his former self. Because grief, in its way, was solace. It was connection to the ones he'd lost. While mired deep in it, he could
forget the real world where Tonia and their son no longer existed. He could remain in the alternate universe of the past where
he'd been happy. Whole.

Every morning, he had to claw his way back from the abyss.

So far, he'd won the battle. But there were days when he
emerged more scarred and worn than others.

Today had been one of them. And though he should've been
down at city hall going over the last-minute details of the town's
annual motorcycle ride and rally, he'd been at Tonia's and Mateo's graves. And then he'd bumped into Sydney Collins.

Grinding his teeth together, Cole advanced on the punching
bag once more and jabbed at it. Again. And again. As if each
punch would drive thoughts of the woman he hadn't seen in almost a decade from his mind. The beautiful, wild, hurting girl
she'd been had matured into a stunning woman.

Thick, dark brown hair that formed a crown of curls on top
of her head. Smooth, walnut-brown skin. Big, chocolate eyes
with a dense fringe of long lashes. The mouth that had been too
sensual for a girl now fit…and would have a lesser man imagining all the things the woman had learned to do with it. The
petite frame with curves a blind man couldn't miss.

And she was pregnant.

A ghostly hand seized him by the throat, squeezing, and his

trembling arms dropped to his sides like three-hundred-pound weights. He staggered back a couple of steps, his feet as heavy and unwieldy as his suddenly useless arms.

"Whoa, Cole. Jesus. You all right?" A big, hard hand steadied him as his brother appeared before him, a frown tugging down his thick eyebrows over green eyes swimming with concern. "What the fuck, man? Here."

A bottle of water smacked Cole in the chest, and Cole reflexively closed his fingers around the room-temperature drink. Shaking his head, he concentrated on shrugging off the sense of suffocation and drew in a breath, twisting the cap off the bottle and downing a gulp. The liquid slid over his dry tongue and down his tight throat. Like a man crawling out of a desert, he guzzled the water, not stopping until only a drop remained.

"Thanks," he said, tossing the bottle toward the recycling bin claiming the far corner of the garage. The plastic hit the rim before tumbling inside. He flexed his fingers, opening and closing them repeatedly before nabbing the end of the wrap. Unbinding his hands, he glanced at his brother, who watched him through narrowed eyes. "What're you doing here?"

"Apparently saving you from ass-planting it." Wolfgang Dennison stalked over to the one window and jerked it open. A refreshing, fragrant summer breeze immediately filtered in. "It's like a damn sauna in here. What're you trying to do? Pass out from the heat? You sure as hell don't have any weight you can afford to lose."

His brother's critical gaze scanned Cole, and he clenched his jaw, imprisoning the clapback that scaled his tongue. The worry threaded through Wolf's voice aided Cole's restraint. His older brother by two weeks loved him, as Cole did him. So instead of saying something sharp, he focused on finishing the removal of the black wrap from his hands.

"I hate to break it to you, but all of us can't be lumbersexual-Aquaman-wannabes," Cole drawled.

Wolf's mouth, surrounded by a thick beard, quirked at the verbal jab. "Oh, but your scrawny ass wishes you could be."

They grinned at each other, and the love and brotherhood that connected them as tightly as if they'd been born from the same mother weaved through Cole like a cooling balm.

Cole's biological mother, Abril Burgos, and his adoptive mother, Billie Dennison, had been best friends since they'd been children growing up in Boston's Dorchester neighborhood. They'd done everything together, including getting married to men they loved, moving to Rose Bend and becoming pregnant. The two women had even planned their children's names; as music fanatics, they'd decided to name their babies after the greats. Hence, Wolfgang after the famous composer and Coltrane after the jazz saxophonist. When Cole's parents' car had been T-boned on the way to pick him up from Billie's house after a date night, Billie and Ian, her husband, had adopted Cole since Abril and Mateo had named them his guardians.

Though he owned pictures of his biological parents, he'd always considered the Dennisons his parents. And Wolf, as well as the children that came after him, his sibling. Maybe not by blood, but by love, loyalty, sacrifice and devotion. And choice.

Still… Damn good thing both Cole and Wolf had been popular when they were younger. Or else, with names like theirs, they would've been fighting every day.

"Not that I don't enjoy staring at that thing on your face that you call a beard, but what brings you by?" Cole asked again, tossing his wraps on the weight bench against the wall.

He glanced over his shoulder, and once more noted the concern that flashed in Wolf's eyes. Cole stifled his tired sigh. His family had been his rock after losing Tonia and their son, but sometimes his family's worry could be smothering. Well, that wasn't exactly accurate. Cole's guilt over causing them anxiety because he couldn't seem to move forward—that was smothering. At times, it was easier to just retreat than glimpse the pain and fear he inflicted on them.

"Let me guess," Cole continued, snatching up a towel and rubbing it over his head and face. "Moe sent you over to check on me."

For as long as Cole could remember, Billie Thomasina Dennison had been "Moe" to their large clan and most of the town. Family lore maintained that Cole had thoroughly jacked up the word "mother" when he'd been a toddler, and he'd shortened it to Moe. It'd stuck, so now nearly everyone called her by the nickname.

"Maybe," Wolf as much as admitted with a shrug. Cole and his brother might both stand at six foot four, but with their father's muscled weight in his shoulders and chest, Wolf was huge. Didn't help that he spent his days hauling and working with wood as a carpenter. The lumberjack crack wasn't far off. "But if you answered your damn phone, I wouldn't have had to drag my ass over here."

Cole arched an eyebrow, slapping the damp towel over a shoulder. "It's literally a five-minute drive down the road, not a journey to the middle of the Earth."

"It's a pain in the ass is what it is," Wolf grumbled, shoving a hand through his long, dark brown hair, pushing the strands out of his face. "Besides, I'm not coming from the inn," he said, referring to Kinsale Inn, the bed-and-breakfast his family owned and ran. "I was over at The Glen, finishing up the stage. I was calling to see if you wanted to come down and make any last-minute changes."

Since Rose Bend had hosted its first motorcycle rally fifteen years earlier, The Glen, a wide, open field on the edge of town, had become the epicenter of the activities. For two weeks, both world-renowned and local musicians would grace the stage, playing everything from rock to country to R&B. Vendors from all over the country would also travel to town to set up booths and sell merchandise to the many riders that flocked to Rose Bend. The annual rally and ride had become huge, and unlike its cousins in Sturgis and Daytona, it'd retained a festival atmosphere where families could—and did—attend.

Proceeds from the event benefited the This Is Home Foundation, an organization that ran the youth home for foster children in town. The charity held a special place in Cole's heart. Not only because if he hadn't been blessed with Dad and Moe in his life, he could've easily ended up in the foster care system. But three of his siblings had been adopted from that home. One of his goals as mayor was to ensure the rally and ride continued to thrive and grow. It'd been one of his promises when he'd run for the office. Because more revenue meant more funding for the youth home.

"I went over there yesterday, and everything looked great. Better than great. Did you still need me to check it out?"

Wolf shook his head. "No. Jasper Landon happened to drop by. And when he complained about it being too large and vulgar, and how it wasn't how they'd always done it, I figured it was perfect." Cole smothered a groan but must not have been too successful in schooling his expression because his brother grinned. "Yeah. Good luck. I'm sure he's going to drop by your office tomorrow to complain."

Shit. Jasper Landon, former mayor of Rose Bend, hadn't taken well to losing to a younger, less experienced and—hell, might as well admit it—Puerto Rican candidate. And he hadn't been quiet about his criticism of Cole since he'd taken office seven months earlier.

Bottom line, the man was a sore loser—and an asshole.

And another reason Cole had decided to run for mayor. He had become a lawyer to do his part in ensuring everyone received fair representation under the law. *Everyone.* Regardless of race, culture, sexuality or religion. And the people of Rose Bend needed someone who would do the same for them as mayor. They needed a person who would go to bat for all of its residents. Not just those from a certain tax bracket or with low melanin.

"Anyway," Wolf continued, "when you didn't answer your

phone, I went by the firm and city hall. Since you weren't at either of them, I came by here."

"I'm fine, Wolf," Cole murmured, hearing the "to make sure you were okay" even though it'd been left unspoken.

"No, you're not, Cole. You can run that bullshit by some people, but I'm not 'some people.' You haven't been fine in two years."

One thing he'd always admired and loved about his brother was his ability to cut through lies and get right to the heart of a matter. Today was not one of the days when he loved that ability.

"Guess who's back in town?" Cole asked, switching the subject he had no intention of touching. Crossing the few feet to the door that led to the kitchen, he pushed it open and entered, leaving Wolf to follow.

"Okay, I'll play along for a few minutes," Wolf said as Cole pulled open the refrigerator and grabbed another bottle of water. His brother shook his head, when he stretched one out to him. "Who's back?"

"Sydney Collins." Cole twisted the cap off and drank deeply.

Wolf frowned. "Leo's friend? Luke and Patricia's youngest?"

"The very same."

"Well damn. It's been a long time since she's set foot in Rose Bend. Is she still sexy as hell?" Wolf asked, propping his hip against the counter and crossing his arms over his massive chest.

"She was a teenager when she left here," Cole snapped, his fingers tightening around the water bottle. "Why the hell were you noticing if she was sexy or not?"

"Because I have eyes. And a dick," Wolf replied. "And she was eighteen. Legal." Wolf cocked his head to the side, peering at Cole in that way he had when studying a piece of wood. Measuring it. Seeing beyond the block to what lay beneath it. With cedar, that scrutiny was inspiring, mesmerizing. Focused on Cole, it was unnerving, intrusive and a pain in the ass. "Why do you care what I call her or how I looked at her? Because it definitely seems to—" his gaze dropped to the bottle Cole clenched "—bother you."

Fuck. It did.

But damn if he could explain why. Maybe because she had been so vulnerable beneath that tough-girl exterior? Maybe because she'd been his sister's friend? Or because he understood how it felt to question if you belonged?

His family was wonderful; his parents had never differentiated between him and their biological children. He'd never doubted their love for and dedication to him. But still… He was a Puerto Rican boy, now man, adopted by white parents in a diverse, unusually tolerant but still predominantly white town in the very Caucasian Berkshires. Every town had its racist assholes and Rose Bend wasn't any different. He'd been called names that had no place in supposedly progressive and enlightened twenty-first-century America. So yes, he'd doubted if he belonged before. But he'd had a support system in his family, and then in Tonia's, that had eased those uncertainties. From what he'd witnessed with Sydney's parents, she hadn't experienced that comfort.

Maybe it was that affinity that had forged a sort of connection with her.

At least, with Wolf's probing stare pinned to Cole's face, he was going with that.

"She's pregnant," Cole stated. And watched as surprise, then a terrible, pitying understanding flared in his brother's eyes.

Cole hated that understanding. Detested the pity more.

"She's what? In her mid to late twenties now? Old enough to know about and have sex. And isn't she married? That's usually a thing married folks do. And you've been around pregnant women since Tonia died. So, I repeat," Wolf murmured, his too-gentle voice belying the almost callousness of his words, "why do you care?"

I don't fucking know!

The shout ricocheted against Cole's skull, gaining speed and volume with each bounce. He fisted the fingers of his free hand

and barely contained the urge to hurl the water bottle across the small kitchen.

Because he lied to himself.

He knew why seeing her rounded belly had made him run like a man possessed. Had driven him home to pound on the punching bag.

Because she was pregnant—and he'd gotten hard for her.

Behind the old Catholic church, his body had stirred like Rip Van Winkle, awakening and stretching, coming to life. For someone who wasn't his wife.

Still hadn't stopped him from staring. From fucking throbbing in *want*.

And the guilt. Jesus, the guilt…and the fear. He might have been able to escape Sydney today, but he couldn't outrun the crushing weight of shame or the visceral terror that tore at him. Guilt over his betrayal of his wife's memory, of the love they'd shared. And fear for Sydney. For the childbirth that could snuff out her life as it'd done Tonia's. Fear for himself, if he ever let himself get attached to another woman who could be stolen away so easily.

Yes, he was a coward. He had every right to be.

"I don't care," he lied to Wolf, turning away on the pretense of downing the remaining water in the bottle and throwing it away. "Just that you'll most likely see Leo before I do, and you can let her know. I figure Sydney could use a friend about now."

Wolf remained silent for several seconds, and when Cole turned back to him, his brother's gaze snagged his, as if he'd just been waiting for Cole to look at him.

"All that lying must get exhausting," Wolf murmured. "When you're ready to be honest with me and yourself, I'll be here. I'm always here."

With that parting shot, Wolf pushed himself off the counter and strode out of the room. Leaving Cole alone.

Always alone.

Just like he preferred.

CHAPTER THREE

There were all kinds of disasters in life.

Like coming down with mono right before the senior prom.

Or going on vacation to a tropical island only for a tsunami to hit.

Another season of *Keeping Up with the Kardashians*.

So many more cataclysmic events than sitting down and sharing dinner with one's parents.

But for the life of her, at this moment, Sydney might risk all those other disasters rather than this hell.

Because this. Was. Hell.

"So, tell me again why you packed up, left your husband and returned here with no plans, no means of support?" her father demanded, setting down his knife and fork on either side of his plate and apparently forgetting about his perfectly cooked, medium-rare steak.

"And pregnant," her mother added, her silverware clutched in tight fists. Her gaze dropped down Sydney's torso to the table that blocked her stomach. Then, as if she couldn't bear the evidence of Sydney's transgression—divorce, single motherhood, she didn't know—her mother jerked her scrutiny back to Sydney's face. "Sydney…"

Okay, here we go…

In spite of the circumstances, and her doubts, when she'd first arrived at her childhood home, Sydney had been happy to see her parents. It'd been three years since they'd last visited North Carolina. And that had been because her father had been on his way to Charleston, South Carolina, for a medical conference. As strained as their relationship was, she loved them. And until setting eyes on them again, she hadn't realized that she'd missed them.

Initially, her parents had been shocked to see her on their doorstep. That shock had quickly melted into confusion and then the expected disappointment when Sydney informed them of her divorce and her pregnancy.

Yes, she'd anticipated their displeasure, but witnessing it had still been a strike to the chest. She should be used to it by now, letting them down. And not because of her rebellious behavior as a teen. No, she'd failed them years before then.

When she'd refused to save her sister's life.

"God, I could use wine right now," she muttered, staring a resentful hole through the water glass in front of her plate.

"This isn't a laughing matter, Sydney." Dr. Luke Collins scolded her in the same tone he'd used when he'd caught her sneaking back in the house after curfew. Most times, she'd felt like a difficult patient for whom her father had struggled to determine the correct diagnosis. Instead of what was causing her cough, though, he couldn't figure out why she wouldn't just act right. "That's always been a problem with you. Everything's not some careless joke. People are hurt by your rash decisions. Daniel, his parents, not to mention your child."

God, there was so much to tackle in those few sentences. But she focused on the last part first. "Trust me, Dad." *Hah!* her brain crowed. *Trust me. Good one.* "My decisions about filing for divorce and having this baby weren't rash. I understand your shock because you're just finding out about Daniel and me, but we've been done for six months. If I'm being truthful, a while before that. Some marriages don't work out. And unfortunately, ours was one of them."

"Then why are you having a baby with him?" Patricia Collins demanded, an eyebrow arched high.

Because of a self-sabotaging mixture of loneliness, why-the-fuck-not sex and Moscato. Somehow, she doubted her mother would appreciate that answer or consider it a good excuse.

"It just happened," she said, inwardly cringing at the cliché reply. Dammit, she sounded like the irresponsible teen they'd known rather than the capable woman she'd become.

"It just happened," her mother repeated, that eyebrow arching higher. "Not rash at all."

"What do you want me to say, Mom?" Sydney leaned back in her chair. "That one night my ex-husband and I had 'one for the road' sex that resulted in an unplanned child?"

"Sydney," Luke snapped.

She sighed, briefly closing her eyes. How quickly they'd fallen back into old patterns—the stern, censorious parents and the re-calcitrant child. This…dysfunctional dynamic was part of the reason she hadn't returned to Rose Bend in eight years. And why her parents' visits to North Carolina had been sporadic at best. The middle ground they'd once shared no longer existed. So, they constantly fought over the scraps. She'd come back here with hopes that the unconditional acceptance and love they withheld from her, they could give to her baby. Her parents were capable of it. She'd witnessed it.

Lifting her lashes, she shifted her gaze to the framed pictures on the far wall and focused on one in particular.

Carlin.

Her sister couldn't have been older than ten, and it must've been one of her healthier periods. In this image, the cancer that had plagued her since she was a toddler hadn't sunken her skin or made it appear sallow. Her eyes were bright, shining, not fuzzied by the pain or medications. Her cheeks were full, her little body slim but not fragile—not bones draped in damn near transparent skin.

Yes, the picture captured a happy moment in Sydney's older sister's short life.

What kind of woman would Carlin have been if she'd survived? Brilliant. Charming. Kind. Loving. Oh no doubt, Carlin would've been successful, perfect—the kind of daughter her parents would've been proud to brag about, to shower with their unconditional adoration. Carlin would've been a great woman...

If only Sydney had given her the chance.

"I don't understand why you and Daniel can't work it out," Patricia said, and when Sydney glanced back at her mother, she just managed not to look away again from the quiet pleading in the dark brown depths of her mother's eyes. "No marriage is easy, Sydney. It requires work. And now you have more of a reason than most to try." Her gaze dipped down Sydney's body again. "A baby deserves two parents. Stability is as important to a child's well-being as love. You and Daniel could give that to your son or daughter."

"And what about love for each other?" Sydney countered softly. "What kind of stable environment would it be to raise a child in a loveless home? You don't think he or she wouldn't notice that? Wouldn't be affected by that?"

Forget that her dignity, her very *person*, would die a slow death if she remained in a marriage that suffocated her independence, her voice. Her choice. What kind of example would that be to a child? To a little girl, especially?

But she didn't vocalize those thoughts. Not when she would be accused of thinking of only herself, her needs.

Mercenary.

That had been the word Daniel had flung at her, along with selfish. She was willing to sacrifice their child's future for her own.

Of all his accusations, that one tormented her the most. When she'd rejected his proposal to remarry, he'd called her selfish, and it'd dug beneath skin and bone, excavating old hurts and insecurities. For years, she'd been proud of how she'd matured. She wasn't the rebellious girl she'd been when she'd left home all those years ago. But with one hurled insult, Daniel had relegated her back to being that teen. Still… His words wouldn't have shaken her, if somewhere, in the darkest corner of her heart, she didn't already question herself.

Pain and, God help her, a sliver of shame sliced through her chest, straight to her heart. Because his accusation had contained a kernel of truth.

An image of Cole standing so alone in that cemetery snapped to mind. No doubt he and Tonia would've raised their child in a warm, nurturing family. Because even as a teen she'd witnessed their love for each other—had even been envious of it. No one would ever accuse Cole of being selfish. The kind of devotion he possessed for his wife wouldn't allow room for it.

It seemed unfair that he'd lost his marriage by the whims of Fate, and she'd thrown hers away.

"We all make sacrifices for those we love, Sydney," her father said, and she ground her teeth together against another blast of pain.

Who was he referring to? What loved ones? Daniel? Their child?

Carlin?

Because Sydney *had* sacrificed. For her marriage. For her sister. Over and over. But in both circumstances, it hadn't been enough.

"So, what's the plan, Sydney? You haven't been back home in almost ten years," Patricia reminded her with a shake of her head. "What do you plan to do? Where are you going to live?

How are you going to support yourself and a baby? What about prenatal care…"

"No, I haven't been back here in a long time, and I admit it. If not for being pregnant, I don't know if I would've returned. But I'm here. Regardless of my personal experience in this town, it's a good, safe place to raise a family. I want him or her to have that sense of community, that tight-knit closeness that's next to impossible in a city. I want my baby to have…family." She wanted her baby to have *them*. To be loved and accepted by them. Needed them to give her child what they hadn't been able to give her. It couldn't be more abundantly clear that she and her parents shared a strained relationship and that might not change. But she knew them; they wouldn't take their disappointment out on an innocent baby. They would love their grandchild.

She'd bet on that when she came home.

Home.

She thought of the house she'd passed on the drive into Rose Bend. A white, two-story Victorian on a corner lot. Gorgeous— with a steeply pitched roof, a lovely turreted tower, wide bay windows and a wraparound porch. It'd been breathtaking, yet still managed to appear homey, welcoming. Perfect for a loving family. A pang of longing echoed in her chest even now, as it had then, and she rubbed her knuckles against the ache. She would love to raise her baby in a house like that with both parents. A house meant to be filled with laughter, joy and affection. Maybe she couldn't give her baby that house or two parents, but she could offer her child the unconditional love of a mother, security and stability.

Contrary to what her parents thought.

Sighing, she lifted her hands, palms up. "I know what my showing up here unannounced seems like to you. That I'm being impulsive and thoughtless. And I'm responsible for that opinion. I should've spoken to you about the divorce, about the baby. But I didn't because…" *Because you might've talked me out of it. Because I couldn't bear letting you down. Again.* "I just didn't," she finished quietly. "I've prepared for this move. As a grant writer, I can work from anywhere. And I make enough to support myself and the baby. Daniel and I agreed that while I'm pregnant, he will keep me under his insurance to cover my medical expenses. And then after he or she is born, Daniel will add the baby. I already contacted Moe Dennison on the drive here, and she agreed to lease me one of their rental cottages for the next couple of months while I decide on a permanent place here in town."

"Basically live in a B&B? No," Luke balked, frowning. "What would people think? That we kicked our own daughter out of our house? No," he repeated, with a decisive slap of his palm to the table. "I won't have that kind of talk."

A small, humorless smile curved Sydney's lips. "Right. Can't have the Rose Bend townspeople gossiping about us. Glad to know that's the first reason that pops into your head for inviting me to stay here."

"You know that's not what I meant," her father objected.

"Sydney," her mother murmured at the same time, but she held up a hand to still their protests.

"I'm tired," Sydney said, a soul-deep weariness winding through her veins and infiltrating every muscle. The baby, she silently convinced herself. Fatigue came with the territory. It had nothing to do with her parents' not-so-warm welcome. Pushing back from the table and her barely touched dinner, she stood. "If it's okay with you, I'm going to crash in my old bedroom for the night. I'll head out to Kinsale Inn in the morning."

"Sydney, really," her mother pleaded.

And in that moment, Sydney desired nothing more than to circle the dining room table and lay her head on her mother's shoulder as she'd done as a little girl. Have her mother wrap her arms around her and whisper everything would be okay, that God never gave them more than they could handle.

The need for that embrace, for those words, throbbed inside her chest like a barely healed wound. One that had just scarred over and could be ripped open with just a careless movement.

But Sydney didn't round the table. Didn't seek the hug, the comfort that most likely wouldn't be offered.

Instead, she murmured good-night and left the room, climbing the stairs she hadn't treaded in years. What was the saying? You can't go home again? Thomas Wolfe had meant a person could try to return to a place from their past, but it wouldn't be the same as they remembered it.

Oh, Thomas.

If only that were true.

CHAPTER FOUR

"Dammit," Cole swore as freshly made coffee sloshed over the rim of his mug and scalded his fingers. Gingerly lowering the cup to the kitchen counter, he lifted his hand to his mouth and sipped at the drops of the dark brew.

Because it was a crime to waste good coffee. Any amount.

The pounding at his front door that had caused the accident in the first place echoed through the living room and into the kitchen, as the two rooms were separated only by a long breakfast bar. He didn't have long to wonder who waited on the other side of the door. Not when his thirteen-year-old twin brother and sister yelled his name through the wood.

"Cole! Hey, Cole! Open the door!" Sonny boomed.

"We know you're in there!" Cher added, following it up with more obnoxious knocking.

Yes. Sonny and Cher.

Moe and Dad had named Wolf, Leontyne and Sinead at birth, and Cole's biological parents had given him his musical name. Florence, his second to youngest sister and now eighteen, had come into the family when she'd been four. The twins had arrived six years later, when they were five. Upon their official adoption, Moe and Dad had allowed them the choice of keeping their birth names or selecting new ones. Each child had decided on a musician-inspired name like their older siblings. At least Florence, obsessed with the Supremes at the time, had chosen the gifted but tragic figure of Florence Ballard as her namesake. But the twins…

Cole shook his head as he strode across the room. That should've been a time when his parents put their collective feet down. He smiled as he unlocked the cottage door and pulled it open.

The fraternal twins grinned up at him. Though they shared the same, tall-for-their-age height and dark eyes, all similarities ended there. Sonny's light brown skin shone with a summer tan even though it was just the middle of June, in contrast to Cher's gleaming, beautiful, mahogany skin. Sonny wore his dark brown hair cut close like Cole's, while his sister's thick, almost sandy-colored corkscrew curls haloed around her head. Both were beautiful kids, but Sonny's features were already losing their boyish curves and maturing into stronger, bolder masculine lines.

Both of them still remained boisterous, a bit wild and totally fun and loving.

Yeah, he adored his baby brother and sister.

Even though they really tried him on Saturday mornings when he'd planned on nothing more strenuous than a good book and reruns of *Gunsmoke*. With the motorcycle rally nearing, this would probably be his last free weekend, but staring down at the twins, he abandoned plans for a lazy day. Especially since he'd lay odds they were on a mission from Moe. Maybe because she'd run a B&B for the last thirty-plus years or she'd raised seven children, but his mother didn't believe in idle hands—or his ass planted on his couch when she could find things for him to do.

"What's up, monsters?"

"What took you so long to answer the door?" Cher demanded, throwing herself against him and wrapping her arms around his waist. She continued smiling up at him, but her hug was tight. His heart clutched as he squeezed her back. Tonia had been the twins' first real experience with death as they'd both been so young when their parents died. But since then, Cher had been just a bit clingier, and he suspected fear of losing someone else she loved lay behind her behavior.

Sonny snickered. "It's because he's smart. He knows why we're here." He shook his head. "Dude, just give in and come quietly. And no one has to get hurt."

"Moe or Leo?" Cole questioned, walking back inside, his arm wrapped around his little sister's shoulders.

"Both," the twins answered in stereo.

"Shit," Cole muttered.

Sonny snickered, and it sounded disturbingly close to an evil cackle. "Exactly."

Several minutes later, he loaded his brother and sister's bikes up in the back of his pickup truck and they headed back toward Kinsale Inn. Out of habit, Cole slowed as he rounded the last turn in the road. Like it always did, his breath caught at the beauty of the place.

His parents had bought it a year before he and Wolf were born. To the townspeople and tourists that flocked to Rose Bend, the three-story building with its slanted roof, many windows, wraparound porch, red door and green shutters was a charming, beautiful landmark and five-star place to stay. For him, it'd always been a haven. The place where he'd been cared for, chastised, learned an invaluable work ethic and grown into the man he was today. It was a place of overflowing love where even those not born to Moe and his father had found security, stability and family.

It was and always would be home.

He'd barely braked at the end of the circular drive when the twins clambered from the back of his truck where they'd opted to ride with their bikes. Before he could yell "be careful," the front door of the inn opened, and Moe appeared in the doorway. All five feet of her. Born a decade too late to really enjoy the sixties, the woman still had never met a pair of bell-bottoms she didn't love or fringe anything she didn't wear. Like today, she'd adorned her small frame in a white-and-blue peasant blouse and a worn pair of denim jeans that seemed to swing around her ankles even though she stood still.

Hands planted on her slim hips and green eyes narrowed, she shouted, "If you fall from there and bust your head, don't expect me to clean it up."

Cole choked back a laugh. That made exactly zero sense. But damn if he would be the one to point that out to her. He loved Moe and had over a foot on her, but all she had to do was toss one of "those" looks in his direction, and he knew to shut up. He had no desire to take his life in his hands. Cue another one of her favorite nonsensical Moe Proverbs: I brought you into this world, I'll take you out.

Technically, she hadn't birthed him. And she'd never raised a hand to any of her kids. But she also hadn't raised a fool, and he wasn't trying her on the "take you out" part.

"Cole told us we could ride back there," Sonny tattled in his best "I'm totally innocent here" voice.

"Snitches get stitches, kid." Cole scowled at him as he lifted his sister's bike out of the truck's bed first.

Not at all intimidated, his brother grinned up at him before turning an impressively contrite hangdog expression to Moe. Who wasn't buying it in the least. The woman had a built-in bullshit radar that never went on the fritz.

"Save it," she said, but the smile twitching the corners of her mouth and the gleam in her gaze belied the brusque order. "Put those bikes away, you two. I'm cleaning up from breakfast while our guests are still on their trip into town. Cher, take over the

Leo until she gets back. And Sonny, you're going
the cottage to help with unpacking for Sydney."

his brother's bike hovering several inches off the
ground. His body locked even as his mind raced around that
one word.

Sydney.

Moe couldn't mean... No, that didn't make sense... Surely,
she meant someone else...

And dammit, could he finish even one thought?

Sonny grabbed his bike from Cole's still numb hands and
took off around the house with a mumbled, "Yes, ma'am," his
sister on his heels.

"Thanks for coming over, sweetie," Moe greeted Cole, shooing him forward with a finger wiggle. "Come give me a hug so
I can put you to work."

His paralysis melted, and he climbed the wide steps to the
porch on pure muscle memory because his mind still whirled.
He schooled his features but couldn't do a thing about the unease pumping through his veins.

Moe pulled him into a tight embrace that lasted just a couple
of seconds too long, her familiar baby powder and lavender scent
enveloping him. "What's wrong with you?" She pulled back,
squinting up at him, her long, elegant fingers wrapped around
his biceps. "Is everything okay?"

God, that note of worry in her voice killed him. He'd put
it there.

"I'm fine, Moe," he said, kissing her cheek. "Yes, I'm sure,"
he added before she could ask.

She smiled. "Smart-ass. I've raised a bunch of smart-asses."

"I wonder where we got that from?"

"Your father. It's always his fault."

Cole laughed, picturing Ian Seamus Dennison's response to
this familiar casting of blame. "Yes, dear," he would've drawled
with a roll of his eyes he would've ensured his wife didn't catch.

"Well, thank you for giving up your Saturday morning for me," she said, releasing him after another squeeze.

"Anything for you, you know that. But what's this about unpacking?" Cole asked, although he already suspected he knew the answer.

"That's right. C'mon."

She turned and headed toward the front door, leaving him to follow. Which he did. The coolness of the open, high-ceilinged lobby immediately welcomed him. The beautiful crystal chandelier that Leo had found at an antiques store a couple of towns over shone brightly overhead, reflecting off the dark, gleaming hardwood floors and staircase. Sunshine poured in through the huge picture windows of the living room that opened off the entryway.

But he didn't pay much notice to the light or the warm charm of the place. No. Every sense, every damn cell of his body focused on the curvy, *pregnant* woman seated next to his sister Leontyne on the overstuffed couch in the middle of the room.

"Cole, you remember Sydney Collins, don't you?"

His self-protective instincts screamed a blaring, banshee-like warning at him to keep his distance. To conjure up any excuse to throw his mother's way—work, mayoral responsibilities, a zombie-fucking-apocalypse—to get out of here.

But then Sydney started to push to her feet and his own carried him swiftly across the lobby and into the living room; his hands, of their own volition, cupped her elbows, and helped her stand from the deep cushions, steadying her.

"Uh, thanks," she said on a chuckle. That low contralto seemed too deep, too husky for such a petite woman. It caressed the skin bared by his short-sleeved T-shirt. "I'm not so far along yet that I can't rise from chairs, but I appreciate the sentiment," she teased.

The reference to her pregnancy scalded him, and before he could rethink what it would imply to her or his mother and sister, he snatched his hands away from her, dropping his arms back to his sides. And taking a step back.

"I'm sorry," he murmured.

Something flickered in her eyes, there and gone before he could decipher it. No doubt the same confusion that had dwelled there last night just before his abrupt departure. Or disgust. Hell, he was disgusted with himself.

"No worries," she said, giving him a slight smile before turning to his mother. "Moe, I can't thank you enough for accommodating me at the last minute. With summer and the rally so close, I know you have to be pretty booked. I doubt things have changed that much."

Moe waved her gratitude away. "Nonsense. It was nothing but a word. Besides, the cottage was sitting empty, and you're practically family."

"No 'practically' about it." Leo cradled Sydney's baby bump. "I'm going to be an aunt to little Arwen or Aragorn here and plan on spoiling her or him rotten."

Moe rolled her eyes. "Good Lord. She's not naming her baby after some Lord of the Realms characters."

"*Lord of the Rings*, Mom. Seriously? Whose child am I?"

Cole ignored their byplay, focusing on nothing but "accommodating me at the last minute." Apprehension skated down his spine. "You're staying here?" Yeah, he was a coward. But it didn't change the fact that avoiding her would be a hell of a lot harder if she was booked into his family's inn for the foreseeable future.

"She's renting one of our cottages. The one down the road from yours, actually," Moe informed him.

Well, damn.

"Which is why we need your help," Leo added, unaware of his panic. His sister slung an arm around Sydney's shoulders and hugged her. "We need your big muscles instead of your big brain today. Call it your civic duty, Mr. Mayor." She scrutinized his arms. "Well, biggish muscles." Her brow crinkled in a mock frown. "Well… Ah, never mind. You'll do."

Any other time, he would've snapped an equally derisive comeback as that was how siblings exhibited their undying affection for one another, but he couldn't speak. Couldn't do anything but stand there and mentally scramble for a reason why his mother shouldn't rent Sydney one of the properties that would place her in much-too-close-for-his-sanity proximity.

But he suspected *She makes me fucking feel* wouldn't fly with Moe. On second thought, it just might. And seeing that hopeful light enter his mother's eyes only to watch it extinguish would break him.

The only other choice would be moving back to the house he'd shared with Tonia. Back to the house and the empty, decorated nursery.

So, yeah, he was shit out of luck.

And stuck.

"It's okay, really," Sydney said, glancing at him before shifting her gaze to his sister and then to his mother. "I don't want to inconvenience anyone. I didn't bring that much with me. Just what I could manage to stuff in my car. Between Wolf, Sonny and Leo, we should have everything covered."

"Nonsense. What's the purpose of having brothers if I can't put them to use? And I refuse to let my recently returned best friend—who has a lot of explaining to do about why she didn't let me know sooner that she was coming home—tire herself out." Leo batted away Sydney's objections with a flick of her hand. "But I mean it. As soon as you get settled. Girls' night. Wine for me, Moe's special non-alcoholic cocktails for you, caramel popcorn and movies. Just like old times."

Leo's plans slid right over Cole's head, because he'd latched onto Sydney's words and they were all he could hear.

She didn't want his help—didn't want him there.

Not that he could blame her. Shame and anger clutched his

gut. Twisted it. What kind of man had he become? *One who makes an innocent woman feel unwelcome and uncomfortable because of your own hang-ups and issues.* The answer echoed in his head like a struck gong.

It wasn't her fault that she'd dragged his body out of hibernation kicking and screaming.

Wasn't her fault that guilt streamed through his veins like a caustic acid.

"No, I'm glad to help," he murmured. Then turning away before she could—rightfully—tell him to go home, he kicked his chin up at Moe. "Where's Wolf?"

"He's loading up his truck with some food I'm sending over with Sydney," she replied, studying him in the same contemplative manner that had dragged the truth out of him the first time he and Tonia had sex all those years ago. The CIA could uncover secrets of states, nuclear codes and the location of Jimmy Hoffa's body with her stare. She was dangerous.

Not willing to spill any of the confusion swirling inside him, he dipped his head in a nod and with a, "I'll go see if he needs any help and ride over with him," he stalked toward the kitchen and the driveway that reached around the back of the house.

Maybe physical labor would ease some of the tension riding him. Besides, he was looking at, what? Three hours of work at the most? He could assist in transporting food and unpacking Sydney's belongings without it being a big deal.

In and out. Hell, he could be back at his house by early afternoon, his original weekend plans resumed.

Not a problem.

He had a problem.

"Why can't Moe or Sinead get the rooms ready?" Cole demanded of Leontyne, thrusting his hand through hair that no longer existed on his head. Damn, after almost two years, he still wasn't used to not having longer curls. Instead, he scrubbed his palm over his head, the soft, short strands grazing his skin. "Or I can go, and you can stay here."

Dammit, he sounded panicked. Panicked and desperate. If the anxiety kicking a hole in his gut wasn't enough of a clue, the worried glances Leo and Wolf exchanged would've been a huge red flag.

"So let me get this straight," Leo said slowly, as if talking to a child—or someone unstable. "You—who hasn't actually worked at the inn in the last seven years—should return to air out and ready the rooms for an unexpected influx of last-minute guests? Rather than me, who runs the place every day along with Moe and Dad? 'Cause, y'know, it's my job. Sounds legit." She shrugged a shoulder. God, who knew a half shrug could carry so much attitude? She lanced him with a narrow-eyed stare that was eerily reminiscent of their mother's. "And to answer your other boneheaded and insensitive question, Moe's already starting to prep food for dinner and Sinead is manning the front desk since Moe let Cher go hang with her friends and Florence pulled another shift at Six Ways to Sundae. So that leaves me and Carrie to ready the guest rooms," she explained, mentioning the young woman the family employed as a part-time maid. "And yes, I need Wolf to drive me back since, as you know, I rode here with Sydney. Now. Any more questions?" She arched an eyebrow, popping her hands on her hips, her vibe fairly screaming, *Go 'head and ask one more thing. I dare you.*

No thanks.

Leontyne might be twenty-seven, but she was a Moe mini-me. And he'd prefer to keep the remainder of the ass he had left after that nice-nasty chewing out.

"What's the problem with you staying here?" Wolf asked, driving straight to the heart of the matter. Damn him. "I thought you and Sydney were friendly back in the day."

"We were, and there is no problem," Cole objected, and tasted the grime of the lie on his tongue. "For God's sake, can you two stop doing that?" he snapped when his siblings exchanged another glance. "It's creepy as hell and just rude. I said I have no issue staying to help Sydney settle in, and I don't."

His vehemence and show of affront did nothing to erase the skepticism from their expressions. And being the Dennisons that they were, neither tried to hide it.

"First, you damn near bit my head off yesterday after mentioning how sexy she used to be—"

"Eww, Wolf." Leo screwed up her face. "Gross. She was a teenager."

"Again. She. Was. Legal." He scowled at Leo before refocusing on Cole. "As I was saying, you bit my head off, and now you're acting like Sonny does when he's trying to get out of eating okra—"

"In his defense, who doesn't want to get out of eating okra?" Leo interjected.

"If you're not going to be a contributor to this conversation, I'm going to put you in time-out in my truck," Wolf threatened their sister.

Her lips turned down in a pout that would've done the twins proud. "I'm a grown-ass woman. You can't put me in time-out like I'm a child… But fine," she grumbled. "Wolfgang has a point, though," she said, her voice rising over his ominous rumble at the use of his full name. "Is there a reason you don't want to be alone with Sydney? Did she somehow offend you in the eight years she's been gone or the two and a half hours you've been in her presence today?"

"They saw each other last night."

Leo jerked her head toward Wolf at his revelation, her lips forming a perfect O on a sharp gasp. "Shut. Up."

"Nope, I think he was the first person to see her when she returned to town. He's the one who told me she was pregnant," the gossiping rat bastard supplied.

"You knew before me? That's such a violation of the girl code!

Why didn't you mention anything?" Leo asked, her head whipping back to Cole. "Did something happen between you two?" An avaricious gleam entered the gray-blue eyes she'd inherited from their father. Dad's eyes only glittered like that when he talked about football, fishing and his wife. Gossip, drama and a sale at the local farmer's market put it in his sister's, and since he wasn't presenting her with half-off tomatoes, he had to guess it was the whiff of a story to carry back to his mother and sisters that had her stare practically glazed over.

Fucking Wolf and his big mouth.

"Because there's nothing to tell and no," Cole said through gritted teeth.

"Uh-huh." Leo squinted at him. "Say what you want, but I'm definitely getting a 'there's something to tell' vibe."

Cole sighed. "I'm going back in now." He turned around and headed back up the short walk that led to the cottage's front door.

"Only the guilty flees when no one pursues," she sang behind him. Now she was quoting Proverbs. Brilliant.

He held up his arm and let his middle finger do his talking.

Bellows of laughter rolled after him, and though his brother and sister were annoying, he couldn't stop his lips from curling. Not that he would turn around and let them see, though. That would just encourage them.

"Is that your mayoral finger?" Wolf snickered.

"We should take a picture and—"

Cole opened Sydney's front door, stepped inside and closed it on his sister's reply. He wrote a mental note to himself. Confiscate Leo's cell later tonight and make sure she hadn't snapped a picture of his one-finger salute. He didn't put it past her to print copies and post them up at city hall right next to the First Presbyterian Church flyer for their annual clothing bazaar.

"Sorry about tha—" Cole's apology broke off when he spotted Sydney in the small kitchen. "Stop. What are you doing?" he barked, rushing through the living room toward her. The layout of her cottage mirrored his, and he maneuvered the space quickly, reaching her within seconds. Without thinking, he cupped her waist, steadying her on the short stepladder where she was perched. "Sydney, the hell? Get down. Carefully."

She glanced over her shoulder at him, her arms still raised, hands clutching the cups she'd been in the process of stashing in the glass-front cabinets.

"I'm fine," she assured him with a small frown.

"Well, seeing you on top of this thing, I'm not. Come down. Please," he added, the plea softer than his demand. His fingers tightened on her, the tips denting firm flesh.

For a long moment, she studied his face and though he wanted to turn away to avoid that penetrating stare, he didn't.

And he hated the part of himself that enjoyed looking at her more than it desired escaping her scrutiny.

"Okay," she finally murmured, slowly descending the three short steps. He guided her, not letting go of his grasp on her hips until her feet met the kitchen floor.

Then, as if her flesh singed him through the layers of her clothes, he released her, shifting backward—as much as he could in the tiny kitchen—and inserting much-needed space between them.

But he'd miscalculated; he should've never touched her. And now, it was too late to fix the error. Much too late.

Unless he could cauterize the nerve endings in his fingertips, he now knew the dichotomy of firmness and softness in her hips and the dip of her waist that hadn't fully disappeared yet with her advancing pregnancy. His hands contained the knowledge of just how wide those hips flared and how perfectly they fit his palms. In the moment right after her feet hit the floor, his body learned exactly how it would cover her, surround her. With the top of her curls brushing the base of his throat, and his chest easily spanning the width of her shoulders with plenty of room… With his cock inches from nestling against the small of her back directly over the delectable swell of her ass... Yeah, in bed, with her on her hands and knees in front of him, his bigger frame would swallow her smaller one. He could fuck her and protect her at the same time.

Jesus Christ.

His heart thudded against his rib cage.

Where had that thought come from?

This was *Sydney.*

Leontyne's friend. The young girl with the wide heart and wounded eyes that he'd once comforted next to her sister's grave. Even if he was ready to be with another woman—which he wasn't; no way in hell was he ready—she was pregnant by another man and married.

This inconvenient and unwanted attraction had turned him into a deviant who lusted after another man's wife.

"I know Leo most likely browbeat you into staying with me, but you don't have to." Sydney's husky voice tore him from the self-loathing he'd been circling like a drain. "I can finish unpacking on my own. You can go. I won't rat you out."

She smiled. The gentleness in the gesture and the words dug under his skin and burned like live coals.

"I don't need handling, Sydney." And though he felt like an asshole for snapping at her, he couldn't stop himself. "Contrary to whatever Leo or Wolf might've told you, I'm not fragile."

Sydney tilted her head to the side, studying him silently before giving him a slight nod and crossing her arms over her chest.

Don't you fucking look down, he silently ordered himself. But his eyes shot him a "To hell with that," and dipped. Taking in how sweet, rounded flesh swelled over the neckline of her tank top, that shadowed cleft a siren's call. Had she been smaller before the pregnancy? Was she sensitive?

None of his. Damn. Business.

"All right then," she said, tone still gentle with a new vein of steel barely running through it. "First, let's clear something up. Leo and Wolf didn't say anything about you. As a matter of fact, other than telling me you'd volunteered to help me move in here—which was obviously a lie on their part—your name didn't come up in our conversations. Sorry to disappoint your sensitive ego there," she drawled. "Second, I don't need anyone to tell me what I can ascertain all on my lonesome. Me being pregnant bothers you. Don't deny it." She thrust up a hand, palm out as if jamming the denial he had been about to vocalize back down his throat. "Yesterday, you couldn't get away from me fast enough after realizing I was pregnant. And today, you can't even bring yourself to look at my stomach."

He started to contradict her, to reassure her that no, he didn't have a problem. But the words couldn't squeeze past the constriction of his throat.

She was wrong…but she wasn't.

How did he explain that it wasn't just her pregnancy? Rose Bend had seen its fair share of pregnant women in the last two years, and as mayor he'd encountered babies as well as expecting mothers. No, the explanation became murky and difficult when he tried to introduce his dick into the mix. Being attracted to a pregnant woman scared the shit out of him.

But that enlightenment would also mean he had to talk about Tonia and Mateo. And he couldn't do that. Not today. Not with her.

Not when a noxious cauldron of emotion—shame, guilt, betrayal, lust and an unforgivable thread of excitement—brewed and bubbled just beneath his sternum. No, he couldn't bring his wife's name up here when the woman who'd kindled that storm of feelings stood not even feet away from him.

That seemed like even more of a betrayal.

Especially since Sydney was another man's wife. About to be the mother of that man's child.

"I'm not judging you, Cole," Sydney continued, lowering her arms to her sides. He caught the slight twitch of her right hand. As if she'd been about to stretch it toward him but decided against it. "And while I might not know the details, I think I understand."

"You do?" He arched an eyebrow, hating the caustic bite in his tone. "What do you think you understand?"

She didn't bat an eye at his sarcasm. "I saw you over at the cemetery, Cole. And you told me yourself you were visiting your wife and son." She glanced away, her throat working. But when she returned her gaze to him, her eyes were clear, her voice steady. "I don't need the details. They're yours, not mine. Especially if you're not ready to give them to me. But all that to say, I don't need excuses if you don't want to stay... If you *can't* stay," she murmured.

Part of him leaped at the out she offered him like it was a rapidly unraveling lifeline. But then, a shadow flickered in her chocolate eyes. There and gone like a bend in light, but he recognized it. Was intimate with it.

Loneliness.

Sydney was lonely.

No.

Something deep inside him roared the denial. He couldn't abide her hurting. Couldn't abide being a perpetuator of that pain.

"I'm good, Sydney," he said, choosing not to analyze the impulse, the urge that demanded he remain here with her. "Put me to work." He threw a pointed glance at the step stool. "I'll start with the cups."

"Okay," she finally conceded after a long moment. "Thank you."

For the next hour, they worked in companionable silence, finishing the kitchen and moving to the living room.

Sydney had been truthful; she hadn't brought a ton of belongings with her. The cottage had already come furnished for guests, and most of the things they unpacked were dishes, clothes, small pieces of furniture like artwork, a scratched but beautiful rocking chair, knickknacks and one of the best record collections he'd ever had the pleasure to lay eyes on.

"You're kidding me," he muttered under his breath, holding up a blue album cover with bright red lettering and an image of John Coltrane playing a saxophone. "You have *My Favorite Things*?" he asked Sydney, incredulous. Picking up the next black-and-white cover with another image of the famed jazz saxophonist, he held it up. Stared at it as if he'd never seen it before. And to be honest, he never had—in person. "And *Love Supreme*?" He didn't care if envy layered his tone. "How did you come by these? Sell a kidney? Knock over a collector? What are you not telling me, Sydney Collins?"

She chuckled, pausing in the middle of adding books to the novels already occupying the tall bookshelf against the far wall of the living room.

Shaking her head, she warned, "I would tell you, but then I'd have to murder you in your sleep. No witnesses and all that."

Plucking *Giant Steps* from the box, he stared at the original 1960 album and muttered, "It might be worth the risk."

"Careful there, Cole," she teased. "You're sounding a little jealous."

"More than a little," he admitted, flipping the cover over and studying the details on the back. "I'm a lawyer, but I'm still over here mentally preparing my defense just in case I decide to perform a little B&E."

Her laugh, full and as husky and sultry as her voice, filled the room, and he had to look up from the LP to glance at her. Delight suffused her lovely features, softening her chocolate eyes and curving her pretty mouth.

"I have to admit, I would've never taken you for a jazz fan."

"Jazz enthusiast, thank you very much." She smirked. "I think I'm a little offended. And disgustingly curious. What kind of music did you 'take me' to be a fan of, then?"

Yeah, he'd clumsily tripped into a minefield. A "how much do you weigh?" kind of minefield. And he had no one but himself and his big mouth to blame.

"Oh no, Coltrane Dennison. Don't get judicious on me now. You've put your foot *aaall* the way in it. Like, I'm three-point-two seconds away from a 'bless your heart.' Which in Southern speak means, fuck you." She grinned, arching a dark eyebrow high. "So you might as well ride this one out."

He held up his hands, palms out. A snicker escaped him before he could trap it inside. "Well, hell. Don't 'bless your heart' me. I just seem to remember you and Leo blasting a lot of Maroon 5, Fall Out Boy and even some One Direction back in the day. Forgive me if I assumed you still worshipped at the altar of pop."

"One. Adam Levine is a sexy, tatted beast with the voice of an angel and the flexibility of a gymnast. Yum. Two. I still love Fall Out Boy and I deny that One Direction accusation. You have no proof, and counselor, you of all people should know any allegation without evidence means nothing. Although, I would watermelon *and* sugar the hell out of Harry Styles."

Cole shuddered. "That is…disturbing."

"Look here, Judgy McJudgerson, you don't see me giving you side-eye over your Celine Dion obsession—"

"She's a legend," he interrupted.

"—so I'll thank you to keep your opinion about my only slightly unsettling fantasies about Harry to yourself. But to satisfy your nosiness, I've always loved jazz. Dad owns a huge collection himself, and I used to sit in the study with him and listen to it. He would quiz me on what instrument I heard or which artist was playing." A faint smile whispered across her lips. "It's one of the few things we have in common. Our love of music." Clearing her throat, she slipped the book in her hand onto the shelf and grabbed another one from a box. "But c'mon," she said, her voice a little huskier, a little rougher. "You're named after one of the most celebrated artists in jazz history. Please tell me you have his music."

He nodded, stroking a reverent hand over the cover before setting it aside and picking up the next one, simply entitled *Coltrane*. "I have CDs, even some old tapes. But nothing like this. None of the originals. I would've loved having them, though. Especially when I was a kid." Lifting his head, he stared out the large picture window next to the entertainment center. The serene view of the empty street, trees thick with summer green leaves and yards of green grass greeted him, but he didn't really see any of it. Instead, hazy, sepia-toned images of the kid he'd been wavered in front of his eyes. "Moe and Dad have never treated me differently from Wolf, Leo or Sinead. Ever. Yet, they made sure I knew who my biological parents were, even if it meant taking me over to the Riveras' and Narvaezes' homes to learn and appreciate my Puerto Rican heritage. And I loved Moe and Dad for that. It made me feel closer to my biological parents. But about thirteen, I became obsessed with them."

He sensed movement out of the corner of his eye, and he shifted his gaze from the window to Sydney. She still held a book in her hand, but she'd turned completely toward him, settling her shoulders against the bookcase and giving him her full attention.

And though the instinctive need for self-protection ordered him to draw back, to shush, he continued speaking. Continued sharing with this woman something he'd never told anyone else.

"Florence hadn't come to us yet, and regardless of the unconditional love and acceptance of my family, I felt...different. And I became consumed with finding out everything I could about my birth parents. And not just about my culture, but *them*. Their likes, dislikes, their habits, what they were like as children, teenagers... What their dreams were together—what they were for me. That information included why they named me after John Coltrane. Turned out, my father was a huge jazz fan. From what Moe told me about him, I think he would've lost his mind over your collection."

He thumbed through the stack he'd pulled out before spotting Coltrane's music. Straight-ahead jazz, as they called it. The greats. Thelonious Monk, Miles Davis, Freddie Hubbard, Ahmad Jamal. And even some Sarah Vaughan and Ella Fitzgerald. Oh, most definitely Sydney and Mateo Burgos would've bonded.

"So anyway, one obsession led to another, and anything John Coltrane I could get my hands on, I snatched up. Records, tapes, videos. He was gone, but I so desperately wanted to bond with my birth father through the music of the man he admired so much he named me after him."

"Cole," Sydney whispered.

The low sound of his name snapped him from his tumble into the past.

"Anyway, I started out listening to 'Trane' for one reason, but ended up loving his music for his absolute genius." He shook his head, releasing his breath on a short huff of laughter. Embarrassment trickled through him as he ran through what he'd divulged to Sydney. *Jesus. Where had all that come from?* "I must've driven Moe crazy with playing those records and tapes over and over. And then the endless questions. But she answered every one and never made me feel guilty for asking. Even though, sometimes, I could tell in her eyes, it hurt her."

"I'm sure she understood," Sydney said. "That's how Moe is, *who* she is. You probably don't remember because you were gone away to school, but on Carlin's birthday and on the anniversary of her death, my parents would go to the cemetery to spend time at her grave. I've never gone. When I was younger, I'd pitch a fit so bad, they left me with babysitters. And when I was older, I would leave the house and not return until later that day. One of the places I would go was your house. Moe never asked me what I was doing there, or made me feel guilty for being there instead of at the grave, or tried to convince me to go like other adults did. She just let me hang out with her, Leo and your family, offered me a safe space and fed me. God, did she feed me." Sydney laughed, but after a moment, the warmth faded from her eyes and her mouth lost its curve. "There were times I…" She paused, frowned and fidgeted with the book in her hands before turning around and sliding it on the bookshelf.

"Times you…" he gently pressed.

Her hand lingered on the book, her shoulders so stiff with… whatever was rippling through her, he knew before she even pivoted to face him again that she wouldn't finish that sentence.

Hypocrite that he was, he almost stood up and stalked over to her, insisting she open up to him, share with him.

But then she might demand the same from him. And that wasn't happening.

"Your mom sent lemonade over with us. Would you like a glass?" Sydney asked, swiping the back of her hand over her forehead.

Alarm sizzled through him as he narrowed his gaze on her slightly glistening skin, noticing the tautness around her lush mouth. In an instant, he shot to his feet and covered the distance between them.

"Hey," he murmured, peering down at her and studying the signs of fatigue he couldn't miss from this close. The haziness in her espresso eyes and the faint smudges underneath them. Earlier in the kitchen, he vowed not to touch her again, to keep his distance. But he broke that promise to cup her elbow. Hell, it was safer than putting his thumbs to those bruises that denoted lack of sleep and trying to smooth them away. "You okay?"

"I'm fine," she maintained. "Just a little thirsty—"

"And tired," he interrupted with a wry smile. "You won't be any less of a superwoman if you admit it, you know," he teased. "I remember—"

His swift intake of breath cut off the words that had been

ready to tumble so easily from his mouth. *I remember how tired—and cranky because she was tired—Tonia would get.*

Oh dammit.

The memory of leading his wife to their bedroom and cajoling her into lying down by offering to nap with her pummeled him with meaty fists, leaving him emotionally bruised and his lungs constricted.

Where had that come from? Why would he think about her here of all places? Now? He swallowed, panic scraping his throat. With… Sydney?

"Cole." A hand on his upper arm snapped him back, centered him. He focused on her face, not realizing until that moment that he'd shifted his gaze over her head and stared blindly at the far wall. "You're right. I am a little tired. Would you mind if we called it a day?"

She was giving him an out. Again.

And this time, he accepted it.

Because that crack into his past had him open, raw. And bleeding.

"Are you sure you're okay? Do you need anything before I leave?" he asked, his voice rough. Jesus, he felt like he was seconds away from flaming out. He had to get out of here.

She nodded, her pretty eyes solemn.

"I'm good."

He returned her nod, his jerkier.

"Moe has my number if you need," his throat closed on *me*, "anything," he rasped.

He didn't wait for her reply. Twisting on his heel, he strode across the room and exited through the door without glancing back.

And tried to convince himself he wasn't escaping.

He failed.

CHAPTER FIVE

"Since you just had an appointment with your OB-GYN last week, we don't need to do an exam today. So, I'll see you here in another two weeks for your five-month checkup," Dr. Kelly Prioleau said, tapping the screen of the tablet she held. Wow, her dad's clinic had stepped into the twenty-first century. How 'bout that? "And since you mentioned not having an early non-invasive prenatal test, you can find out the baby's sex during the ultrasound, too. If you'd like."

"Oh, I'd like," Sydney agreed. "The pregnancy was surprise enough. I don't need the baby's sex to be one, too."

The lovely Black woman with the short, gorgeous twists and wide smile laughed. Just another reason Sydney liked her father's new partner. Well, that and she could take a joke instead of getting all judgy, and her bright, popping red lipstick. The doctor obviously had style.

And a wonderful, warm confidence that had immediately set Sydney at ease when she'd entered the doctor's office this morning. In the time since she'd left Rose Bend, her father had hired the woman who appeared to be in her late thirties as a partner. Sydney couldn't help but think her mother had something to do with that. As in laying down an ultimatum—cut back on work or else.

Luke Collins was a dedicated and great doctor…and a workaholic. At least, that's how Sydney remembered him. Aside from the hospital, the Rose Bend Family Practice was the only clinic in town. The residents adored him, and most would rather see him before going to the larger, more impersonal hospital. Which meant the chairs filling his waiting room were never empty.

The thriving practice provided more than its fair share of patients, and as Dr. Prioleau had assured Sydney, she was kept much busier here than she'd ever been in her bigger, fifteen-plus medical group in Charleston, South Carolina.

Regardless, Sydney was glad the other woman had made the move because it meant her father wouldn't be checking her cervix.

Yeah, she'd always desired to be closer to her father but not *that* close.

"I definitely respect that." Dr. Prioleau smiled, pushing back her chair and rising from behind her desk. "If you don't have any more questions, I look forward to seeing you in a few weeks."

Sydney stood from the visitor's chair and shook the doctor's extended hand. "Thanks, Dr. Prioleau. I'll see you then."

She exited the spacious office, the doctor beside her. As soon as they entered the lobby, a tingle started at the nape of Sydney's neck, marching over her skin like an army of fire ants. She didn't glance behind her to verify, but it seemed as if every eye in the packed waiting area was trained on her. No doubt, in the span of seconds—as long as it required to tap out a text or make a covert phone call—most people would know she'd visited her father's office.

This—the avaricious curiosity and gossip—she hadn't missed about living in a small town. There'd been a certain freedom and peace in living in a city the size of Charlotte. Except for her small circle of friends, anonymity had meant she could be whoever she wanted without comparison to who she used to be. No judgment. No condemnation.

Dr. Prioleau patted Sydney's hand one last time. "I'll see you soon, but remember, if you have any questions, concerns or feel any discomfort, please don't hesitate to call or come in, okay?"

"Got it."

Seconds later, Sydney stepped outside the clinic. The late morning heat warmed her upturned face, and she closed her eyes, breathing in the clean air. Fresh coffee and the scent of pancakes from the diner down the street. The sharp taste of acrylic from the workers painting the dentist's building next door. And underneath it all, the faint, nebulous fragrance of home. Even though she'd lived in Charlotte for eight years, even with her complicated feelings about this place, that particular fragrance had always been missing.

Sighing, she headed toward her car. Just as she hit the key fob to open her doors, her cell buzzed against her hip.

"This better not be you, Katherine," she grumbled, pulling the phone free.

Katherine Rhys owned Grant Resources, the organization Sydney worked for as a contractor. The company posted requests from agencies and corporations seeking grant writers. In the five years she'd been working with Grant Resources, Sydney had written more than a fair share of successful grants. But she'd informed Katherine that she wouldn't be accepting any jobs for the next few weeks while she settled into a new—or old—home. She could afford not to work right now. Old-fashioned in his view of marital roles, Daniel had refused to allow Sydney to pay any of their house bills. Hell, if it'd been up to him, she wouldn't have worked at all. But she'd put her foot down hard on that position. So, all of her earnings had gone into savings. If she chose not to work for the next year, she could. But being stagnant that long would drive Sydney crazy.

You could always work on that urban fantasy book you've been too chicken to finish.

Sydney flipped two middle fingers at the irritating sneer in her head. Leave it to her to not only talk to herself, but to have that voice be a know-it-all bitch, too. Since she was a teen, she'd harbored the dream of writing and publishing a book set in a seemingly not-too-distant, apocalyptic world. But it was just that—a dream.

She'd shared the desire with Daniel once, shortly after they'd married. And once was all she'd needed to decide never to make that mistake again. He'd been so patronizing, so damn *logical*, that she'd ended up agreeing with him. The time for childish things had passed, and grant writing, which actually earned her money, should be her focus. And in the end, he'd been right. It would be her job that provided a stable, secure home for her and her baby.

She glanced down at the cell phone screen.

Speak of the devil.

Grimacing, and then immediately feeling guilty about it, she swiped her thumb across the answer bar. "Hey, Daniel."

"Hello, Sydney." Her ex-husband greeted her in his cultured, deep baritone.

In spite of the strained terms they'd parted on, a rush of affection and maybe a little nostalgia trickled through her. Yes, they'd divorced, and he hadn't agreed with her moving hundreds of miles away, but she'd been with him since she'd been twenty years old, married to him at twenty-one.

An image of her ex-husband solidified in her mind's eye. Tall and lean, skin a beautiful mahogany, his strong, fit body clothed in one of his customary tailored suits with a tie. A handsome, distinguished, successful man who made the perfect dean of students at a prestigious private high school.

Nine years older than her, he'd been her rock, her support system, her friend for over five years. It wasn't his fault she'd grown and decided she needed—something different. Something more. She'd hurt him with her decision to separate and then divorce. And for that, she would always bear regret.

"It's good to hear from you. Did you get my text about getting here safely?" She'd taken the coward's way out and dashed the text off the night she'd arrived, a week ago.

"I did. Thanks for letting me know." An awkward pause that was becoming their norm. "How're you feeling? And the baby?"

"Good. Both of us. As a matter of fact, I just left my dad's clinic after meeting with my new doctor. My first checkup will be in two weeks. I'll find out if we're having a girl or boy," she said, injecting a cheer into her voice to counterbalance the guilt. *Selfish*. There was that word again. Was she selfish for stealing these sorts of milestones from him? As the father, he had the right to share them. Pinching the bridge of her nose, she squeezed her eyes closed and fought against the urge to apologize. Again. "If you'd like, I can record the appointment for you. So, you can still...be there."

"Sure, sure. I'd like that," Daniel said. But his pause vibrated through the open line with tension, with frustration and anger. All directed at her. Not that she could blame him. Because she didn't. "God, Sydney," he exploded, but just as quickly, cut himself off. She could easily picture him straightening, composing himself, submerging his emotion behind that polite mask. To Daniel, emotion was messy, a sign of being out of control. And Dean Pierson was never out of control. "I respect your father, but a *clinic*? You should be going to a hospital with all the best and most advanced technologies. Your OB-GYN here was one of the best in the state. But instead you're at a clinic being cared for by a doctor you don't know. A doctor who—"

"Who graduated from Harvard Medical School, completed her residency at Johns Hopkins and was one of the top physicians at MUSC Health-University Medical Center before deciding to move here," she said, quietly reciting Dr. Prioleau's credentials. "My father wouldn't have taken on a partner in his practice unless she was the very best. I did my homework, Daniel. Our baby's health is just as important to me as it is to you."

His sigh echoed in her ear. "I know that, Sydney. I didn't mean to imply…" He trailed off. "You shouldn't have left. We could've made it work."

"Daniel," she interrupted, tired. So damn tired of this conversation. Of how she just couldn't make him understand how she'd been disappearing in her marriage. He didn't get it. Would never get it because his big, forceful personality wouldn't allow him to grasp how she couldn't have been happy being by his side as his wife, all her needs taken care of, wanting for nothing.

Wanting for nothing except her identity.

Happiness.

Love.

To Daniel, they'd been happy, enjoyed a good, solid marriage. For her? She'd been slowly suffocating.

The breaking point hadn't been an argument. She hadn't caught him cheating. It hadn't been his antiquated ideas of gender role assignments—though heaven forbid he wash a dish, or she take out the trash.

No, it'd been none of those.

The catalyst had been when she'd attended one of many school fundraising functions with him and one of the board members had introduced Daniel and her to a potential benefactor as Dr. Daniel Pierson and his wife.

Just his wife.

As if she had no identity, no, no…*purpose* other than being an extension of her husband.

In that moment, the restlessness that had been hounding her for months crystallized inside her chest like a diamond of truth. Clear. Sharp. And precious.

She couldn't do it anymore.

But the realization had blindsided Daniel. Her request for a divorce had left him frustrated and confused.

"No," he insisted. "You walked away instead of trying. That's what married couples do. They work hard at their relationship. They don't just quit. You quit on me, Sydney. On us."

She didn't say anything. Couldn't. Because he was right. And even though guilt blasted her like a furnace, she still wouldn't have stayed.

He'd called her impulsive, immature for ending their marriage to seek something that only existed in the movies.

To her, it'd been the most mature decision she'd ever made.

"Even if you didn't want to stay married, we could've co-parented here. But now, I don't even have that option with you nearly a thousand miles away. I have no say when it comes to you. Not in our life together, not in my child's life."

"Daniel, I'm sorry," she whispered, giving him the words she'd uttered so many times over the last six months that they should be tattooed on her tongue.

"I know. So you've said many times," he murmured, suddenly sounding weary. Pain spasmed in her chest that she'd brought this proud man to that. "Look, Sydney. This isn't the reason I'm calling. I…" He paused, and when he spoke again, his voice was firmer, stronger. Dean Pierson. "I've been seeing someone."

She stared straight ahead, not really seeing the black-and-gold awning of Mimi's Café across the street. His words rattled in her head, and she even mouthed them to herself. *I've been seeing someone.* She waited. Waited for the burst of jealousy, the flash of resentment that he could berate her for leaving him and in the next breath announce that he'd moved on.

But nothing.

No, that wasn't true. Relief stirred behind her sternum. If he'd fallen for someone else, maybe it would ease the anger he harbored toward her. Maybe…

Maybe it would absolve her of some of the shame weighing her down like a cinder block.

And maybe she really *was* as selfish as he'd called her to turn this around and make it about her.

"I'm happy for you, Daniel," she said. "I really am. She must be a wonderful person."

"She is," he agreed. "Veronica is a special education teacher with a master's and is currently working on her PhD. We have a lot in common." In other words, she was everything Sydney wasn't. She tried not to allow the petty jab to find purchase, but no such luck. "I've also told her about the baby. She's excited to be a part of his or her life if we continue to move forward."

"That's...nice." Sydney found it hard to breathe past the feelings swirling inside her. The jealousy that had been missing over his new relationship now punched her in the gut, winding her. Another woman in her child's life? Possibly claiming her baby? That didn't sit well. Logically, Sydney understood that most likely she and Daniel would one day have partners who would be potential stepparents. Still... Shit. She wasn't ready to deal with this. Not today. "Congratulations, Daniel. I have to go, but I'll be in contact."

"Fine. Please make sure you do, Sydney." He paused. "I won't be kept out of my child's life."

Without a goodbye, he hung up, and for several seconds, she stood there, the phone still pressed to her ear.

Slowly, she lowered her arm and tucked the cell back into her purse. Disquiet lodged in her chest.

She was being silly. Paranoid, even.

And yet...

Why had that sounded faintly...ominous?

What was the saying?

You're only paranoid when you're wrong.

She needed to be wrong.

Sydney shook her head, calling herself a fool. But it didn't stop her from pulling open the entrance door to the big brick building that housed the offices of Coltrane A. Dennison, Esq., and walking into the quiet, elegant lobby.

Yet the gleaming woods, shining glass and inviting furniture did very little to calm the tumbling of her stomach. Nothing could accomplish that but answers.

And as much as she would've liked to continue avoiding Cole, as she'd done for the past week, he was the person who could give her answers. It showed her desperation that she'd peeled out of the clinic parking lot and headed straight here. Without granting herself time to consider how she would face Cole after he'd hightailed it out of her cottage like his firm ass had been on fire.

Did it hurt knowing she made him uncomfortable? God, yes. It ached in a place she wished she could shut off. That place was right next to the one where a wholly inconvenient and unsolicited lust resided for the man with the tragic angel's face. Too bad she couldn't evict both squatters. Because neither one of them boded well for her.

That day in her kitchen, when his strong, big hands had grasped her hips—powerful hands that had been so gentle as they guided her down the ladder and to the floor—her heart had thudded against her breastbone, pumping a languid warmth through her veins. He'd been both dominant and tender. And the combination was devastating.

She'd read somewhere that after the first trimester, a woman's sex drive soared. Well, she'd chalked that up to a myth. What could possibly be sexy about swelling boobs, a big belly and a temperamental bladder? Turned out all she needed to shatter that belief was encounter Coltrane Dennison. Now, she couldn't turn her damn body off. Just one thought about his haunted, amber eyes, that wide, carnal mouth with its slightly fuller bot-

tom lip, that stubborn, solid jaw and large, rangy, sexy body…
She stifled a shiver that whipped through her like a hot flash.

She missed sex.

Not just the act. She missed the intimacy, the cuddling, the connection. Physical attraction had never been an issue between her and Daniel—hence the one night together that had landed her here—but in the last year or so of their marriage, that quiet closeness had been absent.

One glance at Cole on that rise behind the church had reminded her of its absence.

One touch from Cole in her kitchen had made her ache for it.

She shook her head, attempting to clear it of the thoughts that had her nipples standing at attention and the sensitive flesh between her thighs pulsing in equal parts sympathy and deprived outrage. Her body hovered on the verge of a full-out rebellion, and she didn't have time for that now. Not with a pregnancy, a brooding ex-husband and reacclimating to a new town. She needed help more than an orgasm.

But, dammit, the two were running neck 'n' neck.

Good thing she could handle the latter herself.

She approached the wide, cherrywood front desk. It was empty. Frowning, she leaned forward and to the side, peering at the dark computer monitor. Either the receptionist had stepped away or no one manned the lobby today.

"Damn," she whispered. What now? Someone had to be here because the entrance was unlocked. And she'd spotted Cole's truck in the parking space out front. Did she leave and wait until a later time? Like when she could schedule an appointment.

No.

The answer boomed in her head, immediate and adamant. The nerves writhing in her belly like a nest of snakes wouldn't allow her to wait another five minutes, much less a couple of days.

Before she could talk herself out of how impulsive and rude this might be, she strode down the hall to the left of the receptionist's desk. Several closed doors marked the way, but only one at the end of the corridor bore a gold nameplate with Coltrane A. Dennison etched into it. Inhaling a deep breath, she knocked. Several seconds passed. She raised her arm to rap the wood again when the door swung open.

Cole stared down at her, confusion and surprise darkening his golden eyes.

"Sydney?" he asked. "What are you doing here?"

Worrying and trying not to beg you to hug me against that big chest.

She swallowed those foolish and pathetic words and forced a smile to her lips. "I'm sorry to just show up without an appointment, Cole. But if you have a moment, can I take it?"

He stared at her for several seconds, his narrowed gaze a heavy caress she imagined stroked over her cheekbones, nose and jaw. She fought the tremble that tried to work its way through her.

"Of course. Come in."

He stepped back, granting her enough space to enter his large office. Sunlight streamed into the room through the huge floor-to-ceiling casement windows, spilling onto the wide desk. Even though concerns swarmed her, she couldn't prevent curiosity from creeping in.

A giant bookcase packed with legal volumes and books encompassed one wall. In front of it sat a round table with several chairs pushed up to it. A small sitting area with an overstuffed black leather couch, armchairs and a beautiful oak coffee table took up the other half of the room. The requisite framed degrees dotted the wall above the furniture, but right next to them hung gorgeous paintings of town landmarks—St. John's Catholic Church, city hall, Mimi's Café, Winter Elm Ski Resort and Kinsale Inn.

Then there were the smaller, less obvious details that captivated her attention. The intricate carvings of roses in the legs of the coffee table. The green-and-white paperweight on the end table that appeared to be a misshapen blob with a large *C* and

D carved into the base. Several picture frames front and center on his ruthlessly neat desk. An open ring box on the top shelf of his bookcase with two gold bands nestled on the black velvet.

Cole Dennison was a man who appreciated beauty and order and loved family.

The knowledge only increased her ill-advised fascination with him.

Dammit.

"Here," Cole said, extending an arm toward his sitting area instead of the visitor chairs in front of his desk. "Can I get you something? Water? Coffee? Tea?" He frowned. "I don't have decaffeinated coffee, though."

"No, I'm good." She waved off his offer with a small smile and crossed the room, settling on one end of the sofa. "You don't have to go to any trouble. Especially since I showed up out of the blue. And I promise not to keep you long, I just…" She twisted her fingers in her lap, staring down at them for a moment before meeting his gaze again. "I just need to ask your opinion on something. Your legal opinion."

His eyes sharpened with awareness as he lowered to the middle of the couch. "All right," he murmured, propping his elbows on his muscular thighs, his big, elegant hands hanging between his knees. "Are you in trouble, Sydney?"

"No," she hurriedly assured him. "Well, not how you're thinking. Actually, I'm probably being paranoid and making an issue out of nothing. I'm sorry if I'm wasting your time with this—"

"Sydney, you're babbling," he softly interrupted, the corner of his mouth lifting in a faint half smile. "Why don't you let me be the judge of whether or not you're wasting my time. Which you're not, by the way. Just tell me the nonproblem that you may or may not need legal advice for."

"Right." She inhaled and drew his fresh scent into her nose and lungs—rain and earth. It both calmed her nerves and set them ablaze. Shifting her gaze away from his gold-and-brown stare, she studied the fine grain of the coffee table instead. "My ex-husband called a little while ago—"

"Ex-husband?" he repeated sharply, dragging her attention back to him. His thick eyebrows nearly met in a confused but fierce frown. "You're divorced? Since when? You never mentioned..."

"Yes, I've been divorced for nearly six months now. I told Leo, I assumed she would've told you."

"She didn't." His firm lips flattened into a stern line. "Your parents never said anything either."

Sydney sighed, not really wanting to go into her completely dysfunctional relationship with her parents. "That's because they didn't know until I returned to town." Surprise flickered in his gaze, and she held up a hand, forestalling the inevitable question. "That's a long, probably petty on my behalf story, and not one I'd prefer to go into right now."

"Fair enough. But," his gaze flickered to her stomach before returning to her face, "you've been divorced for six months, which means you must've been separated longer than that. And you're what? Four or five months along?"

"Eighteen weeks today. So yes, I was with my ex after we split up. Too much loneliness, too much wine and too long without sex. And here we are," she announced with a wry smile and a sweep of her hand over her belly. "Please don't judge," she whispered, and stifled a groan, appalled that she'd allowed that plea to slip. She didn't need anyone's approval. Her actions were her actions, and she refused to apologize for them or the result. Yet, without her permission, her tongue kept moving. "I know what people thought about me when I left Rose Bend. The wild child. Uncontrollable and zero fucks to give. Some of that is true, but I wasn't as out of control as some of these folks most likely believed. I didn't give head behind the high school bleachers or fuck the quarterback in the boys' locker room. I've only been with one man, and that was my ex-husband. So, when I had a drunken, sexual itch to scratch, it was him I went to. Sex with him was familiar, comforting." She puffed out a self-derisive chuckle. "God, that sounds awful, doesn't it? Instead of passionate and consuming and hot as hell, sex was 'comforting.' Don't get me wrong, though. It's not like we ever had problems in that area…"

"Sydney."

"Yes?" she asked, the sound of her name in that quiet but hard voice cutting off her mortifying jabbering. *Thank God.*

"Move on."

"Right," she breathed, zeroing her gaze back on the coffee table, unable to look at Cole after that case of verbal diarrhea. "Anyway, when I found out I was pregnant, we were both shocked. But Daniel being Daniel recovered faster and immediately went into planning mode. He wanted us to remarry, but I didn't." *Couldn't.* "He wasn't happy about that or my decision to move back home."

"Why did you decide to come back here?" he asked.

She paused, analyzing his tone for the disapproval and criticism that often saturated this question when it was broached. Daniel. Their friends. Her parents.

But she heard only curiosity, sympathy. Compassion.

Briefly closing her eyes, she sank into that voice, allowed it to wrap around her like a warm blanket. But seconds later, she lifted her lashes, tossing that warmth, that shelter away.

Because it wasn't hers to keep. Not even to borrow.

"Because the moment I realized I wanted to keep this baby I knew he or she deserved the very best I could give them. My own childhood was…complicated. But this town…" She moved her attention to the large windows and gazed at the quaint scene that greeted her. Tree-lined Main Street with its light, midday traffic, charming shops, and the chatter and laughter of shoppers that filtered through the glass. In one more week, with the

advent of the motorcycle ride and rally, the traffic—both auto-
motive and pedestrian—would increase, but the town wouldn't
lose its picturesque, close-knit appeal. "This town is home. Even
with all my complaints—and as a kid, I had plenty—I never felt
unsafe here. People care about one another. They're the true
definition of community. Regardless of how it was in my house,
in Rose Bend, a child can be a child. I want that for my baby.
He or she might not have a two-parent household, but they'll
have love, security, people who know them, who will care for
them and watch out for them when I'm not able to."

A place to belong. Family.

God, she wanted family for her child. Whether it was biological or one of their choosing.

"Then I'm glad you came back, Sydney," he murmured.

She jerked her gaze to him, and the genuine warmth and
honesty there—the lack of judgment—both stunned her and
caused a twist of heat to unfurl deep inside her chest. Had she
become so guarded, so jaded that she approached people with
her emotional fists raised, ready to defend, to fight?

Maybe. Probably.

Yes.

"Thank you," she said softly.

"You're welcome," he replied, just as gently.

Silence fell between them, one thick with a steadily rising
tension. Her eyes dipped to his mouth, lingered on the carnal
curves with the slight indent in the middle of that full bottom
lip. Her fingertips tingled, itching to trace the faint depression.
Desperate to. She curled her fingers into her palms, lifting her
gaze back to his.

But he stared at her hands.

And when he slowly drew his gaze up, his eyes peering into
hers, the heat there…

She blinked, air snagging in her throat.

Gone.

In the next instant, nothing but concern and patience shadowed the amber depths. The same concern and patience that had been in his expression since she'd entered his office.

She must've imagined that smoldering intensity, the *need* in his gaze. Or she was projecting her own lust onto him. Drawing in a deliberate breath, she held it, willing her body to calm, to get a grip. Ordering the glide of liquid desire in her veins to cease. Commanding her nipples to stand down and stop being so damn thirsty. Demanding her thighs to stop that futile clenching that seemed to just aggravate the pulsing between her legs.

Because Cole Dennison did not want her. Not only did he probably still consider her just his younger sister's friend, but he could barely look at her belly without flinching.

Even if those two hindrances didn't exist, one undeniable and unescapable fact persisted. Cole remained deeply in love with his dead wife.

And imagining anything different—believing that he could want her—only set her up for an emotional bruising.

"Now it's my turn to apologize for distracting you. Back to why you're here," he said. "And how I can help."

She nodded and swept her tongue over her suddenly dry lips. And pretended not to notice his attention fleetingly dropping to her mouth. "Like I said, my ex isn't—happy about my not remarrying him and then moving here. He called this morning, and though he didn't come right out and say, well," she waved a hand, frustrated, "anything, there was a *tone*. Threatening, maybe? Although, not. I don't know," she huffed out. "But I just can't shake the feeling that he might…that he could…"

"Sue you for custody?" Cole finished. "Is that what you're afraid of?"

"Yes…and no." When Cole arched a dark eyebrow, she loosed a short, harsh laugh. "I know, I know. I'm not making any sense. And I'm most likely overreacting and being all up in my feelings."

"Or you could just be very intuitive and sensitive to the mannerisms of a man you were with for five years."

"Or that," she conceded, scrutinizing his composed facial features. "Or are you just patronizing my hormonal ass?"

A smile teased the corners of his mouth. "Seeing how admitting to patronizing you or agreeing that you're hormonal could possibly place me in imminent danger of injury, I plead the Fifth on both."

"Very lawyerly," she drawled.

"But as it happens, I'm not doing either. And it doesn't really matter. It's smart to prepare yourself for anything, especially when it comes to your welfare and your baby's. Part of that welfare is finding out your legal standing when it comes to custody and your rights as the baby's mother."

"Yes," she whispered. "All of that. Daniel isn't a bad guy. Conservative and very firm in his beliefs, yes. Still, not bad or spiteful. But he's also not used to people disagreeing with him or going against him. In his position as dean of a prep school, he's accustomed to students, teachers and even parents deferring to whatever rule or decision he lays down."

And for a long time, she'd been the same. He'd made it comfortable for her to do so by paying for most of their financial obligations, providing a well-off lifestyle, including a beautiful home in an affluent, upper-middle-class neighborhood. She hadn't had to ask for anything.

And that's where the problem existed. That's why the blame could be placed squarely on her shoulders.

She'd stopped asking. She'd stopped demanding. She'd stopped *speaking*.

One day, she'd woken up and her voice had become his.

No, Daniel wasn't guilty of silencing her. She'd been complicit.

Not anymore, though. She couldn't afford to be quiet anymore. Because it wasn't just her. She had to be her baby's champion, their warrior. And warriors roared, they didn't whimper.

"Anyway, all that to say, I never intended to keep the baby from him. This morning, he said he wouldn't be kept out of the baby's life. I *want* him to be part of our child's life. Just because we're no longer married doesn't mean our child shouldn't have him as a father. But I'm afraid..." She trailed off, twisting her fingers harder before forcing them flat over her thighs. "Can he force me to move back to Charlotte? So we can co-parent?"

"A judge can block a parent from moving out of state, but this is usually after the children are born and custody is being decided. Because you two are already divorced and you're pregnant now, no one can stop you from relocating. Also, by the time the baby is born, a court will most likely consider your new residence as the status quo. In other words, the judge wouldn't issue an order to disrupt the child's daily schedule or existing residence if keeping the status quo is in the best interest of the child. This is especially true with a newborn."

Relief flooded her, pouring through her like a swollen, unchecked river. If she hadn't already been sitting down, her weakening knees wouldn't have been able to support her.

"Thank you," she said. "I really needed to hear that. I was so afraid..." She rested a hand over her stomach, closing her eyes. Tears pricked her lids, and she inhaled a deep breath, battling them back. After several seconds, she lifted her lashes, blinking rapidly. "Sorry," she murmured.

"I'm glad I could ease some of your fears," he said, nodding. "I need to caution you, though. This doesn't mean he won't still petition the court to adjudicate him as the father. If you two were still married, presumption would be that he's the legal father. But you're not, so he'll need to request a paternity test. Once paternity is established, then he can ask the court for custody. But even then, a heavy burden would have to be met in order for a judge to change custody."

"Okay, I understand." Sydney leaned back against the couch's arm, the sudden release of the tension that had been riding her since Daniel's phone call leaving her tired. "I'll keep that in—*oh!*"

A flutter. Like the softest brush of a butterfly's wing against the wall of her belly. She'd felt it. Unlike the heat in Cole's gaze, she hadn't imagined it…right?

She stiffened, going still. Not even daring to breathe.

"Sydney?" Cole leaned forward, the concern coating his voice etched into the frown darkening his expression. "Baby girl, are you okay?" He settled a hand just above her knee, studying her. "What's wrong? Is it the—"

She shook her head, not even concentrating on his murmured "baby girl" or how damn sexy that was. No, every bit of her focused on her body, on feeling that sweet sensation again. But, after several heartbeats, nothing. Disappointment rippled through her. Dr. Prioleau had assured her everything was okay, that this milestone in her pregnancy could come later. Still…

She stifled a sigh. "I'm good. I just thought—*oh shit!*" She pressed both of her palms to the slight swell of her stomach, eyes stretched so wide the skin pinched at the corners. Joy, indescribable joy, surged within her, pressing against her chest, her throat. And love. Jesus, how could she possibly love so much that her body almost seemed incapable of containing it? "I knew it! The baby. The baby just moved. *Oh my God.* Feel it!"

Without thinking, she grasped Cole's wrist and lifted his hand from her leg and planted it over her belly. Only when his long fingers splayed wide over her did the impact of her impetuous actions slam into her.

"Oh God, I'm sorry, Cole. I'm so sorry," she breathed, nearly shoving his hand away in her haste to undo the harm she might've unintentionally caused in her excitement. "I wasn't thinking."

His body had gone as still as the statue of W.E.B. DuBois outside of city hall. She couldn't detect the whisper of a breath or the rise and fall of his chest. But his eyes. Jesus, his eyes.

They flared wide, as if deep within the cage his body had become, he'd plummeted into a full-blown panic attack. And the amber depths swirled with so much pain, so much grief, that she couldn't contain her gasp.

It could've been that soft sound that snapped him from his paralysis.

Cole slowly tipped his head down and inspected the hand she'd tossed aside as if it were a separate entity from his body. His fingers curled into a tight fist against the cushion. Then, slowly, he stretched them out.

And raised his arm until his palm hovered over her stomach.

"I'm…" He paused, swallowed so hard his Adam's apple bobbed up and down in his strong throat. "Can I?" he whispered.

The request sounded as if it'd passed through ten pounds of chewed-up gravel before it emerged, rough, jagged and worn. As if he asked, not because he truly wanted to touch her—touch the place where her unborn child lay—but more so to prove a point. Prove that he could.

And because of the almost grim determination in the clench of his jaw and in his pain-drenched golden eyes, she took his trembling hand and guided it to her belly.

Once more, his big hand spanned the length of her.

And once more, as if greeting him, or maybe even congratulating him for his bravery, her baby moved. That butterfly caress brushed against her, and she didn't even try to contain the soft puff of delight, of wonder, over this proof of the precious life within her.

His fingertips flexed against her, but he didn't jerk his hand away. The trembling didn't cease either. Her gaze followed the length of his arm, up over his shoulder until she reached his face. Eyes squeezed closed, his beautiful mouth pressed into a flat line, his cheekbones in striking relief against taut skin, he appeared in pain. An answering ache twisted inside her, and she covered his hand with hers, prepared to end this torture he seemed intent on inflicting on himself. For her? For himself? For the wife and child he'd lost?

As the last question echoed against the walls of her mind, his thick, unfairly long lashes lifted. The soul-deep agony still shadowed his gaze, as did the grief. But the same wonder that shimmered in her chest glistened in his golden eyes.

"This is the first time?" he whispered, as if they were in church instead of his office.

"Yes." She grinned, and once more those damn tears threatened again, but this time, she let one fall, too overwhelmed to care. And too eager to feel that flutter again to risk moving her hand to wipe it away. "I was expecting it, you know? Waiting on it. My doctor told me it could happen anytime between now and twenty-five weeks. And of course, I'd read books and articles about what it would feel like, but this…" She shook her head, unable to lose her smile. "I wasn't prepared for this. No article came close to describing the beauty, the perfection of…*this*."

They both sat there, their hands stacked on her belly for— God, she didn't know how long. Minutes, hours, an eternity. And they were rewarded by two more shy movements.

"I think she might've gone back to sleep," Sydney murmured after several more moments passed with no more action.

"She?" Cole asked, arching an eyebrow. "You found out the sex already?"

"No." Sydney rubbed a small circle over the last spot she'd felt her baby brush against. "It's still too early for that. Up until today, I've been saying he or she. I really don't have a preference. But today…" She shrugged a shoulder at her fancifulness, the corner of her mouth quirking. "Your sister insists on calling the baby Arwen, the elven princess from *Lord of the Rings*. I think she's rubbing off on me."

He snorted. "Yeah, I remember that. Even if it is a girl, I hope you don't plan on calling her that."

"Not even if Tolkien was my baby's daddy."

Cole snickered, and the sound warmed her as much as if it'd been a full-out belly laugh. He used to have the best of those. She hadn't heard it since returning to Rose Bend. If he even did let go like that anymore.

Something whispered to her that he didn't.

"No, I'm waiting until I see his or her face when they're born to determine their name," she added. "Then I'll know for sure."

For the second time in a matter of minutes, Cole stiffened as if electrocuted. In the next second, he snatched his arm back and jackknifed to his feet. He stood there, his long fingers curling into his palm. To preserve the sensation? Or to eradicate it?

She was putting her money on the latter.

"Cole?" What had she said? She slowly rose from the couch, running her words through her head like a recording. But no. Nothing in their conversation stood out as something that would garner *this* kind of reaction.

"I'm sorry," he said, frost sheeting his voice. "I have an appointment in ten minutes that I need to prepare for."

He gave her his broad back as he headed toward his desk, his white dress shirt stretching across wide shoulders and molding to the sleek lines of his tapered waist. She jerked her gaze up, but not before it glanced over the firmness of his ass and the strength of his powerful thighs.

Good God. What was wrong with her?

Not yours to ogle. Just a friend. Or rather, the brother of a friend.

If there was ever a man who embodied the definition of unattainable, it was Coltrane Dennison. She needed to keep that reminder front and center and stop staring at the man like he'd transformed into 75%-off chocolate the day after Valentine's Day.

Especially when he was dismissing her from his office.

Clearing her throat, she wiped her damp palms down her denim-covered legs, then silently cursed herself for the telltale betrayal of nerves.

"Of course." She summoned up a smile, but her lips barely moved. Confusion and embarrassment streamed through her. "I'll just get out of your hair. Thank you, though." She tried for the smile again. Failed again. "I really appreciate your advice and help."

"No problem, Sydney," he said, standing behind his desk, his hands deep in the front pockets of his pants. The stoic expression belied his words and increased her need to escape.

Escape before she questioned him about what she'd done or said to catapult him back to the place where darkness claimed his golden gaze. A wall had shot up between them that she couldn't scale.

Didn't think she *should* scale.

With a last nod at him, she turned and exited, closing the office door behind her. The relief he'd given her still lingered, but more emotion crowded in. Hurt and bewilderment at the abrupt change in his demeanor. The kindling of anger for the same reason.

And then the persistent residue of that damn desire. A desire she wanted no part of.

As she pulled the door open to the law office and stepped back out into the summer sunshine, she paused on the top step and swept a hand down her belly.

"It's me and you," she whispered. "And that's more than enough."

It would have to be.

CHAPTER SIX

Cole gripped the steel bar with eighty-five pounds of weights on each side of it. Exhaling, he bent his elbows and deliberately lifted the equipment from the rest and pressed it toward his garage ceiling.

I'm waiting until I see his or her face when they're born to determine their name.

He paused, muscles straining, holding the weight aloft. Then slowly lowered it.

I'm waiting until I see his or her face when they're born to determine their name.

The bar clanged against the rest, but he didn't stop. After several moments, he repeated the exercise. And then again. Trying to exorcise Sydney's voice and her love-softened words from his head with pain and exhaustion.

Two hours of slamming his fists into the punching bag, jumping rope, running on the treadmill and lifting weights hadn't worked so far. But he wasn't a quitter.

For the last time, he set the weights down and levered off the bench. His arms were jelly, the muscles trembling in protest. They might be screaming "What the hell did we do to you?"

but his mind, whirling with snatches of his conversation with Sydney at his office earlier that day, assured him they had this. *Keep going. Don't stop until nothing works.* Not his body. Not his brain. Not his fucking heart.

His breathing sawed out of his chest, a rough, labored sound that reverberated against the cement walls. He closed his eyes and immediately an image of Sydney's face snapped into vivid detail. The shocked hurt. The confusion. He'd caused that by leaping away from her like she'd contracted a disease. Guilt pounded away at him, aching and relentless.

Sydney couldn't have known how her innocent declaration would be a sucker punch to his chest. Couldn't have known that panic had seized him in its razor-sharp teeth.

...when they're born...when they're born...

He'd felt his son move in his wife's belly. Had shared the joy and awe when that life they'd created brushed and rolled. And then, when his child was born, he should've rejoiced in each wave of his tiny foot and fist, should've delighted in his enraged cry. Instead he'd held a devastatingly still baby. Heard nothing but silence.

In that moment, with his hand on Sydney's belly, with her words echoing in his head, fear had ripped through him. What if he became attached to this baby that grazed a caress under his palm? What if he grew to care for them...love them?

And what if he lost them as he'd lost his own boy?

No. He couldn't. He *couldn't.*

Yes, he'd shot to his feet, backed away from that new life and his or her mother. But it hadn't been about disgust. It'd been pure self-preservation.

But trapped in the grip of the past, of his own personal terror, he hadn't been able to assure Sydney he wasn't an asshole who ran hot and cold. He hadn't meant to ruin what should've been a sweet, memorable moment for her as a mother.

He was just a scared man who couldn't stop his bruised heart from beating.

"*Mijo?*"

Cole jerked his head up and glanced toward the door that led from the garage into the tiny mudroom off the kitchen. As his gaze settled on the petite, older woman standing in the entrance, he rose. A warm glow settled in his chest. Love only tinged a little by sadness. Because looking at his mother-in-law, Valeria Narvaez, was like peering into the future and seeing how his wife would've appeared if she'd lived another twenty years.

"*Bendiciones*, Mamá," he greeted, smiling and crossing the small garage in several steps. "What are you doing here?"

She scoffed, rolling her eyes. "Making sure you're alive, what else? You haven't been by to see me and Ramon in a few days, so I know your refrigerator is probably lonely and pathetic." She shook her head, tsking. "Bony is not sexy, *mijo*. Why do you think I keep feeding Ramon? A woman needs something to grab a hold of and keep her warm at night."

He groaned, swiping up his towel off the top of the dryer and scrubbing it over his face and head. "Please, stop. My tender ears can't stand any more of that. And I'm fresh outta bleach to cleanse my mind."

"*Ay dios mio*, when did you become so sensitive?" She snorted. "Get in here so I can feed you. But first," she scrunched her nose up as he neared her, "shower. I can't have that stink in my kitchen."

"Actually, it's my kitchen," he reminded her on a playful smirk.

Valeria sniffed. "I'm in it. My kitchen." Then she disappeared through the doorway.

And he went to shower.

Fifteen minutes later, clean and dressed in a fresh T-shirt and pair of black sweatpants, he approached the small kitchen where Valeria stood over the stove—barely. While Tonia had inherited her height from her father, her mother just crested five feet. But what she lacked in inches, she more than made up for in personality and love. He'd known Valeria and Ramon since he'd been a tall, lanky fifth grader. They were second parents to him, and in the two years since Tonia's and Mateo's deaths, they'd been his sole connection to the woman who'd owned his heart from the time she'd run up to Branson Greggs on the playground at recess, kicked him in the nuts and called him a *pendejo* for spitting "spic" at Cole.

The memory was only edged in pinpricks as he sat at the breakfast bar and smiled. Tonia had been a firecracker when riled, as the hints of red in her dark brown hair had hinted. And nothing set her off more than someone coming after those she loved and considered under her protection. At ten years old, he'd become one of those people to her.

"I was right about your refrigerator," Valeria gloated, tossing him an arch glance over her shoulder. "Good thing I brought groceries along with dinner."

"Mamá, you didn't have to do that," he murmured, her generosity never failing to touch him.

"I know I didn't." She returned to the food warming on the stove, and in minutes, slid him a plate piled with his favorites, *ropa vieja* and *arroz con gandulez*. He groaned at the delicious aroma wafting from the shredded beef and rice with pigeon peas and dug in. Humming, Valeria patted his free hand. "Slow down, *mijo*. There's plenty more."

"Thank you for this." He pointed his fork toward the food. "I wasn't even aware I was starving until I smelled your cooking."

"Mmm-hmm." She perched on a stool across from him, her gentle but perceptive gaze fixed on him. Sometimes, it was difficult looking into the brown eyes that she'd bequeathed to her daughter. "I tried calling you earlier to let you know I was headed over. Now I see why you didn't answer. Working out again."

He nodded. "I'm sorry. I left my cell inside the house and didn't hear it ring."

"That's not the problem, Cole." She tilted her head to the side, studying him. "When I walked into that garage, sweat practically poured off your body and you were shaking. Which means you'd been at it for a while. Something is on your mind. Or something happened. Which is it?"

He considered lying. And even parted his lips to give the standard "nothing." But that didn't emerge.

Before he could reply, she softly asked, "Is this about Lacy Mitchell? I know she called and left a message for you today. She contacted me when she didn't hear from you."

Cole frowned. "The real estate agent?" He shook his head. "No, but I haven't checked my messages in the last few hours. What did she want?"

His mother-in-law didn't respond, but just stared at him, love and a mild reproach in her gaze. In that instant, the answer plowed into his head, and he flinched. "I hope you told her I'm not interested," he said.

"No, Cole. I didn't tell her that. I said I would talk to you about it." She tilted her head, a small, melancholy smile curving her mouth. "It's time. It's been two years."

"No." He shook his head. Hard. Adamant. "No."

"The house is just sitting empty, Cole. You're not going to live there again. Let someone else bring the love that you and Tonia shared back to it. Let a family—"

"No," he interrupted. Then, immediately winced. "I'm sorry. I didn't mean to disrespect you by cutting you off. I just... I just can't..." He knew his family believed he should sell the house that stood as a monument to his life before Tonia died in childbirth. The thought of someone else laughing, eating, making love in the home where he was supposed to have lived with his wife and his infant son... Bile raced an acidic path toward his throat. "I'm not ready to let her go."

"It," she murmured. "You mean, it. You're not ready to let the house go."

His slip hit him, but he again shook his head. Slower this time. "Same thing."

"Okay, Cole," she said, that terrible kindness and understanding in her gaze. He glanced away from it. "What were you going to tell me before?"

Once more, especially after this conversation, he almost blurted out "nothing." But his tongue didn't cooperate with his brain. And the truth rebelliously slipped from him.

"I… I touched a pregnant woman's stomach today. Felt her baby move." He didn't say any more and from the glistening in his mother-in-law's eyes, he didn't need to.

"Oh, *mijo*," she whispered, covering his hand with hers, squeezing and holding on. "It gets easier, I promise."

"Has it? For you?" he asked.

She smiled, but sadness stained it and her dark brown gaze. "Some days, yes. And then others?" She shrugged a shoulder. "Others, I'm faithing it until I make it. But I have to remind myself that I had my beautiful Tonia in my life for twenty-nine blessed years. God knows, I would've loved more. To me, it isn't the natural order of life for a child to die before her parents. Still, I'm so thankful for the time I had with her. I try to think on those days, those years, instead of the ones I won't ever have. And more and more, I'm finding comfort in that. Enough that I'm starting to find joy again, even in the little things."

He didn't reply. Couldn't. Because part of him yearned to be where she was. But the other half of him… He feared moving on. Finding joy without Tonia and the son they should've been raising and loving. It felt like a betrayal to forget her and the life they'd planned together. Logically, he understood this didn't make sense. But his heart? His heart clung feverishly to her memory and terror bit at him like a rabid dog when he couldn't recall her light, floral scent. Or the Tinkerbell sound of her laughter.

No, moving on meant losing her all over again. And he couldn't…he couldn't face that pain again.

"Who was the woman?" Valeria asked, jerking him back to his kitchen and the bright curiosity in her eyes. "The pregnant woman whose baby you felt move."

"Sydney Collins."

"Collins. Collins." She tapped her bottom lip in thought. "Dr. Collins's daughter?"

"Yes." He nodded. "She just returned to town after being gone for almost ten years. Do you remember her?"

"Vaguely." She nabbed his plate and crossed the small area to the sink and placed it inside. A chuckle escaped her. "Mostly, I remember how she was accused of hanging tampons on the big red oak outside the high school like Christmas ornaments. I know I was supposed to be scandalized, but Tonia and I had a huge laugh over that. They used to call her rebellious and un-ruly, but I liked her. She was an individual, had spirit."

True, Sydney had been labeled as "the wild one" by most of the town. And the girl had done everything she could to live up to that reputation. From painted-on jeans or denim short-shorts and cropped T-shirts to being escorted home drunk by the police from the lake parties that had been going on since before Cole was a teen, she'd flouted the rules.

Yet, Cole had looked beyond the revealing clothes, sassy mouth and I-don't-give-a-fuck attitude to the vulnerable, hurt girl beneath all the bravado. To most she had been rebellious, but to him, she'd been hungry for attention. Because as good of people as her parents were, Luke and Patricia Collins weren't the warmest residents of Rose Bend. The town doctor and his wife might be among the most solid and respected, but Cole had never seen them put their arms around their daughter. Never witnessed a loving moment between them. Not even during her sister Carlin's funeral.

Though he'd been thirteen, he clearly remembered the sad

service. Luke and Patricia had stood together as a unit beside their daughter's casket as it hovered above that yawning hole in the earth. And off to the side had been Sydney. Alone. No one to comfort her.

So yes, he understood her mutinous behavior as a teen. He imagined for her, negative attention had been better than no attention.

And Sydney had demanded attention.

Leave it to his intuitive mother-in-law to see beyond the antics to the heart of the girl.

Opening his fridge and grabbing a bottle of beer—beer she must've stocked because he hadn't bought any—she crossed the kitchen and set it down in front of him.

He shook his head, smirking. The woman thought of everything. Valeria propped her crossed arms on the breakfast bar and leaned forward, studying him as he twisted the cap off the bottle and lifted it to his mouth.

"Are you involved with this woman?" she asked.

He choked on the gulp he'd just downed. His mother-in-law silently handed him a napkin to wipe his mouth.

"No," he objected, vehemently. Maybe too vehemently because Valeria's eyebrows rose high on her forehead, her mouth quirking as if trying to hold back a smile. "No," he tried again. "We're just friends. If that. I was several years ahead of her in school, and she was close with Leo when they were kids."

"Uh-huh," she drawled. "Coltrane Alejandro Dennison, what aren't you telling me?"

"Nothing." He set the bottle down with a hard plunk. "There's nothing to tell."

More seconds of silence spent under that unwavering, piercing stare. "It's okay to be attracted to another woman, *mijo*," she finally murmured. "It isn't a betrayal to Tonia."

"Mamá—"

"No, you need to hear this whether you want to or not," she

interrupted, her tone gentle but with a thread of steel in it that shouted, *I'm the elder, sit your ass down and listen.* "There was no woman more loved than my daughter by you. Except me by Ramon," she added with a smile. "And that is such a comfort to me. She's gone, but I know with every bit of my heart that she left this world cherished by a wonderful man. But your capacity to care didn't die with her. You have so much to give, and you deserve that affection in return. Don't close yourself off from it."

"You…" He trailed off, unable to squeeze the words past his suddenly constricted throat. "You wouldn't…"

"*Dios*, Cole, no," she whispered, stretching her arms across the bar and cupping his face between her small palms. "I would *rejoice* for you, not be angry with you."

He shook his head, her hushed words pounding against his chest like the strikes of an anvil. "Doesn't matter." He covered her hands with his, tenderly drawing them down and cradling them. "She's just a friend. And I'm not ready. No one could ever take her place."

She flipped her fingers over, squeezing his. "It's not a competition, *mijo*," she softly assured him.

Releasing him, she returned to the sink and twisted the faucets, running water in the sink. He lifted the beer bottle to his lips again, drinking the ale down. His mother-in-law was right. It wasn't a competition.

Because no one could compare to the woman who had died and taken his heart with her.

CHAPTER SEVEN

Sydney paused in front of the shop, staring up at the pink, white and yellow striped awning and the gleaming storefront windows. Many of the shops that had lined Main Street when she'd left town still remained, untouched. But there were new additions, keeping Rose Bend revived and fresh.

Like this ice cream shop. Six Ways to Sundae.

Tongue-in-cheek and adorable.

She smiled just as a familiar and loud voice called out her name. Sydney glanced to the side, her grin widening at the sight of Leo headed toward her in that clipped, no-nonsense stride of hers. Like their time apart had been mere hours instead of years, their friendship had fallen right back into place. When not working, Leo hung out at the cottage, and sometimes, Sydney had gone over to the inn and claimed her old spot in Moe's kitchen.

God, she was grateful for Leo. This friendship helped to beat back the doubts over moving back.

"You made it here before me," Leo greeted, tugging Sydney into her arms for a quick embrace. Another thing she'd missed about her best friend—the unconscious and unashamed displays of affection. Guess it came from being part of a loving and demonstrative family. It'd always been one of the things she'd enjoyed when going over to the inn. "See? Here is where I'm being an amazing friend and refraining from the cliché comment about pregnant women always eating anything that isn't nailed down. Aren't you blessed that I'm so kind and considerate?"

Sydney snickered. "Yes, kind and considerate were the exact words I was thinking of."

Leo laughed and, still cupping Sydney's upper arms, tilted her head to the side and smiled. "If I haven't told you lately, I'm really glad you moved back. I've missed you, Syd."

Sydney blinked. Freaking hormones. Again.

"Thanks, Leo. I've missed you, too. At least I know coming home and having you back in my life is definitely a mark in the pro column for returning here. But I swear…" She laughed, but it possessed too much of an edge to be considered humorous. "One minute I'm certain that I'm doing the right thing. And then the next? The next I'm second-guessing every choice I've made for the last six months. Was I wrong to divorce Daniel? Should I have remarried him after I found out I was pregnant? Should I have stayed in Charlotte, the place that's been a home to me for almost a decade? Am I being impulsive? Am I placing my own needs above the baby's? Am I being—" she paused, then pushed out the last, damning word "—selfish? God, sorry." She pinched the bridge of her nose. "I didn't mean to unload on you like that."

Leo stepped back and jammed her fists on her hips, an eyebrow arched high.

"I need you to listen to me, okay? Hell no, you are not selfish. And I don't know your ex, but just from the little you've told me about him, I can take an educated guess where that bullshit came from."

"Leo." Sydney shook her head. "Daniel's not a bad guy. He's just…set in his ways."

"Sydney, you're my girl, but he sounds like he has a stick lodged so far up his ass, he shits splinters."

I will not laugh. I will not laugh.

"Oh, just go on and laugh. You know you want to." Leo grinned, but a moment later sobered. "God knows I'm not an expert on men. I'm like the anti-relationship whisperer. But I *have* learned this. Whenever anyone—a woman, especially—makes a decision that is beneficial to her but inconvenient to another person, she's selfish." She snorted. "Living for yourself, making your own decisions—that doesn't make you selfish, it makes you strong. Bold. Independent. It's *you*. And don't you forget that. Or let anyone try and convince you differently."

"That's just it, Leo," Sydney protested on a whisper. "I'm not bold or strong. I'm—"

"Scared shitless," her friend finished softly. "Yeah, I get it. I do. Returning here after so long must be terrifying. But being afraid doesn't determine your strength or your courage. Acting in spite of that fear, persevering, pressing forward—that's courage. It would've been easy, comfortable, safe for you to stay in your marriage."

Yes, it would've been, Sydney silently agreed, staring over Leo's shoulder at the gleaming storefront windows of Sunnyside Grille. And all the while, she would've slowly suffocated, lost her ambition, her voice—*lost herself*—as the years passed. That had been the wake-up call for her to walk away from her marriage of almost five years.

And now, she was returning to the place where she'd initially experienced that same sense of drowning. Returning to Rose Bend.

"It takes balls to start over, Sydney." Leo grasped Sydney's hand and squeezed it. "Lady balls. And you, my friend, got a brass set."

Sydney's bark of laughter sounded a bit waterlogged from the damn tears that refused to go away. Good Lord, she had five more months of this emotional upheaval?

"Thanks... I think." Clearing her throat, she switched the subject before she started bawling right here on Main Street and really gave people something to gossip about. "Okay, ice cream. I definitely need ice cream now."

"Done." Leo stepped past her and pulled open the entrance door, still holding Sydney's hand, tugging her inside. As the cool air rushed out to greet her, Sydney didn't bother to hold back her groan.

Oh, thank God. Right now, air-conditioning was better than an orgasm.

"Um, either it's really hot outside or you haven't had sex in a while," an amused, lilting voice observed on the tail end of a snicker.

Crap. She squeezed her eyes shut and pinched the bridge of her nose.

"Oh yes, sister." Leo cackled. "You did indeed say that aloud."

"It's the heat," Sydney muttered. "It's attacking my brain cells as well as my sweat glands."

"Uh-huh." Leo jabbed Sydney in the shoulder with a fingertip. "Just so you know, the topic of your apparently questionable sex life is shelved only until I get ice cream in me. In the meantime, meet the owner of this fabulous establishment, Cecille Lapuz. Cecille, Sydney Collins."

The lovely, petite woman grinned. With long, gorgeous light brown hair, smooth, toffee-colored skin and beautiful brown eyes that spoke of an Asian heritage, possibly Filipina, she could've been anywhere from her midtwenties to her late thirties. An eggshell-blue apron with the shop's name embroidered on it partially covered the white long-sleeved T-shirt and dark blue skinny jeans that adorned her slim figure.

If not for that engaging, playful grin and the tray of delicious-looking ice-cream-topped brownie samples she held, Sydney might've hated her.

"Nice to meet you," Sydney said, plucking up one of the minuscule desserts. She popped the treat in her mouth. Then moaned good and long at the chocolate, pecan and vanilla goodness that melted on her tongue. "I have never met you before in my life, but right now I want to pledge my undying love. And I would offer you my virginity but, hello." Sydney waved a hand down her baby bump that her lilac sundress didn't conceal. "That ship has not only sailed but been torpedoed into the deep."

"How do you like that?" Leo grumbled. "I'm only your childhood best friend. But she gives you chocolate and is offered your love. No loyalty at all."

The other woman's husky burst of laughter bounced off the bright walls of the shop. The handful of customers sitting at the cute pastel circular tables must've been accustomed to Cecille's bouts of hilarity, because they only glanced up with smiles, then returned their attention to their conversations and ice cream.

"I see the rumors about you didn't lie," Cecille said. "It's a pleasure to meet you, too."

Some of Sydney's delight dimmed, her old but familiar protective shields reinforcing themselves. "I'm almost afraid to ask what you've heard."

"Oh, let's see." Cecille squinted, tilting her head to the side. "That you pulled the best pranks, could sell kryptonite to Superman and convince him it was for his own good, could charm a polar bear out of its fur coat, and that you were a beautiful girl who returned to town a gorgeous woman with a body to die for, even with a baby bump. And, woman, they were not wrong." She wiggled her fingers directly over Sydney's breasts, which, admittedly, were looking pretty fabulous in the halter-style top of her dress. "I'm fighting a severe case of envy right now. My two kids sucked the elasticity and perkiness right outta mine," she grumbled.

A giggle tickled Sydney's throat at Cecille's wholly delightful inappropriateness. A freaking *giggle*. But even as she battled back more laughter, surprise cascaded through her. Pulled the best pranks? Charming? Beautiful? *That's* what people had been saying about her? Disbelief crept under the trickle of shocked pleasure.

You don't expect Cecille to tell you the mean things they've shared with her, do you?

No. No, she didn't. And the knowledge endeared this effervescent, kind woman to her even more.

"Part of me feels like I'm being sexually harassed, and the other part is like, tell me more about how pretty the girls are. I'm so conflicted," Sydney said, frowning in mock confusion.

"Eh, figure it out over ice cream." Leo hooked an arm through Sydney's, guiding her to the long glassed-in freezer that stretched across one side of the store.

On the adjoining wall, a tall refrigerated dessert case displayed beautiful sheet and multilayered cakes of all flavors and colors as well as different fruit pies. A free-standing counter containing several toppings, from sprinkles to syrup to candy, occupied one corner.

When she'd left Rose Bend, Mabel Lawson had owned this place, and it'd been nice but a little old-fashioned, offering nothing more exotic than vanilla, chocolate, strawberry and rocky road ice cream. Maybe butter pecan once in a while. Cecille had obviously renovated the space and transformed it into something straight out of a Willy Wonka fantasy.

Including so many flavors, Sydney's stomach released an embarrassing rumble as she stared down at the variety of tubs.

"Forget what I said about my undying love," she said. "I'm going to build a shrine and dance naked around it at midnight, sacrificing waffle cones in your honor."

"What is happening here?" a new, younger voice asked.

Sydney looked up, spotting the newcomer stepping out of the double doors that led to the rear of the store. The pretty Black girl—well, not a girl, but huddling on the cusp of womanhood—glanced back and forth between Sydney and her employer, smiling.

That smile.

Even if Leo hadn't tossed out a "Hey, baby sister!" Sydney would've guessed her identity.

An image superimposed over the girl's features. Rounder cheeks, almond-shaped light brown eyes, a wide mouth, ebony skin and a tall frame of long lines and pointy angles. The cheeks had thinned, and the eyes and mouth were no longer too big for her face, and curves had softened the angles, but that smile with its tiny gap between the front two teeth remained the same.

"Florence?" Sydney whispered.

Leo's younger sister grinned. "Hey, Sydney. Long time, no see."

"Oh my God." Sydney reached across the glass counter and Florence grasped her hands in hers. "You have to be, what? Eighteen or twenty now?"

"Eighteen." She squeezed then released her. "Moe mentioned you were back. It's so good to see you."

Sydney laughed, still wading in disbelief. "You're so…big."

"True that." Florence laughed. "Almost a decade will do that to a person."

"Flo works here, and the brat that she is won't bring home any of the goods. Some sister," Leo teased.

"I'm just thinking of your waistline so you can catch that husband Moe has been on you about." Snickering past her sister's exaggerated groan, Flo turned back to Sydney. "What can I get for you?"

"God." Sydney leered down at the multicolored vats of ice cream. "I don't know what to choose."

"Take your time, Sydney," Cecille said to them, walking away to ring up a customer. "And it's on the house."

"I can't—"

"Of course, you can't. But as the owner, I can. It's the welcome-home special. I just created it." She flashed a smile and turned to her customer.

"Good Lord, is she different from Mrs. Lawson," Sydney muttered, switching her focus back to the cold treats laid out before her in a smorgasbord.

Florence laughed. "Mrs. Lawson would've charged you for

those samples. Cecille and her husband moved here from Ohio about five years ago. Nate is a math teacher over at the high school, and she bought this place from Mrs. Lawson, who retired to Georgia to live with her daughter and grandkids." Flo slipped on gloves. "Decide what you'd like yet?"

"I'm going to go with one scoop of salted caramel and another scoop of strawberry cheesecake."

"Great. Cone or cup?"

Sydney shot Florence a *get real* look. "Flo, don't play with me. Cone. The waffle cone with the chocolate edging at the top."

Florence chuckled. "Gotcha."

As she moved toward the case to grab Sydney's requested cone, the bell above the entrance tinkled. On instinct, Sydney glanced over her shoulder. Then barely managed to stifle a groan. And this one was not of pleasure.

She slowly turned, using those few seconds to shore up her defenses—both facial and emotional. Even as she fixed a polite smile on her face, she drew on every ounce of her *I don't give a fuck* reserve. This particular cache she only drew on when forced to deal with Daniel's uppity coworkers, salespeople who followed her around stores because she committed the crime of shopping while Black and, at times, her parents.

And now for Jenna Landon.

Daughter of the town's former mayor. Spoiled. Mean girl.

To be fair, the willowy, beautiful redhead could've changed during the last eight years. People did that occasionally...

"Well, if it isn't Sydney Collins. I'd heard you'd made your way back to town," Jenna purred, the sneer in her voice as crystal clear as her blue eyes—and the glitter of spiteful glee in them.

Nope. Same ol' stank attitude she'd always had.

"Good to see you, Jenna," Sydney lied, voice carefully bland.

"You remember Karina, don't you?" Jenna waved to the brunette standing next to her, a carbon copy of herself, complete with the same stylish blouses and shorts that hit their slender legs midthigh, and platform wedges. Even their pedicured toes were the same shell pink. "Karina Bloom."

"I sure do." Sydney nodded at the silent brunette. "Nice to see you again, Karina."

How could she forget her? The other woman had trailed behind Jenna like a puppet attached to her master with strings. And it looked like that hadn't changed either. How awful for her. Too bad Sydney couldn't drum up any sympathy since it was Karina's choice to be attached at the hip to Jenna.

"You, too," Karina practically cooed. "Even under these... circumstances."

"Circumstances?" Leo echoed from beside Sydney, an edge creeping into her voice. God love her, Leo had always been ready to throw down on Sydney's behalf. Didn't matter who it was—mean girls, even Sydney's parents.

Sydney arched an eyebrow, unobtrusively settling a hand on Leo's arm. "Not sure what you're referring to."

"We heard about your," Jenna's gaze and voice dipped, the former landing directly on Sydney's stomach, "state. And it's so sad you have to go through this alone...and abandoned by your husband."

Phony sympathy dripped from Jenna's tone, and Sydney forced her face not to move. Ordered her lips not to tremble or allow the curve tilting them to slip. Even as she tightened her grip on Leo's arm.

Even as her heart slowed to a deliberate, aching thud against her sternum. Even as a light buzz droned in her ears. Even as heat swept up her spine and spilled over her skin as if she'd stepped into a sauna.

Nope. She refused to give this chick the satisfaction of knowing she'd dented her shields.

But she had. God, she had.

"Did you two want to order something?" Florence asked from behind Sydney, anger thrumming in her voice.

"No, I know some of us don't have to worry about our figures, but I'm very conscious of mine. And besides, I'm just visiting an old friend, here." Jenna slid the dig in with a saccharine smile.

Sydney smothered the urge to grimace. Hard to believe that during their freshman year of high school, they'd actually been friends. Something happened that summer before their sophomore year, and Jenna had turned into such a mean girl she could've starred in her own movie. And Sydney had been one of her favorite targets.

"Really," Leo drawled. "I wasn't aware you had those." She flicked a glance at Karina. "No offense, babe."

Forcibly holding back a grin, Sydney twisted around and wiggled her fingers over the glass countertop. "Well, Florence. Give me Jenna's scoop. I'm eating for two, after all. As for being alone and abandoned," she returned her attention to Jenna and her sidekick with a half shrug, "I'm divorced, not Oliver Twist. And I'm afraid you'll have to be more specific about my husband. Which one are you talking about?"

Karina's nose scrunched in disgust, her chin tipping up. "Exactly how many have you had?"

"Technically, one," Sydney said, narrowing her eyes and tapping her bottom lip. "Because, legally, I could only marry one man. Polygamy laws, and all that."

Leo frowned. "I thought you told me you didn't marry any of them because you couldn't possibly choose between the three?"

Sydney shook her head, tsking. "No, you remember. I married one, but I called the other two my husbands as well."

"Riiiight." Leo snapped her fingers. "I believe the kids nowadays call it a reverse harem situation."

"Yes, but we called it *love*." Sydney heaved an exaggerated sigh and tried not to loose a grin at the strangled bark of laughter behind her. "Anywho, I became pregnant—let this be a lesson to you about safe sex—and rather than tear my men apart with insecurity and jealousy over who fathered my child, I decided to leave for the good of us all."

Applause broke out, and she glanced over her shoulder to wink at Cecille, who'd apparently finished ringing up her customer. Beside her, Flo choked on her laughter.

"You think you're so smart," Jenna sneered. "And yet, here you are, with your tail between your legs, back in Rose Bend when you declared to anyone who would listen that you'd never return. Like you were too good for us. Tell me, Sydney. What flavor is crow?"

"Chocolaty with a nougat center," Sydney shot back. "And while this little welcome-home party is making me misty, I have some ice cream to chug. So, it was nice seeing you again, Jenna, Karina. It warms my heart to know some things never, *ever* change."

"So sad. Some people could do with a change—for the better," Jenna jabbed with a sniff, before spinning on her platform heels and striding from the store, her lapdog right on her heels.

"No, what's sad is she came in here with the sole purpose of dumping crap on you," Leo raged. "And it's even more pathetic that at her age she's still a bully. Not a good look. She's only halfway decent to me and Flo because she's been panting after Cole like a dog in heat." She sniffed. "I'd disown my brother if he ever even thought about dating her. Right after I put a beating on him."

"And then castrate him," Flo added with a snarl.

Sydney snickered, ignoring the nosedive her stomach took toward her feet at the mention of perfect, beautiful, non-pregnant Jenna with Cole.

"Meh." She waved a hand toward the exit, pretending that the women's barbs hadn't struck deep. Pretending that in those moments, she hadn't been hurled back to high school when she'd been the target of petty taunts and cruel words from Jenna and other students just like her.

Pivoting to face the other women, she shook her head, inject-ing a flippancy into her voice that veered so far from the truth, her pants should be on fire—if she were wearing any.

"My mother has a word for someone like her—*mataray*," Ce-cille added. "And I'm not talking about her angelic disposition."

"You really have to feel compassion for people like Jenna," Sydney said with a shake of her head. "Bullies aren't just born, they're created. Can you imagine the misery, anger and pain a person must feel to always be so unhappy and mean? What must it have been like for her growing up in a household where perfection wasn't just expected, but anything less wasn't toler-ated? The burden to live up to that impossible standard must be exhausting. I can see people taking their hurt and rage out on others. I get it."

Leontyne, Cecille and Florence stared at her, wearing match-ing incredulous expressions.

"You really believe all that?" Leo blurted out.

"Maybe." Sydney flip-flopped her hand back and forth. "But truthfully? She's a bitch."

Barks of laughter burst from the other three women, and Sydney grinned.

"Like I said, *mataray*," Cecille announced, still chuckling. "Just for that, your next two ice cream cones are on the house."

"Welcome home, Sydney," Florence murmured, before scoop-ing ice cream out of the tubs.

Leo wrapped an arm around Sydney's shoulders, squeezing her close. She smiled her thanks to her friend for the silent show of support, but inside...

Inside, she ached.

Because the encounter with Jenna showed her in vivid Tech-nicolor that some people in this town wouldn't allow her to live down her past, to be the woman she'd matured into.

Moving back here...had she given her baby a fresh start or a life sentence?

CHAPTER EIGHT

"Oof."

"No, no. Not the ice cream!"

Even before he heard the husky voice lamenting her dessert, Cole identified the person he'd bumped into, the person whose arms he currently grasped. The sultry scent of orchids—sweet chocolate and spicy citrus—teased him, soft but heady with a natural heat that he suspected emanated from smooth, beautiful skin. He smelled that scent in his sleep, woke up to it still in his nose. As impossible as it was, the sweat on his own skin captured its essence, coating him in that special fragrance. So yeah, he knew whose firm breasts pressed against his chest, whose thighs grazed his…whose rounded belly nudged his lower abdomen before he even looked down.

Cole ground his teeth together, and a dull ache bloomed along his jaw. But he forced himself to breathe past the first ripple of panic, the initial dissonant vibration of pain.

Not Tonia. Not Mateo inside her.

He silently chanted the mantra to himself for what seemed like hours but was only seconds. Still, by the time he lowered his head, the red-tipped emotional claws had gradually receded. Leaving bloody, ugly welts behind, but they'd receded.

Tight, dark brown curls grazed his throat and his chin. An almost too lush mouth tilted down at the corners. Espresso eyes narrowed on her outstretched arm and the hand that clutched a waffle cone with three scoops.

Whoa. Three scoops. Of different colors and flavors.

"What's wrong?" he demanded.

The question caught them both off guard. Her head jerked back, her gaze locking with his. He hadn't meant to ask, but that much ice cream? He recognized a DEFCON-3 situation when facing it.

"I have a mother and four sisters," he explained. "I know emotional eating when I see it."

A frown flirted with her eyebrows, but then she shrugged. "Fine," she grumbled. "I'll give you that one. Speaking of your sister, you just missed Leo. We had a dessert date." Reeling the cone close, she gave the ice cream a long, self-indulgent lick.

Fuck.

Impossibly, he felt that lick straight up his dick. Felt that lustful moan vibrate down his flesh. If she'd been anyone else, he might've accused her of doing that on purpose. Of blasting fire through his veins and turning him into one massive, six-feet-plus, hungry ache.

Releasing his grip on her arms, he stepped back, interjecting much-needed space between them. He didn't want to broadcast to Sydney the state of his rapidly hardening erection. Dammit, part of him wanted to snatch that offensive cone from her hand and hurl it across the street.

The other half demanded he reclaim the space he'd placed between them, curl one hand around the feminine flare of her hip and wrap the other around the fingers clutching the cone—and press it against her mouth, demanding she take another lascivious stroke. Put on a show for him.

Jesus.

He plowed a hand over his head, scrubbing his palm over his short hair. Where had *that* thought come from? Voyeurism had never been his kink, but damn if she couldn't turn him onto that.

With ice cream.

This damn inconvenient and all *wrong* attraction to her was getting out of hand.

"I'm glad I bumped into you," he said, dragging his filthy mind kicking and screaming from the edge of the carnal abyss. "I wanted to apologize for being so abrupt in my office earlier this week. I…" *I was an asshole who couldn't handle my emotions and took it out on you.* "I'm sorry about that," he finished quietly.

"That's fine." She nodded, but didn't meet his eyes, instead focusing on the cone. He jerked his gaze away when she went in for another lick. There was only so much a man could be expected to handle. "It was my fault for intruding on your time without an appointment. I should apologize."

"No, you shouldn't," he replied. "Sydney, look at me." He couldn't explain what compelled him to issue that order. Something in her voice. In the choice of words. Whatever drove it, he waited until she complied, the thick fringe of her lashes lifting, her chocolate eyes locking onto his. "I don't know if it's a habit to accept the blame for other people's bad behavior. If so, it's one you need to break. It's not your fault or your responsibility how others act. You need to start letting people own their shit."

She didn't say anything, but her gaze shifted, flicking to their right. He followed the direction of that glance, settling on the two women standing across the street in front of the Second Time Around consignment shop. The two women obviously pretending hard not to be studying them.

"Jenna Landon. She the reason for the ice cream binge?" Though she was a few years younger than him, he knew the woman. Hell, in a town the size of Rose Bend, he couldn't help but be familiar with her. Not to mention, the statuesque, striking redhead was the ex-mayor's daughter.

"It's nothing." He narrowed his eyes on Sydney and she chuckled, shaking her head. "No, really. She's just…being herself."

"You mean spoiled, catty and arrogant?" he asked, sliding his hands in the front pockets of his slacks. Either that or pinch one of those pretty corkscrew curls and rub it between his thumb and finger to determine for himself if that beautiful hair was soft as satin or if it possessed a coarser texture that would lightly abrade bare skin.

"Oh, so you're familiar with her." Sydney shrugged a shoulder. "It is what it is, though. Some things and people change. But most don't."

"That's true, but for the most part, Rose Bend has progressed and grown. And so have the people. I hope you don't allow one person to color how you see the whole town. Even Mayberry had its Nellie."

She tilted her head to the side. Blinked. "Um, I think you're mixing up your classic TV show metaphors."

He shrugged a shoulder. "Yeah, I couldn't think of a mean character on *Andy Griffith*."

"There's Ben Weaver."

Cole considered it. "Nah. He was actually more crotchety than mean."

She scrunched up her nose in an adorable moue. "Good point."

They stared at each other, grinning.

"C'mon," he said, jerking his chin up. "If you don't have any plans, come with me. Let me show you how much we've changed."

Without conscious thought, he stretched out his hand toward her, and as his hand hovered between them, his brain yelled, "What the hell are you doing?" Caution argued that he not touch her, that even the simplest and most innocent of touches was a slippery slope.

But he didn't lower his arm.

Sydney studied his hand for several moments, and just when he thought she would reject him, turn away from him, she slowly slid her soft palm against his. Wrapped her fingers around his.

And Cole exhaled, his chest falling on a breath he hadn't realized he'd been holding.

Friends. Friends held hands. Friends shared affectionate, yet platonic touches. Friends controlled their baser, inappropriate desires to enjoy a real relationship without sex muddying the waters. All he had to do was convince his dick that she was off-limits.

Because she was.

She might not be married as he'd first thought, but she was still pregnant, fresh out of a divorce, starting over in a town she had to relearn. And there were shadows in her beautiful eyes. Shadows of old hurts and bruises that needed healing. With his own wounds that had barely scabbed over, he would only inflict more harm. Besides, even if none of those obstacles existed, he wasn't free. Yes, his body might be awakening with a vengeance, but his heart... It'd shattered into so many pieces, he would never be whole again. The man who'd boldly, fearlessly dove headfirst into the euphoric bliss of love without care of risk, pain or uncertainty no longer existed.

"How're you doing?" he belatedly asked, shooting a glance toward her stomach. He curled and straightened his fingers, still feeling that beautiful, terrifying flutter over his palm even days later. "Everything okay with the baby?"

Miraculous how he could ask that without flinching, without his throat tightening up.

"We're good." She smiled. "I'm feeling more movement, too. And I'm still knocked on my ass by each one." She chuckled, shaking her head. "So, are we just meandering along or are we headed someplace special so you can regale me with the power of hearth and home?" she asked, giving their joined hands a small swing.

"Regale? Hearth and home?" He smirked. "You certainly have a way with words. What are you, a writer?"

He'd been teasing and had expected a smile or laugh. Mission half accomplished. She emitted a short, muted chuckle that fell flat. "Sort of. I'm a grant writer."

"What do you mean, 'sort of'?" He nudged her arm with his. "I've worked with a couple while on the town council, and it requires discipline, communication and writing skills, a talent for research and an exacting eye for detail. You should be proud of that."

"I am," she said with a nod. "Especially since when I first went to college, I didn't know what I wanted to do. I changed my mind about my major so many times, I confused myself." This time her burst of laughter emanated warmth, if not a little self-deprecation. "But about junior year, I ended up taking a class in grant writing, and part of the curriculum included writing one for an actual company. They told us their mission, and we had to come up with the purpose for the grant, research and identify funding sources, contact organizations for partnerships and endorsements, create the budget… At first, I was like, what the hell are you doing? But the challenge was kind of exhilarating. And I was helping people. Well, helping an organization help people but still—I was making a change in my small way."

"Felt good, didn't it?" he murmured.

"Yeah, it did." She studied him with an insightfulness that both stirred and unsettled him. "Is that why you ran for mayor?" she asked. "To help bring about change?"

Oh God, wasn't that a loaded question. "One of the reasons," he hedged. "I'm not allowing you to change the subject, though. What happened? Did you get the grant?"

She laughed. "Hell no. Even the most seasoned grant writers receive rejects, and I was nowhere near seasoned. But I discovered what I wanted to do. And in taking that class, I changed my major from communications to English and added another one in marketing. It meant another semester in college, but I didn't care. And all that time, I continued to take grant writing classes. Unlike a good many of my fellow graduates, I walked out with my degree, self-employed, working in my field."

"That's amazing, Sydney," he said, gently squeezing her fingers. "I'm happy for you. And I'm proud of you."

She shook her head, smiling wryly as she offered him her half-way demolished ice cream cone. He accepted it and sampled it, heat eddying low in his gut. Of course, it was just his imagination that he could taste the sweetness of the salted caramel and her own chocolate and citrus flavor. But the knowledge that his tongue followed the same path as hers had a twisting need prowling through him.

He'd just grazed that boundary line he'd mentally drawn for himself. As long as he didn't cross it... No matter how hard he tried—and failed—to keep his gaze from tracing the elegant slope of her cheekbones, the sinful bow of her mouth, the lush curves of her breasts, he couldn't cross that line.

"Proud of me? Why?" she scoffed, waving a hand. "Because I did what I was supposed to do? Granted, probably not many people here expected even that much out of me."

"Stop." He gently tugged on her hand, drawing her to a halt. "Look around you. What do you see?"

She tossed him a look that he clearly interpreted as *what the hell*, but she still glanced around the busy downtown area, packed a little more than usual with shoppers, tourists and traffic because of summer and the upcoming motorcycle rally. But the places that marked Rose Bend as a small, close-knit community still stood, impressive in age yet humble in simplicity.

"What am I supposed to see?" she retorted. "I feel like this is a trick question."

"Do they teach suspicion in the South along with genteel manners?" He surrendered to his desire and allowed himself a gentle tug on a brown curl.

"Yes. It's free, along with the master class on the War of Northern Aggression."

"Smart-ass."

"Not the worst thing that I've been called."

Delicious. Perfect. Worship-worthy. All things he would—and had—said himself. *Goddamn, stop.* "Not touching your ass," he said, then pinched the bridge of his nose, inwardly groaning at his words.

Sydney grinned. "You don't sound at all happy about that fact," she drawled.

"Focus," he grunted.

"I was." She lifted her shoulders in a shrug, a wicked smile tugging at the corner of her mouth that completely ruined the innocence she was obviously striving for. "Then you started in about manners and asses, and it all went left quick."

He couldn't help it; he threw back his head, laughing. Long and hard. And damn if it didn't feel good. Warm and...cleansing. He brought her hand, still clasped in his, to his mouth and pressed a quick kiss to her knuckles in gratitude.

Her soft gasp reached his ears. Without his permission, his gaze dropped to her mouth. How would that puff of breath feel across his lips if he bent his head over hers?

"What do you see, Sydney?" he asked again, choosing not to acknowledge the question in those liquid brown eyes.

She jerked her head away, obeying his request. For several moments, she studied their surroundings, and when she returned her attention to him, she shook her head. "The same place I left eight years ago."

"No," he objected. He held the ice cream cone out to her, and when she shook her head, he tossed it into a nearby garbage can. Then, stepping behind her, he settled his hands on her slim shoulders. "You're looking out the eyes of that hurt, misunderstood teenage girl. What does the mature, successful woman see now?" When she remained quiet, he offered, "Let me help. See the pharmacy?" He slightly turned her to the left where the store had stood since his parents had been born. "Mr. Price used to run it with an iron fist and pretty much bark at every kid who came in there. Talk about crotchety." The corner of his mouth quirked at her "hell yeah." "But now, he has grandkids, twin girls, and you wouldn't recognize the old man. He actually—wait for it—smiles. And his daughter helps run the pharmacy. She's enlarged the cosmetics and toy sections, and even added audiobooks."

With slight pressure, he pivoted her in the opposite direction, so she faced across Main Street.

"Remember Sunnyside Grille?" he continued, referring to the diner that, while not the only one, was the most popular. "About five years ago, Ron and Grace decided to renovate. Got rid of that old Formica floor, the '50s decor that had probably been dated even back then and that ancient jukebox that played nothing from the last six decades. Even got a new jukebox that plays everything from the Andrews Sisters to Lizzo and switched up their menu to add gluten-free options as well as organic and farm-to-table food. At first, some people complained. They liked the old design with the old music and familiar meals. Definitely didn't want marble counters, wooden booths or fancy food. But after a while, they adapted. They changed, and Sunnyside Grille still remains the most popular diner in Rose Bend."

Again, he turned her, so they both surveyed the sprawl of the town and the breathtaking view of Monument Mountain and Mount Everett soaring above it.

"We have a new nondenominational church and a synagogue. The resource center hosts several advocacy programs for our LGBTQ community, to provide support for their mental and physical health, and help them lead successful lives in an often intolerant world. We have a Puerto Rican mayor." He nodded. "What I want you to see, Sydney, is that yes, we're still the same in the way that you're still the same person who left here. But just like you've grown and changed, so have we. Just give us a chance to show you. To welcome you."

Several beats of silence passed between them, and he was about to release her and continue on their walk when her quiet voice halted him.

"What if the woman is still hurt?"

He barely caught that low whisper. It throbbed with old wounds. But he did catch it. And he lowered his head, bracing his jaw against the side of her head, her curls tickling his chin, mouth and cheek. Vanilla filled his nose, and he subtly inhaled the scent.

"That's okay. Because she's not too old to be healed. And she'll find healing right here in the very place she ran from."

Like you did.

But he ignored that taunting voice. Her situation and his were different. There was no redemption or miracle cure for him. The best part of him was buried in the cemetery behind St. John's.

He shifted from behind her, taking her hand again. This time she didn't hesitate to enfold her fingers around his. That tiny show of trust shouldn't have struck him in the chest like a fist. Shouldn't have had him battling the need to tunnel his fingers through those thick, sexy curls to tip her head back and brush her lips with a kiss of thankfulness.

He shoved those feelings deep. Like he did lately with most things he didn't want to dwell on. Pretended they didn't exist.

They walked in companionable silence for the few minutes it took to reach the edge of downtown. At the last stoplight, the businesses fell away to a vast open field that the long-ago founders of Rose Bend had agreed wouldn't be spoiled by construction. The Glen. In the spring and winter, the town's annual festivals were held there. And in the summer, The Glen's rich green grass became the grounds for one of the Northeast's largest motorcycle rides and rallies. Men, women and families traveled from all over the country to this part of the Berkshires to celebrate the freedom of the road with concerts, games and special events all centered around Rose Bend's very special guests.

Since the town's businesses benefited from the flood of visitors and proceeds from the event went to the This Is Home foster care youth home, Rose Bend went all out to welcome them. From special prices at the hotels to the Sunnyside Grille temporarily changing their menu to include the Hog and Cog breakfast and the On Any Sunday dinner plate.

But The Glen was the heart of it all.

As mayor, Cole had made the rally a focal point of his platform. And standing here with Sydney by his side as they surveyed the transformation of the wide field, pride slid through him like sun-warmed molasses.

"Damn," Sydney breathed, dropping his hand and stepping farther onto the carpet of fragrant green. "This is *nothing* like how I remembered." She shook her head, spreading her arms wide. "When did it get so...more? No, wait." She whirled around, pinning him with a narrowed stare. "You. You're the *more*. All of this..." She swept her arm out, indicating the rows of vendor booths, the huge stage with state-of-the-art equipment, the large barrel grills ready to be manned, the play area complete with slides, rides, bouncy houses and toys to entertain children of all ages. "It's because of you."

"Not just me," he corrected, sliding his hands into his pockets and rocking back on his heels. "It was most definitely a team implementing the ideas and a town that got behind it. But yes—" he nodded "—I challenged all of us to think bigger, be more inclusive. I researched what Daytona, Myrtle Beach and Sturgis offer and how we could do the same but also provide some things they don't. Not that Rose Bend is trying to compete with those rides, but there's something special about this town, so we should offer the people who travel here that 'special.' Family. A home away from home. A diverse and inclusive community. Show them that even though they're here for two weeks out of the year, for that time Rose Bend is theirs as much as it is ours. So yes, we have the daily rides and the concerts with both famous and local acts, but now they can also bring themselves to us by selling their art, jewelry, clothes. We have a place for their children to safely play. We enlarged the camping ground, provided the best facilities and security. And I think we've accomplished it."

When she didn't reply, he ducked his chin and met her intense scrutiny, which didn't match the almost sweet smile curving one half of her mouth. Again, he forced himself to focus on her eyes.

"What?" he asked.

"Don't think I didn't notice how you skated around my question earlier. The one about why you ran for mayor," she continued before he could ask what part of their conversation she was referring to. "I see right through you, Coltrane Dennison. This," she said, twirling a hand in the direction of the booths, the stage, "is why you did it."

He glanced away from her, strolling over to the empty booths, standing ready. He didn't have to hear her follow behind him to know she did. He could sense her. In the visceral awareness that skated over his skin like dancing fingertips.

I see right through you, Coltrane Dennison.

The words reverberated through him, humming deep in his chest, echoing in his head. They both terrified and...liberated him. Terrified, because he'd become so used to hiding in plain sight. Pretending to be fine, to be on the mend. Giving people answers that made them comfortable, happy, relieved, when all along he was lying. The words scared him, threatened that wall he'd erected around himself. He worried she might be able to peer past it into the real him. Into the darkness that hadn't abated since his family's deaths. While the pain, the grief and anger were ugly, they were his. Not to be spied on, not to be shared. In a completely toxic and illogical way, they connected him to his wife and son.

But even as he felt threatened, he also felt liberated, because he didn't have to pretend with Sydney. She hadn't been here to witness his breakdown, so he didn't need to make her believe he was fine.

Fine. God, he hated that word. For once, he could be honest in a way he couldn't with his parents, brothers and sisters.

There was a certain freedom in that.

"You're half right. I love this town. The family it gave me. The security and sense of safety it offers me." He paused in the middle of the aisle bisecting the booths, staring into the distance so he didn't have to look at her when he added, "The wife and child it gave me. And my way of thanking Rose Bend for those gifts is to make sure it's a refuge. A place where its residents know their welfare always comes first. Honestly, though?" He turned around, facing her. Looking at her when he gave her this truth. "Another reason I ran for mayor—the reason I couldn't include in my campaign—is I needed to lose myself in work, or else I would've been lost. To the bottle. To the grief. To the depression. But that sounds much less altruistic or heroic than the first reason."

"No," she said. Emotion flickered in her eyes, that same something spasming quickly across her face before she moved to stand in front of him. Until her fingers tangled with his. Until her small, warm palm cupped his cheek. Shock, jagged, bright and almost painful, whipped through him, freezing him in place. "It makes you even more heroic in my eyes. It would've been easier to crawl into bed and not get up. And if you had chosen to do that, Cole, I couldn't judge or blame you. But you didn't. You pushed through and even in your pain, decided to enrich a town and empower the people you care for. What's that saying about courage not being the absence of fear but acting in spite of it? Well, your kind of heroism isn't about the lack of grief but persevering and making lives better in spite of it."

He briefly closed his eyes and barely managed not to turn into her hand and brush his lips across the palm. Just stopped himself from groping for her other hand and placing it on his face, his throat, his chest, hell *anywhere*. Hunger for more of her touch roared so loud inside him, he damn near shuddered with it. Not just for the physical. But for the sense of not being so fucking alone. Her touch, her scent, her voice—they beat back the loneliness. For a few precious moments he didn't fear going under.

This wasn't good.

Not for him.

Not for her.

He stepped back, away from her heat, her kindness.

From the temptation of her.

Because if the press of her palm to his face called to him so strongly he had to physically resist it, what would the silken, tight embrace of her sex around his cock do to him?

Undo him.

Air shuddered from between his lips, and he tunneled his fingers over his head.

"You keep doing that," she murmured. "Running your fingers through hair that isn't there anymore. You must miss it."

Her softly uttered observation crashed over him like a frigid wave of salt water—freezing, punishing.

Leaving him shivering and numb.

"Cole?" She recovered the space he'd placed between them, her fingertips glancing the back of his hand, but he drew back. Somewhere deep inside him a dull throb of shame pulsed at her flinch.

Later…later, when his heart thawed and this moratorium on feelings lifted, he would regret hurting her with his abrupt rejection. But right now? Now, he was haunted.

"I shaved it off after Tonia died. She used to love to play with my hair." She'd constantly run her fingers through it, tease him about his curls and how they were prettier than hers. He clenched his jaw, worked it for several seconds while the memories flooded him. "After she was gone, I didn't want it anymore. Couldn't stand to touch it or look at it in the mirror."

Only the faint drone of traffic and the distant hum of voices punctuated the silence that fell between them. Whereas before the silence had been easy, comfortable, now a ragged tension existed, crackling like electrified currents.

"When Carlin..." Sydney's voice trailed off. She rarely mentioned her dead sister, and when she spoke again, a rasp deepened her voice. "When Carlin's hair fell out while going through chemo, my mother saved it. She'd gather the strands from her pillow when Carlin wasn't looking and store them in a plastic bag that she kept in her top dresser drawer. Carlin had such beautiful hair. Soft, dark brown natural curls with hints of red. If she spent any length of time outside, the sun would bring out those red highlights. Which didn't happen often, so I learned to treasure those streaks, because they meant my sister was feeling well enough to play outside with me."

She inhaled a shaky breath, her hands lifting to her stomach and cradling the small mound. Her face wore a composed expression, but her gaze, fixed somewhere over his shoulder...was stricken. Bruised.

"About a week after Carlin died," she whispered, "I found the bag in the garbage. Mom had thrown the hair out. At first, I left it. But later that night, when my parents were asleep, I snuck into the kitchen and dug it out of the trash. I hid it under my mattress. I don't know why. At the time, I told myself it was to keep my sister near. But now, I think I did it because even then I subconsciously knew Mom had thrown it away out of pain, grief. She couldn't open her dresser drawer and constantly be reminded of the child she'd lost. One day, though, when the good days eventually outweighed the bad, and she didn't sob at pictures or memories of her daughter, she might regret throwing that bag away. So, I saved it for her. And years later, I don't remember why I looked under my mattress, but the bag was gone. I don't know exactly when Mom found it—the week before or years before—but I went to her room, looked in the dresser, and there was the bag. Back where it belonged."

Her eyes shifted, focused on him. How had he believed himself numb? Staring into that ruined gaze, he was seared by the—Jesus, what was it? Not something as simple as pain… No. Heartbreak. God, yes. The utter *heartbreak* in those beautiful eyes. It churned his gut, screwed it so tight he clenched his teeth against the heated shimmer of anger, against the need to protect her.

"Sydney," he whispered.

She shot up a hand, palm out, warding him off. "Don't," she murmured. "I'm okay. I only told you that so hopefully one day you'll look in the mirror, like my mom did, and not just see loss. Maybe you'll let your hair grow back because you'll remember how much Tonia loved it. I—" She briefly closed her eyes and pressed her thumb and finger to them. "I should head back," she said, dropping her arm to her side, again not looking at him.

He'd done this—placed this distance, this discomfort between them. Inadvertently, yes, but the blame still sat on his shoulders.

It's for the best.

Possibly, he silently agreed with the soft warning that coasted through his mind. But they were friends. Or on the verge of being friends. And he couldn't allow her to walk away like…this.

"Sydney," he tried again.

And again, she shut him down.

"Thank you for the walk and the…" She pinched her forehead, breathing out a low, harsh chuckle. "Thank you. I'll see you later."

With a taut smile that barely curved her lips and came no-where near reaching her eyes, she strode past him. He didn't turn around and watch her leave. Instead, he closed his eyes and in-haled. Capturing the sultry, warm scent of orchids. Listening for her soft footfalls on the grass. Soon enough, both disappeared.

And as he followed, moments later, returning to his office, he convinced himself the hollow pit inside wasn't loneliness.

After all, he'd become an expert at lying to himself.

CHAPTER NINE

Sydney exhaled heavily as she pulled open the door to her father's clinic. The twisting in her stomach had nothing to do with her baby's active movements—which had steadily increased in the two weeks since she'd last seen the doctor—but with her reason for being here.

Today she'd find out if she was having a boy or girl.

Joy spilled through her, effervescent like the lightest champagne. And if underneath that feeling nerves bubbled, well they were expected and couldn't temper her happiness.

She stepped into the coolness of the lobby out of the early afternoon heat, and walked up to the receptionist's desk.

The pretty young blonde who'd checked her out after her first meeting with Dr. Prioleau greeted her with a smile. "Good afternoon, Ms. Collins."

"Afternoon." Sydney nodded, returning the smile and the kindness. "And please, call me Sydney. With my mom coming around here, Ms. Collins might get a little confusing."

The blonde, whose desk plate identified her as Lauren Grahame, grinned wider. "All right, Sydney. You filled out paperwork last time, so all I need is your co-pay."

"Sure thing."

Sydney dug into the purse she had slung sideways around her neck and handed the receptionist her credit card. While waiting for her to run the payment, Sydney glanced at her watch and frowned. Then plucked her phone out of her overalls and checked the lock screen. No missed calls. She'd asked Leo to come with her to the appointment, and her friend had happily agreed. But one o'clock had passed by ten minutes ago, and she still hadn't arrived and hadn't called or left a message. Maybe Leo was running behind.

Just as she tucked the phone back in her pocket, a nurse opened the connecting door and announced Sydney's name.

"Great timing," Lauren said, handing Sydney her card.

"Thanks." Sydney smiled. "A friend is supposed to meet me here for the appointment. When she arrives, could you just show—"

"I'm here."

Surprise crackled through her, and she stiffened, her hands freezing over the front pocket of her purse.

Several things Sydney knew for certain.

The finale to *Game of Thrones* sucked.

Lisa Bonet went to bed *every* night with a smile on her face.

And *that* voice definitely did *not* belong to Leontyne Dennison.

Hands still clutching her purse, she slowly turned around.

And came face-to-face with Cole.

Nope. Not Leo. In her place stood the Dennison Sydney had been avoiding for the last week and a half. Their encounter outside the ice cream shop and then at The Glen had been such an emotional roller coaster, she'd walked away craving mood stabilizers. And wine. And a good, long, ugly cry. A cry she couldn't blame on her pregnancy hormones but on the pain and grief of the past.

Gorgeous and composed, he wore a light blue shirt that stretched across his broad shoulders and chest and skimmed his flat stomach. He slid his hands into the front pockets of navy dress pants that emphasized his tapered waist and muscled thighs. His amber eyes revealed none of his thoughts, that carnal mouth flat, in an almost grim line. But even that couldn't detract from the lushness of its curves. She suspected nothing could do that.

"What're you doing here?" she hoarsely demanded. Then, glancing around and taking in the avid attention focused on them from the receptionist and others in the waiting room, she edged closer to him and lowered her voice. "Where's Leo?"

"She couldn't make it. One of the guest bathrooms flooded, and she has to wait at the inn for the plumber. So, she called me, and I told her I would meet you here."

"You don't have to do that," she insisted.

For a variety of reasons. The main one being, he seemed to have an aversion to anything having to do with her pregnancy. Hell, when the man had touched her stomach in his office, it'd seemed more like an act of torture than affection or curiosity. He'd lost a child; taking him to that examination room and subjecting him to hearing a baby's heartbeat and seeing the image of that baby on a sonogram was cruel and unusual punishment. She refused to inflict that agony on him.

"I know I don't have to," he said. "I'm here because I want to be."

But she was already shaking her head and poking a finger into his abdomen. And damn, were those rocks? Seriously. Who had abs like that outside of Dwayne Johnson? "No, you're here because you're doing that 'heroic' thing again. When it's not necessary. I got this."

Truthfully, she needed to get used to being on her own. She wouldn't deny Daniel access to their daughter or son, but being hundreds of miles away, Sydney would be primarily raising their child as a single mother. This was her choice, and she was strong enough to do this.

Regardless of what Daniel or her parents thought.

"Sydney." He gently cupped her prodding finger. "I don't doubt that you 'got this.' I also don't doubt that you could do this on your own and be just fine. But the fact is you don't *have* to. I'm here for you. Just like Leo would've been if she could. Just like any friend would."

Any friend would.

Yes, because they were only—could only ever be—friends. If the other day had revealed anything to her, it was that.

"Cole," she said, inching closer and tilting her head back so she wouldn't miss any nuance in his expression, in his eyes. "Leo shouldn't have asked you. Because she might not realize this is going to hurt you. But *I* do. And don't try and tell me it won't. I can't be responsible for causing you more pain. I *won't*."

He didn't immediately reply, instead he studied her with shadows darkening his gaze to nearly brown. Then he lowered his head over hers so his lips nearly grazed the tip of her ear, and his delicious, earthy scent surrounded her.

"You're a strong woman. And you're also a soon-to-be mother who is about to experience one of the most emotional moments of her pregnancy. You're going to look at your baby on that screen and find out if you're going to have a gorgeous little girl or a precious boy." His voice thickened, roughened. "Now, your baby will have a face, even if it's in your head. He or she will be more real to you than ever before, and you might cry. You might do nothing but stare in awe at that black screen with the image of your child. Either way, you're going to be overwhelmed with emotion because it's an amazing, special moment. And it's a moment you should not spend alone. Regardless of how I feel, I'm going in there with you. You won't be alone. Not on my watch. So, get it through that beautiful, thick head. I'm. Staying."

Thick head? She glared at the base of his throat. Well, he could… Oh damn. Beautiful? He thought her head—was beautiful? A ball of warmth dropped into her stomach, detonated, radiating pleasure. Hell, it even tingled in her toes, and she curled the digits into her sandals. She blinked, a little dazed that an offhand compliment from him could make her feel like the sun was rising inside her.

He'd left her speechless. Because, really, what in the hell did she say to that?

Or to his willingness—no, his insistence—that he wasn't leaving her side, regardless of the cost to his own heart, his own pain?

Obviously, the only thing to say was "Okay," because she whispered it just as the nurse called her name again.

Spinning around, she moved forward. She didn't have to glance around to see if people were staring at her and Cole, because those curious gazes prickled her skin. Good Lord. Rose Bend's gossip grapevine would be burning up today.

Speculating if Cole Dennison had taken up with pregnant black sheep Sydney Collins.

Or worse, the mayor was taking pity on poor Sydney and accompanying her to her doctor's appointment because the father of her baby couldn't be bothered.

As embarrassing as the first one was, the second rumor was even more humiliating. Because it contained a kernel of truth.

"I'm Sydney," she said to the nurse.

"Nice to meet you, Sydney. I'm Jackie," the nurse greeted. Her gaze flicked behind Sydney. "Hi, Cole."

"Hey, Jackie," he replied, and a big hand settled on Sydney's shoulder. "I'm with her today. I hope it's okay."

"If it's fine with Sydney, it's good with me." The nurse smiled. "Follow me. We're in Room 3 at the end of the hall and to the left." Moments later they entered an exam room. "You can put your purse down here," Jackie said, gesturing toward a chair in the corner. "I'll take your weight and vitals."

Sydney narrowed her eyes at the scale, then shifted her glare to Cole. "You. Over there." She jabbed a finger at the window on the far wall of the room. "And if you look before I tell you to, you'll turn into a pillar of salt."

Jackie grinned while Cole arched his brows high but complied. Only then did she lift her purse over her head, slip out of her shoes and step on the scale.

"Every little bit helps," she explained to the nurse, who sagely nodded her head. Of course she understood. She was a woman.

Then Sydney sighed at the scale's digital reading. She couldn't decide if that was baby weight or those fresh glazed doughnuts from Mimi's Café that she'd become addicted to since returning home. She swore the owner slid crack up in there. Nothing else could explain her obsession with them.

"You can turn around now," she said to Cole as she stepped off the offending piece of equipment and into her sandals.

He returned to her side as she perched on the paper-covered examination table. Moments later, Jackie finished taking Sydney's temperature, blood pressure and heart rate, recording everything into a handheld tablet.

"Dr. Prioleau will be with you in just a few minutes," Jackie said, smiling before leaving the room and closing the door behind her.

"Is it weird that I'm nervous?" she whispered, as if the butter-yellow walls were the stained glass of a church instead of a doctor's office. "I mean, this isn't my first appointment. Not the first time I'll hear the baby's heartbeat. I should be excited, right? Not feeling like I'm about to dive off a cliff with only a questionably stable cord preventing me from plunging to my death."

"Wow. That's specific…and graphic."

She met the teasing light in Cole's amber eyes. "It's a side effect of this pregnancy. I cry at the drop of a hat, pee when I cough, have an unhealthy relationship with fried dough and have a scarily vivid imagination."

He smiled, and his arm rose from his side, his hand hovering between them for a second before he reached for her, cupping the back of her neck. He gently squeezed, and she briefly closed her eyes, accepting and savoring the comfort he offered.

"So, I'll need to have tissue, diapers and doughnuts handy whenever I'm around you. Good to know."

A snicker slipped out of her. Then, she shook her head and whispered, "Thank you, Cole."

He didn't ask for what. Didn't ask her to explain. Which was good because she couldn't have articulated the answer. Instead, he tenderly squeezed her neck again and dropped his hand away from her. "You're welcome."

The door opened, preventing anything else she would say—or not say. Dr. Prioleau entered, smiling wide. Today, she wore a dark berry lipstick along with a deep purple sheath dress and nude pumps. The woman had style, and Sydney really needed to have a side conversation about what conditioner the doctor used to keep her twists so shiny.

"Hi, Sydney, it's great to see you again," Dr. Prioleau greeted. "You, too, Cole." She shook first Sydney's hand then Cole's. "Your vitals are perfect," she said, then tapped on her tablet and studied the screen. "Weight gain is on target. Everything looks good." She set her tablet down on the counter and stepped over to the sink and washed her hands. "Today, we're going to do a sonogram so I can have a look at your uterus and ovaries and check the baby's growth. And if you haven't changed your mind, we'll see if he or she will be cooperative and let us see if you're having a boy or girl."

Sydney inhaled a breath and slowly exhaled it. "I'm ready."

"Great." The doctor grabbed a paper towel and dried her hands. "Let's get started. Can you lie back and lift your shirt for me? I want to measure the baby's growth. And then we'll listen to the heartbeat."

A second of indecision and misplaced modesty struck Sydney as the doctor dipped her hand in her coat pocket and withdrew a tape measure. Which was silly. The first thing she'd learned to let go of since finding out she was pregnant was modesty. Someone was always exposing her stomach, touching it or inserting things inside her vagina. Yeah, Daniel hadn't seen as much of her sex as her doctor and nurse had. But still…

She slid a sidelong glance at Cole, who'd stood by silently so far. Not like it would be the first time he'd seen a pregnant woman's stomach, but not *hers*. And then there was the fact that most likely the last time had been his wife's. His intentions to accompany her so she wouldn't be alone were admirable, but faced with the reality of this, could he bear it?

"Sydney?" Dr. Prioleau asked, her concern etched in her slight frown. "Is everything all right?"

"Yes, I'm fine. Just a little slow today. Decaf coffee should be outlawed and then run outta town for being a dirty little tease," Sydney muttered, unhooking the top of her overalls and hiking up her tank top while the doctor chuckled.

The cool air brushed over her skin, and she looked down her torso to her bump. With efficient and quick movements, the doctor set the tape at the top of her pubic bone and stretched it over her belly to just under her breasts.

"Twenty centimeters," the other woman said, tucking the tape measure back in her pocket then recording the note on her tablet. "Good size."

Once more Sydney glanced over at Cole. He wore the same stoic expression, his thick, dark lashes hiding his eyes from her. But she didn't need to see his gaze to guess how this was affecting him. The tense line of his jaw, the firm press of his lips, the fisting of his fingers—they all telegraphed the emotion roiling inside him.

"Cole." She waited until his scrutiny flicked toward her. "You okay?"

Her hand ached to wrap around his, to anchor him just as he insisted on being here today. Instead, she curled her hands into the paper-covered table beneath her.

"Yes," he replied, the answer short, but then his tone softened. "Don't worry about me, Sydney."

Right. When pigs flew and Taylor Swift stopped making songs about her exes.

Dr. Prioleau didn't give any indication that she listened to their exchange but walked to the sink/counter combo and removed a handheld Doppler from the drawer along with a tube of gel.

"Ready to hear this baby's heartbeat?" She smiled, squeezing a generous dollop onto her belly, and pressed the end that looked like a small microphone to Sydney's belly.

Static filled the room for several seconds, and the breath in Sydney's lungs stalled. No, this wasn't the first time she'd heard her baby's heartbeat, but every time nerves flurried inside her. What if that beautiful proof of life didn't echo in her ears? What if the doctor couldn't locate it? What if—

A rapid pulse like a horse's gallop reverberated in the room, a *swish-swish* sound throbbing beneath it. Sydney exhaled, a grin spreading across her face as relief poured through her. "I don't think I'll ever get used to hearing this," she breathed.

Dr. Prioleau chuckled. "Confession? Neither do I." She winked, removing the wand from Sydney's stomach. Quickly, she grabbed a handful of paper towels and wiped down Sydney's stomach and then cleaned her medical equipment. "Be right back," she said, storing the Doppler back in the drawer. "I'm going to grab the ultrasound machine."

Suddenly feeling vulnerable and exposed, Sydney tugged her shirt back down. And then dared to peek at Cole again. A little scared of what she would glimpse.

His face could've been a wall of stone with two amber jewels set in it. A fine tension ran through his big body, stringing him so tight, one touch looked like it would shatter him.

"Cole," she whispered. His gaze shifted from her now-covered belly to her face. "Talk to me. Tell me what's going on inside your head."

She halfway didn't expect an answer to her plea; she *definitely* didn't expect him to shift forward and slowly set a shaking hand on her belly. His large palm and long fingers spread across her bump, and each one of his tiny trembles ricocheted through her like sonar waves.

But he didn't move his hand.

"I forgot…" He swallowed hard. Shook his head. "I forgot how beautiful that sound was. How…" Again, he trailed off, slid a tongue across his full lips, dampening them. "How amazing and incredible it was. That proof of a new life. Every time I heard it, I imagined what my son's face would look like. How it would feel to finally hold him in my arms. Every. Time. Was a miracle."

"What was his name?" Sydney dared to ask.

"Mateo," he whispered. His gaze jerked from his hand to meet her eyes. "He—"

Dr. Prioleau opened the door, and he snatched his arm back to his side. A hollow pit opened low inside her as he strode over to the window, cradling his hand against his chest and rubbing a thumb into the center of his palm. As if trying to erase the feeling of her belly…or trying to capture it.

"Here we go," the doctor said, holding the door while Jackie pushed the ultrasound machine into the room.

The two of them situated it next to the exam table, and within moments, had everything set up and working. Sydney lifted her top again. She stared at the black screen while Dr. Prioleau poured more warm gel on her stomach.

"Are you doing okay? Comfortable?" she questioned, pulling up a wheeled stool and sitting down near Sydney's shoulder. "I know lying on your back can cause a little discomfort."

Sydney shook her head, anxious to see her baby's image fill that screen.

Just as the doctor lowered the probe to her belly, a knock reverberated on the door.

An instant later, her father poked his head through the opening. Shock sucker punched her in the chest, and her breath escaped her on a low gasp. She'd fully expected her father to avoid her just as he'd done the last time she'd visited the clinic. Seeing him for the first time since she'd left her parents' home the morning after she arrived in Rose Bend catapulted her into a swirling morass of surprise, anger, longing and love.

Had he believed Dr. Prioleau was with another patient instead of her?

Was he here to speak to the other doctor?

Was he...could he be here...for her?

Her heart thudded against her chest, beating almost as fast as her baby's. Because she wanted the answer. And she didn't.

"Hi, Dr. Collins," the other woman greeted with a warm smile. "What can I do for you?"

Her father glanced from his partner to Sydney, and on any other person, she would label the glint in his eyes as uncertainty. But no, this *was* her father, and he didn't do uncertainty.

"I heard Sydney was here for her twenty-week checkup." He looked like he would continue, his lips parted, but no words emerged.

"Yes," Dr. Prioleau said. "We're just about to start her sonogram. Sydney, is it okay if he stays for it?"

Yes, Dad I need you, that little girl cried out inside her. But the hurt, scared-of-rejection grown woman couldn't voice that yearning for her father. Instead, she nodded and murmured, "If you want to."

After a brief hesitation, he stepped fully into the room. He nodded at Cole and approached her. With her doctor on her right and Cole standing to her left, her father took position near the foot of the table, sliding his hands into his front pants pockets.

Staring at him and remembering who they used to be to each other before Carlin died had a snarled ball of emotion lodging in her throat, so she looked away from him and focused on the black screen.

Her baby. Today was all about her baby. Not her messy relationship—or lack of one—with her parents. Or the despair, regret and pain it caused her.

"Here we go." Dr. Prioleau moved the wand over her abdomen. "Dr. Collins, could you hit the lights for me?"

A second later, the room dimmed, and quiet descended on the room as they all waited for the grainy image to appear.

And when it did…

She gasped. Couldn't help it. Her hand shot out of its own accord and clutched Cole's. His fingers immediately wrapped around hers, and for a moment, their eyes clashed, connected, before she tore her gaze away and returned it to the monitor. It wasn't the first time she'd received a sonogram, but it felt like it was as her baby appeared, tiny. She laughed, the sound breathy and full of the joy that welled and spilled over, infiltrating every part of her.

In this instant, with her eyes glued to her baby, she *became* joy.

"She's beautiful," she said, her voice like sandpaper against her throat. She heard the scuff of feet over the floor, then felt a warm, familiar hand on her knee.

Dragging her attention away from the screen, she glanced down, and her father, his focus fixed on the screen, had moved closer, touching her affectionately for the first time in… God, longer than she could remember. Tears pricked her eyes, and she briefly closed them before returning them to the screen.

"So sure you're having a little Arwen?" Cole teased, and she shrugged a shoulder, smiling.

"One, she will never be named that. And two, I just have a feeling."

"We haven't had a boy in our family since your uncle," her father murmured. "I'm betting on a girl, too."

She and her father agreed on something. Wow. And they said miracles didn't happen anymore.

"Here's your uterus." Dr. Prioleau circled the arrow over a dense-looking place at the bottom of the image. "The baby is in a good place. So that's awesome. Your placenta is healthy. Wonderful," she murmured. She located all the baby's organs, checking them and steadily capturing images. "An active baby," she added.

Sydney grinned, tears pressing against her eyes, stinging them as the baby flipped just then, presenting them her spine and the back of her head.

"If I didn't know any better, I'd swear your kid just told us to kiss its ass," Cole drawled.

She laughed, the sound watery, and squeezed his hand tighter. "Aww. She takes after me already."

Her father snorted, and she smiled at him. That moment of connection bloomed inside her chest, mingling with the happiness that swamped her to capacity.

"And what we've all been waiting for," Dr. Prioleau said, still capturing more images. "Your baby is moving a lot, which is awesome. Now if he or she will turn just so..." They all waited, and the baby did turn, but with its legs curled, hiding the sex.

"You did the same thing," her father said. "Wouldn't cooperate for anything." No censure or sharpened words. Just the opposite. They were packed with warmth and fondness and even a hint of laughter.

"Oh wait... Here we go," Dr. Prioleau announced. The baby had turned again, and her bottom faced the screen from underneath. "A girl," she said, laughing. "Seems you were right, Sydney."

"A girl," she breathed. This time, she didn't even attempt to bat back the tears. They fell from her eyes and tracked down her cheeks. Glancing at her father, she repeated just as softly, "A girl."

"A granddaughter," he whispered, voice thick. He cleared his throat, but when he spoke again, it remained just as scratchy. "How about that?"

"I think it's fair to say she's going to be a handful. And probably spoiled." A half smile curved Cole's lips. "Isn't that right, Luke?"

"My wife is going to be awful," he said. "I'll try and keep her in check, but I can't make any promises."

Cole laughed. "Right." He arched an eyebrow. "Says the grandfather who already looks like he's wrapped around that tiny, alien-looking finger."

"Hey." Sydney chuckled, lightly slapping him in the abdomen with the back of her hand. "That's my alien-looking little girl you're talking about."

"If the UFO fits…" He shrugged, but she caught the quirk at the corner of his mouth.

"That's just wrong," she protested on a burst of laughter. And then, because she couldn't look away too long, she returned her gaze to the monitor. The sonogram would end soon, and she had to soak up every moment she had left. "She's so real. I knew she was, of course, but looking at her here, seeing her move. She's real, and God, I love her," she whispered, not aware she'd uttered the vehement words aloud until a thumb gently wiped away her tears.

"She's definitely real, Sydney," Cole whispered. "And you're going to be a wonderful mom."

"I hope so," she murmured, and tipping her head to the side, she found his face hovering inches above hers.

She could pinpoint the striations of brown and gold in his eyes, feel the puff of his breath on her mouth. Inhale his earth and fresh rain scent. Desire coasted through her, setting every part of her on simmering fire. *Not here*, she scolded herself. She shouldn't have to place a stranglehold on the need to lift her head those few inches, press her lips to his beautiful mouth and taste him. Tangle with him. No, she shouldn't have to wrestle this need, because she shouldn't have it in the first place.

"Do you really think so?" she asked, doubts and uncertainty crowding inside her, crouching like a troll beneath a bridge, waiting to attack.

"I know so," Cole replied softly.

His words reverberated through her, the warmth they generated competing with the desire mingling with it. He straightened, but the hand that wasn't still clutched in hers brushed over her hair. And though it was impossible and fanciful on her part, she would swear under threat of perjury that she felt it. On her cheek. Her shoulder. Her breasts...between her thighs.

"We're all finished here," Dr. Prioleau said, snatching Sydney's attention from her body's wayward response to this man and back to the ultrasound machine.

She studied the image of her daughter one last time before the doctor removed the scope from Sydney's belly. Efficiently but gently, Dr. Prioleau wiped away the gel, and Sydney tugged her shirt down and refastened the straps of her overalls.

"I need to get back to work," her father said, and when Sydney looked at him, she didn't miss the slight frown that marred his brow as he glanced from Cole to Sydney. When their eyes met, the frown cleared, and he almost awkwardly patted her knee again. "See you soon, Sydney."

She hadn't expected her normally reserved father to say, *I love you*. But damn the part of her that held its breath waiting for it, longing for it. Damn the part that ached because she didn't hear the words.

"Bye, Dad," she said, and watched his back as he disappeared through the door.

Let it go, she ordered herself. At least he came in to be with her, to see his first grandchild. Given the state of their strained relationship, beggars couldn't be choosers. And if it struck her that a child shouldn't have to beg for her parent's affection, well...

She'd accepted that a long time ago and yearning for something wouldn't change it.

She should know.

But one of her doubts could be laid to rest. Her father would love and accept his granddaughter. That glimmer of tears had been real.

"Here you go, Sydney." Dr. Prioleau handed Sydney a long printout of the sonogram images she'd captured. Releasing Cole's hand, Sydney cupped the paper, cradling it as if it might poof into thin air any second. "Congratulations. I'm happy for you. You can set up your next appointment date at the front desk. Do you have any questions for me?"

"No, not at the moment. But believe me, as neurotic as I am, I'll reach out if I do."

The other woman laughed. "I'm here. I'll see you next month."

Dr. Prioleau left, her heels clacking against the floor. Damn, she really did need to find out where her doctor shopped. Those heels were bangin'.

"Ready to get out of here?" Cole asked, cupping her elbow as she pushed off the table.

"Yes." She strode over to her purse and carefully stowed the sonogram printout inside. "And I know you're probably sick of me saying this, but thank you," she said, continuing to fuss with her purse so she didn't have to look at him.

With the shenanigans her body insisted on doing whenever he was within breathing distance, and the emotional gauntlet she'd traveled today, she didn't trust her face not to betray her.

"You're welcome, Sydney. Thank *you* for letting me stay."

She finally turned around. The smirk on her lips felt more like a defense than a true show of amusement. "Like I had a choice. 'Get it through your thick head. I'm staying'," she mimicked him, dropping her voice several ranges. She shook her head, and then sobered, studying his face. "Are you sure you're okay? Regardless of what you've said, this cost you, Cole."

He didn't immediately reply, his focus switching from her to the wall behind her. "Yes, it did," he finally said. And her stomach bottomed out.

"I'm so sorry—"

"No," he interrupted, his eyes shifting and clashing with hers. She nearly flinched at the intensity there, the stark emotion that had her wanting to back away and insanely, cuddle close. "Don't apologize. This was my decision, and I'd make the same one again. I don't know who convinced you that you're not worth putting first, but you are. And you deserve that. Demand it."

She blinked, his words punching straight to her heart. Had anyone ever told her she wasn't a priority? No. But they'd hammered that message home her entire life.

Her parents, first with Carlin and her illness, and then with their grief.

Daniel, with his career and his opinions and needs.

And then herself. She was the biggest culprit of not placing herself first in her own life.

But admitting that to herself had her cringing and backpedaling. No way she could confess it to Cole. Not the town golden boy. Not the beloved mayor. It smacked too much of self-pity.

So, she said nothing. And as she pulled the door open, she couldn't help but mentally chuckle, and even in her head it sounded razor sharp. The irony remained that if she ever allowed herself to do something as foolish as falling for Cole—which she would not—he would just be one more person on that short list. She would never be first with him.

His wife already occupied that place.

And no one ever had a hope of displacing her.

CHAPTER TEN

"Oh my God. Are you having sex?"

Sydney jerked to a halt outside of Mimi's Café, coughing and almost spitting out her bite of glazed doughnut.

"What?" she nearly shouted. "What the hell are you talking about?"

Leo cackled like a hyena in her ear. "That moan sounded particularly dirty. And since I've read that pregnant women run hot..." Her friend laughed again.

Sydney finished chewing the treat and swallowed before answering. "You're crazy. And I nearly died because of you. Death by glazed doughnut. I would've haunted your ass, too."

"You're at Mimi's, aren't you? Only a doughnut from Mimi's makes a person moan like that. I secretly call them orgasms in the mouth."

"Dammit, Leo." Sydney choked on another burst of laughter. "Really?"

"What? All I do is work, and it's been a while," she whined, then ruined it by snickering. "Stop punishing me for missing your doctor's appointment! Which I'm so sorry for, by the way. If I could've been there, I would have. And I hate that I missed seeing the baby for myself. So put me out of my misery! Tell me! What're we having? A little Arwen or Aragorn?"

"Well, I'm having..." Sydney dragged out the last word into five syllables.

"Tell me!"

"A girl." Sydney laughed, the delight that hadn't dissipated in the slightest spilling out of her. All over Main Street. "I'm having a little girl."

Leo's scream rang in her ear. Grinning, Sydney held the phone away from her until the squeals stopped. Or rather, lowered in volume.

"I'm going to need the hearing in that ear, thank you very much," Sydney griped to her friend.

"Oh, stop bitchin'. We're having a girl. I'm going to be an aunt. I get to buy her dresses and take her for mani-pedis. And teach her that women rule the world!"

"Oh Lord." Sydney groaned, even as she smiled. Several people passed by her and smiled, even waving hello, but none appeared scandalized. "Can she get here first before you plan global domination?"

"It's never too early to think big, sweetie. And she's going to love her Aunt Leo. I'm going to be the cool one," her friend boasted. Then, her voice lowered, softened. "I'm so happy for you, Sydney. And it's so good to hear you sounding happy. Or at the very least, content."

"I am content. Or getting there, I guess." Sydney paused and stepped aside, out of the way of the foot traffic on the sidewalk. Briefly closing her eyes, she sighed. "This place is different than what I was expecting when I came back. I can't say that everything is great, because I'm still...feeling my way. But for my baby..." She thought of Cole holding her hand in the exam room. Her father's teary smile as he stared at his granddaughter's image on the sonogram screen. Leo's unconditional love and friendship. "For her, I've made the right decision."

"Good." Leo released a shaky breath. "Well, dammit. Something's happening with my eyes. They're fucking leaking. And all over my planner."

Sydney threw her head back, laughing. "You're crazy, woman."

"Another reason Arwen is going to adore me." Leo hesitated. "Have you told Daniel yet?"

Sydney grimaced, shards of guilt lodging in her chest. In truth, she hadn't been able to extricate them since she got off the phone with her ex-husband thirty minutes earlier. "Yes."

"Oh God," Leo snarled. "What? What did the Great American Joy Snatcher do now?"

In spite of the shame and remorse swirling inside her like a cesspool, she huffed out a dry laugh. "No, this was all on me. I promised to record the sonogram for him since he couldn't be at the appointment. And caught up in my nerves and excitement, I forgot. I sent him pictures of the images, but that wasn't enough. He was furious, and you know how he gets when he's angry. Ice cold. And I can't blame him. He's missing these milestones in his baby's growth, and I forgot to do this small thing."

"Okay, you messed up," Leo conceded. "But you can't beat yourself up over this. And please don't let him steal your joy."

"I know. You're right. But I need to make sure he doesn't feel excluded." She sighed and, glancing around, stiffened. For the first time, noticing where she stood.

Right next to the crafts store. One door down was her mother's boutique. Her heart thudded against her sternum. Nerves crowded into her throat, throbbing in her pulse. But underneath the nerves lurked something precarious, something fragile—hope. Maybe it had been ignited when her father had walked into that examination room. Or when he'd whispered, "A granddaughter," with an almost reverent note in his voice.

Or it could've been neither of those things. But memories assailed her as she stared at her mom's store—the place where she used to spend her afternoons reading behind the counter or hiding under the racks pretending they were the many rooms of her fairy-tale castle. Memories of a time before Carlin's death when her mother had been her heroine, her rock, her everything.

She sucked in a breath and crossed an arm under her breasts. God, what she wouldn't give to have that mother back. To have that closeness and respect back.

"Sydney? You still there?" Leo asked, worry threading through her voice.

"Yes," she said. "Hey, I need to take care of something. I'll hit you back later tonight."

"Sure thing." Leo paused. "Is everything okay?"

"Everything's good." She nodded, even though her friend couldn't see the gesture. "Talk to you later?"

"Absolutely. Love you, Sydney."

"Love you, too."

Sydney ended the call, clutching the phone to her chest for a long moment before exhaling. Before she could talk herself out of this, she tucked the cell away in her purse and strode toward Elegant Occasions, the boutique that her mother had owned since before Sydney was born. Its pink-and-light-gray awning with the graceful scrollwork was as familiar to her as her childhood home. It starred in some of her best memories…and her worst. Including the last argument she and her mother had engaged in before Sydney hightailed it out of town.

Squaring her shoulders, she grabbed the handle and pulled open the door. The same bell that she remembered tinkled above her, announcing her entry. Her mother, standing behind the front counter, looked up, wearing a welcoming smile. A smile that dipped and trembled when she met Sydney's gaze. That shouldn't have sent pain shooting through her—Sydney should be accustomed to the trepidation and hesitation that wavered in her mother's eyes—but, it did.

If Carlin was alive, would you be happy to see me? If I'd been will-

ing to give blood, tissue, hell, even a kidney, to save your first daughter, would you still love me?

The questions howled in her head like a furious storm. She glanced away from her mother on the pretense of surveying the store. Truthfully? She was afraid she might find the answers to those questions in Patricia's dark gaze.

"Hi, Mom," she greeted softly. "I hope I'm not disturbing your day."

"No, it's been pretty quiet around here," Patricia murmured.

"That'll change in the next week with the motorcycle rally approaching."

"I'm sure it will."

Polite. They were so painfully polite with each other. If not for sharing the same eyes, facial features and curvy build, a passerby might've mistaken them for strangers. Proprietress of a boutique and her customer.

"I'm sorry to just drop in without..." A call? A text? A warning? Sydney shook her head. "Well, I should've called first."

"Why?" her mother asked, rounding the counter and striding forward, crossing the space that separated them. Like it was a war-torn no-man's-land. Sydney didn't like to think of her and her mother as enemies, but it'd been so long since they'd been allies. "You're my daughter. You don't need to call or make an appointment. I'm glad you came by."

"You are?" Surprise and skepticism saturated her voice, and when her mother's mouth tightened at the corners, Sydney hated that she hadn't been able to contain it. "I'm sorry, Mom. I didn't mean that like it came out."

Patricia arched an eyebrow. And though guilt fluttered inside her, Sydney lightly chuckled. That gesture had been a staple in Sydney's childhood. No one or nothing called bullshit like her mother's right eyebrow.

"Okay, how about I didn't want it to come out that way," she amended with a dry laugh. "Can I start over?" When her mother nodded, she sighed. "Hey, Mom. I got some amazing news today, and I wanted to share it with you."

"You did?" Now surprise colored her voice. So did pleasure. "Well, don't keep me in suspense. You know how much I love secrets. What's happened?"

Sydney smiled, a smoky curl of wistfulness uncoiling inside her chest. Yes, she'd forgotten that about her mother. She'd had a big mouth as a child, and often, especially around Christmas and Patricia's birthday, her mother would bribe Sydney with freshly baked cookies or the promise of trying on some of the clothes in the boutique in the grown-up dressing rooms to spill about the presents her father had bought. Sydney silently snickered, but that amusement mellowed, softened into a melancholy glow. There'd been a time when Sydney had actually giggled with her mother, conspiring like thieves.

She'd forgotten that, too.

"I think it's better if I show you," Sydney murmured, digging into her purse. She plucked the carefully folded scroll of sonogram images from the depths and handed it to her mother. "Pictures of your granddaughter."

Her mother's eyes rounded as she released a hushed gasp. Almost tentatively, she accepted the printout and after a long moment, wrenched her gaze from Sydney's and dropped her head, all her attention focused on the black-and-white pictures.

"Oh my God," she whispered, straightening the long row of images and studying them one by one. "A little girl. I'm going to be a GiGi." She laughed softly, the low sound a little damp, shaking her head. "I always said that if either of you girls had kids of your own, I didn't want to be a boring grandma or nana. I wanted to be a glamorous GiGi."

Sydney braced herself against the offhand mention of Carlin, nearly rocking back on her heels. Other than asking Sydney if she intended to visit her sister's grave with them every year, her parents never—*never*—talked about Carlin. That her mother had, here...and so easily...with *her*...

Sydney swallowed past the lump of emotion—cautious hope, timid delight, dulled sadness—in her throat, a little afraid to speak. Because history reminded Sydney that she and her mother tended to fuck up when they attempted to do things like talk. It never failed that one or both of them would emerge from the occasion scratched and bruised by words, frustration and disappointed expectations.

But in this store, with her mother's joy evident in every excited coo over the image, Sydney stepped out onto that shaky ledge called faith.

To hell with it.

She leaped.

"I mean, you own a boutique. I think it goes without saying you're already glamorous, Mom," Sydney teased. "But I'm suddenly realizing this baby is going to be beyond spoiled," she grumbled. But her grin ruined the irritated tone.

"Pshaw." Her mother waved a hand in her direction, never removing her gaze from the images. "Spoiling is a grandmother's prerogative...and right."

"Did you really just 'pshaw' me?" Sydney snickered. "Mom, I thought I was the one who lived in the South for the last eight years. Are you going to offer me a big glass of sweet tea next?"

"Ha ha. I blame it on Kelly Prioleau. Since she started working with your father, I've become addicted to grits, and have been bingeing them by the pot."

Sydney blinked. Fought back a grin. Lost the fight. "Have you had them with shrimp yet?"

"God. Yes." Her mother loosed a frankly lascivious groan.

Their eyes met.

And they burst out laughing.

Good. Sydney felt *good*. How long had it been since she'd done *this* with her mother? She couldn't remember. That first year after Carlin died had blurred into a haze of grief, guilt and hot rage. And later? Cold. Their house had been plunged into a deep freeze marked by pockets of angry outbursts, silly rebellions and bitter defiance. The distance between Sydney and her parents—especially her mother—had grown and grown until trekking around the globe in a broke-down Winnebago would've been easier than crossing that emotional divide.

But in this moment, with her mother smiling at her, clutching sonogram pictures of her granddaughter and a warmth in her brown eyes that had Sydney's breath catching in her lungs, that divide shrunk just a bit.

"I have something for you." Her mother retraced her steps to the counter, and seconds later, reemerged holding the straps of a large paper bag with her store's logo scrawled across the front. "I ordered these for you last week and they just came in yesterday. I hope you like them."

Astonishment rippled through her, and Sydney gaped at Patricia. A gift? For her? Of course, for Christmas and her birthdays, her parents had sent cards and even small presents. But a just-because gift? And given how their last interaction had gone...

"For me?" she whispered.

Her mother tilted her head to the side, a small smile curving her mouth even as what could've been a hint of sadness gleamed in her eyes. "Yes, for you."

Swallowing hard, Sydney slowly reached out for the offered bag. And just as slowly, she opened it and peered inside. Clothes. A stack of tops, dresses and pants. Still unbelieving, she stroked a hand over an eyelet blouse in a lovely shade of teal.

"Mom..." she murmured.

"Maternity clothes," her mother explained. "Not my usual inventory, but when you came home..." She lifted a shoulder in a half shrug that struck Sydney as a little self-conscious. "Well, what's the point of owning a boutique if I can't provide clothes for my daughter? I had my buyer order these for you. I hope you like them."

"I love them," Sydney said.

Her mother chuckled. "You haven't even seen all of them."

"Doesn't matter." *They came from you.* Sydney didn't utter those words, but they echoed in her head, her heart.

"Well, I'm glad." Clearing her throat, her mother glanced down at the printout she still held. "Oh, Sydney. A little girl. Does your father know?"

Sydney nodded. "He was there for it."

"That's wonderful. Have you..." Her mother hesitated, paused. "Have you spoken with Daniel? Does he know?"

"Yes and yes. But unfortunately, he's a bit angry with me right now," Sydney confessed. Ordinarily, Sydney wouldn't have shared this with her mother—it'd been a long time since she'd felt emotionally safe enough to do that. She told her how she'd neglected to record the appointment and his reaction.

"Oh, Sydney," her mother tsked softly. "You do understand why he's upset, don't you? With you moving and him living so far away, he's missing out on these important moments and feels like he's not even a father because he's not an active part of this pregnancy."

"I know all this, Mom," Sydney said, impatience creeping into her voice. She *did* know. And the guilt hadn't abated at all. It was that shame that lent her tone an edge. "I'm sorry. I didn't mean to snap. I made a mistake, and I've already promised that I'll do better in the future. It's all I can do given the circumstances. Especially since those circumstances aren't likely to change any time soon."

"Are you—" Patricia faltered, and she glanced away from her.

"Just say it, Mom," Sydney said, but then held up a hand, palm out. "No, wait. Let me finish it for you. Am I sure that I'm doing the right thing?"

"Sydney, you know I love you. But I'm so worried about you.

The divorce. Suddenly showing up here with no plan. Taking a baby away from her father and raising her alone? How can I *not* question if you haven't thought all of this out? If you're not acting impulsively without weighing the consequences of your actions."

"Why do you just assume that I haven't weighed them? Assume that I don't have a plan? Maybe I haven't shared my plans with you. Has it occurred to you that I'm *afraid* to share them with you?"

Heat scalded her face, prickled over her skin, under her arms. Fear—of hurting her mother, of being hurt *by* her mother—pumped through her, mingling with the resentment and anger that had become an emotional staple when dealing with her parents.

Not good enough. Not the right daughter. Not anything more than a spare parts factory.

The vitriolic mantra hissed inside her head like a venomous snake. A mantra that had firmly entrenched itself deep in the bone marrow she'd once donated to her sister.

"Afraid?" Her mother frowned. "Why would you ever be afraid of me?"

"Seriously?" Sydney asked, incredulous. "Because I know whatever I told you wouldn't be supported but criticized, torn apart and denigrated."

"So, you want me to support you being a single mother?" Patricia demanded. "Support the added stress and pressure along with the financial burden you'll face?"

"Yes," Sydney nearly shouted. Turning away, she clenched her jaw, trying to leash her temper. "If it's my choice," she said, softer but no less vehemently, "then yes. If the alternative is being trapped in a loveless, too-polite, barren marriage where I'm slowly suffocating and losing myself, then yes. You might not agree with it, but I expect you to support me."

"*I...*" Her mother glanced down at the printout in her hand before lifting her gaze to Sydney's. And the disappointment there slashed a cut so deep, Sydney wondered how her mother didn't see the wound. "Everything you said starts with *I*. But it's not just about you anymore. It's about Daniel and this precious baby." Her mother slightly shook the scroll of images. "It became that when you got married. Even more so when you irresponsibly had sex with a man you shouldn't have divorced in the first place."

Selfish. The word echoed in her head, ricocheted off her skull and buried deep into her soul. It raked her, leaving her exposed, pulsing, a living, breathing bruise.

To her parents she would never be anything but that girl who cared only about herself, her needs, her wants.

In an instant, she was transported back to that night eighteen years ago in Baptist Memorial's pediatric ICU when Sydney had screamed and curled into a ball, hysterical at the prospect of enduring another surgery and painful recovery—this time for a partial kidney donation. She'd stolen that from beautiful, sweet Carlin.

And she'd sealed her fate as the selfish, doomed-to-disappoint failure of a daughter. Her parents had never uttered the words, but Sydney knew they'd never forgiven her for that one, irreversible act.

Which was fair, she supposed. Because she hadn't completely forgiven herself.

And here they stood. Constantly hurting one another. Disappointing one another.

"Sydney," her mother continued, her voice gentling. "It's not too late to fix things. I've talked to Daniel. He wants—"

A needle scratched across a record, loud and discordant, in her head. She stumbled back a step, staring at her mother, disbelief and anger filtering through the shock. "You did what?" she asked.

"He was my son-in-law for five years," she snapped, then

heaved a sigh, pinching the bridge of her nose. "He's hurting, too. So, of course I called to check on him."

Sydney chuckled, and it scraped her throat raw. "You called to check on him. And your daughter, who lives in the same town, you didn't reach out to once. News flash, Mom. I'm hurting. I'm scared. I'm alone. I needed—need—you, but it's Daniel who receives your concern…your love."

"Sydney." Her mother lifted an arm. "I—"

"I shouldn't have come here," Sydney whispered. "This was a mistake." As was stepping out on that bitch Faith.

Pivoting, she strode toward the exit, and for every step she took, it seemed like the smothering air forced her back three. With a sob, she finally, *finally* reached the door. Thankfully, no one stood on the other side because she burst through as if chased. Maybe she was. By her guilt. Her conscience.

Not stopping, she barreled down the sidewalk, almost blind and deaf to anything but the pain that throbbed with every heartbeat. She pushed into the pharmacy and blindly hobbled to the book and magazine section at the back. A large rack of the audiobooks Cole had told her about offered a partial barrier between her and the rest of the store. And she took advantage of it.

The air punched out of her lungs on a loud, harsh gust.

She scrubbed her hands over her face, and when the strap of the shopping bag abraded her cheek, she realized she still clutched the gift from her mother. And that she'd left the sonogram pictures behind. A sound between a sob and a serrated chuckle escaped her.

Dammit.

She couldn't go back.

Not now. Not when she so precariously teetered between screaming at her mother to, for once, have her back and begging her to see Sydney, accept her…love her. Not out of obligation because Sydney was her daughter. But love her because she actually *liked* her. Admired her. Saw her as more than a troublesome, rebellious child. Saw her as a strong, capable woman who made her smile.

Today had been the first time in years that her mother had simply *smiled* at Sydney.

How sad did that make them?

Worse…what did that say about Sydney when her own mother couldn't find simple delight in her?

Another sob crawled its way up her throat, and her hand rose as if the gesture could contain the cry that threatened to rip free. Tipping her head back, she sucked in a shuddering breath, blinking against the burn of tears. Jesus, today had started off so well. Joy-filled. Even wondrous. And now… She shook her head, pressing the heels of her palms to her eyes, the shopping bag knocking against her chin.

Now, she huddled in the back of the pharmacy trying to avoid an epic breakdown right between the *Good Housekeeping* magazines and the fiction section.

"Have you been over to The Glen? It looks fantastic. Cole Dennison definitely came through with his promise about making the rally bigger. I know you didn't vote for him, but I'm glad I did," a feminine voice said from the other side of the audiobook stand.

At Cole's name, Sydney stiffened, and lowered her arms and head. Like a tuning fork, every bit of her went on alert. Eavesdropping was a sign of poor upbringing—hadn't that been one of her mother's endless rules?—but that didn't stop Sydney from edging closer to that partition. Focusing on this conversation also provided the added benefit of distracting her from crumbling into an emotional heap.

And if something inside her hungered for any mention of Cole? Well, that was just because he was her friend.

The lies we tell ourselves.

"I mean, I like Cole," another voice, a woman's, a little deeper, joined in. "I just thought he was a little young for the job. Jasper Landon is older, more experienced and has been mayor for years."

"He also hasn't brought any change here in years," the first woman observed dryly. "He made campaign promises to win another election and didn't see one of them through. I should know. The previous election, I voted for him just because he swore he'd update the technology in the school system, including buying Chromebooks for every student. I'm *still* waiting on those," she said.

"Okay, that's one thing—"

"And approving raises for the police department," the first woman continued. "*Which*, I might add, Cole has already done, and he's only been in office months, not years."

"Fine," the deep-throated woman grumbled. "But Jasper hasn't suffered a heartbreak like Cole. C'mon, Lynn, be truthful. Cole hasn't dated since Tonia died. He's not the same man. We both know he's not over it. That kind of thing can make it hard for a person to focus on anything, much less being mayor of a town."

Sydney scowled, glaring at the audiobook she held, Michelle Obama's *Becoming*. This woman obviously knew nothing about Cole if she believed he wouldn't give his all to this town. Hell, he'd proven that.

"Are you kidding me?" the first, and obviously much smarter, woman scoffed. "Who wouldn't be scarred by that? He lost his wife—his childhood sweetheart—and their baby in childbirth. What was supposed to have been the happiest day of his life turned into the most tragic. But that has nothing to do…"

Sydney couldn't hear the rest of the women's conversation. She couldn't hear anything past the deafening cacophony of words in her head, crashing against her skull like thunderous waves.

He lost his wife—his childhood sweetheart—and their baby in childbirth.
…the happiest day of his life turned into the most tragic.

She pressed a fist to her chest, right over the heart beating out a rapid tattoo. But it didn't stop the shock, grief and pain that threatened to rip a hole right through her rib cage.

No one had mentioned...

She'd assumed that Tonia and his son had died in an accident. Like a car crash. Not while bringing their baby into this world.

No wonder he'd paled when he'd first seen her stomach behind the church. And no wonder his hand had trembled like a leaf battered by a summer storm when he'd touched her belly in his office. Jesus. How had he managed it? Had that been the first time he'd touched a pregnant woman since Tonia? Why hadn't he said something? Told her?

Why had he insisted on going with her to her prenatal appointment today?

You're also a soon-to-be mother who is about to experience one of the most emotional moments of her pregnancy.

He'd murmured those words in the clinic lobby, and he would know. And that moment would be branded in his memory because it'd been one of the few times he'd seen his son. One of the joyful times he and his wife had shared during her pregnancy. God, it must've been torture reliving that today.

And he hadn't uttered a word.

Instead, he had been there for her. If she'd known, if she'd had the slightest clue, she would've never...

The sob that she'd managed to suppress when she'd first entered the pharmacy tore from her. Whirling around, she rushed past the two women who'd unknowingly revealed the awful truth and rushed out of the store.

She didn't stop until she reached her car, started it and peeled out of the parking lot.

Cole.

She had to get to Cole.

CHAPTER ELEVEN

Cole perched on the end of his desk, glaring down at the sullen teen slouched in the chair in front of him. Trevor Haynes, with his dirty blond hair, green eyes and tall, lean figure, was a good-looking kid. He would be even more so without the petulant gleam in his eyes and the sulky set of his mouth. Insolence damn near leaked out of his pores, and Cole grit his teeth against yanking him straight in that chair. At least if he was in his law office instead of here at city hall, he could yell. But he had a town council meeting in thirty minutes, so he had to forgo the loud telling-off.

"Can we make this quick, Cole?" Trevor grumbled. "I got shit to do."

"Watch your mouth," Cole snapped, crossing his arms over his chest. "And it's Mr. Dennison to you. At sixteen, you're not a grown man, but you're almost there. And when you're honorable enough to keep your word and make responsible decisions like a man, then you can call me Cole. Until then, you haven't earned it."

The teen flinched but tried to cover it by slouching farther into the chair.

"Fine, Mr. Dennison," he muttered. "Mom's expecting me home by six."

"I know exactly what time she's expecting you since she and I discussed your new curfew."

"You did what?" he snarled, shooting up in the chair and gripping the arms. He scowled at Cole. "You had no right—"

"No right?" Cole repeated softly. "Are you forgetting who went to bat for you and got your felony larceny of a motor vehicle charge down to a joyriding misdemeanor?"

"Mom paid for you to be my lawyer. That was your job," Trevor sneered.

"Listen up, Trevor," Cole said, praying for the patience of Job. "Your mother works at the Sunnyside Grille, sometimes double shifts, to make sure you have food in your stomach and a roof over your ungrateful head. Yet, she took money that could've gone to rent, bills and your college fund, out of her pocket so she could put it toward a retainer for me. And it still wasn't enough to cover what I charge. So yes, Trevor, she might've given me money, but you were more a pro bono than paid client."

Trevor flattened his mouth into a stubborn line, but he didn't say anything.

"And a detective who knows you're my client decided to call me instead of arresting you and turning you in with the rest of that pot-smoking bunch of asses you call friends. The same bunch that got you in trouble last time—"

"I wasn't—"

"Why do you think you're sitting here with me right now instead of being bailed out by your mother?" Cole barked. "But you were there, and technically, you could've been arrested along with the rest of them. Given you're not, I figure that gives me *a right* and a vested interest in what you do."

A thick silence filled the office. Trevor didn't meet Cole's eyes, but studied the scuffed toes of his sneakers.

"I'm sorry." The apology, although gruff and mumbled,

sounded sincere. "I didn't think. I…" He blew out a hard breath and crossed his arms tightly over his chest. "And thank you. For…everything."

Cole stifled a sigh, along with the urge to clap a hand on the boy's shoulder and pull him into a hug he undoubtedly thought he was too grown for. But with his father, a mean drunk who'd possessed an allergy to work, having abandoned him and his mother years earlier, and his mother working long hours to make ends meet, Trevor had missed out on the positive influence of a man in his life. These last two brushes with the law had the teen toeing a thin but pivotal line. He could go either way at this point—to the college his mother was scrimping and saving for or the jail he'd managed to avoid. So far. He was a good, smart kid. A hardworking kid who fiercely adored his mother and had gotten a job at a gas station as soon as he turned sixteen. But his mother and Cole could only do so much. Trevor had to pick a path. Now, not later. And fight to remain on it.

"Don't thank me yet," Cole warned, pushing off the desk and rounding it. He slid his hands into his front pockets. "When you're not at Mr. Wilson's gas station, then you're going to be out at Kinsale Inn, working with my brother Wolf. I've already cleared it by him. And when you're not at either of those places, you'll be home. By six. You have a problem with that?"

"Are you kid—"

Cole nodded and smiled. "Just what I thought. You don't have any problems. Especially since the only alternative is juvie."

"Then no, I guess I don't have any problems," Trevor drawled.

"Right." Cole made a show of glancing down at his wristwatch. "You have about twenty-five minutes to make it home before curfew. Make sure you bring your school and work schedule by my office sometime tomorrow."

"Yes, sir." He shoved to his feet and finally met Cole's gaze. "And again…thank you."

"You're welcome, Trevor," Cole murmured.

The teen didn't waste time crossing the room to the door and pulling it open. And almost plowing into the woman standing on the other side.

"Oh, I'm sorry. I didn't know you had someone with you," Sydney said, lowering the arm she held midair as if prepared to knock. "I can come back later."

"No, you're good," Cole assured her. "We're just finishing up here."

"Excuse me," Trevor muttered, stepping around Sydney and disappearing. Probably eager to get away from Cole before he tacked on another restriction. Like he'd said. Smart kid.

Smirking, Cole waved Sydney inside. "Come on in. What's going—*the hell?*"

The air exploded from his lungs as her compact body collided with his. Before he had time to register that Sydney was pressed against him, her full breasts crushed to his chest, hips notched tight, thick thighs tangled with his and her arms wrapped around him like a drowning victim clutching a life raft, a jagged, wet sob ripped through the office.

He stiffened, his arms rising of their own accord to close around Sydney's shuddering frame, to clutch her close. Try to absorb the tremors that seemed capable of shattering her to pieces. He glanced toward the open door and frowned. Sydney had only been back in his life for a handful of weeks, but he knew she would hate for someone to catch her like this. He didn't view her tears as a weakness, but she would. He couldn't allow anyone to see her so vulnerable.

Carefully, he bent his knees, lowered one arm behind her back and slipped the other under her thighs. He straightened, cuddling her against his chest, and crossed the few feet to the door. Easing his foot out, he nudged it closed, waiting for the click of the lock engaging before returning to his desk and sinking into his chair.

The harsh cries didn't abate, and each wrack of her body had

him clutching her tighter, holding her closer. Had him whispering useless, nonsensical words against her temple. Had a hand
tunneling deep into her thick, coarse-yet-soft curls, cradling her
head to his shoulder. His heart—it ached, throbbed. For her. For
the heartbreak that echoed in every sob. He wanted to beg her
to tell him who hurt her, confess what was wrong so he could
slay it like some inept knight with tarnished armor charging in
to battle a dragon.

He didn't question why that need rode him. Not when this
proud, unbreakable woman was…breaking in his arms.

"I'm sorry," she whimpered, burrowing into his chest as if
attempting to crawl inside him. Her nails bit into his shoulders,
gripping him hard. "I'm so sorry. So sorry."

"Shh." He pressed his lips to her curls, the hand not buried
in her hair skimming up her back to cup the nape of her neck.
"It's okay. *You're* okay. I got you, baby girl."

"Selfish," she rasped, drawing her knees up and releasing his
shoulders to tuck her arms to her body, almost curled into a fetal
position. "Just like he said. Like she said. I'm so fucking selfish."

Self-disgust practically dripped from the indictment, saturat-
ing her thick voice. Anger on her behalf kindled low in his gut.
Using his grasp on her curls, he tipped her head back. Or tried
to. She resisted him, but he didn't let that stop him from con-
tradicting those inflammatory words.

He bent his head over hers. "There's nothing selfish about
you, Sydney," he murmured hotly, fiercely, his lips moving
against her damp forehead. "I don't know what just happened
or who said something so cruel and *un-fucking-true* to you, but
it's a lie. Let it go, baby girl."

But she shook her head so hard, her nose bumped against his
collarbone. "You don't know…"

"Then tell me." He squeezed the back of her neck then slid
his palm down her back, stroking it. "Please tell me. Let me…"

Take it away. But he didn't utter that too revealing plea. Instead, he gently rocked her while her cries continued.

Eventually, she quieted, but her hot, moist puffs of breath bathed his throat. So attuned to her, he caught the slight loosening of her rigidly held frame and relaxed his embrace. But he didn't release her. Not until she was ready. He'd sit here and hold her however long she needed. However long it required until she felt strong enough to face the world again.

"I'm sorry," she repeated, and he winced in sympathy at the rawness of her voice.

"For what, baby girl?"

She exhaled, a tremble quaking through her body. He wrestled the urge to press her for an answer, to demand she let him in. And damn near shook with the effort. But after a long moment, she finally answered. "I didn't know, Cole. If I'd known, I wouldn't have let you stay today. I wouldn't have… I wouldn't have forced my presence on you."

What the hell? "Sydney." He leaned back in his chair, gripped her chin and gently but firmly moved her head back. Unlike before, he didn't allow her to deny him. Only when her chocolate eyes met his did he ask, "From the beginning. What are you talking about?"

"I was in the pharmacy," she began, so softly he lowered his head to catch every word. "I overheard two women talking about you. And about Tonia…and your—your son. I didn't know how they died. You lost both of them in childbirth. Not an accident. You didn't get to spend time together as a family. Didn't get to have him for years. Tonia didn't get to be a mother. You didn't get to be a father. You—" She bit down on her lower lip, cutting off the rapid, almost frantic torrent of words. "You would've been a wonderful father," she breathed.

Cole briefly closed his eyes, leaning his head back against the chair. He permitted the swell of regret and sadness to move through him, unimpeded. Then he exhaled, letting it flow from him. This wasn't about him; it was about her.

"During your last months with Tonia, she was pregnant. Those are your last memories of her. No wonder you could barely look at me. Couldn't bear to be around me. But I was so caught up in my own shit, that it didn't even occur to me…" She shook her head, jerking free of his grip. "I've brought you pain. Inflicted it over and over again."

"Sydney, you didn't know," he murmured.

"That doesn't excuse it," she argued, her tone sharp. Unforgiving. "Doesn't excuse me. And today… God, you must've stood there suffering, and I was so damn oblivious. So wrapped up in me. My pregnancy. My baby. My happiness—"

"Stop it." He didn't mean to snap at her, but as he recaptured her chin and tilted her head back, he didn't regret it. Anger, hot and impatient, licked at him, and he narrowed his gaze on her. "You. Didn't. Know. You're right about why I had a difficult time being around you at first."

Lie.

Well, not the whole truth. But he for damn sure wasn't going to explain to her how it wasn't just her being pregnant that made being around her like walking a quickly unraveling tightrope—complete with the unnerving sense of free fall, fear and a twisted excitement. If only it was just wanting to corrupt that soft mouth and softer body with all the dark, filthy desires that a two-year sexual hiatus had stored up. But it wasn't.

She reminded him of the life he'd lost.

Taunted him with the lust that should've died with Tonia.

But no. He wouldn't be sharing that with her today.

Or ever.

A freshly divorced single mother who had more than enough on her plate with starting over. She deserved more than him fucking her to get his demons out. Because he couldn't give her anything else. Didn't have it to give. While his body might've reawakened after a long hibernation, his heart… That was still buried under a gravestone with two names etched into it.

"But," he continued in the same crisp tone, "I got over that. You're my friend. And friends show up for one another. They support one another, and yes, sacrifice for each other. We talked about this bad habit of yours. Taking on the blame for other people's actions. Today was on me. And yes, it hurt. I would be lying if I told you I wasn't thinking of another time when I'd been there with my wife, looking at my son on that monitor. But to see your smile, your joy, your healthy baby…" He shifted his hand to cradle her face. Swept a thumb over the damp, tender skin above her cheekbone. "I'd do it again. Because whatever I was feeling didn't compare to that. So do me a favor, okay? Don't apologize again. Not to me. Never to me."

She didn't say yes. But she didn't object either. And that horrible starkness had started to disappear from her eyes. Counting it as a win, he snatched up several sheets of tissue from the box on his desk and handed them to her. She accepted them with a murmured "thank you."

"Now, tell me who called you selfish."

Her lashes fluttered, lowering. She tried to duck her head, but his hand prevented it.

"Don't hide from me," he gently ordered. A shaft of pleasure pierced him when she instantly obeyed, giving him her eyes. What other instructions would she follow? Would she put up a token resistance, or would she immediately, so fucking sweetly, submit? He swallowed, but when he spoke, nothing could erase the roughness of his voice. Lust caused it, and he suspected only lust could ease it. "Who hurt you?"

She shrugged a shoulder. "I went to see my mother. I should've known better. Ours isn't the healthiest or most loving relationship. But since things had gone well with Dad, I…"

"You thought she would be happy for you, and the good news about the baby could be common ground you could build on."

"Yes." The tip of her tongue slicked over her bottom lip, and he jerked his gaze from the wanton temptation of it. "I thought… Well, it doesn't matter what I thought. She was happy. Even gave me a gift of maternity clothes she'd bought for me. But then," she paused, cuddled closer to him in a move that he suspected was unconscious, "everything went so wrong. She mentioned talking to my ex-husband and told me I was only thinking about myself and not the baby and definitely not my baby's father by moving here. That I was being impulsive, irresponsible and stubborn. Y'know, the usual." Her mouth curved into a smile that possessed no trace of humor.

"And I'm assuming your ex agrees?" he pressed, unable to keep the irritation from his voice.

"What?"

"When you were crying you mentioned a 'he.' I'm assuming you were referring to your ex-husband."

"Yes," she admitted after a brief hesitation. "That's been Daniel's favorite word to describe me lately. For not remarrying him and giving our baby a two-parent home. For moving a thousand miles away. For preventing him from being a father. I tried explaining to him—and my mother—why I needed to do this. Not *wanted* to. *Needed*. But neither of them understood."

"Try me."

She blinked. Stared into his eyes, and he leaned his head back or risked drowning in those espresso depths. He focused on the lingering pain there, clutching that like a lifeline.

"I told my mother I was suffocating. She probably thought I was being dramatic, but I couldn't find another word to describe the slow, steady death of my independence, my dreams, my voice. My*self*. It's not Daniel's fault, and I'm not blaming him. He never lied to me, didn't pull a bait and switch. But I pulled one on him. I never complained when he wouldn't let me contribute toward the household bills, and I became financially dependent on him. I didn't object when his career took precedence over mine. I didn't utter a word when my opinions didn't hold as much weight as his. I didn't put up even a token protest, but inside? Inside, I was quietly raging. Resenting not just him, but myself for staying silent. For being so desperate for affection, to be one of a two, to *belong* to someone, that I was willing to lose my own identity to have it. But in the end, I guess my survival instincts kicked in. I needed more. Needed to be more than just an extension of Daniel. Needed more than settling for companionship instead of love. I couldn't. And in the process, I hurt a decent man."

"He might've been decent, but he was also older. Jesus, Sydney, you were twenty when you met him. Still had milk on your breath when you married him. Of course you changed. No, not changed. You grew."

She stared at him, then snickered, and the sound, after her heartbroken sobs only minutes ago, warmed him like the morning sun breaking through the elms surrounding his family's inn. And when a small, but real smile curled the corners of her mouth, it required every bit of his control not to trace the edges of that smile with his lips.

"Milk on my breath? That's disturbingly…specific."

He snorted. "You understand what I'm saying, though. Your ex had already figured out who he was, what he wanted out of life and how to get there. He doesn't get to penalize you or hold a grudge against you because you did, too. Or because it didn't include him." Since his hand already cradled her cheek, he gave in and caressed the blade of her cheekbone. Allowed himself that minimal touch. "The lawyer in me argues that you only owe him unfettered access to his child within the bounds of a custody agreement. The man who just held you while you cried your broken heart out wants to tell him that you two are divorced, relationships fail all the time, vagina the fuck up, be a father to his baby and move on."

"Vagina. The fuck. Up. Seriously?" The grin slowly spread over her face, lighting her eyes until the dark brown glowed.

She chuckled, and damn if he didn't feel like he'd won the election for mayor all over again. *It's because I hate to see women cry*, he reasoned, glancing down to grant himself a break from the impact and power of her beauty. But unfortunately, his gaze landed on her mouth. That lush, sinful tease of a mouth. Jesus. He was in trouble.

He shrugged, pretending that he hadn't just been envisioning her dragging her lips over every bare, hard and aching inch of him.

"Have you ever kicked a man in the nuts? He's down in seconds flat, crying for his mama. A vagina is much stronger than a dick."

Her shocked choke preceded a loud crack of laughter that rebounded off the walls of his office. He grinned in response. A gift. He'd given her that gift of laughter. And even if he was condemned to hell for his inappropriate lust, the husky sound of her hilarity would be well worth it.

Her chuckles softened, eventually ebbing away. She smiled up at him, covering the palm still cupping her face, and turned into it. Placed a sweet kiss in the center.

His gut clenched so hard the muscles twinged in protest. Heat swept through him like flames exposed to oxygen, culminating in a rock-hard erection that had him praying like he hadn't since the doctors pushed him out of that delivery room. Praying that she didn't shift the wrong way on his lap and find out just how much that kiss affected him.

"Thank you," she whispered.

He didn't ask for what; didn't need to. "You're welcome," he said, just as softly.

He should've removed his hand at that point. Should've gently helped her stand and insert distance between them. Should've done anything but lift his free hand to cradle the other side of her face. Or rub his thumbs over the corners of her mouth where they still turned up a little with the residue of her smile.

Or lower his head, inhaling her breath. Tasting the sugary sweetness of some treat and her own unique flavor on his tongue. Her low gasp ghosted over his lips, and hunger roared in him to take that directly from the source.

Only a slight shift of his head and that almost negligible distance between their mouths would disappear. He would finally know if she would allow him to lead her in a wet, erotic dance. Or if she would seize control, demand what she wanted in a carnal tangle of lips, tongue and moans. Or maybe, she would fall somewhere in the middle. A hot give-and-take, a sexy exchange of power where they both dominated and surrendered.

Fuck, he wanted to find out. Needed to...

He slid his thumb so it rested beneath that plump bottom lip. He pressed the skin there so her lips parted wider for him, and he could glimpse the pink tip of her tongue...

"Cole." The loud, firm knock on the door followed his name.

As if some celestial being with a screwed-up sense of humor dashed him with a frigid bucket of water, Cole stiffened then jerked away. Stunned. Horrified. And hard...aching.

Jesus Christ.

He'd been about to kiss Sydney.

What the fuck was he doing? His heart scrabbled for his throat, and it throbbed there, hindering his breath. Trapping any words he could've—should've—said.

The same shock that crackled through him flared in her eyes. Followed quickly by a flash of hurt that her lashes hid in the next second. She stood, and just as the next rap echoed on the door, she rounded the desk.

Joints as rigid as a wooden soldier's, he rose as well, the imprint of her body still branded into his arms, chest and thighs. Her orchid scent still filling his nostrils. Her breath still teasing his lips.

Moving on autopilot, he strode past her and approached the door, pulling it open.

Caroline Jacobs, the town's ballet school owner and a council member, smiled up at him. "Hi, Cole," the pretty blonde greeted. "I was beginning to think I'd missed you. I'm heading downstairs for the meeting and thought we could go—oh, hi, Sydney." Her smile dimmed as she glanced at the silent woman behind him. Then her gaze was back to Cole, curiosity gleaming in her brown eyes. "I'm sorry. I didn't mean to interrupt."

"You're fine," Cole assured her, reaching over to his coatrack and nabbing his suit jacket from the hanger. "I'm ready."

He slipped into it, well aware that he was stalling, prolonging the moment when he would have to turn and face Sydney. He needed to apologize. Dammit. What if she believed he was low enough to take advantage of her vulnerability? She'd come to him to comfort *him*, to apologize, to confide in him. And he'd wanted to dirty that beautiful mouth.

He could barely look at her.

Couldn't stand himself.

"Sydney, are you going to the town council meeting?" Caroline asked.

Was she being polite? Or asking to find out why Sydney was in his office? Guilt had him twisting in suspicion.

"I hadn't planned on it," Sydney said. "Town politics isn't really my thing."

That stung. And felt fucking personal. Not that he didn't deserve that dig. But still...

"Well, the meetings are open to the public just in case you change your mind," she added before switching her attention back to Cole. "Ready to go?"

"Yes, I am." Bracing himself, he finally turned but Sydney had stepped past him, giving him a full view of her gorgeous curls. He fisted his fingers, the phantom caress of the thick strands still tingling against his palm. "Sydney, I—"

"No worries, Cole," she said, tossing him a smile that struck him as too bright. Too false. "Have a good meeting."

Murmuring a goodbye to Caroline, she slipped out of the office, and her name lodged in his throat along with the apology he owed her. But with Caroline standing there, staring up at him expectantly and that same curiosity lingering in her eyes, he allowed her to leave. Swallowing a sigh, he moved forward, and pulled the door shut behind him.

"Let's go get this meeting started," he said, forcing a cheer into his tone that escaped him at the moment.

All of his focus needed to be on the next couple of hours. Not the woman whose scent still lingered in the hallway.

Whose almost-kiss he could still taste.

CHAPTER TWELVE

"The minutes have been distributed to all of you," Cole said from his seat in the middle of the table. The five members of the town council sat on either side of him. "Are there any corrections that need to be made?"

Four no's immediately met his question, but one lone person remained silent. Cole smothered an irritated sigh. He refused to let Jasper Landon see that he could get to Cole. The former mayor would jump on that and run with it.

As Jasper took his time and read through the minutes that had been emailed to each council member almost a week ago, Cole leaned back in his chair and reminded himself that his mother and father sat in the hall where the meeting was being held, so he couldn't swear. He scanned the room, locating his parents, Leo and Wolf. While his brother and sisters took turns attending the bimonthly meetings, Moe and Ian had attended each one since he'd been elected to show their unconditional support. He suspected his father came to make sure Moe didn't snatch up Jasper Landon and shake him like a rag doll.

Cole shifted his attention away from her and on to Sydney,

who sat next to Leo. An electrical pulse popped and sizzled down his spine.

It'd been a shock to see her walk in with his family. Even more disconcerting had been the strand of satisfaction that threaded under the surprise, the sense that she *belonged* with them.

She did. Sydney had been an honorary member of his family since Leo had first brought her home.

Yeah, that's what he was telling himself.

"Oh, stop it, Jasper," Eva Wright snapped, releasing the sigh Cole had restrained. "You've had the minutes for a week, just as long as we have. And I know damn well you've ripped it apart since then, looking for something to complain about. Since you haven't voiced your opinion yet, then there isn't anything to change. Just vote already."

Jasper's head jerked up and he slid a narrowed look at Eva. He rolled his thin lips inward, but he didn't reply. Even Jasper, who considered himself better than everyone, respected Eva Wright. Or maybe he was just afraid of her. With her cap of gray curls and whipcord frame, the older Black woman was at least in her midseventies. But her smooth, nearly unlined face and firecracker personality made the longtime Rose Bend resident and day care owner seem much younger. She'd been a council member for years, and she had no problem shutting Jasper down and putting him in his place.

"I see no corrections," Jasper finally said.

"Thank you." Cole nodded at the secretary, who noted the time and approval. "If there are no corrections, then the minutes are approved as distributed. The meeting is now open for new business."

For the next half hour, Mr. Thompson, who had also never missed a meeting as long as Cole could remember, stood and complained about garbage not being picked up as frequently on his street as the one over, and his street hadn't been paved when the one over had been. Another resident suggested nominating St. John's Catholic Church as a state historical landmark.

When no one else stepped up to the mic, Cole propped his clasped hands on the table and leaned forward. "As indicated on the agenda, I've decided on my appointment for police chief." Appointment of certain positions such as police and fire chief as well as several department heads fell under Cole's list of mayoral powers. "I'm appointing Clarissa Ruiz as the chief of the Rose Bend Police Department."

The room erupted in spontaneous applause, and the middle-aged woman dressed in a dark green dress and black blazer rose from her seat near the back of the room. Smiling, she nodded, and her smile widened when Cole's father added a loud dog whistle to the thunderous praise.

When the clapping died down, Jasper cleared his throat, and Cole braced himself, a weight the size of a boulder settling in his stomach. He'd expected this. Was prepared for it. But damn, anger still smoldered behind his sternum.

"If I may," Jasper began, wearing what Cole labeled his "you poor, ignorant schmuck" expression—a cross between a smile and a smirk. "While I respect your choice, and no offense to Ms. Ruiz, but I must respectfully disagree with your appointment." Jasper twisted slightly in his chair, looking out across the room as if surveying his kingdom and its citizens. "I realize it's most likely due to your…limited experience as mayor, but appointment of important positions such as police chief cannot be taken lightly. Yes, Ms. Ruiz is a wonderful policewoman, but is she the strongest candidate? It might be politically correct to place a woman and," he coughed into his fist, "a minority into this office, but is it best for Rose Bend? I mean, diversity for diversity's sake doesn't really benefit anyone, does it?"

"Says the white, straight, wealthy, Christian male," Eva grumbled.

Rage so hot, so bright it could've been its own star, flared inside of Cole. For a moment, it incinerated his voice and con-sumed his vision, hell, his brain. Inside his head, a deafening drum pounded, and he almost lost his composure.

But as Jasper turned back around and smugly stared into Cole's eyes, clarity rained a fine mist over his fury, watering down the crimson veil to a faded pink. His fury. That's what the ass-hole wanted. More accurately, Jasper wanted Cole to lash out and become the Angry Latino Man so Jasper could go, "Look, I told you he didn't have the temperament, the character, the control to be mayor."

While Daryl Barnes, owner of The Ride, the motorcycle ap-parel shop, or Henry Kingston, council member and bank presi-dent, could get away with losing their tempers, Cole couldn't. Angry men of color were to be feared; they were out of con-trol…animals. They lost their intellect and didn't belong in po-sitions of power. The fact was, if Cole allowed Jasper to goad him into reacting, he not only hurt his own reputation as the first nonwhite mayor, but would harm the chances of other men and women of color who came behind him. Sometimes Cole feared buckling under the weight of the expectation, of being the vanguard…of failing.

But tonight, he wouldn't buckle.

"I have to agree with Jasper," Henry chimed in, leaning back in his chair and folding his hands over his ample stomach. Of course Henry agreed with the former mayor. That was his role on this council. Cosigning whatever check Jasper issued. "No disrespect to Ms. Ruiz—"

"But you are disrespecting *Captain* Ruiz," Cole interrupted, stressing the title she had earned. "I hear your concerns, but no offense," and he gave the two men the same insincere smile they'd offered him, "they're not valid. Captain Ruiz has been a member of the police department for nineteen years. She's most likely served or assisted every person in this room and at this table in some capacity over that time. Patrol for seven years. Detective for twelve. Sergeant. Lieutenant. Captain. And in the last two years before Chief Leonard retired, his right hand. There isn't anyone more qualified for this position."

He refused to even lower himself to address that "diversity for diversity's sake" bullshit.

"Not that Cole needs our approval, since appointing a police chief is one of his responsibilities as mayor," Daryl drawled in his deep, rumbling voice. "But I support Captain Ruiz's promotion. She's a fine officer and even better leader. Congrats, Captain. I hate that we're having this conversation like you're not here."

Captain Ruiz nodded, her expression composed, but her dark gaze flicked to Cole, and she offered him a subtle lift of her chin.

"Next for new business, I'd like to discuss the construction of an elder and children's care center," Cole continued. "Right now, we don't have a community center. And with many of our residents being working parents, caretakers of elderly relatives or older citizens who would benefit from programs geared toward their health and welfare, the town needs this kind of facility."

"What location are you suggesting?" Caroline asked from the other side of Daryl.

"Out on Langford Road. The lot there has been available for a couple of years."

"Most of the day cares here have limited space, and not much in the way of after-school care. A center would be ideal for those children as well as provide summer programs for children whose parents work," Eva added.

"I know for a fact my mom and her circle of friends would love a place to meet up, and some short day trips. Sometimes our older generation is forgotten when it comes to care," Daryl said.

"I hate to be a dissenting voice," Jasper interjected with a condescending chuckle.

"Do you really?" Daryl cocked a bushy salt-and-pepper eyebrow.

Jasper didn't acknowledge the other man's question but continued, "I realize this little project was one of your campaign promises, but the budget for the year doesn't allow for construction of this magnitude. Not to mention money to staff a center."

"Oh, Jasper," Eva muttered. "You must be so tired."

He frowned. "Tired of what?"

"Of being a pompous ass."

A few snickers erupted from the people gathered in the room, and Cole slowly counted back from ten, biting the inside of his cheek to contain his own laughter.

Jasper glared at the older woman. "That was uncalled for, Mrs. Wright," he snapped.

"Then stop begging for it," she shot back.

"Okay, order," Cole intervened, although he would've really loved to watch Eva tear Jasper apart.

"Sorry, Cole," Eva said.

She didn't apologize to Jasper. God, he loved this woman.

"As I was saying," Jasper ground out. "It's a nice idea, but not fiscally possible."

"We have the culture and recreation fund just for projects like this. The proposal I emailed to every member clearly outlines an estimate of—"

"Yes, I read your proposal," Jasper interrupted. "And as...informative as it was, the culture and recreation fund is specifically set aside for parks, libraries and our annual festivals. To pilfer that account would be reckless."

Pilfer. The asshole just basically called him a thief.

"Jasper—" Cole growled.

"Um, excuse me."

At the sound of *that* voice, Cole glanced away from Jasper and settled his gaze on Sydney, who stood at the front of the room behind the floor mic.

"Young lady, you're out of order," Jasper objected sharply.

"Jasper, as mayor, I'm running this meeting," Cole said, voice flat. It was one thing to disrespect him, but he'd be damned if he allowed this jerk to disrespect Sydney. "And every citizen of this town who needs to speak has the right to do so. Sydney, please." He waved, indicating for her to continue.

"This *young lady* thanks you," Sydney said, and when she deliberately turned toward the rest of the council, basically giving Jasper her back, she somehow became even sexier to him. "If I may offer a compromise to the funding issue. I am a contractor with Grant Resources, a nationally recognized organization. I've successfully written grants for corporations and nonprofits and am willing to write one for the proposed community center. And you don't have to worry about paying me out of the budget. My fee will come from the grant. If it's not awarded, then I won't charge one."

"Are you sure, Sydney?" Caroline asked. "That's a lot of work with the chance of not being compensated."

Sydney held up a hand. "I have a seventy percent success rate. And I'm also free for the next few weeks. Use me."

"This is highly irregular," Jasper protested loudly, jabbing the table for emphasis. "And besides the breach in protocol, what do we know about her qualifications other than what she's told us? Are we really placing the plans and funds for a town facility in the hands of a—"

"Watch yourself, Jasper," Cole warned the other man, voice calm. Ominous.

The other man's mouth parted, reminding Cole of a gasping fish, before his lips snapped closed, deep brackets appearing on either side of them.

The man could fume all he wanted, just like the overgrown toddler he was. But if he tried to turn that scalpel-like tongue on Sydney again, Cole had no problem putting him in time-out.

"Jasper has a point," Henry began, stammering as he glanced between his friend and Cole. "With a potential project this size, shouldn't we—"

"That's what a résumé is for, right?" Daryl asked, his tone so dry it fairly crackled. "And references?"

"I have no problem providing both," Sydney said.

Cole nodded. "Do we have a motion for Sydney Collins to write a grant for a community center?"

"Yes, I move," Eva said.

"I second it," Caroline affirmed.

"It has been moved and seconded that Sydney Collins will provide a résumé and references to the town council and then work on a grant for a proposed community center for elders and children on Langford Road. Is there any further discussion?" Cole asked.

"Yes, further discussion is needed," Jasper blustered, a red flush staining his face. "I can't—"

"Oh, for God's sake, Jasper." Eva slapped her palms down on the table and leaned forward, peering around Cole to pin the other man with a scowl that would've given Attila the Hun pause. "Is there any more *valid* discussion other than the petty objections you've raised that have more to do with Cole being mayor than an unprejudiced, reasonable position?"

Daryl's soft bark of laughter echoed like a foghorn in the suddenly silent room. At the end of the table, crimson suffused Jasper's face. Damn, the man was apoplectic.

But he remained quiet.

Such was the power of Eva Wright.

"Since there's no further discussion," Cole continued, impressed that none of the laughter that crowded into his throat shook his voice. "We'll now vote on the motion. All in favor say, 'aye.'"

Three "ayes" emerged from Eva, Daryl and Caroline.

"All opposed say, 'nay.'"

Jasper's clipped "nay" preceded Henry's mumbled response.

"With a vote of three to two, the motion is passed," Cole concluded. "Do we have any more new business?"

The meeting progressed, but before Sydney turned and reclaimed her seat, their gazes caught. Satisfaction, relief, admiration, gratitude, pride—they all barreled through him in a turbulent jumble. And just underneath…simmered that ever-present, reckless need. It lingered, like coals that refused to be banked.

Because God knows, he'd tried.

She could so easily destroy him. Steal what little peace he'd managed to amass in the last two years. Plummet him into an abyss of fear and pain.

The terrifying part? He would be a willing sacrifice in his own emotional demise.

And yet, acknowledging that very real and alarming possibility, a part of him still whispered, *take the risk. Take* her.

Use me.

Those had been her words. And just thinking about them caused his cock to thump against his zipper, interpreting those two words in a completely different way from how they were meant. And apparently, his mind was on board because images—images of sweat-dampened sheets, tangled limbs, throaty moans and straining bodies—bombarded him.

Use her.

That's what he would be doing, too. Using her to purge this inconvenient but relentless, grinding lust. Using her to escape himself for a little while. Using her to *feel* again.

She deserved better than to be his receptacle, his drug.

But God help him, he didn't know if he was good enough not to ask her to give him that release. That forgetfulness.

No.

He deliberately turned away from the sight of her. Forced his focus back to the rezoning discussion.

Undoubtedly, he could find sweet oblivion in Sydney's body. He could satisfy the lust that had roared awake inside him since first gazing down at her beautiful face—his sin made even more sacrilegious considering they'd been yards from his wife's and son's graves.

But were those hours of forgetfulness worth the harm, the pain, the possible loss that could bury him?

Hell no. Been there. Done that.

Not looking for a repeat.

CHAPTER THIRTEEN

"Oh my God, I can't believe this day is finally here. I'm so excited!"

Sydney grinned at Cecille's happy squeal that was accompanied by a fist pump and a dance that was somewhere between the twist and a twerk. On the other side of Sydney, Leo snickered.

"She's just excited to be free of her kids for the day," her friend drawled, a smirk tugging at the corner of her mouth.

"Yes, dammit," Cecille crowed. "I have zero shame in admitting it. No kids, no men and a motorcycle rally. How does this day get any better?"

A throat cleared, and the three of them turned to find Wolf, who aimed a mock scowl in their direction. "Excuse me. I am standing right here. Very much a man."

"Oh yes, you are, sweetie. And with a beard and manly muscles to prove it," Cecille cooed, reaching back to pat his cheek. "Now, go get Mama a beer so she can get this day started off right. Oh, jewelry!" With another squeal, she darted off in the direction of the vendor booths.

"Wow." Wolf stared after the jubilant woman, eyes wide and

lips parted in awe. "I'm gonna go get that beer. I want one, too, but mainly because I'm too scared not to."

Leo cackled, and Sydney choked back a laugh at the sight of this big, bearded lumberjack of a man cringing in trepidation at one petite woman who ran an *ice cream shop*.

As Wolf strode off across The Glen's freshly mowed grass, Sydney snatched a moment to survey the changes that had occurred since Cole had brought her here just a short week ago.

A huge, multicolored tent filled with several huge barrel grills and picnic benches hogged one corner. The delicious aroma of grilling meat and vegetables marinated the air, eliciting a rumble from her stomach. Children's delighted screams peppered the air from the play area jam-packed with bouncy castles, slides, swings and jungle gym equipment. On the stage, a local band jammed to classic rock covers. The Glen burst with people of all ages, races, walks of life. They settled on blankets and towels, danced in front of the stage, shopped among the covered vendor stalls or hung out near the grills. And surrounding it all—whether in the sectioned off parking area, the street in front of The Glen or cruising Main Street—were motorcycles. It was a carnival-meets-rock-concert-meets-flea-market atmosphere.

And it was glorious.

Out of habit, she scanned the crowds for a six-feet-plus figure with wide shoulders. In seconds, her gaze found Cole. There'd never been any doubt she would. Maybe there was a magnet buried inside his chest that drew her focus, her *being*. Because he inexorably drew her to him, even though she knew the smart thing—the only thing—would be to keep her distance.

Apparently, her body didn't agree.

She drank him in.

A cream-colored, short-sleeved shirt and khaki pants fit his leanly muscled body to perfection, emphasizing the strength and power in his chest, arms and thighs. His beautiful face with its stark lines and angles. The sensual, full mouth stretched into a smile for the benefit of the people who surrounded him.

She inhaled a shaky breath that had her thighs quivering. Echoing the taut pull deep inside her. Would she ever be able to look at that mouth again without remembering how close it'd been to owning hers? Without recalling how his breath had warmed her lips? Without craving the kiss she'd been denied?

Doubtful.

Because even now, she forced her arm to remain at her side instead of pressing trembling fingers to her flesh. Even now, she couldn't evict him from her thoughts. She should be thankful for that knock on the office door. Without tasting him, without knowing how it would feel to be possessed by him, she battled the need that invaded her veins, her blood, her thoughts. If she had actually kissed him?

She might have become obsessed.

And humiliated.

Because Cole's horror and guilt couldn't have been any clearer. He'd been offering her comfort, and she'd ruined it by allowing her hunger for connection, for intimacy, for *him* to hijack what should've been a moment between friends. And now, other than a quick phone call to thank her for volunteering to write the community center grant, they were back to avoiding one another.

Longing stretched tight and snapped like a rubber band inside her. Not just for what she couldn't—and shouldn't—have, but for the friendship she'd come to count on.

As if he sensed her attention on him, Cole's head lifted, and before she could turn away, their gazes locked. Held. And her heart sank toward her stomach as that smile ebbed then disappeared.

No, he hadn't forgotten. And hadn't forgiven.

Swallowing hard, she did turn away, her pulse jackhammering against her throat. Today was about having fun, enjoying friends, letting go of her worries for a little while. Tonight, when she lay in her bed, with nothing to distract her from her own self—that would be the time to dwell on Cole and the aching emptiness.

She hurried after Leo, who'd entered the area with the covered booths. In moments, her shopper's heart soared in happiness. Over thirty vendors hawked their wares. They offered everything from clothes to motorcycle gear to art to jewelry. God, she could spend hours in here. Happily.

"Look at this, Sydney," Leo said, waving her over to a stall loaded down with gorgeous silver jewelry. "What do you think?" Her friend held up a dangling set of earrings fashioned in the shape of butterflies. "I was thinking about buying these for Moe for her birthday next week."

"They're beautiful." Sydney brushed a fingertip over the tiny, detailed figures. "Wow. She'll love it." Moe had a thing for butterflies, and as far back as Sydney could remember, figurines and paintings dotted the inn. Especially in the kitchen, Moe's domain.

"I think so, too." Leo grinned and turned to the person behind the booth. "I'll take this pair, please."

Sydney glanced up from the other pieces. "You have seriously gorgeous work—oh my God. Cherrie?"

She gaped at the statuesque woman before her. The ends of her dark, tight curls were dipped in red, and sexy curves filled out a leather patchwork vest and tight, dark denim. Tattoos covered an arm from wrist to shoulder. Though eight years had passed, Sydney easily recognized the friend she'd looked forward to visiting every summer since she was eleven.

"Hell no!" the other woman yelled, pushing open a side door in the stall and rushing through it. "Sydney! This can't be you."

"It's me." Sydney laughed as her childhood friend squeezed her tight and rocked her from side to side.

"What are you doing here? I can't believe this. The last time we saw each other you were ready to blow out of here without ever looking back. I can't—holy shit, babe!" Cherrie breathed, her endless stream of words ending on a gasp. "You're pregnant? Congratulations!" Cherrie tugged Sydney close for another hug. "Girl or boy?"

Sydney shook her head, grinning, her head whirling from Cherrie's rapid-fire words. "A girl."

"Hold on." She released Sydney and hustled back behind the booth. A glance around revealed that several pairs of eyes, male and female, watched the other woman, with more than a little lust. Not that Sydney could blame them. What Cherrie did for low-rise jeans should either be illegal or canonized. "Here. A gift for your little girl."

Sydney stared down at the dainty, child-sized bracelet. The silver gleamed, and the tiny flowers, leaves and vines etched into the metal exhibited the artist's talent and attention to detail.

"Cherrie," she whispered, running a fingertip over the engraving. "It's stunning. I can't take—"

"You will," Cherrie ordered, slipping the jewelry into a plastic sleeve and handing it to Sydney. "My welcome-home gift—although I'mma still need that story—and I would be honored if your baby's first piece of jewelry came from me," she added softly.

"Thank you, Cherrie." She squeezed the other woman's hand. "I love it, and I'll make sure my little girl does, too."

"Don't be surprised if I turn up with more, now that I know you're back. Besides, we'll be seeing more of each other since I've made Rose Bend my home base when I'm not traveling."

Sydney studied her friend's cheeky grin with narrowed eyes. Then she grinned, too. Widely. "It's a man, isn't it?"

Cherrie rolled her eyes, sighing loudly. "Isn't it always?"

"I'd like to think it's also my sharp wit and sparkling personality," a deep, rumbling voice said from behind Sydney.

A smile so bright it was almost blinding lit up Cherrie's face.

Sydney pivoted, and cranked her head back to meet the ice-blue eyes of a giant. A gorgeous giant. She blinked. Wow.

"I know, babe." Cherrie snickered. "I had the same reaction."

The man, who might have edged out even Cole and Wolf in height, squeezed between the booths and pushed into Cherrie's to sweep her up into a tight embrace. His head lowered, his auburn hair mingling with Cherrie's darker curls. Though he just brushed his lips over hers, Sydney almost had to fan herself from the heat these two threw off.

And if an emotion that felt suspiciously close to envy crept inside her like an uninvited intruder, well… Her joy for Cherrie's obvious happiness counterbalanced it.

"I think I just got pregnant," Leo whispered, and Sydney smothered a laugh.

Finally, the two separated and Cherrie turned to Sydney and Leo, but still remained glued to her man's side. "Maddox, let me introduce you to a friend of mine, Sydney Collins. And this is…" Cherrie shook her head, her lips curving into a rueful smile. "You must think I'm so damn rude. I'm sorry I didn't even catch your name."

"Leontyne," Leo offered with a chuckle. "But most everyone around here calls me Leo. And I already know your guy here. Hey, Maddox."

"Leo." He nodded, then switched his attention to Sydney. "Nice to meet you, Sydney. We might not have met, but I've heard about you."

"Of course you have," Sydney said, and not defensive about it this time.

Maddox shrugged a huge shoulder. "Small towns," he supplied in way of explanation. And really, it was all that was needed. "I run Road's End, the bar at the edge of town. When you come by, first round's on the house." His eyes dipped to her stomach, her bump more visible in her long, strapless, forest green maxi dress. "The round will be cranberry juice, but still. Free."

"Thanks, I appreciate it, Maddox. And it's awesome to meet you."

"Ooh, we need to make this happen while I'm still in town," Cherrie pronounced. "A girls' night! And don't worry." She leaned forward and patted Sydney's hand. "Leo and I will handle your share of the booze."

Leo sighed. "It's the least I can do for a friend."

"You're all heart," Sydney murmured, arching an eyebrow. "Let's make it happen."

Several moments later, she hugged Cherrie goodbye, and Sydney and Leo continued through the stalls, finally locating Cecille. Wolf, with Cecille's cold beer, rounded out their small group.

For the next few hours, they enjoyed great food, wonderful music and even more wonderful company. Sydney couldn't remember the last time she'd had as much fun as she had with these women and their laid-back guardian. Even when Wolf left to man his booth so he could relieve his help—a teen named Trevor, Leo had informed her—they still remained together until the sun sank and stars—that wouldn't have been visible in Charlotte— glittered in the night sky. As one of her favorite bands from the '90s took the stage and sang about only wanting to be with you, she danced along with her friends, laughing and throwing every worry to the wind along with her arms and hands.

"Aw shit," Leo grumbled.

Sydney peered over at her friend, frowning, concerned. "What's up? You okay?"

"Yeah," Leo muttered. "And no. Incoming."

Slowly, Sydney lowered her arms and turned, a kernel of dread burrowing into her chest. One glance in the direction Leo scowled, and that kernel bloomed, pressing against her rib cage.

Jenna Landon. With a girl crew of three behind her, including Karina, the woman who'd been with her in the ice cream shop the week before.

Hell.

"I swear, I don't hate anyone. Her included," Leo muttered. "But if she was on fire and I had a glass of water, I'd drink it—Hi, Jenna," Leo greeted the slender redhead as she neared them.

"Hi, Leontyne," Jenna purred, stepping forward and gathering Leo in a hug as if she hadn't just seen her the week before in the ice cream shop. Leo returned it with a lackluster pat on the back. And mouthing "help me" to Sydney with wide eyes.

Sydney covered her snicker with a cough.

Releasing Leo, Jenna bestowed more hugs on Cecille, the clique behind her following suit. But when Jenna eventually turned to Sydney, her mouth pulled into a tight and utterly fake smile. No hug for her.

A shame.

"Sydney." Jenna treated Sydney to a not-so-subtle up and down look that clearly relayed she found Sydney lacking. "How nice to see you again."

"Likewise," Sydney replied. Yeah, she wasn't subjecting herself to this high school, mean girl bullshit. "I'll be right back," she said to Leo and Cecille. "Nature calls."

Leo coughed into her fist, and Sydney could've sworn it sounded a lot like, "Liar." Grinning, Sydney wiggled her fingers and walked off.

But not before Jenna called out, "I'll go with you. No woman should be alone among this…riffraff."

"That's not necessary."

"Oh, I insist," Jenna cooed.

Annoyed at both the other woman's doggedness and her snobby attitude toward the people gathered, she didn't say anything, but stalked off. Hoping she could lose Jenna in the crowd.

But no such luck. Jenna sidled up beside Sydney, matching her step for step and sticking beside her. Like a freaking pit bull with lockjaw.

Shit.

Sydney didn't attempt to convince herself that Jenna gave

one bit about her welfare. Accompanying her had a purpose. But damn if she would ask. Nope, if Jenna was going to get her petty on, it would have to be without Sydney's help.

"So, how're you feeling, Sydney?"

She deserved an award for containing her eye roll. "Fine, thanks."

After several more moments, Jenna tried again. "Hmm. I heard you're having a girl. I guess congratulations are in order. Or are they?"

Heat surged up her from her stomach, scalding her chest and throat. Sydney jerked to a stop, fixing her expression into what she hoped was an aloof mask, one that didn't betray the anger simmering inside her.

No way in hell am I giving this chick the satisfaction of seeing she's getting to me.

"You obviously have something you're dying to say to me, so just say it," she ordered, her tone almost pleasant. Almost. Nothing she could do about the thread of *Bitch, please* it contained.

Jenna halted as well, her eyes widening in an innocence that didn't fit her. At all. "I don't know what you mean. I was just commenting on the fact that the news might not be as joyous as it usually would be considering the father isn't here to share it with you."

"Funny, but no matter how I look at it, I can't seem to find how any of my business is yours. Hold on a sec." Sydney rolled onto the balls of her feet, propped the side of her hand over her eyes and made a show of scoping out the open, wide field of people. "Nope." She shook her head, spreading her hands wide. "Still can't find it."

The faux pleasant smile dropped from Jenna's face, and her mouth twisted into a sneer, her eyes narrowing into angry slits. *Aaand there we are, ladies and gentlemen, the real Jenna Landon.*

"You always had such a smart mouth and acted like you were more than what you were. What you still are. An embarrassment. You think we all don't know the truth? That Cole took pity on you and convinced his family to give you a home out of charity because your own family doesn't want you under their roof? You might act high and mighty, but you're not. You're just a charity case."

Her words jabbed Sydney's heart, her self-esteem…her soul. Because though Jenna had the story wrong—if it were up to Cole, his family wouldn't have leased her one of the guest cottages—it still contained elements of truth. Enough that she quietly bled. She did embarrass her family. They didn't want her here—her mother had practically begged her to return to Charlotte.

She shoved the hurt and shame down; she'd excavate them later. But right now? Jenna wouldn't ever get the satisfaction of witnessing her poisonous darts striking a direct hit.

Jenna would never get to watch Sydney crumble.

Even if Sydney silently shook.

"What did I ever do to you?" Sydney murmured, the question escaping her almost without her permission. She hadn't planned on asking it. Hadn't planned on delving into the past. But apparently, her mouth had different ideas.

Jenna stared at her, mouth twisted into a sneer. "What are you talking about?"

"For a while there, we were actually friends. Except for Leo, you were the person I was closest to. What happened between freshman and sophomore year that made you hate me so much that you used every opportunity you could to tear me down and make me feel like shit? What made you hate *everyone* so much?"

Something flashed in Jenna's gaze—something dark, bleak even. But then, her eyes narrowed, and those lips that could actually form a very pretty smile turned up in a deviant version of it. "Hate everyone?" she repeated with a dismissive scoff. "Dramatic much, Sydney? And as for our so-called friendship, what can I say? It's not a mystery. For a year, I was into charity. Just like the Dennisons. But like I did, they'll discover you aren't worth it."

That shouldn't have hurt. Sydney recognized the gibe for what it was—a poisoned dart aimed straight at her confidence. But it struck true with deadly accuracy.

Still… Damned if she'd allow Jenna to see it.

Sydney shook her head. "I almost feel sorry for you, Jenna. Your life must be damn boring and pitiful if you're consumed with mine. Because again. None of. Your. Business."

"Who you hurt with your 'poor abandoned single mother' routine *is* my business," Jenna snapped, leaning closer until her face hovered inches from Sydney's.

You're pregnant. You can't lay her ass out because you're pregnant.

The warning boomed in her head, and Sydney drew in a deep breath, trying to grab her fury and wrestle it into submission. Besides, Jenna wanted her reaction. She sought to put Sydney "in her place."

Like father, like daughter.

Well, fuck that.

"I'm not going to allow you to manipulate the people who are in my town. And they're *my* people. Not yours," Jenna continued. "No one wants you here. They either pity you or have no respect for you. Just like you have none for yourself. Throwing yourself at Cole and his family." The corner of her mouth curled into a disgusted smirk. "I would say you need to be ashamed of yourself, but we both know you don't have any."

Later, she reminded herself. *Lick your wounds later.*

Tilting her head to the side, Sydney arched an eyebrow and smiled, knowing it would piss off Jenna even more. And it provided the side benefit of covering up the throbbing holes where those well-aimed verbal punches had landed.

"That's the second time you've mentioned Cole," she murmured. "Now we're getting down to the truth of it. That's what this little ambush is about—Cole. Hell, Jenna. Why didn't you just come right out and say that instead of pussyfooting around with the 'baby mama' shaming?"

Even in the dark, Sydney could easily spot the red that flooded the other woman's face. Her lips thinned as her slender shoulders straightened and she peered down her nose at Sydney. No denying Jenna's beauty. Too bad it was spoiled by her snotty, condescending, mean spirit.

The memory of that stark, dejected "something" she'd seen flash in Jenna's eyes moments ago whispered that maybe all wasn't as it seemed. But in the next instant, Jenna opened her mouth and banished any hint of sympathy Sydney might've harbored.

"He might not be able to see through you, but I can. It's really sad, Sydney. Your husband—if you really had one, that is—didn't want you, so you're trying to latch onto Cole, for what? Respectability? *Love?*" She chuckled, and the sharp edges of it scraped over Sydney's skin. "As if he could truly want you. He's a respectable attorney, a good family man, the mayor, for God's sake. What could he possibly see in you? And if you weren't so selfish, you would see that you're harming him. People are talking about how you're playing him for a fool by trying to make him a substitute father to your baby. Did you actually think your little stunt at the council meeting would give you an in with him? Make everyone else forget your sad little existence? Not going to work—"

"Sydney. Everything okay?" Cole appeared at her side, his voice reaching her from a distant, hollow tunnel.

She couldn't breathe. Couldn't drag in air past the pulsing agony that radiated from every pore, every organ in her body. Once more, each word dug deep, unearthing every one of her doubts, secret fears and insecurities.

A big palm settled on the small of her back, and she flinched, the touch like liquid fire through her clothes and against her skin. It possessed too much concern...too much pity, just as Jenna had so cruelly, accurately pointed out.

"Sydney," he murmured.

"We're fine, Cole," Jenna assured him in a sugary-sweet voice. Yes, that was her. Saccharin and strychnine. "I was just making sure Sydney made it to the bathroom okay. You can't be too careful. Especially in her condition."

If Sydney wasn't numb from the neck down, she would be in dire trouble of hurling.

"Sydney," he repeated her name, and his voice vibrated through her. Sending fissures and cracks through the shield of ice that coated her. She suspected she would always respond to him. Like her own personal curse. "You good?" he asked again.

"Fine. I'm fine," she replied, even tried to rummage up a smile, but failed. She barely managed to speak past her pain, her fury, her guilt. Smiling...well, that was beyond her. "If you'll excuse me."

She didn't wait for either him or Jenna to respond, not that Jenna would try to stop her escape. Not when it left her alone with Cole.

Jealousy. It slithered through the toxic maelstrom of emotions that whirled inside her. Ridiculous. He wasn't hers. Would never be hers. She had as much claim as Jenna. But on paper, Jenna made more sense than Sydney...

She glanced over her shoulder. Spied Cole's tall frame dwarfing Jenna's. Witnessed the spiteful redhead rest a hand on his chest, right over his heart. And the food Sydney had happily downed all day churned in her stomach, threatening to spike toward her throat.

Swallowing convulsively, she jerked her head back around and weaved a path through the crowd, laughter and chatter bouncing off her. Whereas only minutes ago, she'd felt a part of this gathering, this town and its people, now she was a stranger, wading through their midst, untouched. Unseen.

Unwanted.

She pinched the bridge of her nose, striding to the edge of

the field and heading toward the parking lot. Logically, she understood Jenna didn't speak for everyone in Rose Bend. The fact that she'd just spent all day with two wonderful women belied Jenna's claim. But deep beneath bone and muscle, where her most secret vulnerabilities lurked—where the rejected and lonely little girl still existed—she believed it.

It didn't matter if people were talking about her and Cole or not—that didn't negate the truth. The upstanding, admired mayor didn't belong with the black sheep, the woman who returned home pregnant, single and with her tail tucked between her legs. Didn't matter if those were Sydney's choices and she had her reasons for them. For the people here, it was all about perception. And the princess, the former mayor's precious daughter, made for a glossier, prettier picture. No matter how much of a bitch she might be.

Stupid of Sydney to think she could start over. That people would let the past go.

That she could hope for more…for different.

"Sydney." A firm hand cuffed her wrist, drawing her to a halt.

She didn't need to look over her shoulder to see who had a hold of her. If that low, midnight-and-sex voice didn't identify him, the sizzle and snap of her neurons and the heat pouring through her veins certainly did.

"What?" she asked, hating the waspish tone. Hating that she let any emotion filter through. She tugged at his grasp, and he released her. Only to circle in front of her so his big body blocked her escape.

"Look at me," he ordered, and though irritation sparked inside her, so did that heat. It flared higher, hotter at the demand in his low voice. "I'm right here, not over my shoulder."

Lip curling, she shifted her gaze from the cars packed into the lot behind him and met his eyes. The light from the tiki torches posted around The Glen and the parking lot didn't quite reach back to this pocket of darkness where they stood. They stared at one another, caught in some kind of in-between—in between light and dark. Silence and noise. Reality and an alternate universe where only they existed. A no-man's-land that offered a false sense of privacy. And danger.

Danger to her senses. Her common sense. Her body.

"What?" she repeated.

"You tell me," he said, studying her face. She refused to recoil or duck her head from his scrutiny that veered too close to intrusive. No, she lied. Not intrusive. Perceptive. Which wasn't awful unless you had a lot to hide. And she did. "What happened back there with Jenna? You don't even like her, so why were you with her?"

"As if I had a choice," she snapped. "She insisted on escorting me to the bathroom, just like she said. But her intention wasn't to make sure I made it to the porta-potty safely. No, she let me know just where I stood with this town, with you. Especially you. Seems she's appointed herself your personal bodyguard and she warned me off of you." She shook her head, her lips turning up into a mocking smile. "What did you do? Fuck her and not call the next morning?"

She was lashing out, being a bitch. But she couldn't rein it in. Couldn't prevent the words that probably betrayed her hurt, her jealousy.

"What did she say to you?" he asked, voice flat.

And that sliced deeper than Jenna's accusations. He wasn't denying having sex with her. And why that should bother—no, no. It didn't hurt. It *eviscerated* her. But it shouldn't. He could screw whoever he wanted. Cole was single, sexy as hell and owner of his choices. He didn't have to answer to anyone, least of all her. And given how people treated her over her decisions, she damn sure would be the last person to shame anyone. But god*damn*. Images of him and Jenna together assaulted her. His honey and almond skin dark next to hers. Her vibrant red strands tangled in his hands. That large, muscular body stretched out over Jenna's...

Sydney sucked in a breath. Her belly roiled, rebelled. Closing her eyes to block out his face, she laid a hand on her stomach.

"What's wrong?" he fairly barked, encircling her upper arm. God, he needed to stop *touching her*. "Is it the baby?"

"No, the baby's fine," she murmured through numb lips. "I'm fine. And not your responsibility. You can go back now. I'll make it to my car safely. I'm sure somebody's looking for you."

She moved forward, but his grip didn't loosen. Held her still. She glared at him, her fury mating with hurt and that ever-present lust.

"No, you're not my responsibility," he agreed calmly. Too calmly. Because one glance at his stony features, half enshrouded by shadows, showed he was holding back. He was hiding behind those taut lines, the darkened eyes, the clenched jaw and the grim line of his carnal mouth. The sight of his barely stifled emotion—whatever it was—sent a wicked, perverse thrill spiraling through her. "But you are my friend. Are friends not supposed to be concerned?"

"Friends?" she shot back, yanking at his grip, and like the good man he was, he let her go. But the way her skin burned from the brand of his fingers, he might as well have been still clutching her. "You've been avoiding me since that night in your office. I'm surprised you can bring yourself to look at me. And we're friends?" She scoffed, slicing a hand through the air. "I'm your regret. The reminder of all you've lost. And now, according to Jenna, I'm your charity case."

"Is that what she said to you? Fuck that." He edged closer into her space. "As if she knows anything about charity. You know who Jenna is, Sydney. The kind of person she is. Why would you take anything that comes out of her mouth as gospel? Especially over my word. You are not a pity project. And I would hope my actions since you've returned home would've proven that."

"That's just it," she snapped. "They *have* proven it. Ignoring your own pain to feel my baby's first kick. Placing yourself in the position to suffer more of that pain just so I wouldn't be alone at my appointment. Do you know what else Jenna said? You're a good man. And you are. So good you would take on the burden of your sister's best friend without a complaint."

"I'm not a fucking saint, Sydney. So don't make me out to be one." The darkly rumbled words rolled through her, vibrating in her chest, tumbling and settling lower, much lower.

He was a man. God, she recognized that. But as far beyond her reach as he loomed, he might as well be one of those celestial beings. She could look, but not touch. Want him, long for him. But dare not to hope that he would ever return that desire.

She rubbed her fingers across her forehead, suddenly tired. So damn tired. "This is pointless. All of this," she waved a hand behind her, "is because of you, and you should be enjoying it. Should be celebrating seeing it come to fruition. You claim not to be a saint, but once more you're over here trying to save me. Go be someone else's savior. Like I said, I'm good. And I'm also done."

She stepped forward, and at the same time, he shifted closer. In the span of a breath, they crowded each other's personal space. No part of his body touched her, but somehow, he still surrounded her. His scent, his heat, his intensity. She should backpedal, insert distance between them, so she could think. So his overwhelming presence didn't scramble her thoughts. So it didn't ratchet up the hunger inside her.

"I'm not done. And I haven't addressed the evidence you brought up to prove your very flawed case."

She scoffed, assuming an annoyed nonchalance that was ninety percent bullshit and ten percent nerves. "Using lawyer speak? Really?"

"Sydney."

"What?"

"Shut up. Or in 'lawyer speak,' you're out of order," he tacked on, the steely tone of his voice betraying that he would condone nothing but obedience from her.

She reeled at that hard note; he'd never used it with her before. What did it say about her that it both angered and aroused her? *That you need to get your shit together and check him. Or climb him like a rock wall.* Dammit. Even her conscience was no help.

"As far as avoiding you and not being able to look at you…" He paused, the strong line of his jaw clenching. "That has more to do with me than you, Sydney. You came to me crying, seeking the comfort of a friend. And I…" He bit off the words, scrubbing a hand over nonexistent curls. Turning his head, he stared off in the distance for several silent, taut seconds before returning his burning, golden gaze to her. "And I took advantage of that. I almost stole what you weren't offering. So it has nothing to do with not being able to look at you. It's me I can't stand. Me I'm angry as hell at, not you."

"How do you know I wasn't offering?" she breathed, the question blurting out of her before she could trap it. Or consider the lunacy of voicing it.

She didn't even have alcohol to blame for her lack of control. That heat in his eyes looked a little too close to desire—she could blame her inhibition on that. Hell, just staring into it, feeling singed by it… Yeah, it had her head swimming harder than if she'd downed a bar full of cranberry vodkas.

Cole stiffened, air sucking through his flared nostrils, his eyes narrowing on her. "Don't joke with this, Sydney. Now isn't the time," he commanded, iron still threading through his voice.

"Why do you assume I'm joking?" she pushed, even as her mind screamed *caution* in red, blinking letters. For her, this man was pain wrapped in beauty. Yet, she didn't walk away. Because though she'd matured, she obviously hadn't lost the impulsive streak that didn't heed danger. She would end up wrecked by pressing this. But in this moment, with his glittering, hooded stare licking over her skin and that big, wide body unnaturally still, as if forcibly holding himself in check, she didn't give a damn. She wanted him to break. To shatter. And take her with him.

"If I was anyone else but me, what would you have done?" she taunted softly, tilting her head. "Finished what you started? Taken my mouth? Bruised it? Owned it?" she whispered. Rising on tiptoe, she pressed her forehead against his chin, a breath shuddering out from between her lips. An answering shiver rippled through his large frame, and her eyes closed. "You can't take advantage of what I would've freely given you."

A second passed. Then two. A couple more. And neither of them moved.

Until he did.

Cole stepped back. Away from her. Leaving her brittle and cold in the summer heat.

Slowly, she rolled down to the soles of her feet, humiliation churning in her stomach. Jesus, when would she learn?

She parted her lips, the apology there, ready to be uttered. But it wouldn't emerge. Instead, she tore her gaze away from Cole and turned. Walked away from him before he could do it. Before she could glimpse the regret and guilt that would undoubtedly darken his gaze. Again.

"Fuck."

The harsh, coarse growl reached her only seconds before a hand gripped her hip, spinning her around and hauling her against a solid, wide chest. Another hand stroked roughly up her back, over her neck, and tunneled through her hair. Long, implacable fingers twisted in her hair, tugging her head back, sending tiny pinpricks scattering across her scalp. A moan broke free of her. But before embarrassment at the needy sound could set in, Cole crushed his mouth to hers, swallowing the tail end of that sound.

Oh. God.

She hadn't been ready. No matter how many times she'd dreamed of his kiss, of his rangy, powerful body pressed to hers, she hadn't. Been. Ready.

Not for the hot, demanding thrust and sweep of his tongue. Not for the wet but firm slide of lips against lips. Not for the sensual graze of teeth over sensitive flesh. Not for the deep, ragged groan that poured into her mouth and vibrated against her chest.

He consumed her.

Licking. Sucking. Stroking. Giving her pleasure even as the firm grip and tug on her hair demanded she surrender to him. He took utter control of the kiss, of her passion...of her. He angled her head so he could go deeper. So he had more access, more of a claim.

With a whimper, she circled his wrists, held on. Because that's all she could do. His lust beat at her like hot, living flames, stoking hers higher and brighter. Rising on her toes again, she opened her mouth wider—so wide the corners of her mouth twinged. She would emerge from this with bruised, swollen flesh. And loving it. Craving it. She wanted his mark of passion on her.

As if reading her mind, the kiss turned harder. Wilder. Wetter. Cole crowded impossibly close, his chest pressed against her breasts, and her nipples peaked, beading. Her flesh had grown more sensitive with the pregnancy, and just the minute shift of his body arrowed electric spikes of pleasure straight to her aching, drenched sex. Seeking some relief of that carnal pain, the emptiness, she squeezed her thighs, but it didn't work. Every twist of his tongue around hers, every greedy pull as if he couldn't get enough of her taste, of *her*, increased the lust clawing at her, demanding to be satisfied. Didn't stop her from meeting him thrust for thrust, lick for lick, moan for moan.

And when his hips rocked forward, his thick cock grinding just under her swelled belly, the wide length riding over her clit, she emitted a soft, shocked cry. And when he repeated it, slower, firmer, she damn near erupted. Her knees trembled, almost giving out. So long. It'd been so long since she'd been touched as a desirable woman.

And she'd never experienced this...this intense, uncontrollable need and ravenous hunger that threatened to raze her to the ground and leave only ashes behind. One kiss. This one kiss rivaled the best sex she'd ever had. God. If just a meeting of mouths and tongues could render her a shivering, throbbing mess, what would the actual act do to her? Would she be the same after he slid into her body, stretching her, molding her, burning her...

Damn, she wanted to find out.

Even if it meant being irrevocably changed afterward.

"Um... Cole?" The hesitant, feminine voice that shook a little interrupted on their lust-soaked cocoon.

Sydney flinched, the intrusion an icy dousing of reality. Cole's grip tightened on her for a fraction of a second, as if he protested releasing her. But then his hands dropped away as if scalded. Or repulsed. He stepped back. Then back again.

Stunned, eyes wide, Sydney stared at him. At his hooded eyes with just a rim of amber visible, his damp, swollen lips, clenched fists and, *good God*, the bulge in the front of his pants. Big. Long. It had her mouth watering and her flesh spasming. Another whimper of need scratched its way up her throat, and she called on every scrap of her tattered control to lock it down.

"I'm sorry to interrupt," that same voice interjected again, and it shocked her as much now as it did seconds ago.

Turning, she faced Caroline Jacobs. The irony that she'd preempted their kiss last time wasn't lost on Sydney. The woman's timing was either impeccable or left a lot to be desired. At the moment, Sydney couldn't decide which one.

"It's fine, Caroline," Cole finally said, his voice the texture of grit and rubble. Shifting his focus to the other woman, he asked, "What do you need?"

"The concert is about to wind down. You're needed onstage for the closing remarks for the day. I'll just wait over there while you..." She glanced at Sydney before switching her gaze back to him. "Finish up." Clearing her throat, she wandered several feet away, granting them a modicum of privacy.

Sydney averted her eyes, too vulnerable, too raw to continue meeting his. If he apologized… If he told her it was a mistake—that *she* was a mistake… He wouldn't be wrong about this kiss crossing a line they shouldn't have no matter how much she hungered for it, but right now she couldn't handle the rejection. Or the message that she wasn't wanted.

"I should go so you can…do your mayor thing," she murmured.

Not granting him time to say anything or stop her—if he even intended to do either—she pivoted on her heel and headed toward the parking lot.

"Sydney."

She drew to a halt but didn't turn around.

"I've never had sex with Jenna," he said, his low, sensual voice caressing her exposed skin like dark velvet. His admission rocked through her, igniting another quake of shivers. But he wasn't through. "You're the first woman I've touched in two years."

She heard him walk away. Caught the murmur of his deeper tone and Caroline's lighter one. And yet, she still remained in the same spot, his confession ringing in her ears.

She should be terrified by that information. More specifically, terrified by the satisfaction and joy that fizzed and popped in her veins like champagne bubbles.

But she wasn't. Her heart thumped, filling her head with its ecstatic rhythm.

And that… Well, that should've scared her most of all.

CHAPTER FOURTEEN

Sydney glared at the one-cup coffee maker as the fragrant brew poured into the waiting mug. Decaffeinated. It was a crime against God and nature. But the thought of going cold turkey had her body screaming in mutiny, so decaf it was. The sacrifices she made for this baby.

Sighing, she leaned back against the counter, the cabinet cushioning her head. God, she was tired. After a full day at the motorcycle rally, she should've fallen asleep as soon as her head hit the pillow. But no such luck. Her thoughts had whirled in her head long into the night, filled with instant replays of The Kiss. And also, with the audio of Cole's confession.

You're the first woman I've touched in two years.

Even now, her belly dipped, an eddying heat rushing in to fill the void. Confusion and arousal—not a good mix and detrimental to a decent night's sleep. Why had Cole admitted that to her? Should she go to his cottage and ask him? Should she just leave it alone? Should she avoid him altogether? Logic cautioned that becoming physically and emotionally involved with a man who clearly still loved his dead wife and deeply grieved her and their son's deaths totaled up to a mistake. And while the woman

she'd been six months ago might've risked it, the mother-to-
be she was now couldn't. Because she didn't only have herself
to consider. She needed to be whole, settled and completely focused on her baby. And a brokenhearted mother indulging in a
doomed fling didn't constitute settled or focused.

And no matter how much her body craved him, was greedy
for his brand of passion, lust didn't transform her into an idealistic
idiot. Anything between her and Cole could only end one way.

With heartbreak and pain.

The coffee machine emitted one final hiss and bubble, and
the last drops plopped into her cup. First, coffee, she prioritized.
Then obsessing.

Just as she lifted the mug to her lips for that first wonderful
sip, a firm knock on her door reverberated through her living
room and kitchen. Frowning, she peered at the clock on the
wall above the stove. Who would possibly be on her doorstep
at seven thirty in the morning? Setting the cup down on the
counter, she crossed the small distance on bare feet. For a second, she hesitated, casting a glance down at her black tank top,
which cupped her breasts and stretched over her baby bump, and
the small pair of pink sleep shorts. She shrugged, continuing toward the front door. Hey, if someone was rude enough to drop
by unannounced this early, then they got what they got. Which
in this case was boobage, big belly and thick thighs.

She paused next to the window, pulling back the cover and
peeking out to see who stood on her dime-sized porch.

"Oh shit," she breathed. Shock gripped her in its icy fist, and
she clutched the curtain, threatening to tug the rod down on
her head. "Oh shit," she repeated, just as breathless.

Daniel.

What the hell was her ex-husband doing in Rose Bend, much
less standing on the other side of the door?

Unease trickled into her chest, dripping down to her stomach.
But with an irritated scoff at herself, she released the curtain and
shifted to the door, clasping the knob. She had no reason to be

nervous about Daniel's appearance, even if it was unexpected. Yes, they were divorced, but he'd never been mean or abusive. Maybe he'd just shown up to see her for himself, make sure her pregnancy was progressing as it should… Yes, she silently admonished, pulling open the door. This was *Daniel*, for God's sake. Not a harbinger of doom.

"Daniel," she greeted warmly, smiling and pushing open the storm door. Because, though still shocked, she was happy to see him. They'd been friends for years, and having his familiar face here brought back memories of those better times. "What a surprise. Come on in."

"Thank you," he said, his slight Southern drawl evident in just those two words. His brown-eyed perusal roamed over her, lingering on her belly before returning to her face. "You're looking well."

"Thanks," she murmured, stepping back and waving him inside.

He entered the little cottage, his tall, lean build clad in what she'd once affectionately termed his "summer uniform." A white polo shirt, crisply pressed khakis with a razor-sharp front crease and brightly buffed dark brown shoes. Funny how the previous evening, Cole had been similarly dressed, and the look had been casual and sexy as hell. Yet, with Daniel, he appeared every inch the stuffy dean of a pretentious prep school—a little uptight, a lot reserved.

Stop it. Tiny needles of guilt pinpricked her. How unfair to compare the two men. How unfair to find Daniel lacking. The men were different. Especially since one elicited a fondness and friendly affection. And the other, a conflagration of grinding, insatiable need that tortured her waking and sleeping hours.

Totally unfair.

"Not that I'm not pleased to see you, but what are you doing here? And why didn't you tell me you were coming? I could've planned ahead, and I'm certain my parents would've been excited to see you." Wasn't that an understatement?

"Is this where you're staying?" Daniel asked, ignoring her questions and surveying the room. The corner of his mouth curled in a faint sneer of distaste. "It's kind of…small, isn't it?"

She tamped down a spurt of annoyance as well as the urge to point out that no one asked him to come here to have his senses offended by her residence. Instead, she shrugged and maintained her smile. Even if it felt strained and phony.

"The Dennisons were kind enough to rent me one of their guest cottages while I look for a permanent house."

"And the Dennisons are?" he prompted, sliding his hands into the front pockets of his pants. Even that didn't displace the crease.

"I thought I mentioned them before." She had—she knew she had. But as she'd discovered through the years with Daniel, he often relegated things that didn't directly affect him to the bottom of his Give a Damn list. "My friend Leo's family who owns the bed-and-breakfast. They're like family to me." Well, *almost* all of them were like family.

"That's nice of them. Just how long do you intend to stay here? Shouldn't you be preparing for the baby? You only have four more months," he pointed out, strolling toward the kitchen and peering down the hallway that led to the small two bedrooms and bathroom. "You can't plan on bringing our daughter back here."

"No," she replied through gritted teeth. And suddenly, she recalled another reason why their marriage had started to crumble. This parent/child dynamic. Older, Daniel had treated her more and more like his dependent instead of his wife. And no woman wanted to sleep with Daddy. "Like I said, this is only temporary. I didn't want to impose on my parents. And I know exactly how much longer I have before she arrives. Y'know, since I'm the one who's carrying her."

"There's no need for sarcasm," he said, and immediately, she bit back the impulse to apologize.

Dammit, he's not your husband anymore. You don't answer to him, or anyone.

"Daniel, what are you doing here? I know you didn't just feel like a jaunt to the Berkshires."

"I didn't want to do this over the phone..." he began, and those nine words triggered the unease that she'd denied just moments earlier.

A metallic flavor filtered into her mouth—the taste of fear.

"You didn't want to do what over the phone?" she croaked.

He sighed. "I have to tell you, the entire flight and drive here, I remained on the fence. But seeing this place you're holed up in, this town... It cemented my decision. Sydney, I don't do this to hurt you, but I have to think of our baby and her future over your feelings. I've been in discussion with my attorney. As soon as the baby is born and several months old, I intend to sue for full custody."

For the second time that morning, shock wrapped around her like smothering wool. The air in her lungs stalled, and for a terrifying moment, she feared fainting, further reinforcing Daniel's opinion about her weakness. No. The objection wavered in her head, but it was enough to beat back the thunderous roar deafening her. She couldn't do a thing about her rapidly pounding heart or the panic tearing at her throat, but she refused to add one more sin on his undoubtedly long list.

"You can't do that," she whispered, hating that her voice hadn't emerged strong, certain.

"I can, and I will," he affirmed, his gaze unwavering and, worse, determined. "I don't want to hurt you—"

"You've said that already," she snapped. "But what do you think snatching a baby from her mother would do? Or threatening to remove a baby before she's even born? How do you suppose that doesn't inflict harm?"

Another one of his world-weary sighs escaped him, and she wanted to shove it back down his throat. She was sick and tired of being the one cast as immature and unreasonable. Right now, he posed a hazard to her motherhood, her relationship with her baby, their happiness and well-being. Hell no. She wasn't going to allow that.

"There's no need to exaggerate or become overemotional about this, Sydney," he murmured. The patronizing, ignorant ass. "This isn't personal or an attack on you. I have to put my baby's welfare first." For the first time since he'd entered her home, he revealed an emotion other than stoicism or disdain. Frustration flickered over his face, gleamed in his dark brown eyes, and absurdly, she was grateful for it. That meant he wasn't a complete, unfeeling asshole. This person, who briefly glanced away from her and whose jaw ticked, she could reason with. "Look, I accepted that we were not going to remain married. I respected your decision, but as you've shown with forgetting to keep me in the loop with doctor's appointments and not sending me video of the ultrasound, I can't trust you to include me in this baby's life."

"That was a mistake, and I've apologized for it. I promised you it wouldn't happen again," she argued. "I can't believe you would take my child away from me because of a mistake."

"It's not just that mistake, Sydney," he shouted. Then, inhaling a deep breath, he paced away from her to the window, staring out of it for several long moments. When he turned and faced her again, the composed professor stared back at her. "It was just the latest of your thoughtless and irresponsible decisions. Driving here this morning, I couldn't comprehend how you could prefer this small, country village that's not close to any kind of civilization."

"Seriously, Daniel," she scoffed. "Now who's exaggerating? Boston is two hours away and this isn't damn Walnut Grove. There're cars instead of horses and buggies and even a Walmart," she snapped. "Just because it's not your preference, doesn't make it a throwback to a time before indoor plumbing."

"Sarcasm duly noted. But it doesn't change the fact that it's not a place our daughter should live. If this is where you want to live? Fine. You grew up here. But don't forget even you couldn't get away fast enough when you turned eighteen," he reminded her, jabbing a finger in her direction. "In Charlotte, so many things will be available to her. The best medical care, a better school system, accessible art, culture, amenities that aren't available in this backwater town. And that you can't see that has me questioning your priorities and your ability to raise her."

"And your priorities are better?" she threw back. "Your ability? You have just as much experience as I do with raising children."

"But I can give her what you can't." He paused, and she braced herself, instinctively sensing he was about to deliver his final blow. "I can give my daughter a two-parent home. What you selfishly refused her."

She blinked. Stunned, reeling from this news.

"What are you talking about?"

"I told you about the woman I've been seeing," he said, his shoulders drawing back, straightening. "I've proposed to her. By the time the baby arrives, we will be married, and will be able to give her a family. Stability. Financial security. My daughter deserves that, and even if I have to sue for custody to give it to her, I'm ready to. I *will*, Sydney."

"Fuck you," she whispered.

He grimaced, as if exasperated or pained by her profanity. Of course. Because, as he'd often told his students, profanity denoted a lack of vocabulary and creativity. Well, just one more thing he could add to the list of reasons why she wasn't good enough to raise their baby.

"Really, Sydney. I'm trying to have a mature conversation with you. Is that necessary—"

"Fuck. You," she reiterated, slowly and succinctly. Just in case he didn't catch how much she loathed him in this moment. "Fuck you for coming into my home and looking down your nose at it. For threatening to rip away my baby—the baby I've been carrying, nurturing, and have already fallen deeply in love with. And fuck you for daring to say that some woman you've known for five minutes would make a better mother to *my* child than me." She took a step toward him, shaking from head to toe. "You're a bully, Daniel. And you can wrap it up in any way that makes you feel righteous, but this is about penalizing me for not falling in line with your dictates."

She shook her head, her lips twisting into a bitter smile. "I won't let you do it. If you thought this little visit would have me running scared back to Charlotte, have me giving in to your demands, your edicts that are all about making everything comfortable and convenient for *you*, then I hate to break it to you. This was a wasted trip. Get out." She marched over to the front door and hauled it open. "Consider this my overemotional reply to you and your attorney. As a matter of fact, send me his email address, since that is where I will be sending any further communication between us."

Daniel stared at her, his expression stony, implacable. Dipping his head in a rigid nod, he stalked across the room, but paused on the threshold.

"It doesn't have to be this way, Sydney," he said, quietly.

"I don't know what other way you expected it to be, Daniel," she returned, just as softly.

She closed the door behind him.

And then slid down the wood until her behind hit the floor.

Only then, did she allow the fear to roll over her, swamping her. Tears stung her eyes, and she squeezed them closed. Now wasn't the time to break down. She had to be strong not just for herself, but for her baby. But *God*... Did Daniel really hate her that much? Would he actually replace her in her baby's life?

She wasn't certain about the answer to the first question, but "yes" boomed in her head in reply to the second. Yes, he would. Because one thing she knew about her ex-husband. When he believed he was right, nothing could change his opinion or his course of action.

No. Sydney pushed herself to her feet, wiping away the few tears that had managed to escape. She definitely could not afford to break down, because she had a fight to prepare for.

And win.

CHAPTER FIFTEEN

"I need you."

Cole stared, lips parted in surprise, as Sydney blew past him into his living room.

Slowly shutting his front door, he couldn't decide what concerned him more—the iron fist of lust that plowed into him at those three words or the tiny pink shorts and oversize hoodie she wore that simultaneously clung to her voluptuous curves and dwarfed them.

He briefly closed his eyes, his fingers curling around the doorknob. Maybe if he still couldn't taste her kiss... Maybe if he still couldn't feel the soft imprint of those lush lips on his mouth... Maybe if he hadn't fisted himself to her memory last night...

Maybe if those damn shorts didn't reveal so much...

Then, maybe he could turn around and look at her, find out what she was doing here at eight thirty in the morning, obviously upset. But then he did face her, and his gaze dipped to her blue-painted toes in flip-flops, up her deliciously bare, thick legs, over the hooded sweatshirt that didn't hide the fact that she wasn't wearing a bra.

"I need you."

Those repeated three words were imbued with a desperation he'd missed when she'd pushed into his home. He jerked his scrutiny to her face. His worry surged, shoving the desire down to a manageable simmer. His dick didn't matter as much as whatever caused her eyes to darken to nearly black, or what incited those faint tear tracks on her cheeks.

"What's wrong?" he demanded, his voice rough with concern and rage at whoever had placed those haunted shadows in her eyes. She didn't immediately answer. She inhaled a breath, her arms crossing over her chest and her chin dipping in a self-protective pose.

"Sydney?" he prompted, trying—and failing—to keep the edge out of his tone.

"Daniel," she replied, voice hoarse. Then, clearing her throat, she lifted her head, and said, louder, "Daniel was here."

"Your ex?" Cole stalked forward, erasing the distance between them. His fingers itched like fire, needing to touch her, to soothe away the pain, the fear. "He called you?"

"No," she said with a vehemence that was a little alarming. "He was *here*. In Rose Bend. At my cottage." Her lips trembled, and she bit down into the full lower one.

He couldn't have stopped himself from reaching for her if he'd wanted to—and right now, he didn't want to. He cupped her jaw and absorbed her flinch. Murmuring soothing nonsense, he pressed his thumb to the middle of her lip and gently tugged, releasing the abused flesh. He rubbed the pad of his thumb back and forth over the small imprints left behind by her teeth. Because that hungry beast inside of him demanded he not let go, he dropped his arm. Took a step back.

"Go ahead," he ordered, needing her to continue so he could help in any way he could—and so he didn't surrender to the need that insisted he slip that thumb inside her mouth. Feel her tongue again. "Finish."

"He showed up unannounced this morning. He…" She faltered, her arms tightening. "He intends to sue me for custody of the baby after she's born. He's engaged and believes he can give her a two-parent home with more financial stability. His lawyer assures him he can win. Cole—" Her voice cracked, and she abruptly stopped. Closed her eyes. Visibly gathered herself. But when she lifted her lashes and met his eyes again, panic glittered in the brown depths. "Cole, I can't lose her. I can't…"

"And you won't," he snapped, claiming the space between them again and cradling her elbows. "We talked about this before, Sydney. He has to establish paternity first, and he can't do that until after the baby is born so the pregnancy isn't endangered. Once that's done, he can petition the court for custody, but if his lawyer is assuring him this is a slam dunk because he's married and has more money, then that attorney is overconfident or lying. The burden to prove that a mother is unfit enough to remove a child—particularly an infant who needs her—is heavy. And it's all on him to prove it."

But she was already shaking her head. "That might've been true before, but with the way this country and the laws have been changing—especially laws and opinions toward women and their control over their own damn bodies—what you're saying isn't a given. A return to traditional values. Traditional families. With the right judge, the right connections, the right argument… Daniel has those connections. And knowing him, he'll expend any amount of money to get what he wants. No, Cole. I'm scared. And I have a right to be."

"I'm not telling you what to feel, Sydney. I'm not discounting anything you've said, because it's true. But he wants you to think he has all the power here, when he doesn't. Unless the judge can determine why it would be in the best interest of this child to separate you from your infant daughter, then you being this child's mother carries a lot more weight than Daniel's marital and financial status. If anything, because of his financial status, his child support would help solidify the disparity in your wages. I understand how you, as a woman, would feel vulnerable in today's world. But there is law and precedence, and Daniel's money can't supersede either."

Her lips twisted into a skeptical, sad smile. "I wish I could be as optimistic as you. Your job is to defend that law, but with my baby's welfare and future in the balance—my life with her on the line—I can't afford to be that confident. I—" She broke off, swaying slightly, her eyes widening a fraction and her walnut-brown skin paling.

"*Sydney,*" he damn near shouted, hauling her into his arms.

His heart raced, and fear pumped through him until he breathed it, became it. *She's okay*, his mind whispered. *She's not Tonia.* But the logical reassurances did nothing to ease the terror.

Bending his knees, he swept her up, rushing to the couch and sinking down to the cushions.

"Sydney," he rasped, cradling her against his chest, rocking her back and forth. The primitive part of his brain had taken over, and it screamed *protect.* "Are you okay? Baby girl, tell me you're okay," he whispered.

"I'm fine, Cole," she said, her voice shaky, but gaining strength. She patted his shoulder, even giving him a quivering smile. "Honestly, I'm good. I just felt a little light-headed for a moment. Probably a combination of all the emotion and I didn't eat yet. It happens, Cole," she assured him. She cupped his cheek, her thumb caressing his cheekbone. "I promise you, I'm okay."

Bending his head, he pressed his forehead to hers, breathing in her rich, unique scent. Indulging in her touch. He silently ordered his heart to slow, his pulse to ease. His mind to stop feeding him images of worst-case scenarios.

"You can't forget to eat," he said. "Let me fix you something."

"You don't have to—"

"Yes, I do." Carefully, he shifted her off his lap to the couch. "And I was about to fix me something anyway."

A lie. He'd been on his way downtown to the rally. The first ride kicked off at eight, but the vendors' booths opened at nine. He wanted to be there just in case they needed assistance or had questions. But the rally could wait; everybody could wait.

He strode to the kitchen, his brain whirling, fed by the anxiety that hadn't fully abated. As he removed the carton of eggs and the package of turkey bacon from the refrigerator, her words spun in his mind like a cyclone.

How sad was it that he couldn't deny her assertions? He loved the law, had made it his life's work. But he would be a blind, idealistic fool to believe it couldn't be twisted, to believe it was infallible. Sadly, he'd witnessed that kind of manipulation himself. But what he'd told her remained true. Precedent stood in her favor. If the case was being filed here in their county, where he was familiar with the available judges likely to hear the case, he would be even more confident. But that wasn't the case. This would be filed by her ex-husband in North Carolina where, according to Sydney, he had connections because of his job and reputation. His attorney had similar relationships within that particular court system.

The scent of frying bacon filled the air, and on autopilot he flipped the meat, continuing to mull over the situation.

He could not—*would not*—see another woman lose her child. Would not stand by while another life was destroyed. No, losing primary custody of her daughter wouldn't lead to Sydney's death, but it would devastate her. Her baby meant everything to her—she'd sacrificed so much for her daughter already and was prepared to give more. All for the love of her child. If Sydney lost her... He would do anything to prevent that. Anything. Even if it meant fighting fire with...fire.

He stilled, the spatula in his hand hovering over the scrambled eggs. His breath stalled then stuttered in his lungs. He blinked, staring sightlessly at the wall in front of him, both shocked and terrified at the direction of his thoughts. Shocked, terrified and...resolved.

Oh hell. He was going to do this.

There wasn't another choice. Not for him, at least. He would do this for Sydney.

He had to.

"What are you thinking about so hard over there that your eggs are in danger of tasting like a rubber tire?"

His shoulders tensed even more at the teasing behind him, but he deliberately inhaled a breath past his taut chest and forced his body to relax. To convince Sydney to agree with his admittedly wild plan, he had to appear as if it weren't a big deal. As if he wasn't going back on a vow he'd sworn to himself.

To his wife.

Grabbing a plate, he quickly scooped the food onto the dish. He turned, fixing a smile on his face and nabbing a fork from the drawer before sliding the breakfast in front of her.

"Eat," he gently instructed, then he sat down on a stool on the other side of the bar. He waited until she'd eaten half of the meal then spoke again. "I have a suggestion, a proposition."

She set her fork down on the plate, eyes narrowing on him. "Let me stop you. Retaining you was why I came here. I need the best, someone I know will fight for me," she said, unknowingly echoing his thoughts from moments ago. "But I don't know how long this will drag on, so don't even think about suggesting a discount in your fees. I won't hear it. Contrary to Daniel's opinion, I'm not a pauper. I can support myself and the baby on my income. That includes paying your fees."

"That's not what I was going to say, but of course, I'm going to represent you. And we'll discuss payment later." As in never. "Sydney, I want you to completely hear me out, okay? Let me finish before you say anything."

A faint frown creased her brow, but she nodded.

"Okay." He paused, all of the eloquence he employed as an attorney abandoning him when he needed it most. "Marry me."

Well, fuck.

Shock slackened her beautiful features as she gaped at him. Her lips moved, but nothing emerged, and he jumped in, holding up a hand, palm out.

"You promised to hear me out first." She didn't reply, but that was probably due more to being rendered speechless than acquiescence. "I know it sounds impulsive, but it's not. Daniel's main argument for custody is providing the baby with the stability of a two-parent home. We could do that. Also, with our combined incomes, his claim of having better financial means doesn't hold water either. Plus, throw in that I'm the mayor of a small town with a low crime rate, a nationally recognized clinic run by top medical organizations—which Daniel would've discovered if he'd bothered to do his homework—and a superior school system just to name a few things. And you have a core support group with my family, yours and a network of friends. We counter each point and give back our own."

"Cole, stop. Just...stop." She held up her hands, mimicking his gesture. "Are you listening to yourself? People in romance novels or rom-com movies do what you're suggesting, not rational adults in the real world. A marriage of convenience is a trope, not my *life*. My baby's life. Hell, your life. I can't even believe..." She trailed off, staring at him.

"I've listed the pros," he said calmly, settling into litigator mode. A curious calm settled over him, and he didn't question it. Didn't analyze why he was fighting so hard for this. "Give me your cons."

"Are you serious?" she scoffed, bewildered. "A huge con is it's crazy as hell."

"That's opinion, not an argument. But okay, I'll counter with people still marry all the time for reasons of convenience—companionship, finances, expectations, even business. Next."

"I just returned to Rose Bend. No one here is going to believe that we married for love, least of all a court or Daniel."

"If we get married sooner rather than later, we'll be married longer than Daniel and his fiancée. And why wouldn't a court believe our marriage is legitimate? Besides a very real certificate proving it is, we've known each other for years. On paper, we make more sense than your ex and his partner. And the bottom line is, it doesn't matter what Daniel believes. It only matters what the court takes into account to rule in our favor."

"When you say 'sooner rather than later'…"

"Next week."

She shoved back from the breakfast bar, nearly teetering on the stool before righting herself and shooting off the seat. On instinct, he stood, reaching for her but she backed away.

"I don't know what the hell this is. But no. No way in hell."

"Sydney."

"No," she repeated, slamming up a hand. He obeyed it, respecting her space. Digging her fingers into her hair, she loosened the crown of curls piled on top of her head. Spinning away from him, she paced across the limited expanse of the living room. "I refused to head back into a marriage that would have been a loveless, emotionally sterile household. After Carlin…" An arm lowered, and delicate fingers circled her neck. "I grew up in that. I couldn't do that to my child. I chose to raise my baby in a single-parent home rather than put that burden on her. The burden of being my happiness. And now you're proposing that I undo those choices. That they're no longer valid. I can't…"

"I'm not saying any such thing. You made the decisions you did at the time, and they were right for you—for both of you. But here, now, it's time to make another decision. Your baby wouldn't grow up in a barren home. You and I are friends. We have mutual respect and affection for one another. There's… attraction there."

Jesus, wasn't that the understatement of the century? As if attraction could accurately describe the greed and lust that consumed him whenever he was within breathing distance of her.

Even the ever-present guilt couldn't extinguish it. In a perverse way, the guilt inflamed it.

He got Tonia pregnant. *He* failed her and his son when they needed him most. He deserved this guilt, this shame. He didn't deserve to be free of it when he was alive, and their bodies were interred in a cemetery. Like a masochist, he craved it—guilt connected him to them. Kept them forefront in his mind, his heart, his conscience.

And maybe he was just a desperate addict trying to find a way to justify having Sydney.

"Right." An edge entered her voice, curling a corner of her mouth, glinting in her eyes. "About that 'attraction.' Do you intend for this marriage of convenience to be a platonic arrangement? Sexless?" She scoffed. "I might be pregnant, but I need to be touched. I want the connection that comes from physical intimacy. I want the pleasure. You know what, Cole? I want orgasms."

Burning hot.

How the fuck did he just instantaneously combust while still standing here?

Desire licked every inch of his skin as if his clothes had evaporated under the heat of his lust. His skin prickled, and awareness of her—of each breath, each rise and fall of her chest, each blink of an eyelash—danced over him as if he'd become a tuning fork set to pick up only her frequency. His cock pounded, blood streaming to it like all his veins had changed course and now charged to one destination. He ground his teeth against the wicked, goddamn delicious throb. Craved the only thing that would ease it, make it disappear...for a while.

He craved *her*.

"Can you give me that?" she demanded, sarcasm as thick as cream.

"Is that what you want from me?" he asked quietly.

For the first time since she'd backed away from the breakfast bar, her anger faltered. And uncertainty, along with a bruising vulnerability, flickered in her eyes.

"Does it matter?" she murmured. "It's not what you want from *me*. You've made that very clear. A kiss is one thing, but sex? Sharing a bed? Sharing a life? You've only desired that with one woman, and she's not me. That woman is gone." Her shoulders slumped a fraction, and on a weighty sigh, she turned. Several curls of hair had escaped her bun due to agitated fingers and they sprung around her head, glinting in the sunlight that streamed through the large living room window. "Your heart belongs to Tonia, and we both know that."

"Sydney, look at me. Please," he softly tacked on, approaching her.

He should deny her statement, reassure her—hell, say or do anything to get her to agree to his proposal. At some point between him laying out his proposition and her turning him down, it'd become vital for her to accept. He needed to give her this future with primary custody of her daughter.

He needed to protect her.

But as she pivoted and met his gaze, he couldn't lie to her. Couldn't allow her to walk into this under false pretenses, believing, hoping he could give her something he was incapable of offering anyone.

"You're right. Love is not included in this. I can't..." He ground his teeth together. *Man up*, a furious whisper hissed inside his head.

"I understand, Cole," she said. And he sensed that she truly did...and didn't.

"No, let me finish." He lifted a hand, but at the last moment, he curled his fingers into his palm and lowered it back to his side. He couldn't touch her. Not yet. Not while there were things left to be said. "I was with Tonia since we were kids. I loved her so completely that being with someone else was never even an option in my mind. And after she died... Sydney, I don't want to love someone like that again. Even if it were possible. And yes, I know how much of a coward I sound like right now, but losing her...broke something inside me. Something that can't be fixed. And I came so close to losing my mind from the pain, the fucking pain." An echo of it shimmered in his chest, so much that he absently rubbed the burning spot. "I don't—*won't* go through that again."

"That doesn't make you a coward." Her eyes roamed his face. "It makes you human."

Instead of arguing, he scrubbed a hand over his mouth. "We can agree to disagree, but either way, I don't want to mislead you about what I'm offering. Sydney, while you're right about love, you're also wrong. I want you." Her sensual demands still rang in his head, and the residual desire flared brighter, hotter, deepening and roughening his voice. He shifted closer, dipping his head to ensure she could look directly into his eyes. See as well as hear the truth. "I may not be able to give you a heart that no longer exists, but I can give you pleasure. Intimacy. Orgasms." He inched closer until his nose nearly bumped hers, until their breaths mingled. "It would be not just your pleasure, but mine to give that to you, baby girl."

The echo of their jagged breathing filled the room. For several long moments, they just stood there, neither speaking, neither moving. Shock and an answering lust darkened her eyes, and it required every scrap of his control not to cup the back of her head, grip those curls and devour that sweet, sinfully pretty mouth. Sate himself and finally trace the graceful length of her collarbone with his tongue. Then discover for himself if those beautiful breasts would fill his hand. Determine how heavy they were, how sensitive. Find out if she could break and come for him just from his mouth and hands teasing and sucking her nipples.

He bet she could.

He wanted to test the theory.

"You don't mean…" she breathed.

"Mean it?" he finished, dipping his head an inch lower. When he spoke his lips ghosted over hers with the merest of caresses. Now that he'd admitted his desire not just to himself, but also to her, he was greedy for her. A leash had been loosed from his restraint. Hell, from his mouth. It was…freeing. "Baby girl, I'm not in the habit of saying things I don't mean. Especially when it comes to this. I'm asking you to accept this proposal, this plan, this protection for you and your daughter. And I'm offering you my body for whenever you need, for whatever you need. If you want my cock, I'll give it to you. As often as you want. How you want it. If you need me to warm you through the night and be there for you to hold, that's yours, too. Let me do all of this for you. Let me be all of this for you."

"Cole." Her lashes fluttered, lowered.

"Say yes, Sydney."

His heart pounded in his chest, mirroring the throbbing in his flesh. Waiting. Waiting…

"Yes."

Relief poured through him, and like a match to gasoline, it set him afire. With a dark, ravenous growl, he tunneled his fingers into her hair, grasping the thick strands and angling her head back and to the side. Like the night before, she clutched his wrists, steadying herself, bracing herself.

Just before he took her mouth.

Captured it.

Conquered it.

On the tail end of another rumble—or maybe the same one— he thrust his tongue between her lips, claiming her mouth with a lick, a stroke and a suck. And it still wasn't enough. He couldn't get deep enough. Couldn't taste fast enough. Just couldn't get *enough*. He was a beast freed from its cage. And he was intent on consuming.

Without lifting his head or removing his hands, he used his

bigger frame to guide her backward across the floor to the couch. Later he might question his dexterity, but now, with her tongue dancing with his and her sexy-as-hell whimpers disappearing into his mouth, he just thanked God for it. Shifting them, he sank to the cushions, cupping the backs of her legs and arranging her in a straddle across his thighs. With rough hands, he grabbed the hem of her hoodie and jerked it up and over her head, tossing it to the seat beside them.

Her breasts plumped against his chest, and the swell of her belly pressed to his abdomen. The lush flesh with the taut, beaded tips. The hard bump that protected the baby she was willing to sacrifice it all for... The curves screamed what kind of woman she was—soft, giving, selfless, nurturing. He tore his mouth away from hers. Dragged it over her jaw, down the line of her throat, paused to indulge in finally worshipping the strength and grace of her collarbone before lowering his head to the mounds pushing over the top of her black tank.

Reverently, he swept his lips back and forth over one breast and then the other. Inhaling her rich orchid scent. It emanated from the shadowed cleft that beckoned him, and he followed, trailing that line with his tongue. Her nails bit into his shoulders, a delicious whimper escaping her. She squirmed on his lap, her sex rocking over his cock. Even though her shorts and panties separated them, he swore her heat seared him. He shuddered beneath her, his fingers digging into her hips, helping her ride him, urging her to work harder. Faster.

"Is that what you want, baby girl?" He grazed one nipple with his lips, then with a hint of teeth. Her breathless cry had his hips grinding between her legs over that so soft, undoubtedly sweet flesh that he'd only sampled in his dirtiest dreams. "Tell me. Give me the words. Is this what you need? Do you want more?" He punctuated the hoarse question by capturing the other peak between the edge of his teeth and tugging. Then treating it to a short, greedy suck.

She bowed tight, her hands flying to his head. Trying to push him back down to her chest.

"The words, baby girl," he ordered, holding her still and rolling his erection over her. He could take her full-body shiver as an answer, but he needed her voice. Needed her assent. Needed to hear that he wasn't alone in this.

Yeah, he was a greedy bastard.

"Yes," she said. "More. Give me more."

That's all he needed. Drawing hard on her, he lashed the rigid tip with his tongue, and she tipped her head back on her shoulders, her hold on him a vise grip. Another of those needy sounds tore from her and vibrated against his lips. Another. He hungered for another. And another. In this moment, his life's mission became eliciting more of them.

Releasing one hip, he brushed his hand over her lower belly and slipped his fingers inside the low-hanging top of her shorts. He paused, waiting to see if she would object. Taking her whimpered "please" as permission, he dipped lower until his fingertips encountered soft, drenched flesh. *Oh fuck.*

"You're so wet, baby girl," he murmured, sliding between her folds, dampening his fingers then returning to that swelled button crowning her sex. He circled it, teasing, taunting, his touch gentle. "For me?"

"Please," she pleaded again, and that word, that tone…

Hell, she could have the damn world right now. She undulated over him, her movements jerky, uncontrolled. He loved that he could do this to her.

"I promised you, didn't I? I never go back on my word," he snarled.

He firmed his caress, drawing tighter circles, stroking and rubbing. Cries spilled from her and she became frantic, bucking and twisting over him, chasing his touch, chasing pleasure. Beneath his fingertips, her clit stiffened, and a feral satisfaction bloomed in his chest. So close. This was his first time with her like this and already it was as if her body was as familiar as his own.

Lifting his free hand, he yanked down the edge of her top, baring her breast to him. Opening his mouth wide, he sucked the flesh into his mouth, curling his tongue and tugging. Savoring. Feasting.

Feverishly shaking her head, she choked back a scream, went rigid and came. With a curse, he worked her sex, giving her every measure of the orgasm. He whispered praise against her breast, urging her to take it all, not to hold back. As if the words spurred her on, she bucked and writhed until her body sagged against his, her face buried in his neck.

His body ached with unfulfilled lust. His dick throbbed, loudly demanding to be buried in the sweet flesh his fingers had just enjoyed. But he did nothing to provide that relief. Because he might not have satisfied his physical needs, but contentment hummed within him.

Gently, he stroked a hand down her back, nuzzling her hair. And he shifted his other hand to the small bump of her stomach. He felt her tension, but he cradled her belly, sweeping a thumb back and forth. Slowly, the rigidity seeped from her, and once more she relaxed, curving her body into his.

His.

She'd agreed to be his. To place herself and her baby under his protection, even if it was in name only.

He closed his eyes, and a trickle of unease infiltrated his peace.

Please let him be doing the right thing.

For all of them.

CHAPTER SIXTEEN

She'd done it.

She'd married Cole Dennison.

In front of God and country. Well, at least the small part of the country that gathered at The Glen. Yep. She and Cole had held their wedding and, now, reception, in the midst of the motorcycle rally. Family, friends and bikers and vendors from all over the country had witnessed their union.

Elation. That's what should be rushing through her, lifting her as high as the group of balloons that bobbed over the crowd of vendor booths. Oh, what she wouldn't give right now to describe this pressure steadily gathering against her rib cage as elation.

But she would be deceiving herself as well as the people gathered to celebrate her and Cole's nuptials. The least she could do was admit that anxiety and unease coursed through her. No matter how big a smile stretched her face. That was for show so no one else guessed that inside she trembled with worry.

Worry over Cole regretting his decision.

Worry over if her parents and his family would accept this marriage.

Worry over her rash behavior.

The last one caused her smile to waver for a moment before she firmed it up. How many times had her reckless and impulsive choices affected and hurt those she loved? Carlin. Because of her refusal to donate part of her kidney, her sister had died. Her parents. Carlin's resultant death had destroyed their family. Daniel. She should've never married him in the first place. She'd been too young.

And now, possibly her baby.

Cole's arguments in favor of this marriage of convenience—Jesus, she couldn't suppress a disbelieving chuckle even as she *thought* the words—had swayed her. They'd been valid. Marriage to him would counter Daniel's reasons for seeking custody of their baby. She possessed zero doubts Cole would make a good husband. After all, he'd been loyal, kind and loving to Tonia.

And wasn't that the crux of why her stomach churned while she'd recited vows to love, cherish and honor him? He'd sworn these same vows years ago to the woman he loved. He could never honestly give them to Sydney. As he'd admitted in his living room a week ago. She was consigning herself to a future of being second in someone's heart. Oh no, he would never neglect or hurt her. At least not intentionally. But all her life, she'd never been a priority. Not for her parents—true, Carlin's illness and medical treatment had come first, and rightly so. And unless Sydney was giving blood, tissue or an organ, she'd always felt like an afterthought, a Plan B, for her parents. And with Daniel, his career had taken precedence.

She didn't know what it felt like to be a priority in someone's life. In their heart.

But oh God, had she always dreamed about it.

Craved it.

It wasn't meant for her. Because when it came down to it—when the choice was between her needs and her baby's welfare and happiness—there wasn't a choice. Her daughter came first.

So, she'd agreed.

She'd settled for affection and sex.

Her cheeks heated and standing amid the hundreds of people celebrating their nuptials and the rally, she forced herself not to fan her face. Just the memories of how he'd kissed her, touched her…

Jesus.

She'd lit up like a torch dipped in kerosene as soon as his mouth crashed to hers. Desire and embarrassment collided and she sipped from the glass of cold lemonade Cole had pressed into her hand just after they finished taking pictures.

Desire, because, whoa. The kiss the first night of the rally hadn't prepared her for the conflagration that had leveled her on his couch. She'd experienced good sex—even great sex—with Daniel. But what amounted to heavy petting had obliterated her preconceived notions of "great sex." And Cole hadn't even been inside her yet.

She might not survive that "yet."

Her fingers tightened around her glass and her thighs tightened around the empty ache.

Embarrassment, because she'd shown her hand, revealed her vulnerability to him. She'd *begged* him to touch her. Now he knew how much she wanted him. She couldn't deny it. She'd basically just given him her weakness.

With her safety, her protection, her child? She unquestionably trusted him.

But with her feelings? No.

And she knew with a clarity that carried heavy resignation, that the more she had sex with him, was intimate with him, the more she placed her own heart in jeopardy.

But again…her daughter was worth any risk.

And Sydney had to guard her heart. Remember who she was fighting for. And believe Cole when he told her he couldn't be more than her friend and lover.

"You okay? Do you need to sit down?" Cole murmured in her ear. To an onlooker, it might appear as if he were whispering something sweet to his new wife. And for the sake of her pride, she hoped that's how it seemed. If anyone knew the truth… Jesus, she couldn't handle the pity or being the topic of hot gossip.

Well, any more gossip.

"No, I'm fine." She turned the wattage up on her smile. "I can't believe you got all of this together in such a short amount of time. I mean, even a photographer?"

He winked. "I'm mayor."

"Which means, what exactly?" she teased. "You have the goods on everybody to make them comply with your wishes?"

"That's called blackmail." He arched an eyebrow. "Besides, in a town this size, where everybody knows everybody's business, I couldn't find any dirt that isn't already common knowledge."

She shrugged a shoulder. "True."

"To answer your question, though, I have six brothers and sisters and wonderful parents. The people I don't know, they do. Between all of us, we got the impossible covered."

"Do they know about…us?" she asked quietly. Leo did. Sydney couldn't have held that truth back from her friend. The other woman had been mad as hell at Daniel and surprisingly accepting of the "arrangement" Sydney had decided to enter into with Cole. Hell, Leo had even insisted on standing up with Sydney as her maid of honor. So, yes, Leo knew.

But the rest of the Dennison clan…

He hesitated, then pinched her chin and tilted it back. "Yes," he said, his voice incredibly—terribly—gentle. "I was honest with them because they love me and had questions and concerns. And because they love you, too, and want to be our support system. I had a difficult time convincing Moe that she could not drive down to North Carolina and 'handle' Daniel, but after that crisis passed, everyone was adamant about being in this with us. You're family, and no one comes for family."

She blinked back the sudden sting of tears and turned her

head away, breaking free of his grasp. Hormones again. Yep, that's what caused the swell of emotion. Definitely not the joy and sadness that battled it out in her chest. The Dennisons had formed a united front behind Cole, even if they might not agree with his choice, and therefore, they backed her as well. How sad was it that she hadn't confided in her parents about Daniel's visit or the truth behind this hasty wedding? Unlike Cole, she couldn't count on their acceptance, their unconditional support. Call her a coward, she'd told them over the phone. She hadn't been up to staring their disappointment in the face. To them, their daughter was making another impulsive decision. Fresh out of one marriage and jumping into another. Hell, until she'd walked down that makeshift aisle where Cole waited in front of a gazebo with Wolf and the minister, she hadn't even been sure her parents would show up for her. But they had. And well, she took small victories where she could.

Scanning the crowded field where people were decked out in their Sunday best, or wearing jeans and T-shirts, she quickly located her parents. They stood talking with Moe and Ian and another older couple. As if sensing her attention on them, her mother glanced in Sydney's direction. Her mother's smile wavered, then firmed. That phone call last week had been the first they'd spoken since Sydney had visited the boutique. The strain between them hadn't lessened, the distance yawning wider.

One she feared even a whole armada of ships couldn't cross.

"We should go over and speak," Cole murmured. She peered up at him, surprised to see a tiny muscle jumping along the hard line of his jaw.

"Cole?" She pressed a hand to his abdomen. And cursed herself for noticing how ripped the muscles were beneath her palm.

He glanced at her, and shadows darkened his amber gaze. "I'd like to introduce you to…" He didn't finish, but cupped her elbow and guided her over to the small group.

Several people stopped them along the way, congratulating

them. By the time they made it to their destination, her face cracking in half from the constant smiling and laughing seemed an imminent possibility.

"Hey, Moe, Dad." Cole leaned forward and kissed his mother on the cheek and drew his father into one of those manly hugs that included back and shoulder slapping. "Luke, Patricia, thank you for coming."

"Of course," Luke said, shaking Cole's hand. "We wouldn't have missed it. Sydney, you look beautiful," he murmured, and her mind—or her desperate heart—must have conjured that hint of chafing in his voice.

"Thanks, Dad." Clearing her throat, she turned to her mother. "Mom. I'm glad you guys came."

Her mother nodded. "Where else would we be? You're our daughter." For several moments, she searched Sydney's face. "This is sudden, but… I hope you'll be happy."

Would her mother be proud or further dismayed if Sydney told her this marriage wasn't about happiness but sacrifice? She honestly didn't know.

"Sydney, I'd like to introduce you to Ramon and Valeria Narvaez." He paused, and a curious tension filled the heartbeat of time. "These are Tonia's parents, my in-laws. Ramon, Mamá, this is Sydney."

God.

The pain damn near blindsided her, and she struggled to breathe past it without cluing in everyone standing there that she'd been dealt a blow. But something told her she'd failed to fully conceal it when Ian winced and Moe's eyes softened, even as she gave Sydney a tiny shake of her head.

Sydney got what Cole's mother was trying to silently convey. Oh, she got it. That had most likely been a slip on Cole's part; she had no doubt it hadn't been deliberate. But that somehow made the slight more hurtful. Hurtful, hell. Devastating. If she glanced down, she might glimpse jagged shards of her pride littering the ground around the hem of her long, pale yellow dress.

My in-laws.

Because Tonia would always be his first and true wife.

Sydney was a watered-down substitute.

Stupid of her to be so wounded. She'd gone into this union with her eyes wide-open, acknowledging her place, her role. And did she really expect him to stop considering Tonia's parents as family just because their daughter had died, and he'd remarried? No. Of course not.

But logic and reason still didn't prevent her from seeking Patricia like a little girl instinctively crying out for her mother when in pain. A crinkle marred the bridge of her mother's nose, but quickly disappeared when she noticed Sydney looking at her. Patricia notched her chin a shade higher, and the pain dimmed, ebbed. *You hold your head up.* Message received. Though a minefield of issues cluttered their relationship, warmth eddied inside her. And Sydney did just as her mother instructed. She hiked her chin, fixed a smile on her face and switched her attention to the older couple.

"It's a delight to finally meet you, Sydney," Valeria greeted, stepping forward with both hands outstretched. She clasped Sydney's in hers and leaned in to press a kiss to her cheek. It'd been years since Sydney last saw Tonia, but she saw the other woman in Valeria's kind brown eyes, thick eyebrows and wide mouth. Tonia had been a beauty, just like her mother. "My husband and I have heard so many good things about you. We've been excited to meet you."

Sydney's smile warmed despite the ache that continued to pulse in her chest. Sincerity and a genuine friendliness emanated from Valeria. And as Ramon moved forward and kissed her other cheek, murmuring, "Welcome to the family, *mija*," she understood why Tonia had been such a loving person. With parents like these, she'd had no choice.

"Thank you. It's wonderful to meet you both." Sydney hesitated, unsure if she should continue but… Forget it. If there was an etiquette for this kind of situation, she'd never read that Emily Post covered it. "I was younger than Tonia, but I remember her well. She was a beautiful person, inside and out."

"Thank you," Valeria whispered, squeezing her hands, then releasing them. "Now I expect you two to come around the house for dinner soon. I need to start fattening up you and this little one as soon as possible. You're so tiny. May I?" Valeria's hand hovered above Sydney's stomach, waiting for permission. Sydney nodded, and the older woman laid a gentle hand on top of the bump. "Cole told us you're having a girl. I would've adored a boy just as much, but there's something about girls. Sweet. Angelic. And so much fun to shop for," she added with a sly smile.

"I think you're going to find competition in the spoiling department," Moe drawled. "Between you, me and Patricia we're going to have one hell of a race for number one nana. You up for this, Patricia?" Moe grinned, extending her arms and cracking her knuckles.

"Oh God," Ian muttered.

"I didn't want to mention that the dress my daughter is wearing came from my shop—one that I specially ordered for her. And I have a matching infant-sized dress on the way. So you ladies have some catching up to do."

Sydney laughed, astonished and…delighted. It'd been a while since she'd witnessed her mother's dry sense of humor. The woman had sarcasm down to a fine art, and it'd always been one of the things Sydney had enjoyed about her mother.

"Hmm. *Atrévete*," Valeria drawled, arching a dark eyebrow. Sydney smothered a snicker. She couldn't speak Spanish, but she sensed the woman had just uttered the equivalent of "come at me, bro." And from the rumble of Cole's chuckle, she didn't think she was far off. Grinning, Valeria asked Sydney, "I don't know if you've started working on the nursery yet. You're five months along, right? If not, we need to get started. We can make a girls' day of it," she chattered, not giving Sydney a chance to respond. Her excitement was contagious, and Sydney found her-self grinning. "We need measurements and colors. Where are you two living? Are you going to move into the—"

"No."

Cole's abrupt, flat interruption dropped an awkward silence between them. Awkward and tense. And vibrating with some-thing unspoken but understood by everyone but her. Well, nearly everyone. Her parents seemed as confused as she was. But as the other two couples exchanged weighty, meaningful glances, she knew she wasn't imagining this…whatever this was.

"For now, we're going to stay in my cottage, until we find a place of our own," Cole said, his voice smooth, but with a flinty undertone that brooked no further discussion.

"You two are welcome to stay as long as you need," Ian mur-mured, his deep rumble carrying a hint of his native Ireland that hadn't abandoned him even after decades in the States.

Cole nodded. "Thanks, Dad." He glanced over his shoulder toward the tent with the huge grills and tables. "I think we're about to serve dinner then cut the cake."

With more hugs, the three couples made their way across the field, leaving her and Cole alone.

"What was that about?" Sydney asked quietly. "And don't tell me nothing," she tacked on.

A beat of silence. "Let it go, Sydney," he murmured. "We're supposed to be celebrating our wedding. Let's just do that and let everything else…go."

The protest backed up in her throat. A part of her wanted to stand her ground. But they stood in a field full of family, friends and rally goers. Now wasn't the time. He won this round. But later? She wanted answers.

"Okay," she conceded. "Let's go join our guests."

Shadows draped the small front yard of Cole's cottage as he parked in his driveway.

Home.

As of yesterday, she'd moved the last of her belongings into his place, and this was now their home. There was no going back. As the hours of the day passed, and the sun sank behind the mountains, her nerves had climbed. Maybe the same had been true for Cole, because he'd become more and more subdued, distant.

Was he regretting his decision? Regretting her?

She wished she had the courage to ask him. But getting married today after a week's notice had sapped every last ounce she had in reserve. Maybe tomorrow. That had become her mantra lately.

Cole exited the car, and she pushed her door open. Before she could step out, he was there, his hand extended toward her. Her heart thumped against her chest, and she shot it side-eye before sliding her palm across his. Long, capable fingers folded around hers, and he guided her out of the vehicle, leading her up the walk to his house. Correction. *Their* house.

Yeah, that would take some getting used to. Because right now, she still had to acclimate to being someone's wife again.

Not someone's.

Cole's.

She stared at his broad, powerful back and shoulders as he opened the front door. As always, she admired his width and build. But she also noticed the taut set of his shoulders. The almost stiff gait that had replaced his normal fluid, sensual grace. The tension that radiated off of him.

The anxiety that had been steadily building crept up her own spine and twisted her stomach. She stood on a fragile edge. On one side loomed her own uncertainties and insecurities. On the other, Cole and her complicated, messy feelings toward him. Both felt like deep plunges into an abyss that offered her no safety net.

Locking her fingers together in front of her, she turned to face him. And took that step off the edge toward him.

"I'm going to get ready for bed, unless you'd rather stay up and watch TV or talk…" God, she had no idea how to maneuver this. Most newlyweds couldn't wait to dive into bed. But they weren't most newlyweds.

"No," he said, sliding his hands into the front pockets of his suit pants. The rolled-up sleeves of his white shirt gathered underneath his elbows, and even that small movement set tendons flexing. Restrained power. Rigid control. She'd experienced how overwhelming that power could be when he loosed just a little of it. The greedy part of her wanted him to let the leash off. To let go with her. "You go ahead."

"I don't mind." She moved toward him. "Really, we can—"

"I can't, Sydney." The words, though quiet, cut through the room—through her—like a scalpel, halting her midstep. "I thought I could…but I can't do this. Not right now. Not—" His lips clamped shut, and he lifted his arms, scrubbing his hands over his short hair.

"Cole," she breathed.

You can't what? Have sex with me tonight? Lie next to me? Can't do this marriage?

Panic scoured her throat, and every breath felt abraded. No matter how she wanted the answers to those questions, she couldn't shove them out. Because a smaller part of her didn't want to hear them. Didn't want the pain the answers would inflict.

"I'm sorry," he rasped. "I'm so sorry. I need—" He glanced over his shoulder at the front door. Reminding her of a trapped animal desperately seeking escape.

"Go."

His head whipped back around, and she almost softened at the obvious torment that darkened his gaze, drew his skin taut over sharp cheekbones, carved lines on either side of his flattened mouth. Almost. Because the pain tearing through her demanded she clutch the remaining shreds of her pride.

Rejected on her wedding night. Jesus.

"Sydney, I—"

"Don't say it again," she ordered. "Just go."

He hesitated, and for a moment, she thought he would come to her, hold her. Tell her he had no intention of walking out that door. And fool that she was, she would allow him to.

But he didn't approach her.

He wheeled around, jerked open the door and disappeared through it.

She still stood in the same spot moments later when his engine rumbled to life and headlights swept across the living room.

Only when she'd convinced herself that he wasn't returning did she unglue her feet and move toward the bedroom.

Alone.

CHAPTER SEVENTEEN

Cole delivered one last brutal blow to the punching bag. When it swung back in his direction, he caught it between his wrapped hands, leaning his sweaty forehead against the leather. Harsh air burst from his lungs, and his bare chest rose and fell on the labored breaths.

Tired.

He was so damn tired.

Sleep had been like a game of finding fucking Waldo. Elusive and with so many other thoughts crowding into his head he couldn't locate it.

Pushing away from the bag, he strode on heavy legs to the weight bench and lowered to it, unwinding the black wrap from his hands. He'd been running, then working out in his garage, since the first hints of dawn. And yet none of the exercise had cleared his mind or eased the restless energy that crackled inside him like a live wire.

But staying inside this garage to punish his body wasn't an option. At least not a long-term one.

Not when his new wife slept inside his house.

He flattened his hands over the black sweatpants covering

his thighs, staring down at the concrete floor. He'd fucked up. No other way he could put it. He'd abandoned Sydney on their first night together as man and wife. Hadn't meant to. Hadn't wanted to. But as he stood in his living room, her wearing that beautiful yellow dress, her gorgeous, thick curls framing her lovely face and brushing her bare shoulders, he'd failed in battling back the grief, the guilt that had slowly been strangling him since the reception.

More accurately, since his mother-in-law had asked him about moving Sydney into the home he'd shared with Tonia. The home that stood silent with a fully furnished nursery that had never been used.

Panic had seized him by the throat, locked its jaw and refused to release him. And it'd been either escape or break down right there at Sydney's feet.

So, he'd left. Even though he'd glimpsed the confusion, the hurt and finally the devastating resignation that entered her gaze. As if someone leaving her, disappointing her, didn't come as a shock. As if, on some level, she'd expected it.

Maybe she had. But she hadn't failed him. He'd failed her.

Still didn't stop him from driving through Rose Bend, blowing past the town limits to the road and mountains beyond, only to return hours later and collapse at his wife's and son's graves. There, knees buried in grass, he apologized for marrying another woman. Told Tonia about Sydney and the situation with her ex-husband. Promised he'd love Tonia forever. Her and Mateo.

He hadn't confessed that he desired Sydney. Desired, hell. He *craved* her. In the past two years, his dick had only throbbed for her. He couldn't admit that. Not when guilt spilled through him unchecked, a landslide that buried his heart under its burden. Guilt because while he'd stared at Sydney last night, lust for her seething under the grief and panic, he couldn't remember Tonia's scent. Couldn't recall the exact lilt of her laugh. Couldn't evoke the timbre of her voice. He was losing all he had left of her, and that felt like the cruelest betrayal of her and their love.

But how could he explain all that to Sydney without sounding like a complete asshole? In the end, his silence had damned him as much as if he'd opened his mouth.

Now, he had to make amends. And if she didn't want to hear his apology? If she didn't want anything to do with him? Well, he couldn't blame her.

Sighing, he rose from the bench and made his way into the silent house, heading directly for the bathroom and a much-needed shower. Thirty minutes later, clean and dressed in a white T-shirt and black jeans, he padded on bare feet to the kitchen. When he'd gone into the bedroom to grab clothes, the bed had been empty and freshly made. Or maybe it hadn't been slept in at all.

What if she'd left him and returned to her place? Alarm had crackled inside him, sliding toward dread. He'd fucked up last night, but even as he'd driven back home, he'd feared her leaving him. He hadn't bothered to analyze the emotion twisting his gut. Yes, he'd married her to provide protection, but it hadn't been those arguments he'd presented a week ago at the forefront of his mind. No, he'd wanted her there. With him. Filling his space. Making him feel...normal.

But as he'd turned toward the bedroom door, the aroma of brewing coffee drifted toward him, alerting him that she hadn't abandoned him as he'd done to her. Selfish relief had flowed through him then, as it did now.

"More active this morning, aren't you?" she murmured.

Cole frowned, pausing just behind the wall that separated the living room from the kitchen. Was she on the phone? He didn't want to interrupt, but no calls this early in the morning were good ones. Maybe she needed him...

He resumed moving forward, but then halted as she started talking again.

"You were probably feeling my emotions, and I've disturbed your sleep. In about four months, you'll pay me back, won't you?" She chuckled, and it hit Cole that she wasn't on the phone; Sydney was having a one-sided conversation with her baby.

On silent feet, he carefully eased around the wall, pausing at the edge of the breakfast bar. Clad in another sleep set, this time an emerald green tank and ass-hugging shorts, she stood at the counter next to the coffee machine, her back to him.

The soft joy as well as the thread of sadness in her voice held him transfixed. If he possessed the barest of manners, he would announce himself with a cough or retrace his steps and let his heavy footsteps declare his presence. But he did neither. He remained there, eavesdropping. And drinking her in.

"I'm sorry, jellybean. But I promise you this. Every time you wake up, I'll be there. Every time you cry, I'll hold you, do everything in my power to fix what's wrong." She shifted to the side, and he caught her hand gently rubbing the small bump. She bowed her head, speaking directly to her stomach, and in spite of the heartbreak in her words, he smiled. "You'll never be alone in this world. Not as long as I have breath in my body. I promise to tell you every day how much I love you. You'll never doubt it. And not just because of what you can do for me or if you make me proud. No, I'll always be proud because you're you. There aren't any conditions attached to my love. If there's one thing you will always be able to count on, it's that."

Cole closed his eyes, his fingers curling into a fist at his side. To avoid punching the nearest wall? Or to prevent himself from reaching out for her? He didn't know. It was a toss-up.

It didn't require Sherlock Holmes–level skills to deduce what she referred to. Her parents. Her ex-husband. Didn't matter if it was true or not, Sydney believed their love for her was conditional.

How could she not see the selfless, brave heart that rendered her priceless? The beauty that tied tongues? The kindness that a blind man could see? And last night he had trampled all over that heart, humbled that strength and probably dented that pride.

Forgive me, wavered on his tongue. But he didn't utter it. Placing the onus of his bad behavior on her wasn't worthy of either of them.

"Morning," he murmured, making his presence known. She spun around on a gasp, coffee spilling over the rim of the cup, splashing on the hand that hadn't been cradling her belly. "Shit," he hissed, rushing forward and nabbing the cup from her, placing it behind them on the counter. Cradling her hand and circling her wrist, he tugged her over to the sink and twisted the cold-water faucet. "I didn't mean to startle you," he muttered, easing her hand under the rushing water. She flinched at the first contact, but didn't pull away from him. He swept a thumb over the reddened area. "I'm sorry."

She stiffened against him and, using her uninjured hand, switched off the water.

"I'm fine. It barely stings." Sydney moved as if to ease away, but he shifted forward, his continued hold on her hand and his chest against her back trapping her in place.

Closing his eyes, he lowered his head, pressed his cheek to her mass of curls. Inhaled the chocolate and citrus scent that had become an obsession for him. If possible, she went even more rigid, her spine ramrod straight and unyielding.

Lips grazing the slightly pointed top of her ear, he whispered, "I'm sorry."

"I heard you," she said, tone as cold as the water that had just doused her hand. "Can you let me loose now? I need to dry my hand."

For a second, he remained standing behind her, crowding her. But then, he did as she requested, and leaned a hip against the counter's edge as she crossed the kitchen. She grabbed a dish towel and dabbed her skin, not glancing at him once.

"I'm going to head back to my cottage to make sure I didn't

leave anything. And I'll probably stay over there to work on the grant for a while."

"You're leaving." Though he'd calmly uttered the statement, inside he felt anything but. Panic, not unlike what had chased him out of the house the night before, raced through him. The primal, instinctive core of him roared not to let her walk out the door. Not to let her walk away from him.

God, he was such a hypocrite.

"No," she said, setting down the towel but still not looking at him. "I think we just need some space."

"And if I say I don't want or need space?"

That brought her spinning around, hands clutching the counter at her hips. He forced himself to keep his gaze on her beautiful but furious face and not dip to the breasts he'd bared and kissed just a week ago. But, goddamn, it was a battle. Her body called to him like the loveliest but deadliest siren's song. Even as he wanted to soothe the anger—the awful hurt—that darkened her eyes, he longed to crash against her like those doomed sailors, and drown in her.

"Did you give me that choice last night?" she asked, the demand low but throbbing with the pain he'd inflicted.

His gut twisted.

"No, baby girl. I didn't," he murmured.

"I'm not an idiot, and I'm not insensitive," she continued as if he hadn't spoken. Like a valve had popped under extreme pressure, she unloaded on him, holding nothing back. "I get why yesterday would've been rough for you. I even get why you would've needed time alone to cope with unexpected feelings that might've overwhelmed you. I would've told you all of that if you had. Just. Talked to. Me." She shook her head. "But you didn't, Cole. Instead, you ran out of here like a cornered animal. And I was your jailer. Like I had forced you to be here. To be with me." Her voice trembled, then cracked and so did his resolve not to touch her until they talked. His heart lodged in his throat as he moved toward her, but she slammed up a hand. "No. Don't touch me. You asked *me* to marry *you*. You asked *me* to move in here. You stood up there in front of this whole town and pledged yourself to *me*. I didn't force you. I didn't guilt you. All I did was trust you."

"Sydney." His fingers curled and uncurled at his side. Fuck, he *needed* to touch her. To hold her. To try and take away the pain he'd caused.

"You said you wanted me, but last night you couldn't even look at me. Like I disgusted you…disappointed you," she whispered. "I'm so tired, Cole. So tired of seeing that look on the faces of people I care about. I can't do it anymore. I won't." She shook her head again, more vehemently, eyes squeezing shut. "I *won't*."

"Sydney, please," he pleaded. "Please, let me touch you." He didn't wait for her answer. He couldn't remain still any longer. Not when she was so tormented. As a man, he couldn't do it. "Let me hold you."

He crossed the last few feet separating them and cupped her face, tilting her head back. But she didn't open her eyes, didn't look at him. And he needed that, too. A part of him acknowledged how he seemed to be making this about his needs, his wants. But he found when it came to her, he was a selfish bastard. He craved her voice, her scent, her company and now, her kiss. Her body. The blessed oblivion they promised him.

Jesus, did he crave that.

And only she could give it to him.

"I'm sorry." He swept his thumbs across her cheekbones then pressed his lips over the left one. "I'm so sorry, baby girl," he repeated against her skin.

"You hurt me." Her hands slid up between them, settled against his chest. But instead of shoving him away, her fingers fisted in his T-shirt, tugging it down. As if it, and he, were the only things keeping her on her feet.

"I know I did." He caressed the tender skin just below her eyes. "Look at me. Please." Relief and a deep, rumbling satisfaction barreled through him when she complied and revealed those beautiful eyes to him. "I know I hurt you," he reiterated. "But my worst sin is walking out that door and leaving you here thinking I regretted you…that I didn't want you. Because, baby girl, nothing could be further from the truth. Last night was about me, not you. And I should've explained that before abandoning you on our wedding night. I owed you that, not just as my new wife, but as my friend." He lowered his head, brushed his lips across the corner of her mouth. "As the man who last kissed you, brought this gorgeous body pleasure." He gave the other corner a kiss. "I'm so sorry, Sydney. Let me show you how much I still want you."

How much I still need you.

But he didn't utter those damning words. They sounded too close to something more than lust.

Because this could be nothing more than that.

He was good as long as he didn't allow his emotions to become involved in this…arrangement. As long as he didn't cross that line, he wouldn't collapse under the fear that haunted him. Because if he did, and he lost her like he'd lost Tonia, there wouldn't be a coming back from that dark abyss for him. He'd managed it once, by the grace of God. But he suspected even God's grace had limits. Or his heart did. He wouldn't make it. The pain would destroy his mind, and he couldn't suffer that agony again. He was fucking terrified of it, and he couldn't go through it again.

He wouldn't.

So, yes, he'd married Sydney. He'd grant her and her child security. But he couldn't love her. Or the baby whose heartbeat he could still hear.

If he remembered that one rule, then they would all be safe, content. Maybe even happy.

With that goal firmly entrenched in his mind, he grazed her chin with the edge of his teeth. Soothed it with a whisper of a kiss.

"Will you, baby girl?" he asked, lifting his gaze to hers. "Let me take the hurt away. For both of us."

Her nod was imperceptible, but he caught it. The relief screamed almost as loud as the lust. The groan barely breached his throat before he took her mouth. And the now familiar taste of her swept over his tongue, flooded his senses. Another hungry sound escaped him, as he feasted on her like a long-starved man. He shifted a hand, thrusting his fingers through the curls that drove him wild—the curls that had caressed his chest, his abdomen, his thighs in his dirtiest dreams. He fisted them as he did in those dreams, tugging her head back so he could have deeper access. And he lowered the other hand to her jaw, pressing his thumb just under her bottom lip, applying pressure to open her mouth wider to him. Give him more of her. Always more with this woman. Never enough.

She rose on her toes, offering him all that he demanded. And then she took in return. Curled her tongue around his, sucked hard so he felt the pull of it in his dick. Licked the roof of his mouth so the wet, luxuriant caress resulted in a twin, phantom stroke over his abdomen. Lightly bit his lip, and his nipples tingled with that hint of pain and so much pleasure.

Wrenching his mouth away from hers, he circled her wrist and yanked it away from his shirt. His chest heaving on his ragged breaths, he led her out of the kitchen.

Or started to.

She tugged on his hold, and dismay punched a hole in his gut. But before he could ask her what was wrong, she flung her arms around his neck, crushed her body to his and opened her mouth against the base of his throat. He shuddered, his arms automatically wrapping around her.

"No," she panted. "Don't stop kissing me."

Unable to resist that request, he dipped his head and parted her lips with his tongue. Tasting her again. And like before, he became lost in it, devouring her in a raw, explicit demonstration of what he wanted from her, wanted to do to her. Grabbing a hold of the scraps of his control, he moaned, tearing his mouth away from her.

"Baby girl, if we don't stop right now, we won't make it to the bedroom." He delivered the warning against her cheek.

"That's fine." She tried to capture his mouth again, but he lifted his head, meeting her pleasure-darkened eyes. But glimpsing uncertainty in their depths.

"What's wrong?" He cupped the back of her neck. "What's going on in that head of yours?"

She sank her teeth into her bottom lip, and he barely restrained himself from licking the curve.

"Sydney," he urged, squeezing her nape.

She huffed out a breath, and he would've smiled at the irritated sound if her lashes hadn't lowered, hiding. "I just don't want you to change your mind," she admitted. "In the time it takes for us to get from the kitchen to the bedroom, if you start to think…"

She trailed off, but he caught her meaning. He released a rough chuckle. When her brow wrinkled in a frown, he planted a kiss in the middle of the vee.

"I'm not going to change my mind," he assured her. When she still didn't meet his eyes, he clasped one of her hands and drew it down between them. Pressed it over the thick, throbbing length of his cock. Her gaze crashed to his, the heat there like an incinerator to his skin. Without breaking their visual showdown, she curled her fingers around him, squeezing. His hips punched forward, grinding his erection into her grip. This time, it was him who closed his eyes and muttered a soft curse. "No damn way I'm changing my mind," he repeated. "But you're pregnant and this is our first time together. I'm not fucking you on the kitchen table. At least not the first time," he rumbled, removing her hand and circling her wrist.

Not giving her time to object again, he guided her from the room, not stopping until they reached his bedroom.

Where she belongs.

The words ricocheted off his skull, but he mercilessly smothered them. Being married, having access to one another, wasn't the same as belonging, he reminded himself. Even as he reclaimed her mouth and plundered it.

She whimpered, surrendering to him. Trusting him with her body. No, she might not have said the words, but the way she tilted her head back, opened for him, melted against him... He didn't need the words when her body did all the talking. She didn't—and shouldn't—entrust her heart to him, but her pleasure, her inhibitions? There was no safer place than with him.

And it was that thought that forced his hands to gentle, his mouth to slow. Each thrust and lick and twist of his tongue was a lesson in savoring, in teasing, in worshipping. He might not have acknowledged it until this moment, but he'd been yearning for this since the moment she'd turned to him on that hill behind the church. Weeks. He'd been alive for weeks, brought to life by hunger, by desire for this woman.

So yeah, he would savor.

He stroked his hands down her neck, pausing to cradle her throat and rub his thumbs up and down the front of the elegant column. Her pulse galloped under his touch, and he lowered his head, pressing his lips there, soothing her heartbeat, assuring it that he was only there to give pleasure, not cause harm.

Or maybe he was projecting. Maybe a part of him yearned to ask Sydney for that same assurance.

He shook his head, attempting to dislodge the foolish and terrifying thought.

"What?" Sydney murmured, trailing the backs of her fingers down his cheek. "What's wrong, Cole?"

He lifted his head, met the warm concern that mingled with the desire in her eyes. "You're so beautiful," he whispered. Not a lie. Slowly, he skimmed his hands down her torso and gripped the hem of her top. "Let me see all of you."

He'd seen and touched her breasts the week before, but this was different. Then, they could still turn around and walk away. Now, with this step taken, there would be no going back. It wasn't a step he would take without her permission. Without her being fully in.

She nodded, her gaze unwavering. "Yes."

Only then did he drag the shirt up and toss it aside. Only then did he go to his knees, placing a reverent kiss in the middle of her chest and one on her rounded belly. He slipped fingers under the waist of her shorts and drew them down her thighs, leaving her completely naked before him. Sitting back on his heels, he stared at her, his heart thundering, the raucous beat filling his head.

Exquisite.

She was exquisite.

Her hands twitched at her sides then started to rise, presumably to hide herself from him. Murmuring something that sounded strangled in his throat, he cuffed her wrists, preventing the movement. He didn't speak. Couldn't. Because she stole his breath.

Dark-tipped, full breasts that almost filled his hands—his palms itched with the memory of their weight, texture and sensitivity. The barest dip of a waist that he ached to trace with his tongue. The swollen, beautiful belly that was still on the smaller side but would continue to grow as the months passed. Fear of that time, of what would come after flickered in his chest, but he locked it away, let the pure wonder of her fill him instead. Round hips that a dark part of him hungered to see marked by his fingers. The thick, toned legs that he wanted wrapped around his waist, so he could experience their strength firsthand.

The wet, plump folds of her sex. His hold on her tightened as he stared at the dark thatch of hair that couldn't hide the moisture gleaming on her flesh and upper thighs. His mouth watered. He wanted to dip his head and taste her—feast on her—so bad his jaw throbbed, his throat worked.

"I'm trying." Damn, was that his voice? The harsh tone resembled an animal's snarl. "I'm trying hard not to dive into you. To take you like a man instead of the starved thing I've become. To handle you gently, like you deserve, instead of hard, rough. Instead of fucking you until my dick cries for mercy. Until your screams of pleasure are all I hear, and you come so hard, you break for me. Fuck, Sydney. I want you to break for me."

"What if I deserve gentle *and* hard and rough?" Fingers lightly stroked his short hair, and for the first time in two years, he fleetingly wished he hadn't cut it. Right now, he would've loved having those clever, delicate fingers pulling on the strands, feeling pinpricks of pleasure/pain skate across his scalp. "Don't hold back with me," she urged, her nails scratching him, and he grunted with the bite of it, not too proud to beg for more. "You won't hurt me because you're you. I trust you to take care of me. Of us both."

Was he worthy of that trust? He couldn't answer that. But here, kneeling before this goddess of a woman, he wanted to be. In this—the exchange of passion—he vowed to be.

"Do what you want. Use me, Cole."

She parted her legs.

Oh fuck.

He squeezed his eyes shut, as if shutting out the erotic sight of her would somehow cool the agony of controlling his baser needs. But her scent—damp, heavy, sweet with that hint of spice. He snapped.

With impatient hands, he gripped her hips, quickly guided her to the floor, arranging her so she reclined on her hands, knees bent and open. Then he dove between her thighs. One, long, greedy lick—from her fluttering entrance, between her swollen folds and up to the pulsing, engorged button cresting the top.

Goddamn. That first taste. Like a hit of the most potent and highly addicting drug. The scent was rich, heady, like he was sampling the undiluted flavor of her—Sydney. Pure Sydney. And he was already hooked. And he took. And took. And took. With short, teasing laps. Long, greedy sucks. Messy strokes. Hard flicks and merciless rubs.

Her cries rained down on him and her legs shook around his head. Palming her inner thighs and spreading her wider, he dove lower, thrusting his tongue into that channel where his cock wept to be. Groaning as her sex spasmed around him, he released one thigh to grip his erection, squeezing through the sweatpants. Pleasure blasted up his spine like a rocket, and for a moment, he feared he would go over without even burying himself inside the flesh he tormented and worshipped.

A glance up her torso, and for a moment, he was enraptured. Sprawled on her elbows, head thrown back, chest heaving, hips twisting and bucking, she embodied sex. A carnal, pagan goddess manifested right here in his bedroom.

Her tortured groan snapped him out of his stupor, and he returned his attention to her slick flesh. Dipping his head again, he lapped at her clit, circling the distended button. Lower, he mimicked the movement with his fingers over the entrance to her body then slowly pushed them inside her. She shuddered and cried out, her back arching high, thrusting her breasts toward the ceiling. That sound, the evidence of her pleasure, the eager grasping of her sex around his fingers… With a moan, he finger-fucked her, the heel of his palm bumping against her folds, her moisture coating his skin.

"Cole," she pleaded, voice ragged, breathless. "Please. God, please."

He couldn't hold back any longer, couldn't hold out on her. Curling his fingers, he rubbed a place high and deep, and sucked hard on her. On a choked scream, Sydney came, writhing and undulating. He kept at her, not stopping until she weakly pushed at his head, whimpering "no more."

Giving her pulsing clit one last kiss, he drew free of her sex and rose to his feet, his own legs trembling with unfulfilled need. He slid his fingers into his mouth, licking them clean, and watching the renewed flare of heat in her eyes. Bending down, he grasped her hands and helped her to stand. Silently, he led her to the bed, helping her onto the mattress.

Gaze fixed on her sweat-dampened, beautiful body, he removed his clothes. He moved to the dresser and retrieved the newly bought box of condoms. She was pregnant, and so they could have sex without protection. But he'd... The box trembled in his hands. He'd only ever been bare with one woman. That particular intimacy—he didn't know if he was ready for it. Didn't know if Sydney was ready for that when she was carrying another man's baby. So, he didn't ask. Couldn't ask.

Nabbing one of the packets, he climbed on the bed beside her. The rich musk of her release scented the air, and he breathed it in, fisting his cock, giving it a healthy, long pump, fisting the tip. She stared, eyes glazed, nipples diamond hard, legs shifting restlessly.

"You need time?" he asked, praying that if she said yes, he could respect it. Hell, survive it.

"No." She shook her head for added emphasis and *thank God.* "I want you inside me," she whispered.

Leaning over, he gathered her hair in his freed hand and took her mouth again, still stroking himself. The kiss was messy, raw, hot, his control shot. Before he reached the point of no return, he released her, tore open the foil, sheathed himself.

"What's most comfortable for you, baby girl?" he asked, shifting and crouching over her. "Do you want to ride me?" His dick twitched in vote for that option. "Do you want me to take you from the back?"

"I want to look at you," she whispered, a flush painting the slants of her cheekbones. "For this first time. I want you on top." She cupped his jaw, swept a caress over his mouth.

He nodded, a little surprised by how much he wanted that, too. To cover her as much as he safely could. Reaching behind her, he arranged the pillows so she wouldn't be lying flat on her back. He knelt between her spread thighs, splaying his hands on her skin, his fingertips grazing her glistening flesh.

"Look at me." Echoing his earlier demands, she lifted her other hand and cradled his face, lifting his head and not giving him a choice but to do as she said. "Only you and I are here. When you're ready, Cole. When you're ready."

He bowed his head, turning to press a kiss to her palm. He hadn't known he'd needed those words—but she had. Granting him permission to let go of any lingering guilt, to be with her in this most intimate embrace.

Bracing one hand against the headboard, he gripped his cock and notched his erection against her entrance. He paused, pressed a hand into the pillow next to her head...and pushed inside her.

The rumble that clawed up his throat rolled out of his mouth and echoed in the room. Jesus. So soft. So firm. She was liquid fire, tighter than a fist and sweeter than a mouth. She was pleasure and pain. Heaven and hell. Shelter and danger.

She was perfect.

Drawing on a will he hadn't known he possessed, he paused. Sweat dotted his brow, trickling down his temple. And yet, he stilled, his cock only half buried in her body. He opened eyes he hadn't been aware of closing and peered down at Sydney.

Curls wild and gorgeous on his pillow, she strained under him, her breasts trembling with the tremors that rocked through her. Lashes lifting, she met his gaze, the dark brown hazy with lust. Her knees squeezed his hips before she rested her heels on the backs of his thighs.

"More. All of you," she breathed. "You promised you wouldn't hold back."

"You sure?" It cost him to ask that, but he had to. Had to make sure. "This what you want?"

"All of you," she repeated, sliding her palms up his arms and shoulders, her nails biting into his skin.

Leaning his head back, he thrust home. Fully sheathed inside her tight, wet heat. Her walls embraced him, kissed his flesh. All of him. Just as she'd requested.

Buried so deep, he burned. Felt branded by her. And it wasn't enough. Not nearly enough.

Pulling free of her until just the tip remained inside and the cool air brushed over his flesh, he levered off of her and watched, damn near hypnotized by the sight of his cock slowly thrusting into her. He gripped her hips, slightly raising her ass off the bed. Again. He withdrew and pushed back inside, electrical currents racing up and down his spine. Gritting his teeth against the ecstasy, he set up a steady pace, riding her, rocking into her, ever mindful of her comfort.

Loosening his hold, he fell back over her, a palm slamming on the headboard, his other cupping a breast and thumbing the rigid nipple. With a snarl, he bent almost double over her, sucking that tip into his mouth. Her sex tightened, tightened, quivering around him and caressing him from root to tip.

"Cole," she whimpered, undulating beneath him, hands clasping his head and holding him close. "Cole, I need—I need, please…"

"I know what you need, baby girl." He reached between them, stroked fingertips over her clit, circling it firmly. "Give it to me."

Her scream ripped through the air, echoing in his ears. Her core clamped down on his dick, squeezing, rippling around him. She twisted, as if fighting to get closer while simultaneously escaping the pleasure that wracked her.

He rode her, whispering demands that she take it all. *Don't fucking stop until you take it all.* And just as her tremors started to ease, pleasure crackled in the soles of his feet, traveling with lightning speed up his legs, zipping up his spine and then pumping into his dick. With a hoarse shout, he came, exploding, letting himself go into the oblivion that he'd been seeking.

The sweet oblivion she'd gifted him.

He didn't think about tomorrow, later that evening or even ten minutes from now.

At this moment, as he fell to the bed beside Sydney, his muscles heavy and thick with fatigue, lungs laboring, he had peace. And as she curled into his side, her palm flattening over his still pounding heart, he welcomed it.

Even as a tiny voice whispered that it couldn't last.

CHAPTER EIGHTEEN

"Okay, this is good. At least I think it's good. Maybe." Sydney squinted at the computer screen and the last few lines she'd just typed. "Dammit, it's crap."

Groaning, she lifted her arms above her head, stretching. The ache in her lower back had nothing to do with pregnancy this time, but because she'd been hunched over her laptop for the last three hours, working on... She huffed out a breath, setting her computer on the couch cushion and pushing to her feet. How sad was it that she couldn't even *think* the words, much less utter them aloud?

"My urban fantasy book."

There. She'd said it.

She'd put it out there. And there was nothing wrong with it. She'd almost completed the grant for the community center, so working on her secret book didn't take time away from that job. Besides, she was a grown woman with great organizational skills. She could manage writing both at the same time. She didn't have to answer to anyone for her choices. Yet, part of her still wanted to snatch that declaration out of the atmosphere and stuff it back inside where it belonged.

But the other half stubbornly ordered herself to stop being such a chicken.

This is my dream. I don't need to make excuses, apologize or be ashamed of working on a project that makes me happy.

Sighing, she strode toward the kitchen, rubbing a hand over her belly. Jellybean—oh how Leo hated the nickname Sydney had given the baby—had been more active lately. And every flutter, every roll and poke, was a treasure. Hard to believe that in just a little over three months, she would be able to hold her little girl. Smell her baby scent. Finally see whose features she'd inherited.

Her smile wavered a bit. It'd been four weeks since Daniel had arrived on her doorstep. And three since she and Cole married at the motorcycle rally. In that time, she'd contacted Daniel's attorney and relayed the information about her marriage as well as her medical records from Dr. Prioleau. Per Sydney's request, the physician would now email over information from her appointments. Cole had advised that she keep all contact with Daniel through him and her ex's lawyer for the foreseeable future. He didn't—and she didn't either—trust Daniel not to record any conversation with her and twist it to bolster his future case. If someone had asked her even five weeks ago if Daniel would be capable of that kind of subterfuge, she would've disagreed. But now?

She frowned, filling the teakettle and setting it on the stove. That she and Daniel had come to this saddened her. Their divorce had been relatively amicable, and she'd hoped that their co-parenting would be the same. She hated that their relationship had turned so contentious.

The front door opened, jerking her from her thoughts. Then Cole entered.

Three weeks, she'd been his wife. Three weeks, she'd been his lover.

So, she should be used to that beautiful, masculine face. That tall, muscled, wiry body.

But even now, her breath snagged in her throat. Her pulse skipped and raced. Pinpricks of awareness danced down her bare arms and spine. Arousal spilled through her like the hot tea that boiled on the stove.

She turned and headed toward the cabinet for a cup. Not that removing Cole from her direct line of sight did anything for the tightening of her nipples or the hollow ache between her thighs. Jesus, the man should be locked up for her safety. She'd read about pregnant women experiencing a boost in their sexual drive, but this was ridiculous. Besides, she suspected this persistent and deep need for him had nothing to do with hormones and everything to do with him. And her reaction to him.

But the question that frightened her most—could she get over it? Would a time come that just looking at him—inhaling his earthy scent, staring into his whiskey eyes—wouldn't leave her hot, hungry and…unsatisfied?

As much as the question frightened her, the answer scared her more.

So, she chose not to dwell on it.

She opened the cabinet door, but before she could retrieve a mug, a hard chest pressed against her back and a long, muscled arm reached over her head and nabbed one. Her favorite "Not today, Mugglefucker" Harry Potter cup. She ignored the flutter of butterfly wings in her stomach. The baby. That was the baby.

"What're you doing?" Cole lightly scolded. "You know you're supposed to be taking it easy and definitely not stretching your arms above your head."

He moved around her and removed a tea bag from the box. The kettle whistled, and he poured the steaming water into the cup with the bag. She stood back, watching him. And trying not to… She shook her head. *Can't go there.* Yet, when he constantly did these sweet, thoughtful things, as if they were just second nature, she slid closer and closer to *there*.

Which presented a huge problem. Because Cole was the definition of heartbreak. The certainty of that grew with each pass-ing day. Her stomach had grown a little bigger in the past three weeks, and unless they were having sex, Cole didn't touch her stomach. Barely even looked at it.

She understood why. Panic had to be setting in. Even know-ing that Dr. Prioleau deemed her pregnancy normal with no complications so far probably did nothing to lessen his anxiety. After all, Tonia's appointments had been the same. He was dis-tancing himself from her; she felt it. Except for when they were naked, and he was inside her. Then, she'd never felt as connected to another person. Not even Daniel. Still… That didn't mean Cole's pulling away didn't hurt.

Especially when she needed him to want her just as much as she wanted him.

She had to guard her heart. Not just for her sake, but also for her daughter's.

Stuffing her wayward—and frankly, depressing—thoughts into the lockbox where she stored all her worries and fears, she smirked. "That's an old wives' tale. I'm *pretty* sure Dr. Prioleau said I should continue to be active. And I think she would file getting a cup of tea under 'active.'"

"Smart-ass," he grumbled. He hiked his chin in the direc-tion of the living room, a smile flirting with his mouth. "I'll bring this in."

She returned to the couch, and he followed, waiting until she was settled before handing her the tea. Blowing across the top of it, she stared down into the mug.

"What's this?"

She glanced up, horrified to see her laptop in Cole's hands. No. Horrified to see her laptop in his hands as he read the doc-ument she'd stupidly left open.

"Nothing." She quickly set the tea on the coffee table and snatched the computer from him. Heart pounding, she mini-mized the novel and closed the top. The whole mantra she'd repeated to herself moments earlier about not being embarrassed or ashamed jumbled in her head.

"Nothing, huh?" He arched an eyebrow. "Scavengers on souped-up ATVs and undead carnivores. What? Are you writing a grant proposal for *The Walking Dead*, now?"

She flinched.

"Whoa, whoa. Wait." He shifted on the couch, leaning forward, a frown marring his brow and concern darkening his amber eyes. "What was that about? I was only kidding."

She pinched the bridge of her nose, briefly closing her eyes. "I'm sorry." She dropped her hand, meeting his gaze. "I guess I'm a little...oversensitive about..." Not able to say the words to him—because a part of her still didn't trust opening herself up to ridicule—she waved in the direction of the laptop.

But she should've known Cole wouldn't just leave it at that.

"What is that, exactly?" he pressed.

"You read enough to guess what it is," she hedged, reaching for her tea again. Anything to deflect attention.

But he clasped her hand, wrapping his fingers around hers. "Sydney."

She scoffed, yanking her hand free and retrieving her tea before he could stop her again. "It's nothing. Stop making such a big deal out of it," she said, grasping for flippancy and landing on irritability.

"Then why are you making it one?" he asked quietly. "And why does the fact that you're working on a sci-fi book embarrass you?"

"Urban fantasy," she mumbled the correction. Then set the tea down again. Damn. At this rate, she would never get to drink it. Well, not before it lost all its heat. "I'm not embarrassed because I'm writing an urban fantasy novel. It's you knowing that I'm working on it that I'm...uncomfortable with."

Cole studied her for several silent moments. "Daniel."

She grimaced and glanced away, unable to hold his unwavering stare. "Yes. No." She blew out a breath, her hand fluttering in a nervous gesture. "I mean, it's my fault, too. It was my responsibility to make my needs known. But it was just easier not to."

"Remember when I asked you if it was a habit to accept the blame for others' bad behavior? I also said it was one you needed to break. Baby girl—" he covered the hand that bunched the front of her skirt, halting the restless action "—if Daniel made you feel so embarrassed about sharing this with him, then that's on him, not you. He must've done something to instill that in you. The blame is squarely on him if his wife couldn't trust him with something important to her. You hid it from him, Sydney. And I know that because you're still hiding it. That's his shame, not yours. But I'm quickly coming to learn that your ex isn't big on owning his shit. So, tell me about this." He waved toward the laptop. "Trust me, baby girl."

How did he dig right to the heart of the matter? How did he…*see* her so clearly, but couldn't do the same for himself? Daniel had harmed her. And the emotional bruise had been so deep, she'd hidden part of herself away, afraid of being injured again. It was lonely living like that. And she didn't want to be that person—afraid to trust, fearful of rejection—any longer. At least, not with this.

She parted her lips, but nothing came out. Apparently being brave didn't just happen because you wanted it to. Licking her lips, she swallowed. Tried again. Forced herself to stop being such a chicken.

"In college, I started a book," she said, finally. "It began as fan fiction for *Resident Evil*, but I kept expanding it until it was my own world, characters and story line. I was excited about it. I was proud of it." A faint echo of that exhilaration and pleasure rippled through her. "I enjoyed grant writing, but the novel… It was my creative outlet, and as the world and the plot solidified, I started to dream about one day submitting it to publishers. I've always read books—it's one of my joys—but I never allowed myself to envision seeing my book next to the authors I admired."

She lifted her gaze to Cole's face and glimpsed…what? Pity? Patronization? Humor? What would've been worst out of that trio? Didn't matter, because she didn't have to choose. His amber eyes held none of those. Just patience and understanding. No judgment. It bolstered her confidence to continue.

"One day not too long after we were married, I told Daniel about the book and shared a couple of chapters with him." The memory of that impulsive decision still retained the power to burn her cheeks with humiliation and hurt. "He read them, then complimented me on my effort and initiative, but said that I was wasting my time on foolish projects. He told me to focus on the grant writing because I was good at it, and it would earn me money."

"Insensitive fucker."

"It's just his—" She cut off the reflexive excuse she'd been about to make for Daniel. But then she frowned, remembering how his dismissive, thoughtless response had been a *shitty thing* to do, and snapped, "Yes, he was. He never asked about my dreams, about my hopes, my inspiration. Even if what I wrote was crap, he never encouraged me to improve. Hell, he's a teacher, that's what he's supposed to do. He could support and inspire his students, but not his own wife. For years, I didn't write after that. I did what he suggested. Put it aside. Was afraid to try again. All because I trusted the wrong person with my dreams."

"Are you willing to trust again?" Cole asked, tangling his fingers with hers and gripping tight. As if he were attempting to infuse courage into her through physical contact.

The "no" leaped on her tongue, hot and immediate. But before it could burst past her lips, she trapped it. Could she? She'd told Cole about the book of her heart, something she hadn't discussed with anyone. But could she take this last step and risk another rejection from another husband?

Cole isn't Daniel.

No, he has even more power to devastate me.

*Go shop for those big girl drawers and pull them on. And stop being
so damn dramatic while you're at it.*

Screw you.

Oh wonderful. Now she was arguing with herself. And losing.

"Okay," she murmured. Before she could change her mind,
she snatched up the computer, powered it back up and set it on
Cole's thighs. Then she rose from the couch and strode toward
the front door.

"Where are you going?"

"For a walk." She threw him a narrowed glance. "And don't
try to tell me I should be taking it easy. A walk will be good
for me, and I can't sit in this house while you read my book."

The corner of his mouth twitched, but he wisely didn't attempt to convince her to stay. "Be careful," he said.

She nodded and, opening the door, headed outside. For the
next hour, she strolled around the beautiful, quiet area that included several rental cottages, along with the buildings belonging to the Dennisons. The late summer afternoon ambled into
early evening, but the sun still spilled its rays over the rich green
yards, filtering through the trees. Peace wrapped around her
like a comforting blanket, and as she stood at the end of Cole's
driveway, peering at the majestic mountains beyond, she gently rubbed her belly.

"I've made some mistakes in my life, jellybean," she said, and
smiled at the little poke that could've been a foot or hand. "But
despite all my initial doubts, moving back here isn't one of them.
I've done right by you in this." As if agreeing, her stomach lifted
in another nudge, and Sydney laughed. Anyone passing by might
wonder why she was laughing to herself, but she didn't care.

As she turned to the house and started up the walkway, that
peace started to ebb, and anxiety waltzed in.

"You can't hang out here all night," she grumbled, march-

ing up the sidewalk to the small porch. "Whatever he's going
to say, he's going to say. And you can take it."

With those determined words ringing in the air, she twisted
the knob and entered the house.

"I wondered how long you were going to stand out there,"
Cole murmured, glancing up from the laptop.

She scrutinized his shuttered gaze and unsmiling face, her
heart thudding against her rib cage. Suddenly, her tongue felt
thick in her mouth and she could barely swallow. *Say anything!
Tell me!*

"There are two things I now know for certain," he stated,
his voice even. A little too even. "One, your ex is a complete
asshole. And two..." He shook his head, and for the first time
since she reentered the house, his eyes softened and a note of
reverence colored his voice. "Baby girl, you're brilliant. You're
fucking brilliant, and I suspect Daniel recognized it and tried
to dim that dazzling light so you wouldn't leave him. He was
afraid you wouldn't need him."

Placing the laptop on the cushion beside him, he stood and
crossed the room. Which was good. Because she couldn't move,
stunned by his passionate, husky words.

You're fucking brilliant.

...tried to dim that dazzling light...

Tears stung her eyes, and she squeezed her eyes shut against
them. Against that gleam in his eyes that had her longing to do
foolish, reckless things like throw her arms around him and beg
him to let her into his heart...to love her.

Because, God help her, she loved him.

As hard as she'd tried to guard her heart, she'd failed.

She'd loved him as a friend. And now she loved this broken,
tortured and walled-off man with the heart of the woman who'd
experienced loss, disappointments, heartaches. A woman who
should know better.

But when he'd put aside his own pain to make sure she wasn't alone at her doctor's appointment… When he'd never been embarrassed about being seen with the town black sheep… When he'd offered his name, his home and his future to protect her and her baby… Each instance of sacrifice, of kindness, of vulnerability had chipped away at her resolve until he'd slipped inside her heart before she'd even been aware.

Now it was too late.

And call it woman's intuition, a sixth sense or just plain superstition, she knew she would pay for that mistake.

"You going to give me those eyes, baby girl?" he whispered. "I need them."

No. Because then you'll see I betrayed our bargain. And you'll run faster.

After a moment, she did as he asked. But not before granting herself a much-needed pause to put her shields back in place. Better than leaving herself so vulnerable to him that she might as well be standing there naked with her arms open, her chest unprotected. No, as much as she loved him, she still didn't trust him with the heart that now belonged to him.

"Good," Cole softly praised. "I need you to look at me, so you see I'm telling you the truth. You're a grant writer, and I don't doubt a fine one. But that's not all you are. Because what I just read? You deserve to be on a shelf in a bookstore, your name right next to your favorite bestsellers. And if you want to pursue it by yourself, I'll support you one hundred percent. Or if you want my help, I'll give it to you and still support you one hundred percent. Because you're that damn good."

Relief spiraled through her, and she clutched his forearms, leaning forward until her forehead pressed against his pectoral muscle. Quick on the heels of the relief, though, surged an indescribable joy laced with equally sharp pain. Joy because of obvious reasons. She hadn't been expecting his reaction. Even though she'd trusted him with her book, there'd remained a tiny bit of her that had anticipated the same reaction she'd received from Daniel. To receive just the opposite from a man she respected and admired? Yeah, her knees wobbled with happiness.

But the pain? The pain because his reaction, his praise and unconditional offer of help, only solidified that she loved him.

And she was going to let him break her heart.

"Thank you," she whispered.

"I'm only speaking the truth." He cupped the back of her neck, his other hand smoothing over her hair. She sensed more than felt his lips brush over the crown of her head, but the caress still hummed through her like a plucked cord. "Thank you for sharing it with me. For sharing *you* with me."

She couldn't say anything that wouldn't divulge just how much she yearned for that which he couldn't give her. Something like, *If you'd only ask for all of me, I'd gladly give it.* Since she didn't dare utter that, she settled for pressing her lips to his chest. Right over his barricaded heart.

A growl vibrated against her mouth. His fingers tangled in her hair, gripping the curls. "I'm being sensitive and supportive here, and you're not letting me."

"You can be sensitive and supportive," she said, then bit the dense muscle through his white dress shirt. "And naked."

"Fuck," he snapped, pulling on her hair and tugging her head back. A moan escaped her, and she arched deeper into his tall frame. "There's going to come a time when just the scent of you," he buried his head in the crook between her neck and shoulder, his heated breath moist against her skin, "doesn't make me hard."

"Is that what you want?" She stared up at the ceiling, her heart lodged in her throat. Right where he placed a hot, open-mouthed kiss.

He lifted his head, stared down at her with solemn eyes and damp, sensual lips. "It's what I need," he rasped. "But not what I want."

The answer was a double-edged sword, and it sliced her both ways. His mind and heart warred with his body. For now, with her blood simmering in her veins, pooling between her thighs, she'd take it. Take him.

Lifting to her toes, she nipped his bottom lip, then sucked on it. His grip on her hair and neck tightened, and when she would've drawn back, he didn't allow it. Instead, his mouth covered hers, his tongue taking possession of hers. This. Oh God, *this* she would never get tired of. Like him, she doubted there would come a time when she would. Because his taste, how he mastered every one of her responses, how he seemed to intuit every caress that she needed—they were every bit as addictive as the indescribable pleasure he bestowed upon her.

Being seen.

It was her Achilles' heel.

Submerging every thought but the heated power under her palms, she met him, thrust for thrust. Until the times—like now—where she just surrendered. Let him take the lead. Let him tug her under with his hungry licks and sucks. Let him be her guide on a sexual adventure into an adult theme park where he was the roller coaster, Ferris wheel and fun house rolled into one.

And damn, did she want to ride him.

She gripped his shoulders, hiking herself higher against him, pressing tighter. Opening wider, granting him more access to the only place she could—her body. With a dark rumble, he tore his mouth free of hers, scattering hard kisses to her cheeks, jaw, throat. His teeth grazed the line of her shoulder before lightly clamping down, marking her with lips and tongue. She tilted her head back, blinking up at the ceiling as molten desire poured through her in a sinuous glide.

Him. She'd been created for him. Like a switch, she came alive in an unprecedented way—an instinctive, primal way. And he was the source.

"Off," he ordered, fisting the bottom of her top and hauling it upward.

She shot her arms in the air, and as soon as the shirt cleared her head, she attacked the buttons on his. One after the other, she freed them, yanking and snatching until his wide, muscled chest was bared to her like the perfect gift.

"So beautiful," Cole murmured, cupping her bra-covered breasts, whisking his thumbs back and forth over the straining nipples. For a moment, she paused, staring down at those large hands on her, enjoying the sight almost as much as the heat racing through her like lightning.

She briefly closed her eyes, shivering from the firm strokes to her flesh. Savoring them. But greed rose, swift and demanding, and she flattened her hands on his ridged abdomen. In her head, she could admit she'd become somewhat obsessed with his body, with touching it. And with knowing that Cole seemed to welcome every caress like a big cat basking under a hot summer sun. She licked her lips, imagining tracing each rung of muscle with her mouth. Feeling those muscles flex under her tongue. *Later.* That promise to herself granted her the strength to refocus and smooth her palms up his torso, over his chest and shoulders and down his arms, taking the shirt with her.

A fine thread of desperation wound through the lust, lending her movements an urgency that hadn't appeared in the previous times they'd been together. Determined to ignore that *tick-tick* in her head, like a clock slowly counting down the time, she retraced the same path. Up his arms, over his shoulders and down his chest until the heels of her palms scraped the small brown discs of his nipples. His big body shivered, and she repeated the caress, rubbing, circling…then bringing her tongue into play.

She moaned just as his own moan vibrated under her mouth, his hands tangling in her hair. The flavor of him—rich, sharp, tempered with a sweet, fresh scent like cold water—filled her, and she lapped at his skin, thirsty and unable to quench it. She got lost in him. Capturing him between her teeth and tugging, then licking, sucking the sting away—these became her reason for existence. Her world. Hard fingertips massaged her scalp, pressing her tighter to him. Each firm twist or pull demanded she stop teasing and give him more.

Which she obeyed.

Because that desperation, it hadn't dissipated no matter how hard she'd tried to shove it out of her mind. It goaded her, and inflamed the need to mark him, force him to feel her—remember her. Here, in this moment, she wanted to possess him...be possessed in return.

Abandoning the stiff tip, she slid her mouth over to the neglected one. She worried it, drawing it between her lips and flicking her tongue over it, hauling one groan after another from him. Pleasure pounded within her like a bass drum, strong, resounding, reaching all parts of her. Especially her achy, wet sex. She clenched her thighs around the empty throbbing, but experience assured her this wouldn't alleviate it. Nothing could do that but his cock buried inside her, filling her. Completing her.

She trailed her lips down his chest, between the ripple of his abs, pausing to trace each ridge of muscle. Slowly, she sank to her knees, hands falling to the thin belt looped through his suit pants. With suddenly uncoordinated fingers, she released it, jerking open the tab of his pants, too.

"Sydney." Cole cupped her shoulders, smoothing his hands up her neck to her face, tipping it up to meet his bright amber gaze.

"Are you going to stop me?" She didn't look away as she continued lowering his zipper and tugging his pants down until they hung loose on his slim hips. When his only response was to clench his jaw, his lips flattening into a hard, carnal line, she dipped her head, nuzzling first one line then the other of the vee that disappeared into his black boxer briefs. "Are you going to let me take you, Cole? Or are you going to be too much of a gentleman to fuck my mouth?" she whispered, yanking on the front of his underwear until the swollen tip of his erection popped free.

Humming low in her throat, she brushed a caress over the

small slit at the top. A barely there kiss. His hands shifted from her cheeks to her hair, his grip tighter, rougher than earlier.

That was all the answer she needed.

Her lips parted over the head, taking him inside. Heat bloomed in her belly, sending tendrils to all points north and south. She'd had him in her sex, but this… This almost rivaled that in intimacy. Though she knelt before him in a submissive position, she'd never felt more powerful. Especially when his fingertips dug into her scalp and his hips jerked. Especially when his breath hissed out. She, curling her tongue around him, sucking and licking, had him at her mercy. And as often as she'd been swept along by his fierce passion, feeling like a leaf carried away on furious rapids, it was absolutely heady.

Hooking her fingers into the band of his boxers, she yanked, baring all of him. And she took swift, full advantage. He was heated steel in her hand, and as she fisted the thick bottom half of his dick, she couldn't help but trace the light blue veins that traveled the long, wide column. Up, up, up to the tip again, where she swallowed him down, taking as much of him as she could. And what she couldn't, she pumped in a steady, tight rhythm.

"Goddamn, baby girl," he said, voice low. Pained. But she was achingly familiar with that agonized quality. It mirrored the one that he ripped out of her when he feasted on her. Now it was her turn…and his. "Your mouth. So sweet. Fuck, I can't even look at you sucking on my cock like you've never had better." Then he belied that statement by tracing a finger along her stretched lips. "Beautiful. So damn beautiful," he grated, returning his hand to her head. His hold tautened, firmed. "Give it to me then. Take me like you mean it. Like you want it."

His words unlocked something deep inside her. Freed her. Raising higher onto her knees, the last of her inhibitions disintegrated. She did just as he'd bid. Took him as she'd always fantasized. She left no part of him undiscovered—not the underside of the sensitive flared tip, not the pulsing, hot stalk, not the wide base or even the heavy sac of his testicles. And when she sucked him in again, not stopping until he nudged the narrow channel of her throat, she exulted in his snarl of pleasure. She repeated it, allowing him to breach her, claiming another of those dark rumbles as her own.

"Enough," he barked, holding her head still and dragging free of her mouth.

Before she could protest, he grabbed her arms, yanking her to her feet. Then steadying her with a hand to the back of her neck and his hungry mouth on hers when she swayed. She wrapped her legs around him as he lifted her and carried her to the couch. Once more, she found herself off-kilter when he abruptly broke off their kiss and jerked down her skirt and panties. Their breath—hers soft and his harsh—broke on the air as he removed his wallet from his pants before pushing them down and off. In seconds, he liberated a condom from the billfold, and a "We don't need that," leaped to her tongue.

But at the last second, she caged it. Just as she'd done the other times they'd had sex in these last three weeks. If they were a normal man and wife, they wouldn't need the protection. But they weren't normal. She was pregnant with another man's baby, and he was still in love with his dead wife—his true wife. So no, she didn't ask him to come inside her bare. Even if the condom left her feeling as if she would never be good enough for him. She tried to uproot the seed of resentment it sowed.

Instead, she focused on his big hands as he sheathed himself. Allowed the passion to overwhelm everything else, silence it. Which, with a very naked Cole standing before her, fisting his dick, was an easy thing to do.

Jesus, he was gorgeous.

Clothed, the man exuded a leashed power and vitality that hummed like a low-level current. But naked, without the restraints of that civility? He nearly rocked her back on her heels with all that visceral sexuality and strength. He was a sleek, formidable beast who'd shaken off domestication, and the way he studied her from underneath those whiskey-colored, hooded eyes… She barely managed the inane urge to bare her neck and let him take her down.

"How do you want it?" He molded his palm to her breast, squeezing. "What's most comfortable for you?"

He never failed to ask her this question. No matter how hot they burned—and God, did they raze each other to the ground—her comfort was always his priority. How she wished that didn't squeeze her heart like a vise.

"I want to look at you," she said, softly repeating the request she'd given him the first time they'd had sex. *I need to look into your eyes and know that you're here with me and only me.* She sank her teeth into her bottom lip, trapping those too-revealing words inside.

Cole nodded and sank to the couch. Tangling his fingers with hers, he eased her down and over his thighs until she straddled him. Their gazes locked; he guided his cock to her folds before sliding between them, nudging her clit. She gasped at the electric strike of pleasure, her head tipping back on her shoulders. Her hips rolled as if of their own volition, seeking more of that brain-numbing ecstasy. Her breath burst out of her on a ragged whimper, and she didn't wait for him to notch his erection at her entrance. Needy, hungry, she lifted and sank down on him.

Once more, she gasped at the stretching, the almost-too-much filling of her sex. They'd been together like this so many times over the past few weeks, but he never failed to steal her breath with how he branded her. Completed her. Not just physically. But in a place so deep inside, she feared ever being able to root him out.

"Ride me, baby girl," Cole ordered, clutching her hips, drawing her off of him, then slowly, so slowly, pushing her back down. His dusky skin drew taut, his mouth pulling into a tight line. "Fuck me and ruin us both."

Ruined? She leaned forward, parting her lips over the base of his neck and pressing a hot kiss there. Already there. Ruined for any other man. Ruined for any future that didn't include him. Ruined from the person she'd been before returning to Rose Bend—before falling in love with him.

If only she could wreck him in the same way.

Wrapping her arms around his shoulders, she rose and fell over him. Leisurely, at first, cherishing each drag of his cock over her sensitive, quivering sex. But as her desire spiked, as he hit a place high inside her with each thrust, her pace quickened, roughened. He whispered encouragement and dirty praises against her throat, urged her to take, ride, fuck with the hard grip of his hands. Pushed her closer to the crumbling edge of release as he lowered his head and caught a beaded nipple between his lips and sucked.

"Cole." His name cracked on the air between them just as she did. Right down the middle.

With a keening cry, she bucked and spasmed, her sex clamping down on his cock as she came, rocking and tumbling like the wildest storm. Beneath her, Cole pounded into her, prolonging the pleasure that threatened to tear her into pieces. Finally, he stiffened, and his flesh throbbed within her. A sob escaped her as she collapsed against his chest. She trembled, and his large body vibrated with those quakes.

Only as they quieted, and she eased off into an exhausted sleep, did she feel the almost phantomlike caress over her belly. Maybe she imagined it. Maybe her mind was playing tricks on her.

Either way, she treasured that fleeting touch. Clasped it to her heart, and as the darkness finally claimed her, so did a trace of hope.

CHAPTER NINETEEN

As Sydney strode down the sidewalk toward city hall, she couldn't hold back the smile curling her lips. Even if it made her look like a grinning idiot. Nope, she honestly didn't care. She'd completed the grant and forwarded it to Cole, and though he would've most likely already seen the email, she wanted to celebrate with him. This grant would make his dream of the community center a reality—and she had full faith that the funding would come through. And her husband definitely would.

Her husband.

God, it still seemed weird saying that, even if only to herself. Weird, new, but…so good.

Smile widening, she approached the front steps of city hall, but paused as her phone rang. Cursing to herself, she hiked the picnic basket containing her lunch for Cole on her hip and reached into her bag for the phone. After some juggling, she removed it from the inside pocket and glanced down at the screen.

And froze.

Daniel.

Her heart thudded. Why would he call her? She'd made it very clear all of their communication needed to take place through their attorneys. Did she answer it? Did she let it go to voice mail? The questions whirled, then, giving her head a hard, short shake, she hit answer and quickly thumbed through to the recording app on her phone.

She'd talk to him, but that didn't mean she trusted him.

Hitting the red button, she said into the phone, "Daniel."

"Hello, Sydney. How are you?" he greeted, and her stomach dipped nervously at that modulated tone.

Then anger flashed through her because of the nerves. She was through being intimidated and afraid.

"Fine." Her fingers tightened around the phone. "But I'm sure this isn't a casual call. Not that you should be calling me in the first place. Are you with your attorney?"

"No, I just left his office, actually," he said. A pause followed his reply, and a thousand questions crowded into that space. But she sank her teeth into her bottom lip, trapping them. He'd reached out to her; she wasn't going to prod him to speak. "I told him that I changed my mind about suing for full custody. I'm dropping the suit."

Shock assaulted her, and she grasped for the stair railing, steadying herself. She couldn't speak. Could barely squeeze a breath past her constricted lungs.

Surely, he hadn't said… No, he couldn't have…

"What?"

"Yes, Sydney," he repeated, voice softer. "I'm not suing for full custody." And because she still couldn't shove anything out beyond that tortured one word, he continued, "My attorney will be contacting yours shortly, but I've told him you will have primary physical custody, and I would still like to share joint custody that would go into effect once our daughter is old enough to travel out of state. A time that would fall under your discretion. Until she's old enough, though, I would also like the freedom to travel to Massachusetts to visit her at least monthly on agreed-upon times. We'll still have to work out other decisions such as child support, but…" Silence beat between them for several seconds. The pounding of it as loud as her heart. "But I won't try and take the baby away from you."

Though joy, relief and disbelief screamed in her head like a howling gale, she didn't speak. Not yet. A part of her didn't trust this sudden turnaround. Daniel had hurt her. To the core. Yes, he'd believed he was only doing what was best for their child. But his idea of best—stealing her daughter from her and installing another woman as her child's mother—made it difficult for her to forgive him for his treatment of her.

"Why the sudden change of heart?" she challenged, her voice harsh. She didn't care. "Is it my new marital status? You realized this fight wouldn't be as easy as you assumed?"

His sigh reached her ears, and she braced herself for his lecture on being "too emotional." But he shocked her by murmuring, "I deserve that. I do. And I would be lying if I said that had nothing to do with me considering this situation more carefully. But I have to be honest, Sydney…" He hesitated, and a frown creased her brow. Daniel didn't do uncertain, and something about this pause smacked of it. "When I came to see you, I didn't expect you to push back. I thought you would see the validity of my arguments and decide to return to Charlotte."

"You didn't expect me to stand up to you and not cave to your bullying," she corrected, anger kindling inside her. "You expected me to be that young twenty-year-old who always bent to your 'wisdom,' your wants and demands. But I'm not that girl anymore, Daniel. I haven't been for a long time."

"I see that…now," he conceded. "After returning home, and then finding out you'd moved on, too, I had to take a hard look at myself. And… And I wasn't happy with who I saw. You called me a bully who was penalizing you for not falling into line. For leaving me. You were right. I hadn't forgiven you, and though I did—and part of me still does—believe you and the baby would have a better life in Charlotte, that doesn't excuse me using my connections and the law to threaten you into compliance. I'm sorry for that, Sydney."

She couldn't say it was okay. Yes, he'd realized he'd been wrong, but that didn't make his actions anywhere near "okay." So instead she said, "Thank you for the apology, Daniel. I appreciate it."

"Maybe I didn't want to acknowledge that we were growing apart. Or that you were growing into your own person, your own woman, and I didn't want to accept it. But you are that woman, and I have to respect your decisions. I have to respect *you*, Sydney. That said," he huffed a breath, and she could easily imagine him squaring his shoulders and lifting his chin in that confident way she'd always admired, "I also have to accept that as our baby's mother, you would always place her welfare and safety first. And if it's your choice to live in Rose Bend, I'll work with you as long as you work with me. I want my daughter to know me as her father," he whispered.

"She will, Daniel," Sydney replied just as softly. "I've never had any intention of cutting you out of her life or to have someone else fill that role. She will be loved by her parents and be blessed to have more people in her life to protect and adore her like Cole and your fiancée. Who," she added, firming her voice, "I really need to meet in the near future."

"And I need to do the same with Cole—and not as your attorney."

She chuckled. "Deal." Inhaling a breath, she slowly let it go—determined to do the same with the resentment. "Thank you, Daniel. You're going to make a wonderful father."

"You're already a wonderful mother," he praised.

They ended the call, and Sydney stood in front of city hall, clasping her cell to her chest. Holy hell, that happened. An effervescent joy bubbled inside her and, not caring if it made her appear crazy, she laughed. She'd come here to tell Cole about completing the grant, and now she could add to that news that this custody battle was over.

Opening her eyes, she swept her gaze over the building before her with its town and state flags, then surveyed the tree-lined street behind her with its scattering of benches. Took in the people who called out to one another or stopped to chat. She waved back to one who noted her gaze and held up a hand in greeting.

And for the first time since crossing the town limits weeks ago, she felt like she belonged. Here. In this town. In this community. With her friends and maybe, just maybe, even her family.

She was finally home.

She hiked the picnic basket on her hip, practically floated up the front steps and pulled open one of the double doors at the top. She moved into the cool lobby, the scent of pine and lemon teasing her nose. The last time she'd been here, her one objective had been getting to Cole, and she hadn't paid any attention to her surroundings. But now, she took in the gleaming, dark brown tiles flecked with gold and the crystal chandelier that shone brightly even in early afternoon. While the piece wouldn't have been out of place in a ballroom, it had been donated by the family of one of the town's founders many years ago. So it remained, lending elegance to the wood security desk, glass billboard case with notes and flyers about upcoming town events and closed office doors.

Though Cole's office resided up the staircase on the second floor, Sydney headed toward the security desk. He hadn't been at his law firm, and when she'd called his cell, it'd gone straight to voice mail. Taking a chance he was here, she'd brought her impromptu celebratory lunch to city hall, hoping to surprise him and convince him to eat with her. Her stomach did a flip and roll as she neared the security desk. Would he be happy to see her? Or irritated that she'd just shown up unannounced? Or indifferent?

Stop it. You're celebrating, so don't be a killjoy.

She mentally shook her head. Since she'd shared her book with him last week, that distance she'd been sensing between them had started to disappear. They were still as hot for each other as ever. That hadn't changed. And it offered her a tentative hope that their physical connection would strengthen their emotional one. She rested a hand on her stomach, remembering his sweet caress days ago. Oh yes. She clutched onto that, too.

Did it make her pathetic that she clasped those...lifelines so tightly? Optimistic, pathetic. Sometimes she swore they were just two sides of the same coin.

"Good afternoon," the older man greeted from behind the desk, his smile lifting up the ends of his bushy, gray mustache. "How can I help you?"

"Hi," she replied, giving him her own smile back. "I wanted to see if Cole Dennison was in. I'm his wife."

"I know who you are," he said, winking. "I was at your reception. Shoot, the whole town was." He chuckled. "I'm afraid you just missed him, though. Cole left for an appointment about fifteen minutes ago. Can I leave a message for him?" He glanced down at the picnic basket on her arm. "Like how he screwed the pooch by missing out on lunch with his pretty Mrs.? Of course, I don't mind being a substitute." He grinned, granting her an unobstructed view of his perfectly white, straight dentures.

She laughed, her disappointment momentarily capsized by his shameless flirting. "Oh, you're good. Your wife must have a time with you." She arched a brow, glancing down meaningfully at the gold ring on his left hand.

He scoffed. "We've been married forty years as of last month. Three children and eight grandkids. She knows better than to question me." He leaned closer, humor glittering in his blue eyes. "Just don't tell her I said that, okay? Forty years, three children and eight grandkids, and she *still* scares me."

Sydney's laughter echoed in the lobby, and she clapped a hand over her mouth, trying to contain the loud sound. The security guard, whose stitched name tag identified him as Bert, chuckled.

Once she had her amusement under control, she nodded. "Deal. I tell you what, though." She set the basket on top of the security desk. "Since I won't need this after all, enjoy yourself. And if you haven't eaten lunch yet, maybe surprise your wife and earn some brownie points."

Surprise and delight filled his gaze. "Well, that's really sweet of you. I think I will." He moved the basket behind the desk. "Thank you, Mrs. Dennison. Very much."

"It's Sydney. And you're very welcome. Enjoy."

"We will. And I'll let Cole know you dropped by."

"Thank you." Waving goodbye, she crossed the lobby and stepped back out into the summer sunshine.

Well, that was that. At least she could make Bert and his wife happy. Her mouth quirked. Plan B then—dinner. Thoughts turning to what she would need to pick up at the grocery store, she started down the steps.

"Well, if it isn't the new Mrs. Dennison," a voice drawled from behind her.

Fuck.

Sydney mouthed the curse, grimacing. Sending up a short prayer for patience and quickly reminding herself that orange was most definitely *not* the new black, she pivoted to face Jenna Landon.

Sydney hadn't seen Jenna since the first night of the motorcycle rally, and in a town the size of Rose Bend that had been a minor miracle. One she'd thanked God for. But now, facing the other woman—who appeared as flawless as always with her sleek auburn hair, slender frame in a body-hugging green dress and nude heels—her miracle had left town.

Forcing a polite smile to her face, Sydney refused to peep down at her own less…sophisticated form clad in a white maternity tank and one of her favorite long, floral skirts. In deference to the heat and her hormones, she'd gathered her hair into a bun at the top of her head. Yeah, Jenna looked like she'd come straight from the country club and Sydney could've been playing in the country.

Oh well. Her flip-flops were comfortable.

But as the other woman swept a condescending survey down Sydney's body and a faint sneer curled the corner of her mouth, embarrassment and irritation surged hot and swift in Sydney's chest. Screw her. Sydney's chin notched up and she returned that sneer with an arched eyebrow. This wasn't high school, even though Jenna hadn't seemed to figure that out yet.

"Hello, Jenna. How're you?" *I could give negative fucks, but let's just pretend that's not true.* Even uttering those words in her head helped lend warmth to her smile.

"Oh, I'm just fine," Jenna drawled. "I saw the basket you left behind in there." Fake sympathy dripped from her voice, her eyes glittering with a nasty glee that sent a ripple of unease tripping down Sydney's spine. "Was that for Cole? How sweet," she continued, not giving Sydney time to answer. "Too bad I saw him leave with Caroline Jacobs several minutes ago. I'm sure it was just a business meeting."

"Since they're both on the town council, I'm sure it was," Sydney replied, dryly. Ignoring the image of how Caroline had seemed surprised and a little dejected when she'd interrupted Sydney and Cole in his office weeks ago. But Cole was… Cole. What single woman—or hell, man—with a pulse wouldn't have a crush on him?

Jenna shrugged a slim, tanned shoulder. "If you say so. I was just wondering, and I'm certain I'm not the only person. Married only a month and already he's 'lunching' with other women. Not a good look, now is it?"

"You know what else isn't a good look? Gossiping. But if you have nothing better to do with your time than talk about my life, then who am I to stop your good time?" Sydney spread her arms wide, never losing her smile, although it felt brittle on her face. "Knock yourself out."

Jenna's eyes narrowed and she stepped into Sydney's personal space. All pretense of civility dropped, she once more skimmed Sydney from head to toe, her derision plain.

"You show up back here knocked up by a man who didn't want you, seeking sympathy like we all don't remember who you really are. A nobody who always thought she was better than she truly was. And somehow you convinced Cole and his family to drink the Kool-Aid. You think being pregnant and writing some worthless grant to help him save face in front of the council makes him indebted to you? It might have gotten him to marry you, but it won't keep him. There're bets going around town on how long this so-called marriage will last. I don't give it three months. Pity and gratitude will only last so long. It won't keep him from one day waking up and seeing what a mistake he's made."

"What is wrong with you?" Sydney murmured, pain at the other woman's well-placed barbs burrowing deep. Unearthing the doubts and worries that had already been sown into Sydney's heart. But damn if she would let Jenna see it. "What have I ever done to you that makes you so vicious? So spiteful?" she asked again, same as she'd done the night of the rally. She hadn't received an answer then, and she didn't expect one now. "Yes, I might have been a rebellious pain in the ass when I was younger, but I've matured, hopefully grown wiser in eight years. But you? Except for one year when you were actually human, you're still the same spoiled mean girl you always were. And for what?" Sydney huffed out a humorless chuckle. "You're beautiful, smart, wealthy, privileged. And yet, you're like a toddler whose favorite toy has been taken, and now you're throwing a fit." Sydney shook her head, and amazingly a seed of sympathy for this gorgeous yet unhappy woman wormed its way into her chest. "I'm sorry if you wanted Cole, and he didn't reciprocate those feelings. I really am. He's a good man. But I refuse to be your punching bag. Find someone else, because I'm no longer interested in the position."

Sydney started to turn and head down the stairs, but Jenna grabbed her forearm, halting her. Anger flared hot within Sydney, and she shook off the hold. *I'm pregnant*, she reminded herself. *I'm pregnant so I can't lay the mean lady out.*

"Don't put your hands on me. Ever," she bit out, narrowing her eyes on Jenna.

Crimson mottled the other woman's face, and an ugly sneer twisted her red-painted mouth. "Let's get one thing perfectly clear. If I wanted Cole, he would be mine. And there is nothing you could do about it." Sydney nearly rolled her eyes at the juvenile retort… Oh hell, screw it. She did roll them. Good and hard. Which served to enrage Jenna further if the furious glitter in her eyes was anything to judge by. "And don't you dare pity me," she spat. "You're so high and mighty when you couldn't even keep your new husband home on his wedding night. Oh yes—" she nodded, her smile cruel, vindictive "—he was seen driving all around town on the night he should've been home with his *wife*. Instead he ended up at the cemetery with the woman he really loves. And that woman isn't you. The fact that the two of you still live in that tiny, ridiculous rental cottage tells me everything I need to know about how real this marriage is and how long it will last. Cole has a huge house, beautiful and fully furnished, and he still hasn't moved you into it."

What?

Sydney flinched, unable to contain it as Jenna's revelation slammed into her with the force of a Mack truck. Cole had a house? Since when? Why hadn't he mentioned it?

Then a memory crashed into her from the wedding reception. *Where are you two living? Are you going to move into the—*

Valeria, Tonia's mother, had been about to mention something when Cole had abruptly cut her off with a terse "no." Had she been talking about this house Jenna referred to? If so, why was he hiding it? Why didn't he want…

The answer burst in her head so hard and bright, Sydney winced.

Because it'd been the house he'd shared with Tonia. The house where they'd planned to raise their child.

Pain stole her breath, nearly choking her. Blindly, she reached for the rail behind her, steadying herself before her trembling knees collapsed under her.

"Oh, this is just perfect," Jenna cooed, chuckling in malicious delight. "You didn't know about it, did you? Probably because he doesn't consider you good enough to live there. Why would he when—"

"Shut up."

The new voice, sharp and furious, had Jenna spinning around and Sydney's gaze landing on Eva Wright. The older woman stood in the doorway of city hall, her small frame stiff with the anger that lined her face and crackled in her voice. She stepped forward, the door slamming shut behind her, and advanced on Jenna. Though she had at least five inches on the older woman, Jenna shrank back, alarm flashing across her face before she assembled her expression into a polite mask that didn't fool anyone. Least of all Eva, who only glared harder.

"You're a nasty piece of work, you know that, Jenna Landon?" Eva snapped.

"Ms. Eva, I don't know what you mean…"

Eva snorted. "Don't even try it. I overheard enough of the poison you were spewing that this," she circled a finger in front of Jenna's face, "won't cut it with me. I would say you ought to be ashamed of yourself, but we both know that would be a waste of breath."

"But Ms. Eva," Jenna said, trying to placate the woman again. "I was just being honest with Sydney…"

If possible, Eva's glare burned hotter, and she nearly vibrated with anger. "It kills me when people try to wrap up their cruelty in that big bow of 'just being honest.' What would you know about honesty? Truth is given in love not spite. Something you know nothing about. You were intentionally trying to hurt this girl, and for what? To make your own petty, small existence better? Take your nice/nasty self out of here before I lose every bit of the Christianity I'm holding on to by the chin hairs."

Jenna's shoulders snapped back, her chin following suit. "You can't talk to me like that," she snarled. And if agony wasn't still throbbing inside her like a fresh wound, Sydney would've rolled her eyes. Again.

"I just did." Eva harrumphed. Holding a hand up between them, she flicked her fingers. "Now get out of here. Run home to tell your daddy what I just said. And make sure you add that maybe if he'd put a paddle to your ass you might not be the spoiled brat you are today."

Maybe it was respect for her elders that bridled Jenna's tongue. Or maybe it was a very real fear of this intimidating woman. Either way, Jenna scowled, then charged down the city hall steps, probably to do just as Eva predicted—running home to tattle to Daddy.

God, later, when it didn't hurt to breathe, Sydney would look back on this and fall out laughing. Right after she traded high fives with Eva Wright.

"Sydney. Honey," Eva murmured, moving forward and clasping Sydney's elbow. "Let me walk you to your car."

"Isn't that my line?" Sydney joked. But the hoarse tone and her inability to force a smile caused the teasing to fall flat. "She was telling the truth, wasn't she?" she asked Eva.

Before the other woman even answered, her sad gaze confessed, telling Sydney everything she needed to know. "Honey, you should be having this conversation with Cole, not me. And definitely not with Jenna Landon. Let me take you to him," she gently offered.

"No," Sydney barked. Then, immediately regretful, she softened her voice. "I'm sorry, Ms. Eva. I didn't mean to disrespect you. But no. That's okay. I can find him on my own. I... I'm going now."

"Sydney, please," Eva insisted. "You shouldn't be driving in—"

"I'm fine. Really," Sydney interrupted. Again, not intending to disrespect the older woman, but she desperately needed to leave. To get away before she crumbled right here on the city hall steps.

"Okay," Eva conceded, worry still heavy in her kind brown eyes. "But promise me you'll talk to Cole. Don't let Jenna poison what you two have."

What they had? What *did* she and Cole have? At best, a mutually beneficial arrangement. At worst... At worst a fake friendship based on secrets, half-truths and pity.

No, Jenna couldn't poison something they'd never possessed to begin with.

But instead of explaining all this to Eva, Sydney nodded, rummaging for a reassuring smile. And failing.

"I promise."

CHAPTER TWENTY

Thirty minutes after Cole received the frantic call from Eva Wright, relaying what she'd witnessed between Jenna Landon and Sydney, he pulled up outside the home he'd spent five wonderful years in with Tonia. His heart pounded, momentarily deafening him, as he opened his car door and stepped out. All the moisture fled from his mouth, and he stopped in front of the hood, for a moment, his feet frozen to the street.

He hadn't been to this house since after the funeral two years ago. Hadn't been able to cross the threshold of the home where he'd planned a future with such hope and joy. His future and his family had both been snatched away from him, and while this house stood as a cruel reminder of all that he'd lost, he hadn't been able to sell it. It was *theirs*—his and Tonia's. To get rid of it—to allow another happy family to live in it when they couldn't—felt like a betrayal. So, he'd closed it up. Except for the cleaning woman he'd hired to go through it once a month, no one entered his home.

And now the front door was wide-open. From his position on the street, he could just glimpse the mantel in the entryway with a vase of long-dead flowers.

Grief, pain and anger, welled up inside of him—so much he damn near shook with the overwhelming cascade of emotion. No one should be there. No one. Not even him.

His fury propelled him up the walk and stairs to the porch. And finally, into the house.

Memories plowed into him, and he shot out a hand, flattening it against the entryway wall to steady himself. Dragging in several deep breaths, he tried to wade through the images of him and Tonia here in this home—sharing breakfast, watching television, hosting family dinners, laughing together, preparing the nursery—and shoved off the wall. He shifted forward, his feet sliding over the hardwood floor. Movement caught his eye, and he glanced to his left, spotting Sydney standing in the large living room, studying the collection of framed photos on the mantel. Photos he'd refused to bring to the cottage.

Nothing had changed in two years. The same light blue curtains hung at the bay windows. The same couch, love seat and coffee table occupied one half of the room and a medium-sized piano sat in the other. Two small armchairs and an area rug claimed the space in front of the fireplace. It was like stepping into a time machine where a happily married couple still resided here. Loved here.

"I saw this house," she announced, as if talking to herself. But she wasn't. The tense set of her shoulders and erect line of her back telegraphed her awareness of him. "On my first day back in town, I noticed it and thought, 'That house is a home for a happy, loving, noisy family.' Instead, it's like a museum," Sydney murmured. "Or a shrine."

That anger sparked again. Thank God.

"What are you doing here? How did you get in?"

She didn't turn around when she answered him but continued to stare at the photos. "Leo. Don't be mad at her, though. I lied and told her you gave me permission to come here. You should've seen how happy she was when she turned over the key and offered me directions. I think your family believes this marriage is starting to heal you, that you'll let go of the past. But we both know that's a lie, don't we?" She shook her head. "You'll never let go."

Finally, she turned around, and again, another blow slammed into him. Though she wore a calm, composed expression, her eyes... Jesus, her eyes pierced him to his soul. All the emotion absent from her face—confusion, betrayal, fury, pain—darkened her eyes. On instinct, he shifted forward, but she moved back. Away from him. And goddamn, if that didn't stab him just as deep.

"You lied to me."

"I didn't lie to you," he objected, hating the coldness of her voice. Part of him wanted to stride over to her, clasp her to him, beg her to rage, yell, curse him. Anything but that chilly tone that gave him nothing.

But the other part... That part hungered to rage itself. To order her to leave this alone. That he didn't have to share this with her.

She arched a dark eyebrow. "Really? We're going to play the semantics game? A lie of omission is still a lie."

Impatience curled within him and he slashed a hand through the air. "This house has nothing to do with you," he snapped.

Her body flinched as if his words had struck her. Shit. He hadn't—

Scrubbing both hands over his head, he turned away, swearing softly under his breath as he paced. Remorse rushed in, swirling in his chest. *Dammit.*

Abruptly, he faced her again, his hands stretched out, palms up. "I'm sorry, Sydney. I didn't mean it like that."

Silence roared in the room. No, not silence. Pain, vibrating between them so loud it was deafening.

"You're right, though," she finally murmured. "This house

has nothing to do with me. Or else you would've told me about it before someone else did."

"Sydney," he whispered, but she continued as if she didn't hear him. Or didn't want to hear him.

"Do you know how humiliating it was to hear about a secret home you owned from Jenna Landon, of all people?" she rasped, shaking her head. For the first time since he'd entered the house, emotion leaked from her voice. Hurt, sadness. Betrayal.

"This house," he swept an arm out, indicating the living room and foyer behind them, "wasn't a secret. I just never thought—"

"Lies." Her tone hardened into a steel he'd never heard from her before. "Valeria brought it up after our wedding and you cut her off. You thought of this house. I'm willing to bet you think of it every day. And every day you made the choice to hold its existence from me, because then you wouldn't have to explain why you couldn't move me and my child into it." She laughed, the sound brittle...bitter. "Jenna was right about one thing. You had no intention of telling me about it because to you, I'm not worthy to grace these hallowed halls."

Rage swelled within him again, not at Sydney, but at the idea of her not being worthy. She was...perfect. And for her to believe otherwise? Everything in him howled to move forward, to enfold her in his arms, shelter her with his body. Protect her from those sacrilegious thoughts.

But one glance at the stiffness of her frame, as if one touch would shatter her, and he didn't give in to the impulse. One look into those beautiful but dull brown eyes, and he knew she didn't want anything from him.

"That's not true," he said instead. "Don't ever say that again."

"Okay, then." She notched her chin higher. Was she bracing herself for another verbal blow? Since when did she have to protect herself from him? "You tell me why. Why didn't you tell me about your home?"

"It's not—" He ground his teeth together, fisting his hands

at his sides. Anything to keep him from reaching for her. "It's my past. And it has nothing to do with us."

The explanation sounded inadequate to his own ears, so he wasn't surprised when her lips twisted into a humorless smile.

"The past has *everything* to do with us. It *permeates* us. This house you've held on to for two years but don't live in and won't let anyone else live in either. The baby you can't bring yourself to talk about or touch. You can't even have sex with me without a condom. It doesn't take a genius level IQ to figure out it's because Tonia was the only woman you've been with like that. You were hers first and only hers. And you're only letting me have so much of you. But I refuse to settle for those crumbs anymore."

Before he could reply—could lie—and tell her she was wrong, she shook her head, holding up a hand, palm out.

"No, I don't want to hear that I'm wrong. You wouldn't just be lying to me, you would be deceiving yourself. Cole, did it ever occur to you that I would understand?" She lowered her arm, wrapping it around herself. "Just like our wedding night, if you'd only talked to me, I would've told you I'm okay with not living here. I get it. I don't even know how comfortable I would've been making this place my home. This was yours and hers, together. A place of love and hope. I don't want to take that away, or Tonia and your son away, from you. I don't want to erase them. I don't even want to take her place in your heart. I just want you to put me next to them. Make room for me. But you won't share. You're locked inside your grief, your pain and anger. And for a little while I thought maybe being there for you...loving you, could free you. But I can't. Nothing and no one can but you."

I thought maybe being there for you...loving you, could free you. Loving you...loving you...

"No," he whispered. Then louder, hoarser. "No."

"Yes," she said, sadness darkening her eyes even more. Sadness and a firm resolve. "I love you. Even though the most foolish thing a woman can do is fall for a man who isn't willing to invest all of himself, I did it. I became that foolish woman. Oh, don't worry." Another sardonic smile dipped in weariness. "I don't expect you to return the words or the sentiment. And I'm not telling you this to emotionally blackmail you, either. It's my choice to let you know that you aren't a rebound for me. You're not just an impulsive whim. You're not just the man who gave me his name in a bargain. You're my heart, my gift. And I need someone who will see me that way, too. For so long, I've been second place in people's hearts, their Plan B. With my parents, with Daniel. Even with myself. And now you. I competed with a ghost for my parents' love for too many years to count. I won't do the same with you. Not anymore."

"Sydney, what are you saying?" he demanded, taking those steps forward that he promised himself he wouldn't. Clutching her arms when he ordered himself not to.

But she didn't wrench away. She didn't encircle him with her arms either. And only when she didn't, did he realize how much he'd come to rely on her welcoming embraces. Her warm, affectionate smiles. Her unrestrained passion. His body and his soul cried out for their return.

But his mind knew they were already gone. They were no longer his to claim.

"I'm saying I can't live in your world of fear with you. You're so afraid of what has happened, what *could* happen, that you refuse to live. To love. I adore you, Cole, but I want freedom to love and be loved in return, not just for myself, but also for my little girl. We both deserve that." She stepped back, forcing his hands to fall away. "Goodbye, Cole."

"Sydney, don't do this. Please," he pleaded. Yes. Pleaded. He didn't care. He couldn't return to the darkness, the loneliness. The emptiness. Not again.

"Oh, Cole," she breathed, pain spasming across her expression. She cradled his cheek and he turned into her hand, pressing his lips to the palm. She touched him. He shivered, hope rekindling. "Can you tell me you love me? Keep the house, I don't care. But do you love me?"

He parted his lips, prepared to shove the words out if she just wouldn't leave him. If she would stay and beat back the abyss. But the words wouldn't come. He couldn't say them. They lodged in his throat, and he choked on them.

She dropped her hand, agony flashing in her brown eyes before her lashes lowered. Shutting him out.

"Goodbye," she whispered, then walked away.

Dimly, he heard the front door shut. But he still couldn't move. Remained rooted, staring at the mantel packed with pictures of the family he'd lost.

While his mind remained fixed on the one he'd let walk away.

CHAPTER TWENTY-ONE

Sydney climbed the steps to her parents' home.

Had it only been a little less than two months since she'd returned to Rose Bend? Since she'd first shown up here on her parents' doorstep? It was like déjà vu. Only then, her heart hadn't been shattered into so many pieces they resembled grains of sand. Then, she'd been single, looking forward to the birth of her child and being a present, caring parent. Now, she was married, on her way to her second divorce and concern for her daughter was the only thing keeping her sane.

Funny how she'd returned here of all places. The inn with Leontyne and Moe would've made more sense. Or even Cecille and a tub of her favorite ice cream. But she'd left that house, that sad museum standing as a living memory to a life two years in the past, and had driven around for hours. When she returned to town, the only thing she'd wanted was her mother.

Sighing, she knocked on the door. Moments later, it opened and when her mother stood in the entryway, Sydney barely restrained the impulse to fling herself into her arms. God, how she longed to revert to that eight-year-old who could go to her mother and hug her, knowing murmured words of comfort and encouragement would be given without reserve. When was the last time she'd laid her head against her mother's shoulder and leaned on her? Too many years ago to count. Too many hurts, harsh words and disappointments inflicted to number.

"Hey, Mom," she said instead. "Can I come in?"

"Of course." Her mother stepped aside, a small frown wrinkling her brow. "Is everything okay? You look upset. Is it the baby? Is she okay?" Worry jacked her voice higher, and Sydney quickly shook her head.

"No, no, the baby's fine, Mom. I promise." Relief erased the concern from Patricia's expression, and with a nod, her mother closed the front door. "Me, on the other hand," Sydney added with a soft but bitter chuckle.

"What's going on?" Her father appeared in the foyer, still wearing his suit jacket and tie. "Sydney, the baby—"

"Is fine," she finished. "Dad, you're home from the clinic early."

And yes, she was stalling as she questioned if she'd made a mistake in coming here.

"Not really. Ever since Kelly joined the practice, I try to be home by five. But my work schedule isn't why you're here. What's going on, sweetheart?"

That did it. He hadn't called her by any endearment in years. That he did now, when she stood there, barely hanging on, so fragile she feared if she stopped moving, she might never get up again... Well, she couldn't handle it.

Tears stung her eyes, then rolled down her cheeks. She didn't try and hide them.

She was so damn tired of hiding.

"Sydney," her mother cried out, alarmed. And when her mother's arms wrapped around her, the tears flowed harder. "Oh sweetie."

How long she sobbed in her mother's embrace, she didn't know. But by the time the crying jag ebbed, and her father wordlessly pressed a handkerchief into her hand, she was seated on the couch and could breathe easier. She didn't remember her mother leading her into the living room or sitting her down, but as the exhaustion weighed down her limbs, she was thankful for it.

"I left Cole." She dropped the abrupt statement like a nuclear bomb and silently waited for the explosion. Because she fully expected one. Sighing, she rubbed her forehead, trying to relieve the headache that her crying hadn't helped. "I know you're disappointed in me. So, I might as well get it all out there."

And she confessed everything.

Daniel's threat to sue for custody. Cole's proposition and the purpose behind their marriage. Falling in love with her husband. Discovering the house. And finally, her telling him it was over.

A thick silence smothered the room, and shoulders tense, Sydney again waited for her parents to speak, to castigate her for being too impulsive, for being reckless and selfish. But as the seconds ticked by, they remained quiet. Torture. Pure torture. Why didn't they just get it over with? Forget it. She had to end it.

"Look, I know—"

"Why would we be disappointed in you?" her father asked, gruffly but gently.

Several answers whirled in her head, but nothing emerged.

"I'm hurting for you. I'm also saddened that you didn't feel you could confide in us about Daniel. And as a father, I'm angry with myself that I wasn't there for you, that I couldn't protect you. But do I blame you? No, I don't. I'm proud of you for making the hard decisions. Then and now."

Sydney whipped her gaze from her father, to her mother, then back to him. Surely, she hadn't heard him right. She couldn't have...

"When did this happen?" she asked, too stunned by their *lack* of reaction to be tactful. "Just a few weeks ago, we sat in that dining room and you both accused me of being rash and impulsive. Why the turnaround?"

"Sydney." Her mother lifted her hand, and it hovered several seconds before Patricia settled it over Sydney's clenched fingers. "We've made mistakes. Plenty of them when it's come to you. Ever since you visited me at the store and we argued, your father and I have been doing a lot of soul-searching. We've had to look back with a critical eye turned not toward you, but ourselves. And we're not proud of what we've seen." She inhaled a shaky breath, briefly closing her eyes. When she reopened them, Sydney almost gasped at the bright sheen of tears in her mother's gaze.

She hadn't seen her mother cry in years—not since Carlin's death and the months afterward. Her heart, which she didn't believe could break more than it already had after leaving Cole, cracked. No matter the distant relationship they'd been locked in, she couldn't bear the sight of her mother's tears.

"Mom," she breathed, flipping their hands over so she now clasped her mother's.

"No, this needs to be said," Patricia said, squaring her shoulders. She glanced at Sydney's father, who nodded, as if offering his support, his encouragement. For what, though? "Your father and I actually planned to come see you this weekend," her mother continued, her voice slightly trembling. "To apologize. To ask for your forgiveness. Not just for our reaction when you returned home. Which was horrible. Over the years, we've been so focused on our concern for you, our hope that you'd find stability and security, find happiness, that we forgot to show you compassion. We forgot to say, I love you and show it to you. Our motivation was love, but the delivery of it has been lacking at the least, abysmal at best. What you said to me that afternoon in the boutique—that we gave Daniel our unconditional support but not our own child—it cut. As the truth always does. You returned home to us for a reason. Because you were looking for a safe place to land, because you needed us. And instead you received criticism and the brunt of our fears. We failed you, and we're sorry. I'm so sorry, Sydney."

A maelstrom of emotion—shock, grief, anger and guilt—crashed inside her, battering her. Surging to her feet, she strode away from the couch, from her parents, thrusting her hands through her curls. She couldn't think. Too much bombarded her. Eighteen years' worth of pent-up feelings. Confusion. Her parents' sudden regret and sorrow. The pain that still tore through her from Cole. And that bitch called Hope. She'd betrayed Sydney too many times, and it was hope that tipped the scale.

"I'm sorry," Sydney whispered. Then louder, a note of hysteria creeping into her voice, "I'm so sorry. You think I don't know why you've resented me all these years? I let your daughter die," she cried, voice cracking.

She wrapped her arms around her belly, cradling the bump as if she held her baby in her arms. Her daughter wasn't even born yet, but just the thought of her dying... She shook her head. It's why she couldn't hate her parents...couldn't hate Cole. Now she understood. With her baby sleeping inside her, now she understood.

"Sydney," her father barked, disbelief coating her name. "What the hell are you talking about?"

She blinked. Luke Collins never cursed.

"Come on, Dad, you can say it," she said, just...weary. Of the things left unsaid. Of the secrets. Of the denials. "You and Mom blame me for Carlin's death. I could've saved her if I had gone through with the partial kidney donation. It might've bought her more time. Might've given the doctors a chance to find another way to help her. To keep her alive. But I didn't. And you've never forgiven me for it. Which is okay. Because I've never forgiven myself."

"Sydney." One moment, she stood there, arms wrapped around herself, and in the next, her father's arms encircled her. Holding her close, his big, gentle hand cupping the back of her head, pressing her to his chest. She inhaled his familiar crisp, woodsy scent, and cuddled closer. "Sydney," he said again, voice thick, hoarse. "No, honey. No. We have never, *never* blamed you." He leaned back and waited for her to lift her gaze to his. "I need you to understand and accept that. At no time have we ever been mad at you, resented you. You are wholly blameless. It's cancer that's responsible. It took Carlin away from us. Not you."

"And sweetie, Carlin was tired." Her mother rose from the couch, approaching them. She smoothed a hand over Sydney's curls, a small, sad smile curving her lips. "She was so tired that when the kidney donation didn't happen, I think she was relieved. Her body had been through so much by the time she was thirteen, she just wanted to let go. To be at peace. She wasn't mad at you, Sydney, and neither were we." Patricia sighed. "But looking back, I can see how you would believe this. Especially with me. I think…"

She paused, swallowed hard, and reached for her husband. He wrapped an arm around her shoulders, brushing a kiss across her hair. "When I came out of the worst of the grieving, I distanced myself from you. Carlin's death left me with a horrible fear of losing another child. When you would disappear for hours or return home late after curfew, I went into a panic, afraid of what could happen to you. So, I unconsciously erected this shield between us. Maybe a part of me believed that if we weren't close, if I kept you at arm's length, then I wouldn't fall apart if something happened. I wanted to hold on to you so hard, Sydney. Not let you out the door. Not let you leave my sight. But in my fear, I pushed you away. And I'm so sorry. I have so much to make up for with you." She cupped Sydney's cheek, the hand shaking. "Please let me try and make it up to you."

"Mom." Unable to say more past the relief, amazement and joy that constricted her throat, Sydney hugged her mother. Tight. And didn't want to let go. For the first time since she was a girl, she felt free to hug her mother without any expectation of rejection. She felt loved, accepted. She belonged. "I love you," she whispered. "I love you so much. And I've missed you."

"Me, too, sweetie." Her mother squeezed her close as if she didn't want to let go. And that was fine with Sydney. "Welcome home, Sydney."

A soggy laugh escaped her, and in seconds, laughter from the three of them echoed in the room. It was cathartic, healing. A fresh start. And in spite of the breakdown of her marriage with Cole, peace stole into her, spreading, leaving her warm and just a little less broken.

"I want—" Heart pounding, she nodded, encouraging herself to continue. To take that last step. "Tomorrow, I want to visit Carlin's grave. I didn't go with you before because…because I was so angry with her for dying and leaving me. For taking your love for me with her to the grave. But," she shook her head, "I blamed her for something that she didn't have any control over. Something that wasn't true. So the first time I go to see her, I'd like it to be with you." She inhaled, smiling at her parents. "Let her know we're all okay and we're starting over as a family. Will you…will you go with me?"

Her father, one arm still around her mother and the other around Sydney, pulled them both close until they formed a solid, unbreakable unit.

"I think we would both love that."

CHAPTER TWENTY-TWO

Cole opened the door to Kinsale Inn, and familiar scents greeted him. Lemon from the furniture polish his mother used. The sugar and chocolate of the cookies his mother baked and set out in the common area for her guests. The aromatic blend of coffee his mother always had on the ready.

They were the scents of home. Of family.

He inhaled, breathing deep—as deep as the smothering weight on his chest allowed.

Clenching his jaw, he strode forward, past the living area, dining room, staircase and the front desk where guests checked in. Too bad he couldn't outrun himself. Because he'd been trying for the past four days, and it hadn't happened yet.

"Hey, Moe," he said, walking into the kitchen.

His mother whirled around the counter where she sliced fresh vegetables with a muffled shriek. "Cole," she gasped, spreading a hand over her chest. "You can't just sneak up on me like that. I'm getting too old to risk a heart attack," she scolded.

He chuckled, hands up in surrender. "Sorry 'bout that. But could you please lower the knife now?"

With a huff, she did as he asked, turning to twist the sink faucets on and wash her hands. "To what do I owe this pleasure? It's," she squinted at the rooster clock on the far wall that had been there for as long as he could remember, "two o'clock on a Thursday. I'm happy to see you, but shouldn't you be at the office or doing something at city hall?"

He shrugged a shoulder and headed toward the wooden island in the middle of the huge kitchen. Platters of chocolate chip and oatmeal raisin cookies along with huge, dark brownies covered nearly half of it. Out of habit, and because they smelled so damn good, he nabbed an oatmeal raisin cookie and bit into it. And didn't bother containing his groan.

"What do you put into these? Crack?" He stuffed the rest of it into his mouth as she laughed, a touch of pink streaking across her striking cheekbones.

"Now, son, why would I do that when the blood of virgins is much handier?"

"I'm a lawyer, you know." He arched a brow. "But you can totally buy my silence and cooperation with more baked goods." He snatched up another cookie, chocolate chip this time. "And to answer your question." He sighed, the weariness that had temporarily lifted, dropping back on his shoulders like an anvil. "I'm coming from a meeting with Jasper Landon."

Her nose wrinkled as if something rancid had just entered the kitchen. "'Nuff said."

"Yeah." Cole bit into the cookie, chewing slower. "The motorcycle rally is barely over, but he's already gearing up to find some way to be the Grinch of the Christmas festival."

"He's such an ass," Moe bit out. Anger tinged her cheeks now, not pleasure. She snatched up a mitt and crossed the kitchen to the large oven. "Most people would just accept losing gracefully, but not him. It's been months since you won, and it still sticks in his craw that not only did he lose, but that he lost to a younger, Latino man. He should be placing the community he's supposed to serve ahead of his own personal agenda, but not Jasper. He'd rather exercise all his energy toward making you look bad. Racist jerk."

Though Cole found it hilarious whenever Moe "got her Irish up" as his father put it, Jasper wasn't worth her ire.

"Most of the people in Rose Bend are good and honest. But then you have some like Jasper. He's not the only one who doesn't believe I'm experienced or white enough for the office of mayor." He smiled at his mom, though a familiar flicker of anger wavered in his chest. "I've just come to accept that not everyone doesn't see color, like you do."

Moe slammed the oven door shut and dropped a pan of fresh, hot cookies on top of the stove with a clatter. Cole jumped at the sound, startled as she whipped around to pin a fierce scowl on him.

"Don't you ever accuse me of that." She jabbed a mitt-covered hand at him. "Of course I see color. To say I didn't would mean I don't see your beauty, don't acknowledge and respect your proud heritage. It would mean I don't see your strength, the struggles you have to face in life and your resilience to overcome them. It would mean that I, as a white woman, don't grasp that I have certain privileges granted to me just because of the color of my skin, and that you will encounter hate and bigotry just because of the color of yours. It would mean that I don't respect that, that I don't need to do all in my power to support you while not making it about me. It would mean I don't *see* *you*. So no, Coltrane, I see color. And I see the power you possess and the weight you bear because of it."

He stared at her, blown away, humbled by this woman who'd raised him as her own. Who had never made him feel any different from the children she'd birthed, but still celebrated his differences.

"I honestly didn't believe it would be possible to love you more than I do, but here we are," he said.

Moe blinked. Then again, and once more. Chuckling, Cole

rounded the island, setting down his half-eaten cookie, and
gathered his mother in his arms.

"Good God, please don't cry," he teased. "If Dad comes in
here and sees that, he'll haul me out of here and demand to
know what I did to 'his woman.'"

"Oh hush," she said, squeezing him tight before pushing out
of his embrace and shooing him away. "Go sit down and stop
saying foolish crap then."

Laughing, Cole smacked a kiss on the top of her head and
grabbed his abandoned cookie before doing as she ordered.

"Now, before everyone returns home, why don't you tell me
the real reason you're here. In other words, tell me what's going
on with you and Sydney." She crossed her arms over her chest and
leveled her patented don't-give-me-no-bullshit stare on him. He
didn't bother asking how she knew, because this was Rose Bend.
Something like Sydney moving in with her parents wouldn't have
remained under wraps for long. "Because that *is* why you're here."

He parted his lips to refute it, but the denial didn't material-
ize. Bending his head, he stared at the surface of the oak table
where they'd shared many meals with guests and family. She
was right. He'd come here seeking comfort, the familiarity of
her presence, the no-nonsense of her advice.

"Sydney found out about the house."

He didn't look up from the tabletop, but he caught the soft
sound of her sandaled feet crossing the floor and the scrape of
the chair across from him as she dragged it from under the table.
Felt the warm clasp of her hand over his.

"Found out?" she repeated. "Or did you tell her?"

"Jenna Landon told her," he admitted, still seeing Sydney's
hurt over that every time he closed his eyes. Not that closing
his eyes had been an issue these past four days. Sleep hadn't even
been an option.

"For the love of… The apple doesn't fall far from the tree
with that one. Hell, I wish we could just saw that whole damn

tree down," she grumbled. Her fingers tightened around his, and he lifted his head, meeting the compassion in her soft gaze. "I'm sorry, Cole. She had no right to do that. But, why hadn't you shared that information with Sydney?"

Gently pulling his hand free of his mother's hold, he leaned back in his chair and scrubbed his hands over his head. Then he tipped the chair back, staring at the ceiling.

"I've tried to convince myself that it had nothing to do with her. But as she pointed out, it has everything to do with her— with us. The truth is I didn't want her intruding on that part of me, of my life. My time with Tonia…it was mine. Sydney accused me of hoarding my memories, and she wasn't wrong. I married Sydney thinking I could keep her in this safe box where she wouldn't bleed over into any other part of my life. But obviously, that didn't happen," he said with a harsh bark of laughter. He splayed his hands wide on the table, studied them. "The house… Moe, it's all I have left of them. I can't remember her voice as clearly. Or her laugh. I can't recall her scent anymore. If I lose the house, it will be like saying they never existed. That they weren't…important to me."

"Oh, baby, how long you grieve doesn't determine the depth of your love for a person. Cole." Moe sighed, and the chair creaked as she shifted her slight weight. "I've never lost a child, but I have had to grieve a grandchild and watch my own son drown in his grief. I didn't understand what being powerless truly was until I could only stand back and let you suffer without being able to fix it for you. I was so worried that we would never have you back. That you wouldn't make it. But you did. Because that's who you are. Strong. Stubborn, yes, but unbreakable. Also so emotionally bottled up, I both anticipated and feared what would happen when or if you ever popped."

She paused, and the silence in the kitchen hummed between them, the bright sounds of a chirping bird filtering through the open windows along with the whine of Wolf's saw from his workshop in the back of the inn.

"When I first saw you with Sydney, I started to cautiously hope again. With her, you weren't…numb. I saw the flashes of the old you, when I was doubting if I ever would see them again. When you told us about marrying her, that hope grew. Even knowing the reasons why and your insistence that it wasn't a love match, that you were just helping a friend, I still *hoped*. And now, seeing the pain you're trying to hide, I'm more certain than ever you're going to be just fine."

Cole jerked his head down, narrowing his gaze on his mother, who smiled at him with the telltale brightness of tears glistening in her eyes.

"What?" How could she say that? He felt a lot of shit at the moment, but *fine* wasn't one of them.

She nodded. "For two years, you've mourned Tonia and Mateo. But finally, you're in pain over someone else. Over losing Sydney. Cole, if you didn't love her, you wouldn't care that she walked away. You would be relieved and eager to return to that lonely existence you've been living. Not sitting here in my kitchen because you don't want to go back to an empty home."

Did she possess some sort of ESP? He had been so fucking lonely since Sydney left him. Before she came back into his life, he'd been perfectly fine with being alone in that cottage. Alone with his memories. But now, he was this ghost rattling around his home. He couldn't even bring himself to sleep in his bed anymore, because Sydney's citrus and chocolate scent lingered on the pillows, the sheets. He'd tried that first night, and the ache of missing her, of not having her there was too much. The couch had become his temporary bed where he stared at the television all night until morning came and he could lose himself in work again.

But love her?

"I don't love Sydney," he protested, voice sharp—sharper than he'd intended. But then, desperation tended to do that.

Moe arched an eyebrow high, the corner of her mouth quirking.

"I *can't* love her, Moe." What had barreled up his throat as a shout emerged as a hoarse, serrated whisper. He squeezed his eyes shut, shook his head. "I can't love them."

"Cole." A small hand with calluses on the fingertips once more wrapped around his. And he held on tight, as if his mother's hand was his lifeline that prevented him from crashing into a churning sea hungry to drag him under and never let him surface. "Cole, look at me." She didn't speak again until he complied. "What are you scared of, son?"

"If I—" He broke off, swallowed hard to moisten his suddenly dry throat. "If I allow myself to love her—if I love her too much, too hard—if I let myself feel any amount of affection for the baby she's carrying, I'll lose them both." He laughed again, and the jagged edges of it scraped him raw. "Believe me, I know how irrational it sounds. But I can't shake it. I'm scared they'll both be taken away from me like Tonia and Mateo. So, I told myself if I didn't love them, if I didn't make them my whole world, then maybe, just maybe, God would let me keep them."

The truth exploded out of him in a furious torrent of words. And once he started, he couldn't stop.

"I feel so guilty. For not being able to save Tonia. For living. For giving Sydney my name when it should've only been Tonia's. For wanting to move on with her. I don't deserve that, Moe. Not when Tonia's not here. *I don't fucking deserve that*," he roared, his fist slamming down onto the table. "I don't—"

His voice broke on the sob that took him by surprise. And he couldn't speak past the next one. Or the one after that. Through the hoarse, agony-filled wails crashing against his skull, he dimly realized they weren't all in his head. They burst out of him, leaving him shattered.

"Shh, it's okay." Familiar arms enclosed him, surrounding him in love, comfort and strength. "Let it all out, baby. Let it all go," she soothed. "I've got you."

She did. She rocked him as she'd done when he was a boy, and in her embrace, he finally emptied himself of the grief and pain that had been festering inside him for two long years. Where it would leave him once it was done, he didn't know.

But for once, he wasn't terrified to find out.

The morning after he broke down in his mother's kitchen, Cole stood on the curb outside his old home with Tonia. Most of the neighborhood still slept as the sun crested the horizon, the sky still clutching to the remnants of violet and gray. But he welcomed the quiet. It was appropriate that he was doing this at the dawn of a new day.

He was starting over.

He was letting go.

He was choosing to love.

Inhaling a deep breath, he released it on a shaky gust. Moe had insisted he stay with family last night, so he'd slept in his and Wolf's old bedroom on the family's floor. Sleep had eluded him again, but this time, instead of running his last conversation with Sydney over and over like a depressing reel, he rewound and hit play on all the moments they'd shared since her return to Rose Bend.

Seeing her for the first time on the hill behind the church.

Helping her move into the cottage.

Feeling the baby move for the first time.

Holding her hand as they gazed at the ultrasound monitor and discovered she was having a little girl.

Seeing her stand up at the council meeting and offer to write the grant so he could see his dream of the community center come to fruition.

Vowing to love, honor and cherish her in The Glen.

Making love to her for the first time. The last time.

Somewhere in all of those moments, he'd fallen so deeply in love with her that it'd caused him to distance himself, to react out of fear and push her away. He could admit that now. And without the panic that had gripped him when Sydney had uttered those words to him or the denial when Moe had pointed it out.

During those long hours, he forgave himself—well, he'd started the process. Because it would be a process. Every day, he would have to wake up and decide to forgive himself and accept that the God he'd believed had abandoned him had offered him a wonderful, miraculous gift—a second chance with a beautiful, kind, selfless woman and a child that he could raise, nurture and love as his own.

And deep in his heart, he knew Tonia would not just approve but be happy for him.

Had his guilt disappeared? No, but that would take time, too. Still… It didn't crush him or taint his every joy.

He was stepping into the future with Sydney. If she would have him. But begging for her forgiveness and for her to return to him would have to wait.

Because right now, he had a house to clean out.

Sighing, he turned around and strode toward the rear of his truck where he'd stowed a stack of flattened boxes and a bag full of tape and markers. Lowering the tailgate, he reached for them but paused as headlights—several pairs of them—cut through the quickly vanishing shadows.

Stepping away from the truck, he stared, stunned, as four vehicles pulled up behind him. After several seconds, the engines cut, and people streamed out of them.

Moe. Dad. Wolf. Leo, the rest of his siblings.

Valeria and Ramon.

He blinked, battling back the sting of tears. Jesus Christ, hadn't he done enough of that in the last twenty-four hours?

Awe and love filled his chest to capacity and beyond it. They all approached and gathered around him, surrounding him in a semicircle of love, support and encouragement.

"How—" He cleared his throat of the emotion clogging it. "How did you know?"

"You're my son," came Moe's reply.

And that said it all.

Smiling, he nodded. "Well, let's get started then."

Started on packing up the house.

Started on his new beginning.

Started on a future with the woman and child he loved.

CHAPTER TWENTY-THREE

"All done, Sydney," Dr. Prioleau said, wiping the last of the gel away from Sydney's stomach. "You can sit up now."

The ever-stylish doctor—sporting a burnt-orange one-piece jumpsuit today with leopard-print peep-toe pumps and dark brown lipstick—crossed the room to pick up her tablet and toss the tissue.

"Y'know, Dr. Prioleau, if I wasn't comfortable in my stretch-marked skin, then coming in here every month to see you giving Mahogany Diana Ross a run for her money would really screw with my equilibrium," she teased.

The other woman flashed her a wide grin. "Well that's sweet of you," she said. "No wonder you're my favorite patient. But let's keep that here, okay?"

Sydney snickered, sitting up and lowering her tank top, then retying the shoulder straps of her dress. "Sure, Doc. It'll be our little secret."

The doctor shook her head, chuckling. "Any questions for me, Sydney? Concerns?"

"No, except for the little bit of heartburn I told you about, I'm good." Sydney patted her stomach. "Jellybean's super active, and sometimes that's a little 'girl, please!' at one o'clock in the morning, but I'm guessing it's normal."

"Jellybean, huh?" The doctor's mouth quirked. "I should mention now's the time to start thinking of names, too."

"I've already been working on that." Sydney grinned.

"Good. If you have any other questions, please don't hesitate to call me, okay?"

"I will," Sydney promised, carefully sliding off the exam table. "Thank you and see you in two weeks." Since she was moving into her third trimester, her visits would increase to bi-weekly instead of monthly. Her stomach dipped in excitement and nerves. The steadily increasing stomach size, cravings and movements made her pregnancy a fact. But moving into the third trimester? Oh, it just got *real.*

"Looking forward to it." The doctor opened the door. "Let me walk you out."

They exited the exam room, and as they passed the closed door to her father's office, she couldn't help but smile. He'd popped into her appointment earlier to hear the baby's heartbeat with her. Her mother had offered to accompany her this morning, but Sydney hadn't wanted her mother to miss work at the shop. She hadn't opened the boutique at all the day after Sydney had shown up on their doorstep. She and her parents had spent the day together—visiting Carlin's grave, eating lunch, playing Monopoly (her mother was a real estate shark) and then binge-ing Netflix over dinner. It'd been…amazing. And if anyone had told her when she'd crossed Rose Bend's town limits weeks ago that she would be close with her parents again, she would've ordered them to stop smoking that stuff around her baby.

These past few days had been awesome. And yet, the empty ache in her chest hadn't dissipated. She missed Cole; she couldn't deny it. Not when she still rolled over in the morning, half-asleep, and reached for him only to find a cold, vacant side of the bed. Or when she worked on her book, and a plot twist popped in her head, but she couldn't call him to share it. Or when she lay in bed at night, longing to be held against his strong body, wanting to be filled by him.

So, God, yes. She missed him. But nothing had changed between them. She still needed more from him, needed more for herself and her baby. For once, she was demanding all or nothing. Because they both deserved nothing less.

Even if she threatened to buckle under the loneliness and hurt.

"Have a great rest of your day, Sydney," Dr. Prioleau said, opening the door that led into the lobby. A grin spread over the doctor's face, and she glanced at Sydney. "Something tells me it will be," she murmured.

Hmm. Enigmatic much?

Shrugging a shoulder, Sydney waved at the other woman and moved past her into the lobby. "Have a great...day..."

Shock robbed her of the rest of the words and her breath.

Cole.

His name ricocheted off her skull, booming louder and louder until she curled her fingers into fists at her thighs so she wouldn't clap her palms over her ears.

Yearning so powerful, so damn visceral, wrenched within her. It almost propelled her forward. Toward him. But she stretched out an arm, steadying herself against the edge of the desk.

No. The word broke past the emotion fogging her mind, squeezing her chest. Obligation. Responsibility. They were so ingrained in him they should be added to his birth certificate. Duty as her husband brought him here, not love. And it wasn't enough. She valued his friendship, but she needed someone who would take her heart and give her his.

Cole was not that man.

"What are you doing here?" she asked, proud when the question came out even if it was quiet.

He stepped toward her, and only then did she notice what

her hyperfocus on him hadn't allowed her to notice before. She gasped, feeling her eyes widen.

Mom. Moe. Leo. The whole Dennison clan. And Tonia's parents, Valeria and Ramon. Crowded into the clinic lobby.

What were they all doing here?

"They're here for you," Cole said, and she winced, realizing she'd uttered her stunned thoughts aloud. "I'm here for you," he murmured.

She shook her head. This couldn't be happening. This smacked too close to a grand gesture that strictly belonged in romance novels and movies. Not to her. Not with...*him*.

But one glance around, noting the rapt faces of the reception staff and the patients in the waiting area confirmed that, yes, this was indeed happening.

"Look, Cole, I don't know what you're thinking or what's going on, but—" she started, but he moved closer, halting just shy of invading her personal space. But near enough that his earthy, sensual scent drifted to her, teased her. Near enough that she glimpsed the dark brown flecks in his amber gaze. Near enough that she didn't even have to fully extend her arm to brush her fingertips over that strong jaw, those full lips.

She swallowed hard. And shifted half a step backward.

His eyes darkened with pain at her movement, and she had to steel herself against it. Either that or she would've kicked her resolve out of the way to comfort him.

"I don't deserve to ask you for a chance to hear me out, but I am. Because for once, I'm going to be brave when it comes to you." He studied her for several long moments, and she could almost see that beautiful mind working. "From the moment I first saw you on that hill, I was changed. And I didn't want any part of it. I'd been numb for so long that it was...comfortable for me. I liked my world just as it was—shades of gray where I could exist. But then you came along, and everything wasn't just color but vivid, high-definition, Technicolor. You were so bright, looking at you, being around you, hurt. In the same way it does when a man has been in darkness for so long that the sun is painful. But I needed to grow, to thrive, to live again. You made me live again, Sydney."

She stared at him, her heart a wild thing in her chest. It pounded, raced, desperate to throw itself at this man. *You made me live again.* But fear crept in underneath, warning her heart not to be a fool again. She'd been led by her emotions before and what had happened? She'd been left rejected and so hurt she'd barely been able to function. Empty. Alone.

It terrified her to give him that much power over her again. Could she trust him with it?

"I admit, I resented you for it. Because I felt too much. I wanted too much. More than I believed I deserved. For so long I felt guilty for Tonia's and Mateo's deaths. Why had I lived when they didn't? How could I move on without them? I didn't deserve to be happy or to laugh or to enjoy life when I couldn't protect my family. My one purpose as a man, and I failed. I failed them and myself."

"No, you didn't," she objected fiercely, the protest bursting out of her before she could contain it. Hell, she didn't want to. Yes, he'd hurt her, couldn't love her like she needed, but he was a *good* man. A great man. "And you're worthy of every happiness and success life has to offer you. Everything."

Humor gleamed in his eyes, temporarily lighting the darkness there. A smile ghosted across his lips, and he inclined his head. "Thank you, baby girl. I believe that now. Thanks to you."

Her guard shot back up, and she shifted her body, leaning away from him, wary. "Since when?" she asked, not hiding her skepticism. "In five days?" She shook her head, softly scoffing. "I don't—"

"I love you," he said, just as softly. But it might as well have been a deafening shout as loudly as it rang in her ears.

"No," she whispered. "You don't. You couldn't even say the

words. You couldn't…" Her voice broke as she clearly recalled begging him to tell her he loved her. And he couldn't.

"Yes, I do," he insisted, tone solemn. "Five days ago, fear kept me from admitting it to myself, but I loved you long before then. I've given it a lot of thought, and I fell in love with you the moment you cried in my arms over the loss of my wife and baby. Your heart, your kindness, your selflessness, the blinding beauty of your spirit… Sydney, loving you was as inevitable as the sun setting then rising again."

He paused, his gaze dipping to her mouth, then lower to her belly, and she froze, time itself halting as he gently spread his fingers wide over her bump, his palm cradling her.

"I fought this because I wanted it so much. The fear of possibly losing you and her…" He briefly closed his eyes, and when his thick lashes lifted, her heart thumped at the emotion that shined past the shadows. "It paralyzed me, and I told myself I couldn't do it again. That if I kept you at a distance, I could have you, but not lose you. Not lose my sanity if something were to happen to either of you. But you told me you didn't want to live in my world of fear anymore. Well, neither do I, Sydney. Bring me into your world where there's hope, joy, love. I need you to bring me there and hold me. Don't leave me to simply exist. I want to live. I want to love."

Slowly, he sank to his knees, and a soft cry of surprise escaped her. What the hell? She jerked her gaze from him to her family. All of her family. Her mother wiped at her eyes, and one of the nurses passed her a tissue. Moe leaned her head against Ian's shoulder, her smile soft, misty. Leo gave Sydney an air fist bump, while Wolf and the rest of the Dennisons grinned widely. Valeria and Ramon, their arms around one another, smiled at each other and her. Tonia's mother nodded, and that blessing meant everything.

Finally, Sydney returned her attention to the proud, beautiful man before her. He took her trembling hand in his, pressing his lips to the solitaire on her ring finger.

"I let go of the past hurt and bitterness because you and this little girl are my future. I have been blessed to find love with two wonderful, beautiful, giving women in this life. Now, I can allow Tonia rest knowing she would be proud of me and happy for us. I'm selling the house so we can buy a home for us—the three of us." He lowered his head and brushed his lips over her belly, and at that moment, her baby kicked, as if giving her full approval. Cole smiled, tipping his head back to meet Sydney's eyes again. "I don't want to go another day without you beside me as my wife, my partner, my friend, my love, the mother of our children."

He released her hand and slipped it into his pants pocket. When he opened his fist, a beautiful, rose-gold band, engraved with a rose, sat on the palm.

"Cole," she whispered, going to her knees, too, cupping his face. Love—so much love—filled her heart. So much it hurt. But a good ache this time. Not of pain, but of joy. Hope. Trust.

She trusted him with her heart, her body, her daughter.

Their future.

"Will you marry me again, Sydney?" he murmured, sliding the jewelry above the solitaire so three rings banded her finger. "In front of our family, will you take me again as the man who adores you, pledges his life and everything he is and has to you? Will you take me as your husband and the father to our daughter?"

"Yes," she declared, no hesitation. No doubts. No fear. "Yes, to everything. I love you." She threw her arms around his neck, burying her face against his throat. Scattering kisses up the strong column, over his jaw and finally, across his mouth, she promised, "Forever. I trust you. I love you."

Two large hands clasped her face and held her still as he took her mouth in a kiss that made her forget they had an audience.

His tongue swept inside, and she parted wide for him, welcoming him. It'd been too long since she'd tasted him, and she'd missed him. Way too soon, he withdrew from her, and pressed his forehead to hers.

"I love you, baby girl," he murmured. "So much. Thank you for returning to Rose Bend."

She covered his hands with hers and smiled against his lips. "Thank you for showing me I could come home again."

★ ★ ★ ★ ★

Look for Wolfgang's story in
The Inn at Rose Bend
Available October 2021!

Dear Reader,

I have a confession. I'm a Hallmark movie junkie. The person who schedules their weekends around the movies coming on TV? Yep. I'm that girl. Whether it's about the bridesmaid at the summer wedding or the seamstress falling for the undercover prince at Christmas, I'm all in. Of course, it's the swoony romance that captures me. But just as captivating are the small town settings.

There's something almost magical about a small town. Yes, the beautiful scenery, the quaint shops, clean streets and cozy homes that often seem untouched, unspoiled by the outside world. But the true magic lies in the people, the community. The love of neighbors—even if that exhibits itself as nosiness. It's the concern for each other, as if all the members of that town know they need each other, depend on each other, to be happy and prosperous. There's beauty in that.

In *The Road to Rose Bend*, Sydney Collins and Coltrane "Cole" Dennison depend on that sense of community, that love of neighbors. I hope you fall in love with the special town of Rose Bend, its residents and with Sydney and Cole.

Naima

ACKNOWLEDGMENTS

Thank you, foremost, to my heavenly Father for pouring Your creative spirit into me every day. You've been my coauthor from day one, and not only can I not do this without You. I don't want to.

Thank you to my husband, Gary. This journey is as much yours as it is mine, and I thank you for being the wind—sometimes the foot—at my back and the stable, unfailing, never-pitted road underneath my feet.

To my parents, Wayne L. Alston and Connie Butts. Connie, thank you for being my cheerleader and always telling me, "Change how you talk!" You won't stand for me being negative about myself, and I love you for it. Daddy, thank you for bequeathing me the gift of sarcasm, your advice, insight and for instructing me in all things John Coltrane.

Thank you to my wonderful editor, Stacy Boyd. I am so grateful for your experience, patience, guidance and never-failing enthusiasm with not just this book and series, but with me as an author. I hope you know just how precious that is to me.

Thank you to my amazing agent, Rachel Brooks. You've been my advocate, champion, reality checker, encourager... I can just go on and on. Thank you for supporting me in reaching for my dreams and doing your damndest to make sure they happen. As my father says, "We have God and we have Rachel!"

Finally, thank you to Dahlia Rose, Fedora Chen and Kenya Goree-Bell for selflessly lending me your time to read this book while it was in process and making me feel like a sparkly, glittery Nalini Singh unicorn with your words of love and encouragement. You are gifts to me, and I love and appreciate you!